Francis Cowley Burnand

The A.D.C.

Francis Cowley Burnand

The A.D.C.

ISBN/EAN: 9783337333041

Printed in Europe, USA, Canada, Australia, Japan

Cover: Foto ©Andreas Hilbeck / pixelio.de

More available books at **www.hansebooks.com**

THE "A.D.C."

BEING

Personal Reminiscences

OF THE

UNIVERSITY AMATEUR DRAMATIC CLUB, CAMBRIDGE.

WRITTEN BY

F. C. BURNAND, B.A.,

TRIN. COLL. CAMB.

"HÆC OLIM MEMINISSE JUVABIT.'

LONDON:

CHAPMAN AND HALL, 193, PICCADILLY,

1880.

TO

.

𝕳𝖎𝖘 𝕽𝖔𝖞𝖆𝖑 𝕳𝖎𝖌𝖍𝖓𝖊𝖘𝖘

THE PRINCE OF WALES.

TO

WHOSE MOST GOODNATURED ENCOURAGEMENT THE CLUB IS MAINLY

INDEBTED FOR ITS PRESENT RECOGNISED POSITION,

THIS BOOK OF

"A. D. C." REMINISCENCES

IS

GRATEFULLY DEDICATED

BY

ITS AUTHOR.

September, 1879.

PREFACE.

SEVERAL Dramatic Clubs have been started, from time to time, either by Town or Gown, in Cambridge, but no one of these has ever achieved the permanent success of the A. D. C., or Amateur Dramatic Club of the University, which it was my good fortune to have had the opportunity of founding in 1855, so that next year, 1880, it will have existed for a quarter of a century, a duration unexampled in the history of Cambridge Dramatic Clubs, whether Academic or Oppidanic.

The most celebrated non-academic University Dramatic Society in Cambridge, called the Cambridge Garrick Club, was started in 1835. Among its members it numbered very few University men, and these were graduates, professors, and fellows of Colleges, who were elected, not *quâ* University men, but as Residents in the town of Cambridge, who, having a taste for English Dramatic Literature, were willing to encourage a Club that could show on its list of honorary members, the names of Charles Kemble,

W. Macready, Sheridan Knowles, Liston, and Douglas
Jerrold.

Whether any of these distinguished characters,
—with the exception of Sheridan Knowles, whom
the Club entertained at a banquet given in his
honour, and Macready, to whom the Club presented a
silver cup,—ever actively assisted at the meetings,
or performances, of the Cambridge Garrick Club, I
have been unable to ascertain. As, however, in the
last published notice of their performances at the
Barnewell Theatre, where Macready played Knowles's
Virginius, the critic of *The Cambridge Chronicle*, Aug. 5,
1836, expresses a hope that the subscribers to the Club
may "see Mr. Tilbury on the next Garrick performance in a character of more importance," it is just
probable that the Cambridge Garrick continued its
representations for some little time after the Great Macready Star had disappeared in that one overpowering
blaze of triumph, which must have been enough to ruin
any ordinary Club; for who would pay their money
to see the attempts of local talent, after witnessing
the finished performance of a great Dramatic genius?

This Club may exist now in some shape, and twenty
years ago there was a town Dramatic Club, but
nobody of any note belonged to it, and its representations, which took place out of term time, as a
rule, at the Barnewell Theatre, were given by Messrs.
Quince the carpenter, Snug the joiner, Flute the

bellows mender, Snout the tinker, Starveling the tailor, and last but not least, Bottom the weaver, all tradesmen of the town, with aspirations, but without aspirates, who, for aught I can recollect, may have been associated together under the style and title of the Cambridge Garrick Club,—but I do not think this was so, neither do I suppose this society had anything whatever to do with the Cambridge Garrick of 1833, which, apparently, came to an end in 1836.

But of all University Amateur Performances the most ambitious was on Friday, 19th March, 1830; at the Hoop Hotel, when *Much Ado about Nothing* was given, with an Epilogue written by Lord Houghton —then Mr. R. M. Milnes—through whose kindness I am enabled to place before my readers the cast of the *Dramatis Personæ* on this occasion, together with the Epilogue above mentioned. It was spoken by Mr. Stafford O'Brien, who then exhibited those admirable dramatic faculties which he afterwards showed to such advantage in the amateur theatricals at Lord Northampton's seat (Castle Ashby), at the Duke of Bedford's (Woburn Abbey), at Lord Lyveden's (Farming Woods), and many other country houses where a fine dramatic taste was then prevalent. The burlesque, *A Knock at the Door; or, Worsted works Wonders*, written and acted by him and Mr. Milnes at Castle Ashby, was privately printed and is now a great bibliographical curiosity.

EPILOGUE

TO

SHAKESPEARE'S COMEDY

"MUCH ADO ABOUT NOTHING."

Performed Friday, 19th March, 1830, and printed at the request of the Performers.

Cast of the Characters.

Don Pedro	E. ELLICE (present M.P. for St. Andrews).
Don John	R. W. BLANE (late Colonel in Grenadier Guards).
Leonato	A. FITZROY (son of the Rev. Lord Henry FitzRoy).
Claudio	R. MONTEITH (of Carstairs).
Benedick	S. A. O'BRIEN (Angustus Stafford, Secretary of the Admiralty in Lord Derby's first Administration).
Antonio	H. ARUNDELL.
Borachio	H. MOORE.
Conrade	J. H. PRESTON (Sir Jacob Preston, Bart.).
Friar	E. B. G. WARBURTON (Eliot Warburton, author of *The Crescent and the Cross;* lost in the fatal fire of the Amazon).
Dogberry	J. M. KEMBLE (son of the eminent actor, Charles Kemble, and author of the *History of the Anglo-Saxons*).
Verges	A. H. HALLAM (Henry Hallam, son of the historian, and author of the remarkable *Memorials* published after his death).
Seacoal	J. B. BOWES (winner of the Derby in 1853, with West Australian).
Oatcake	E. BRUCE (now Marquis of Ailesbury).
Sexton	C. VANDELEUR (Crofton Vandeleur, long M.P. for Co. Clare).
Hero	C. L. KIRWAN.
Beatrice	R. M. MILNES (now Lord Houghton).
Ursula	E. H. BUNBURY (distinguished scholar, Fellow of Trin. Coll.).
Margaret	H. CLARKE.

Stage-Manager   R. M. MILNES.

BEFORE our corps their scenic task renew,
Gentles, I would a word or two with you;
And fear not—Benedick forgets to sneer,
When he remembers he is acting here—
And Beatrice, your graces to obtain,
Anxiously doffs " her Ladyship Disdain."

[*Looking at* BEATRICE.

Some weeks ago we tortured every ear
With the trite nonsense of a scribbling peer,*
To-night we dare the opposite extreme,
And Shakespeare, *Nature's noble*, is our theme ;
But chance if then we sunk our shaft too low,
To-night we aim too high—well—be it so.
Our cause is good, and it may claim some praise
To have restored the forms of Shakespeare's days ;

> [*Pointing to the Ladies.*

When the men-ladies, as their parts might fall,
Were taught to trip and simper, and " speak small "—
And, when delayed, th' impatient Monarch raved,
The excuse was, " Sire, the Queen is not yet shaved."
'Twas thus we chose to act—the risk is run—
Our will has triumphed, and the play is done.
No power has tightened the scholastic rein,
And gate-bill thunders have been hurled in vain.
What ! if we thus our unchecked course pursue,
Who dares to tell us what we may not do ?
Why may we not in living truth upraise
The masquing merriments of antient days ?
Why may we not, at no far moment, see
Juliets M.A., and Romeos D.D. ?
Then shall the witches dance, or Cæsar fall
Stabbed by his Brutus, in a College Hall.
Then in most tender converse shall be seen
An amorous Proctor and an ogling Dean—
While Heads of Houses don the gamesome gear,
And Chafy† makes a grand début in Lear !
Some short time more, the Drama shall replace
Euclid's grim frown, and Algebra's lean face.
And they who, lusting after laurels, now
Gaze with such rapture on a curve's cold brow,
Or who, in deference to a father's word,
Pay forced addresses to an ugly surd,

---

* *The Follies of Fashion*, by Lord Glengall, also performed at the Hoop Hotel.
† Master of Sidney College—then Vice-Chancellor.

Shall find, within our Drama's golden store,
Garlands to win, and beauty to adore.
" You're going out in honours, my dear fellow ?"
" Yes—I shall take my Master's in Othello."
" And I, more humble, for my Senior Op.,
In ' Charles the Second '—take up Captain Copp."
" What, *you* not passed ?"   " No ; for the rascals say
I acted well, but did not know the play."
" Hamlet, our Senior Wrangler—the Buffoon
In Twelfth Night, second—Cato, Wooden Spoon."
Are these the phantoms of a stage-sick brain ?
Well, we have other hopes not *quite* so vain.
Tho' some full sated with collegiate lore,
May tread these boards, or shift these scenes, no more—
Tho' all of us too soon may actors be
On wider stage, with sadder scenery—
Still other Tyros shall give utterance here,
New hands applaud them and new voices cheer,
And fan to flame the fire we humbly lit—
The simple exercise of harmless wit—
While fresh rewards, each rising genius hail,
Till Time itself, or Trinity, shall fail.
But ere *our* artless pageant disappear,
We ask one boon—if, in some after-year,
In evening hours, your eye should chance to light
On any name you recognise to-night—
On some brief record of their mortal lot—
Married, or murdered, ruined, or what not ?
While natural thought returns upon its track,
Just pause, and murmur, ere you call it back,
With pleasant memory, sipping your liqueur—
" Yes, yes, he was a Cambridge Amateur."

The Rivals, Lord Houghton informs me, was also
played, first in Cameron's rooms, over the Combination-
Room, in Trinity. This Mr. Cameron, now an eminent

clergyman in Kent, is the father of the wonderful
African pedestrian. Its second performance took place
in King's College, at the rooms of the Rev. William
Gifford Cookesley, who, by the way, was subsequently my tutor at Eton, in whose pupil-room my
first play was produced. In *The Rivals* Mr. Cookesley
played *Sir Lucius*, besides undertaking the stage-
management; Mr. Bernal Osborne was *Young Absolute*, and he has not belied the character in his public
life; Sir James Colville, now "Right Honourable"
and Judge of the Privy Council, was *Sir Anthony;*
Lydia Languish found an admirable representative in
the Hon. Charles Manners Sutton, afterwards Viscount
Canterbury, to the last "the prettiest man about
town;" and Lord Houghton was Mrs. Malaprop,
which accounts for his being a master of the English language. On this same occasion they played
Bombastes, which explains my tutor's accurate
knowledge of the dialogue and the business, when
we got it up under his superintendence, in his
pupil-room at Eton in 1852. The above-mentioned
performances, however, never resulted in the formation of a Club.

As far as I can ascertain, an endeavour to start a
sort of Dramatic Society was made in 1849 by Mr.
Alfred Thompson, the present editor and illustrator
of *The Mask*, to whom I have alluded in the course
of these memoirs, but it did not succeed.

Until we hit upon the plan of possessing ourselves of our own rooms—giving ourselves a local habitation and a name—the notion of forming a Club had been limited to merely getting together a number of amateur actors, and arranging for a performance, to which each should subscribe his share of the expenses. In this there was not even the permanent bond of union that existed in our ancient University Dinner Clubs, "The Beefsteak" and "The True Blue," and the modern *Quare Hæc*—*i.e.*, "Why this Club?"—to which the members subscribed by the term, and were jointly interested in the Club property of dinner-plate, which had been purchased out of the subscriptions.

The idea of the A. D. C. was an adaptation of the Cambridge Union Club, substituting dramatic entertainment for political debating. I now see that the Society, if recognised and directed by judicious authority, could work for a higher end, and for a far more important object, than was contemplated by its first founders, who will readily admit that their notion in starting the Club was to obtain a fair opportunity for the exercise of their dramatic talents, thus affording themselves novel and intellectual recreation, and their friends a considerable amount of amusement.

In these days when the question of the establishment of a School of Dramatic Art is being earnestly discussed, where could it find itself better placed than in the University, which, tardily but certainly, has already shown itself not unfavourable to the legitimate development of energy in this direction?

Dramatic Art requires that its leading professors in every department should be men of education, of taste, of refinement. Consider for one moment what is involved in the conscientious production of an Historical Drama. What care, what research, what accuracy in details are absolutely necessary. Here are study and work for the painter, for the archæologist, for the designer of costumes, for the musician, and, if there are to be 'mechanical effects,' plenty of exercise for the ingenuity of the machinist.

In a school of Dramatic Art should be comprehended all the above-mentioned studies, while,—but *cela va sans dire,*—first and foremost, should be placed the study of our National Drama, side by side with that of France, Italy, Germany, Spain, past and present,—so that the instruction should benefit the aspiring author as well as the intending actor, each of whom would here master the first principles of his art, while the latter, at this early stage of his career, would learn to appreciate, intelligently, Dramatic Art as a profession, eminence in which demands exceptional acquirements, apart from the possession of exceptional gifts.

Hitherto, into the much-abused 'Theatrical Profession' fools have rushed where angels would fear to tread—being afraid of soiling their wings. Now-a-days there is a growing desire to see the profession of Art generally recognised as bestowing on the artist an honourable status in society.

Ladies, to whom the schools of painting and music are open, no matter how gifted by nature for the stage, are nervously shy of having anything to do with it, except as a *dernier ressort* of absolute necessity. Yet, in these days, when the disabilities under which the gentle sex formerly suffered, are gradually being removed, when they have a College to themselves, near Cambridge, under the very eye of *Alma Mater*, surely they could participate in the advantages which would be offered by a University School of Dramatic Art?

In time there would be burses, prizes, dramatic scholarships of a respectable pecuniary value, with which the aspirant for dramatic honours could make a start.

The University gives its B.A. and M.A., and the Royal Academy its R.A. and A.R.A. If the Arts of painting and sculpture are thus evenly privileged with the University, why should there not be also founded a Corporation of Dramatic Art? Music has its degrees: our Literature its prizes and professorships. Perhaps we may yet hear of a 'Garrick

Scholarship,'—a Roscius' Professor, and degrees of
'*F.R.A.*' (First-Rate Actor), '.M.D.A.' (Master of
Dramatic Art), and so forth.

If these hints, however lightly put forward,
suggest action in the matter, the cause, which so
many of us have at heart, will have been so far
served.

* * * * *

In concluding my 'recollections' I have to record
my thanks to Mr. Ion Trant Hamilton, the most
indefatigable of secretaries, for his notes, and to
Lord Carington, a former president, for his most
cheerfully given assistance; to Mr. Kelly, Mr. Freeman, Mr. Charles Hall, and the Hon. Evelyn Ashley,
for their contribution of 'recollections,' and to various members of the 'A. D. C.,' past and present,
who have kindly aided my memory. Also I must
specially acknowledge my obligation to the Club
generally, which some years back confided to my
care the only records extant. To Mr. J. W. Clark,
M.A., Fellow of Trinity, who has so heartily
and generously laboured for the good of the
Club, I tender my best thanks for the information
he has afforded me during the progress of this
work.

Finally, it must be ever gratefully borne in mind
by our members, that it is to H.R.H. The Prince of

Wales, who, as a member of the University, most goodnaturedly accepted the Honorary Presidency, and is still personally interested in its welfare, the Club owes its first recognition by the authorities, and thenceforward its existence as a *quasi* Institution.

FLOREAT 'A. D. C.'!

CONTENTS.

CHAPTER I.

CHAPTER II.

CHAPTER III.

CHAPTER IV.

CHAPTER V.

CHAPTER VI.

CHAPTER VII.

CHAPTER VIII.

b

PERSONAL REMINISCENCES

OF

THE "A. D. C." CAMB.

CHAPTER I.

THE FIRST STEP.—LENT TERM, 1854.

THE initials "A. D. C." stand for Amateur Dramatic Club. It is composed entirely of members of the University of Cambridge, but it admits as "honorary members" Oxford men who belong to a similar institution at the sister University. I am not aware if this rule has been in any way enlarged, for the sake of exceptional amateurs who may be of neither University.

Although with true Pickwickian modesty, "I cannot put myself in competition with those great men, Plato, Zeno, Epicurus, Pythagoras, who," as Mr. Leo Hunter pointed out to that eminent character, were "all founders of clubs," yet, at least, I may claim for myself the largest share in the original idea; and those of my co-æquales, and contemporaries, whose memories will carry them back to 1855, will not, I think, be inclined to deny me the credit of having stuck to the ship,—certainly to "the boards,"—and of having brought her, with the assistance of good men and true, *per varios casus, per tot discrimina rerum*, into those smooth waters, where, propelled by friendly breezes, she has since held on her prosperous dramatic course. It is about nineteen

B

years since I resigned the direction, and often have I had it in my mind to publish some memoranda of what would, I am sure, be interesting to so many.

The Club has increased and multiplied from very small beginnings, and on its list are to be found names of the highest eminence, whether by virtue of rank, or talent,—names of those who have since made their mark in life.

Fortunately, when the "A. D. C." was started, we kept a record of our doings. At first it appears to have been carefully, but rather prosily, written, and was intended to contain "full, true, and particular accounts" of the performances. Several hands were engaged on this work. Gradually the writers became lazy, and the book degenerated into mere businesslike minutes of committee meetings, elections, and so forth, until, probably, an entirely new volume was purchased, and a fresh system inaugurated.* This early record of the "A. D. C.," as well as many of the first playbills, I have before me for my guidance, and now, without further preface, I will draw upon my own recollections of the commencement of the Club.

In the October term of 1854, my first term at Trinity, the notion occurred to me how much more amusing than cards, drinking, and supper, would be private theatricals, with, of course, supper to follow. Perhaps the fact of my having written a piece—an "original work," compiled from my recollection of farces, in which I had seen Buckstone, Charles Mathews, Compton, Keeley, Wright, and Paul Bedford—was at the bottom of this idea. Besides, I came up to the University with some reputation for this sort of thing, among Etonians at least, as a farce of mine —(another original work composed in much the same way,

---

* This new book which I have now by me—though the kindness of Mr. Brookfield, one of the best amateurs I have seen, either on or off the "A.D.C." stage, is half filled with long-winded descriptions of the performances, and amateur criticisms which are most amusing. But it lacks the fun of our first book of records.

only more so) — had been performed in my tutor's pupil-room, under the special patronage of my tutor himself (the Rev. William Gifford Cookesley),—who was an admirable audience,—and this farce had been not only actually printed in Windsor, and sold for a shilling a copy—(I fancy it must have paid its expenses, as I do not quite see how I could have otherwise settled the printing bill—I hope I am not still in his debt; but anyhow I was a minor, and there is the Statute of Limitations for my protection)—but it had also been played in public, for a benefit, to a crowded house at the Theatre Royal, Worthing, by a company of professionals, for One Night Only! *

So it became known and accepted, at college, that I was an authority in theatricals, and before the term was out, we had contrived a capital little stage in our rooms, opposite Trinity College, over a grocer's shop, now swept away, and its place taken by Trinity New Buildings; we had got together our company, which was quite Shakspearean, in one respect, *i.e.*, its ladies. But here we were most fortunate, as was the "A. D. C." afterwards. Lads between eighteen, nineteen, and twenty-one,

---

* I haven't the heart to dispel the illusive impression in anything but whispering type, which I give as a sort of aside to the reader, but I must in all honesty explain how this work of an unknown author of fifteen years of age came to be acted before a crowded audience at a public theatre. The Worthing Theatre was not at that time much of a place either to speak *of*, or to speak *in*. I am talking of what it was *a quarter of a century* ago, in 1852. The players came and went, and generally managed to pick up something from "bespeaks" and "benefits." The manager called on a relative of mine, and asked him for his patronage for a certain evening. He happened to have my farce lying on the table (all my family, I believe, had been supplied with copies, whether gratis or not, I am unable to say), and stipulated that its performance should be the condition of his patronage. The manager accepted the farce—promised, and played it. I remember seeing the bill. There was the usual "great attraction" and so forth; but I regret not having witnessed the entertainment. So that is how my first farce came to be played in public by the sad sea wave. By the way, I think I have got my dates pretty correct. By reference to an Eton list, I find I left Eton in 1853; therefore, as I matriculated at Cambridge in the following year, my first term was in October, 1854, before I had completed my eighteenth year.

slim and guiltless of whisker or moustache, downy fledgelings whose delight was then not to encourage hirsute growth, but to shave, could easily "make up" for the female characters, and represent them admirably, voice excepted. At that time the "moustache movement" had only barely commenced, and I remember sending up to *Punch* a sketch of a mistaken young undergraduate appearing before the dean, under the impression that he had been summoned to receive a reprimand for his moustache, a mere sprout; and the dean was made to answer sarcastically, "I didn't perceive you had any." Both dean and undergraduate were portraits. That of the dean was, by the merest chance, exact, and in my letter I requested the editor (Mr. Mark Lemon) to request the. artist, Mr. John Leech, not to alter either face in transferring the sketch to *Punch's* page. Mr. Leech executed an inimitable picture, of course, faithfully retaining the likenesses, while giving real life to what had been mere pen-and-ink outline; but I notice that he did not put his well-known signature to the picture. I sent up two other sketches from Cambridge, and on referring to John Leech's collected drawings, I find that his initials are absent from both. In his collection there are many unsigned, so I suppose it was his custom to omit his initials, when he could not claim the originality of the design. At all events, moustaches and whiskers were conspicuous by their absence at that time, and so the difficult question that invariably arises at every amateur performance, of, "Must I shave for the part?" did not give us much trouble.

The performance of this piece in our rooms—rooms belonging to a friend and myself who "kept" together—was such a success as to suggest a repetition of the entertainment. Our little company, the nucleus of the future Club, met together to consider this, early in the following term; but our ambition led us to higher flights, not dramatically, for, if I remember rightly, we only wished to play Morton's immortal *Box and Cox*, Frank Talfourd's burlesque of *Macbeth*, written by him at Eton, and a short burlesque of my own, called *Villikins* *and his Dinah*, of which I had just made a sketchy plan,* and instead of confining our talent to our apartments over the grocer's, we wanted to take the big room at the Bull,† (that was the name of the hotel, I think), where the county balls were held, have a stage down from London, go in heavily for costumes, and—charge for admission !

Nor did we stop at this proposition. The inch had been taken, why not the ell ? Why go to the Bull, when there was a real *bonâ fide* theatre, with real boxes, real pit, real gallery, real scenes, and real lights, within half an hour's walk of us, namely, at Barnwell ?

At the mention of the Barnwell Theatre, the meeting looked grave. There were objections. " There were," I admitted,— " but not insuperable." It was only my second term, and I was, as yet, unacquainted with the unsavoury reputation this suburb of Cambridge had acquired. The celebrated uncle-slayer, George Barnwell, could not have been worse spoken of, as a man, than was *this* Barnwell, as a place.

I stood out for Barnwell. Somehow, my theatrically-attuned ideas associated the name of the place with that of the famous tragedy, whose hero I have just mentioned above, of which I had heard, as usually preceding a Drury Lane pantomime. I stuck to the Barnwell Theatre.

My elders remonstrated, and represented, that, for such a performance as I contemplated, the Vice-Chancellor's permission was indispensable.

This—audacious juvenile that I was—had no terrors for me. I had not an idea what a Vice-Chancellor was like. I didn't believe in him, any more than did Mrs. Prig in Sairey Gamp's Mrs. Harris. I thought he was a sort of Guy Faux figure on a woolsack. I had no reverence. I was for blindly

---

* I find by dates that this burlesque was not actually written until the October term of 1855, but the subject was popular enough in 1854, and had been for years.

† The Bull was suggested in the first instance, as there was some floating vague tradition about a performance which, " once upon a time," had been given there by undergraduates. The Bull was then the chief hotel.

rushing in where my betters refused to tread. I had said in my heart, There is no Vice-Chancellor; and, in fact, I did not, at that time, realize the full extent of University authority. I was going to teach my *alma mater*, not my *alma mater* me. *Alma mater* was to be instructed how to get up *Box and Cox*, *Villikins and his Dinah*, *Macbeth* burlesque, and *Bombastes Furioso*, "which had only one woman in it, and was, therefore, very easy."

All commencing amateurs rush for *Bombastes*: few know anything at all about playing it. But, for the matter of that, even professionals make an utter muddle of it, and misconceive its bathos. I had, however, enjoyed the advantage of instruction from as great an authority on *Bombastes* as he was on the *Antigone*, and that was Mr. W. G. Cookesley, who had insisted upon our playing it at Eton, and who had coached us in the true serious vein of this old-fashioned, genuine burlesque. Talfourd's *Macbeth* was set aside in favour of *Bombastes*, and the Barnwell Theatre scheme was relinquished in favour of the room at the Bull. Then *Bombastes* was supplanted by my *Villikins and his Dinah*, which I undertook to have finished in plenty of time, and which, like *Bombastes*, having only one female character in it, was therefore to be easily managed. We fluctuated between *Bombastes* and *Villikins*, but we determined upon the room at the Bull.*

But, for this it appeared we should also have to obtain the Vice-Chancellor's permission, or the Proctors could come in, ask for our "names and colleges," and report actors and audience to the authorities. Rustication was vexation; and we were not at all sure what penalty might be incurred for acting stage-plays without a licence. Probably rustication would not follow, but we might be "gated" for the rest of

---

* Of course the "A. D. C.," when started, took up its quarters in the rear of the Hoop Hotel; but before the idea was concreted into a club, the projectors of the performance merely thought of hiring a room at the Bull or some other hotel, "for one night only."

the term, and as that meant a most severe restriction on our liberty, no one cared to run such a risk, especially those who lived outside college, and who when "gated" would have no companions to share their imprisonment, and no cheerful quadrangle, or cloisters, to lounge in.

It was finally decided that the Vice-Chancellor's permission should be obtained (we felt confident that it would be granted) for our performance at the Bull, *or*,—I stipulated for this alternative,—at the Barnwell Theatre. For my part, I held firmly to the latter, and, as they unanimously selected me for the mission to convert the Vice-Chancellor to our theatrical views, I undertook the office, on the distinct understanding, that I was to use my own discretion as to the place to be chosen for our performance.

The Vice-Chancellor was to be found at Caius College.

I had some vague idea that in calling on a Vice-Chancellor some official dress was *de rigueur*. I did not know what, and no one could tell me. I decided, ultimately, for cap and gown. Cap and bells would have been more appropriate. As the hour approached for my visit, I began to be nervous. If I had previously treated the idea of a Vice-Chancellor with more than indifference, I now, for the first time, commenced to think of him with something akin to awe. I had not believed in him, and now I was going to see him. He had been in perspective, at the vanishing point, and now I was going to walk up to him and see him *in propriâ personâ*. If I could have visited him by deputy, I would have done so: but I couldn't.

The time came, and hot and uncomfortable, I entered the gate of Caius, and walked to the Vice-Chancellor's house. Of course the entrance to it was ancient and dingy, all such entrances are. I was left in the sombre passage by a clerical-looking butler, who took my card in to his master.

Beyond the present interview which I am about to recount, I know nothing of this excellent man. (Not the butler, the Vice-Chancellor, though the remark applies to both equally.)

I never, to my knowledge, saw, or spoke to, him again. This was our first and last meeting. Presently I was ushered into a dull, dimly-lighted room, and into the presence of the Vice-Chancellor, a short, wizened, dried-up, elderly gentleman, with little legs and a big head, like a serious Punch doll, wearing his academical cap, and with his gown hitched up under his elbows, which gave him the appearance of having recently finished a hornpipe before I came in. He had the fidgetty air of a short-sighted person who has just lost his glasses. This I believe was the truth : he *had* mislaid his glasses. After saluting me, as I stood, timidly respectful, cap in hand, in the middle of the room, he commenced the conversation.

"You want to see me, I believe, Mr. —, Mr. —," here he referred to the card, but, the light being unfavourable, he was unable to read it without his spectacles, and so gave it up as a bad job. I did not feel inclined to help him. Somehow, why I don't know, I felt that my name would be against me. It was like one of those *obiter dicta*, about which you have to be very careful, lest it should be "used against you at your trial."

"Yes, sir," I said, twiddling the tassel of my cap, which had been cut off rather short.

Then there was a pause. I didn't see how to plunge *in medias res*, and he wouldn't help me.

"I've got a meeting of the Heads in a few minutes," said the Vice-Chancellor, taking out a large watch, pretending to consult it, and then returning it to his fob.

A "meeting of the Heads" had a pantomimic sound about it, which was, in view of my errand, reassuring. I hoped that the "Heads" in "Meeting" would not hurt themselves. In my mind's eye I pictured those Heads, and I remember now how the unfamiliar use of the word "Heads" struck me, and how I formulated a sort of riddle to myself about "how many Heads together make one body." Had I been allowed to chat with the Vice-Chancellor about these "Heads," and could

I thus have gradually proceeded to the object of my visit, I am sure we should have got on quite pleasantly. If I could only have said, "Never mind the *Heads*, listen to my *tale*," the ice would have been broken. But I was too nervous for this ill-timed levity.

I felt I must begin. I began accordingly, very hot, and uncomfortably parched: and in a husky voice, as if I had been breakfasting on nuts.

"I've come, sir, to ask you, sir," I said, "for your permission"—my sentence was not as clear as this, but confused and jumbled: "for your permission, to—to—" and then I thought I could put it better, and so tried back. "I mean, sir, we had some idea of getting up a—a—a—" like Macbeth's amen, the words "theatrical performance" stuck in my throat. If there had been a trap-door at my feet, and I could have been let down easily into the cellar beneath, startled the clerical-looking butler, and then escaped, I would have given a trifle to have done so at that moment. Never shall I forget this interview.

"Yes," he said, taking my sentence up at the point where I had dropped it. "You are getting up a—subscription, eh? For what object?"

I had a great mind to adopt his suggestion, and make it a subscription, instead of theatricals. The idea struck me, "How about saying, we propose to play for a charity. The Something Hospital. I know there is one"; but on second thoughts I discarded this notion, as a detail to be subsequently considered, and made for my point, by the shortest and most direct route in my power.

"No, sir," I replied; "not exactly a subscription, though the object," and here the charity idea again recurred, as softening it all down, "would be the benefit of some hospital—the Adenbrook Hospital, for instance," I added, so as to interest him, as it were, with a certain local colouring. He merely nodded, and peered at me; he was peering at me during nearly the whole interview; and at first I could not

make out why—absence of glasses and nearness of sight
would not sufficiently account for his searching regards.
It was not long before I discovered the reason of this
scrutiny.

"And, sir," I went on, rather vaguely, "I thought—at
least we thought — that a theatrical performance —" he
started, as my cat jumped thus suddenly out of the bag,
and his start frightened me, but I managed to resume as
steadily as I could, "a theatrical performance—of—in fact
—ahem!—some one or two plays—or one—perhaps,"—
thinking not to overpower him with too large a programme all
at once—"and—and—and—" here I came to a standstill.
But I breathed more freely now. The first step had been
taken, and the words "theatrical performance" had been pronounced.

The Vice-Chancellor peered at me, as though I were gradually melting before him in a mist.

"Um!" he said, so portentously, that it sounded to me
like an awful rebuke of my rashness, in daring to thrust myself forward, and disturbing the peace of the University. If
I could, even then, have begged his pardon, and have said,
like Mr. Toots, "It's of no consequence," I would have with-
drawn. But I was not acting for myself, I was a Deputy
with a mission.

"Um!" said the Vice-Chancellor; and, giving his gown a
good hitch up over his elbows, he put his head on one side,
as though he were meditating the commencement of another
hornpipe on the spot. Had he done so, I could have joined
him in a breakdown. Of course, his dance would have been
"the College Hornpipe." On second thoughts, however, he
gave up the idea of dancing, and after some consideration,
during which he seemed to be trying to realise, in his academical mind, the full scope and bearing of my request for a
"theatrical performance," he said,

"And where do you propose giving this dramatic representation?"

The question was more than my wildest hopes could have expected. In effect, he had granted the application, so it seemed to me, and was now going into details. At once I was more at my ease, and answered, with an inquiring, perhaps almost a patronizing, smile, as if rather inviting a suggestion from *him*, than making one myself,—

"Well, sir, we had thought of the—the—". I hesitated a little—but out it must come, and it came—"of the Barnwell Theatre," and seeing his severe expression, I hastened to add, as if I in no way insisted on the Barnwell Theatre as the only place—"or the large room at the Bull."

Somehow I felt that I had put my foot in it—that Barnwell and the Bull had done it between them.

His manner was courteous, but very grave, when, peering at me more intently than ever, he said,—

"I have not the pleasure of being personally acquainted with you, I believe, Mr.—Mr.—Mr.—" and he referred to my card, which he could not see to read.

I was bound to help him. My name, I informed him, was Burnand; somehow it didn't sound to my own ears as if I said it well; in fact, I pronounced it so badly, that I should have been prepossessed against myself, on the spot, had I been somebody else hearing it for the first time. He went on with his examination, as though I were trying to keep something back from him.

"Of Trinity?" he asked, persuasively.

"Of Trinity," I answered.

"A—um—a Fellow of Trinity?" he inquired, with a courtesy of manner, and an emphasis on the word "Fellow" that implied a doubt.

"No, sir," I answered, respectfully, but with as much carelessness as I could muster at the moment,—"no, sir, I am not a Fellow." I tried to give myself the air of saying this, as though I *could* have been a Fellow if I had liked, only that, somehow, it had not suited my purpose.

His manner towards me changed visibly. He became stiffer, and more decidedly the academical Don.

"Um!" he said, with decreasing courtesy, and increasing emphasis on the test word, "A *scholar* of Trinity?"

"No," I replied, getting rather tired of this; "I am not a scholar."

I did not like to tell him I was an undergraduate, and that this was only my second term.

"Oh," he said, with some asperity, as though he resented my having obtained an interview with him under false pretences, "I did not see your gown."

That was what he had been peering at. At first he had thought that I was wearing the gown of a Master of Arts; now, he was not quite clear whether it was a Bachelor's, or not.

"You have taken your degree and are staying up?" he suggested, inquiringly.

It was like a doctor's guesses at a patient's health, and being wrong every time.

"No, sir," I was obliged to admit; "I have not yet taken my degree."

"Oh!" he said, with a sort of pitying air. "Still an undergraduate?"

He had guessed right at last. The opportunity for presenting him with a pun on his own name—which was *Guest* —was almost too good to be lost. But the interests of our dramatic scheme were at stake, and I felt, that, at this critical moment, a false step on my part would ruin our not very bright prospects. Somehow we seemed to have wandered away from the subject, to which I saw no road back. This time *he* took the initiative. Now he was quite the Don. His uncertainty had vanished. It was no longer an interview between a colonel and a captain, or a lieutenant, but between a colonel and a private. Once more he hitched up his gown, but this time it was not with the air of a man who might be going to dance, but with the determined action of a truculent counsel, who is not going to be browbeaten by a witness.

"So you want my permission for a dramatic performance?"

"Yes," I said, humbly, that was what his petitioner, &c., and if he granted it, then, in effect, his petitioners would ever pray, &c., &c.

"Um!" he said, giving another violent hitch up to his gown. "And—ahem!—what play do you propose?"

"What play?" This was an unexpected question. We had, as I have said, fixed on *Box and Cox, Villikins and his Dinah*, if done in time, or *Bombastes*, and perhaps Talfourd's *Macbeth Travestie*.

"Well, sir," I replied, diffidently, "we have not yet quite decided," but, as I didn't want him to make this a pretext for deferring his answer, I added, "but we are considering two or three."

"Ah!" he said, with a more satisfied air, which argued well for my success,—"ah! Of course," he went on, most seriously, "there's a large field for selection."

I was delighted to agree with him.

"There is," I observed, with the authority of a student of dramatic literature, "a very large collection of plays."

My thoughts reverted to "Lacy's Acting Edition," in many volumes, and I thought what a choice we should have, if we once got permission, and how we might play, *Did you ever Send your Wife to Camberwell?* * *My Precious Betsy, That Blessed Baby, Betsy Baker, Domestic Economy, Grimshaw, Bagshaw, and Bradshaw*, and a heap of others, in which Wright, the Keeleys, and Buckstone had been so inimitably funny.

"Yes," the Vice-Chancellor continued, very gravely, and balancing himself alternately on his toes and heels; "there is a large choice. Is it a Greek play that you propose?"

* This was one of the first farces performed by the "A. D. C."

I might have been knocked over with a feather. I saw it was hopeless ; I saw he was on the wrong tack ; I saw, that, unless he granted permission, without further inquiry, there was an end of the matter.

" No," I replied, as if I were most reluctantly divulging a deep secret ; " it is *not* a Greek play." And I wondered to myself what he would think of *Villikins and his Dinah*, if I had mentioned the subject to him.

" Well," he continued, as if inclined to yield a point in my favour, " perhaps you are right. Terence is a favourite. You have, you say, selected a Latin play ?"

" No, sir, I,"—I hesitated,—" it is—it is *not* a Latin play."

I devoutly wished I could have said *Box and Cox* was a Latin play. It flashed through my mind, " If I could only call it *Balbus et Caius*, or *Castor and Pollux*. But it won't do : he would find it out afterwards."

" Not Greek, or Latin !" he exclaimed, as if these were the only two languages he had ever heard of anywhere. " Then what *is* the play you propose ?"

" Well, sir, it's—it's English," I answered ; and I began to have my doubts as to the truth of *that* statement now.

" English !" he repeated, with an air of surprise. " One of Shakspeare's ? Surely that's rather an undertaking ?"

I admitted most readily, for it was the first loophole he had given me, that Shakspeare would indeed have been far too much of an enterprise for us, and that, in fact, we did not aim *quite* so high.

" Then what do you propose to play ?" he asked, severely. I looked at him to see if I could detect the slightest tremble of humour in his eye, or the pucker of a smile on his lips. No. He was as hard as granite. He had suggested Greek plays, Latin plays, and had conceded Shakspeare. Evidently, as Vice-Chancellor of the University, he could not be expected to take cognizance of any compositions outside these three, or rather these two, for Shakspeare was a concession. From

Sophocles to Terence, from Terence to Shakspeare, was all very well, very proper, and both classical and correct; but, from the *Antigone* to the *Adelphi* (Terence's, not Webster's), from the *Adelphi* of Terence (who, when I first went to Eton, was, I thought, an *Irish* dramatist) to the *Comedy of Errors*, and from that to *Box and Cox*, and thence to *Villikins and his Dinah*, the fall was too great for serious consideration. Still the truth had to be told.

. "Well, sir," I began humbly, "we were not thinking of attempting anything great. It is merely among ourselves."

"Members of the University *only*, of course," interrupted the Vice-Chancellor.

"Oh, of course!" I returned, quite cheerfully, being delighted to find myself at one with him on any point. "And, sir, we were thinking of merely playing a little—a little piece."

A grand idea struck me. I would not mention the name, *Box and Cox*, which might only make the Vice-Chancellor think I was laughing at him, but I would mention the name of its author, Mr. Maddison Morton, by which, I fancied, he would be impressed; for I knew that *I*, personally, had always been impressed by the name of Maddison Morton, which, I still think, does sound wonderfully imposing; only it sounds better without the prefix of "*Mister*," which rather vulgarizes it. However, I felt that the Vice-Chancellor was bound to give the "Mister." So I finished up thus,—"We are thinking of playing a little piece by Mr. Maddison Morton."

"Perhaps," it occurred to me, "the Vice-Chancellor may know Maddison Morton; and, if so, all right!"

But Dr. Guest only appeared puzzled, and repeated several times,—

"Morton—Morton!" as if he were either trying to recall an acquaintance of that name, or were learning the word, by heart, like a parrot.

"Maddison Morton," I explained, affably.

" Um ! " he considered.   Then he paused and examined the carpet.   Receiving no assistance from that quarter, he looked up suddenly at me, and asked, " Fellow of Trinity ? "

" No," I said.   I was not aware,—he might be—but—in fact, Maddison Morton had never presented himself to me in that light.   For *me*, it had been sufficient that Maddison Morton should have been the distinguished author of *Box and Cox.*

" *Not* a Fellow of Trinity ? " said the Vice-Chancellor, suspiciously.

" No ; I don't think so."

" Um !   And you propose acting a play written by Mr. Morton, who is *not* a Fellow of Trinity ?   Yes ; what is the name ? "

I could not help it.   It was bound to come out at last.

" It is called *Box and Cox.*"

Even then I was afraid he would ask me if ' Box and Cox ' were Fellows of Trinity, without which qualification their fate, I felt at once, was sealed.   I even regretted not having introduced them as *Mr.* Box and *Mr.* Cox, the other title sounding so familiar.   If I could only have metamorphosed them into the Rev. Mr. Box, M.A., Fellow of Trinity, and Dr. Cox, D.D., Fellow of Caius, it would have been perfect.

But the Vice-Chancellor was very grave and serious over it. He did not know either Box or Cox, by name.   They were not members of the University, any more than Mr. Maddison Morton was a Fellow of Trinity, and so he could not recognize them, officially.   Box, *and* Cox, might be, he seemed to think, very worthy persons, without a stain on their character, but he could not countenance them, as performing in this University.   He had misunderstood me; and thought I had proposed a theatrical entertainment to be given by Messrs. Box and Cox (of the London theatres) in a play written by a Mr. Morton,—*not* a Fellow of Trinity.*

---

* How I subsequently wished that I had been acquainted with the fac
of Mr. Tom Taylor having been a Fellow of Trinity.   I was acquainted with

I thought he was going to ask me for the name of the other piece, and I would rather have relinquished the whole affair, there and then, than have given up the name of *Villikins and his Dinah*, and have avowed myself the author. No: I had got into a difficulty, and made myself a martyr for the sake of *Box and Cox*, and that was ridiculous enough for one morning. If I added *Villikins*, he would think that there was a lunatic undergraduate at large in Trinity College.

Fortunately the clock reminded him, that, at that hour, a council was sitting,—where his attendance was imperative.

"I will lay this matter," he said, solemnly, "before the Heads, and will forward you our decision."

The idea of the Heads again struck me, only this time in connexion with the tossing shilling and the lucky sixpence, in "Box and Cox." "Heads I *don't* win," I thought to myself as I thanked the Vice-Chancellor for his polite attention, and so withdrew. Through an open side-door in the hall, as I passed out, I saw the "Heads" assembling, and I could not help feeling intensely amused at the notion of the Vice-Chancellor's gravely submitting for the careful consideration of this august body the names of Box *and* Cox, not being members of the University, associated with that of Maddison Morton (*not* a Fellow of Trinity), and of F. C. Burnand, undergraduate, Trin. Coll. Cam.

This was the first step taken towards obtaining official recognition for an amateur University performance, with what result remains to be seen.

And this interview, which should form the subject of a fine historical cartoon, took place in the early part of the Lent Term—it must have been quite at the commencement of the Term, while the fervour of the previous Term's theatricals was still warm within us, and before I had settled down to the routine of University life.

some of his plays, performed, I think, by the Wigans, and then there was *Our Clerks*, with the Keeleys in it. But, advanced as I was in theatrical matters, I did not know everything at eighteen.

CHAPTER II.

THE "ATHENÆUM" PERFORMANCE AND THE FIRST
INSPIRATION.

I HAVE never felt any profound veneration for a Don—I
mean, of course, a University Don, as the regular Spanish
Dons, or, rather, the irregular Spanish Dons, as, for example,
Don Quixote or Don Cesar de Bazan, have always commanded
my admiration, if not my esteem and respect.

But for the representative, typical, college Don, I have not,
and never had, I say it boldly, the slightest atom of respect,
and the sentiments of my youth, as regards Dons in general,
have never been modified, or altered, by the experience of
middle-age. What was at first a very natural undergraduate
instinct, has grown into a most firm and honest conviction.

Of course I am aware that there are Dons *and* Dons ; but
when a Don, who *is* a don by position, is at the same time *not*
a Don by disposition, then he ought not to be a Don at all ; he
is so clearly out of place, that, when you inform your friends
that the gentleman in question is a resident fellow of S. Boni-
face, they will hardly credit your assertion.

There is no such creature, properly speaking, as a young Don.
If a man is a Don by nature, he is never young. There are
no such comfortable places anywhere as those held by the college Dons in residence. Their life is simply a luxurious
development of bachelor existence in club and chambers, but
their chambers are above suspicion, and the obligations of
their state are a guarantee for their individual local respecta-
bility, while their public morality is as unexceptionable as

their dinners at the high table in Hall, and their wine in the common room of the College.

Dons seem to forget they have ever been undergraduates; and, for the matter of that, they have very little to forget, as they, probably, never partook of the generally hilarious undergraduate's temperament,—the healthy outburst of youth and the overflow of animal spirits, peculiarly English in its boisterous character, easily directed for good by judicious control, and turned off into various channels of harmless recreation, where a discriminating superior, if he chose to trouble himself about those placed under his care, would be able to detect the bent, inclination, of many a young man, whose peculiar talents might be then and there fostered with the most beneficial results.

The " A. D. C." has had some valuable assistance from Dons, but these belong to the exceptional class, who were not Dons by Nature, but by Grace of the senate,—that is if a Grace of the senate be required for the creation, which I doubt; but the sentence turns itself well, and has a theological air suited to the gravity of the subject, and so, right or wrong, with Grace or Graceless, let it stand.

The Vice-Chancellor who wanted to know if *Box and Cox* were "Fellows of Trinity," and who seemed to ignore all dramatic literature, except what was strictly classical and within the limits of an ordinary examination paper, was, and has always been, my *beau-idéal* of an English University Don. Why have we not Schools of Dramatic Art, and Schools of Painting within the University? Why not a professorship of Dramatic Literature, the lecturer explaining the art of construction, the method of development of plot, and the examination requiring a competent knowledge of the English drama first and foremost, and then of the French, the Italian, the German and the Spanish?

Have we all of us a natural taste for mathematics, or for the military tactics of the ancient Greeks and Romans? Let the usual grounding, as we have had it—and as it still is, and *must* be,—be retained, and our sons will be more interested in Balbus and Caius building their wall, if the wall itself is made an object of interest to us in the first instance. If Balbus and Caius, both authors, actors, and managers, and joint proprietors of a theatre, having purchased the suitable plot of ground, commence their work with a wall——why here, at once, is more than a field,—a number of provinces of knowledge,—open at once to the art student, who would pick up incidentally an acquaintance with practical business, and be directed to the schools of Law to master the questions of freehold, copyhold, tenancy, sale and purchase, ancient lights, compensation, &c., &c., to the school of architecture for the best models, to gain information in various languages concerning the theatres in various parts of the civilized world —and so on—*ad infinitum.*

Would not many of us have taken a personal interest in Caius and Balbus—from this point of view?

Directly a lad finds a line of study that interests him, he will study.

The lad who has not got the taste for the studies which go to make a senior wrangler, will never arrive at that degree, no matter how good his will, how hard his work. It will be all up hill and against collar, and, as in a crowd of competitors there must be some one to whom the work is pleasant and comes easily, the misplaced student will expend his energies to no purpose—save one, which I admit *is* an important one. I mean the exercise of his will in obedience to a call of duty. But what would not such a young man have done with congenial work? What eminence would he not have attained, early in life, in that line for which nature had fitted him?

*　　*　　*　　*　　*　　*

Which disquisition and inquiry after all comes to this, that if the Vice-Chancellor had been struck by my application for a performance to be licensed by the University, he might have gone a step farther and have instituted a Dramatic College, whence in the course of a few years, would have issued highly educated Keans, Kembles, Macreadys, and Garricks, with an English Sardou or two, and an Alexandre Dumas *père et fils* to write for them. But *that* was not to be.

In what form the Vice-Chancellor presented my request to The Heads—oh, those Heads !—always a pantomimic idea to me—I have never been able to learn, nor can I easily imagine.

Whether he got confused in his names and told them that Mr. Maddison Box, who was *not*, he regretted to say, a Fellow of Trinity, and Mr. Morton Cox, of No College as far as he could learn, wished to give a theatrical entertainment for a charity, with his (the Vice-Chancellor's) sanction, and that of the Heads,—whereupon they all shook them solemnly, and the request was negatived by the whole lot,—or whether he only casually alluded to it as an insignificant matter, which, as coming from two undergraduates of Trinity, whose names were Box and Cox, who had deputed another foolish undergraduate of the name of Burnand to interview him (the Vice) on the subject, was not worth their consideration—I have never inquired. Suffice it that three days after,—why three days? there must have been some sort of ceremony—some delay—some formalities—unless the Vice had forgotten all about it, and had suddenly found my card three days afterwards, and determined at once to answer me—three days after my interview, a very polite formal note was left at my lodgings, opposite Trinity, to the effect that " the V.-C. presented his compliments to Mr. Burnand, who would inform his friends "—(he hadn't got Cox and Box out of his head—he evidently pictured me with Cox and Box at wine in my rooms,—" that after due consideration the Heads were unable to grant their sanction for a theatrical performance."

Well, now we were in a worse position than before. Without having gone to the Vice-Chancellor we could have given a performance, and if interfered with could have pleaded *bonâ fide* ignorance of all statutes in that case made and provided. But *now*, if we gave a performance, we knew that it must be in direct violation of the University Law.

Our application for permission virtually amounted to a recognition of the law against theatrical performances in the University.

And the V.-C.'s explicit refusal—a refusal coming from the collective wisdom of the University—came as an utterance from the Talking Head. The representative of all authority settles the question. If *we* performed now—we, Box, Cox, and Burnand, at least those were the parties addressed through me, by the Vice—if *we* performed now, we defied the law, and ran no slight danger of excommunication, I mean of rustication, loss of term, or gating for a term, or some such penalty.

We had the available talent at hand. What was to be done ? We consulted together.

I have already mentioned our first performance in our rooms opposite Trinity Gate—rooms that have now vanished and the space occupied (worthily, I am glad to say) by an annex of Trinity—and therefore we had, as I have said, the beginnings of a *corps dramatique.*

The great difficulty of obtaining a fitting representation of the " Spindle side," had been got over, and in Mr. F. C. Wilson of Trinity, who subsequently figured in the "A. D. C." Bills as " Mr. C. Digby," we had an artist who, in Shakspeare's time might have been chosen by the poet himself to represent his Audrey or his Lady Macbeth,—for strange to say, but fortunately for us, he was excellent in burlesque though his forte was undoubtedly tragedy, of which quality, except in the course of burlesque, he was never called upon to give us a taste. Those who may be inclined to remark, goodnaturedly, that at that time we probably mistook tragedy for burlesque, and burlesque for tragedy, must remember that we were constantly seeing Robson in his best days at the Olympic, when in his burlesque he touched the very boundary line of tragedy—indeed in Shylock and Medea he passed it, instantly returning, however, to burlesque—and in *The Miser's Daughter* we saw the intensity of his dramatic power.

Burlesque there was not a mere leg-display, for the ballet was still in existence as an attractive part of the entertainment, but it was acted, with a purpose, by the Keeleys, the Wigans, Charles Mathews, the Frank Matthewses, James Bland, Miss Horton, Harley, Madame Celeste, and Mrs. Mellon, and the burlesque, or extravaganza, occupied an important position in the evening's programme.   Therefore our notions of burlesque were rather different from what prevails now-a-days, and even from what was in vogue a few years after the "A. D. C." was started, that is when Strand burlesques were made popular by the charm of Miss Swanborough, the pretty faces and the inimitable fun of Patty Oliver and Marie Wilton (Mrs. Bancroft), the earnestness of Charlotte Saunders, the grace of Fanny Josephs, and the original humour of 'Jimmy' Rogers, and 'Little' Clarke.

But at Cambridge in my time our ideal of burlesque acting was Robson; of light comedy, Charles Mathews; of farce, Buckstone.

Of Dramatic Authors, except Maddison Morton, we knew very little.   We spoke of any play as "one of Lacy's"— meaning that it was in the catalogue of plays sold by the late Mr. T. Hailes Lacy, of 89, Strand.

Besides F. C. Wilson there was a Mr. Llewellyn who appeared—in the private theatricals at our rooms on this occasion only, with singular distinction, but who took his degree and his departure soon after, and never belonged to the "A. D. C."   So that F. C. Wilson and myself were in effect the entire company.   Neither of us wished the idea to be dropped, but besides being my senior, he was in a totally different set from that in which I lived and moved,—and, as the only bond of union between us, at this time, was our taste for theatricals, and as there appeared just now very little chance of our being able to indulge this taste, we seldom met. But when we did, it was to talk about the possibility of establishing a Dramatic Club, which he promised to join if it could be once started.

The Vice-Chancellor had puzzled me. For a time he had paralysed my action.

I confided my difficulties to some friends, Etonian undergraduates belonging to the Athenæum Club, which was *the* swell University Club, for which only the University Tufts were eligible. The Tufts naturally attracted the Toadies, as Athenæum membership—the rooms were over a tailor's shop in Trinity Street—conferred a dignity on the privileged undergraduate, and for that matter on the privileged graduate,—for there were, I fancy, one or two youngish Dons, recently in orders, who thought more of their position as members of the Athenæum, than of their status as Fellows of Trinity.

A generously disposed young nobleman might be of considerable service hereafter to an agreeable and reverend Don, who in such a patron saw the first sign-post directing him to a bishopric.

The next thing I heard was that the Athenæum was going to give a performance at the Red Lion, an hotel in Petit Curey, where there was a first-rate room, generally used for masonic lodges and county balls.

The Athenæum made no secret of it.

They pretended to do so just as a show of such deference as—*noblesse oblige*—was to be expected for dukes, earls, and other titled members of the aristocracy who had kindly consented to come up to the University and patronise the ancient Institution.

This undoubtedly vexed me, considerably.

The Vice-Chancellor had refused permission to Box and Cox, and to commoners, plebeians, anybodies, and here were Viscount Box and Lord Cox, with Sir Bluster Bouncer, without a ' with your leave,' or ' by your leave,' flaunting their theatrical programme in the face of the University, or at all events of Trinity College, which to *us* (of Trin. Coll., Cam.) was about the same thing.

To quote the immortal work, "Should I curb my indignation? should I falter in my vengeance? No!" (vide Box's or Cox's speech, when one throws the other's breakfast out of the window).

But I *did* curb my indignation. I did not falter in my vengeance, but I postponed it.

One of the Athenæum men, an Etonian,—who was to play Frank Matthews's part in *The Bachelor of Arts*, paid me the compliment of coming to me to be coached. As I have already explained, I had brought with me from Eton this theatrical reputation. I coached him with an imitation of Frank Matthews from memory, and then proffered my services to assist any one else.

I had seen the play more than once, and remembered most of the business.

My usefulness entitled me to a free admission on both nights—for there were two—*Charles the Second* and *The Original* being the first bill, and *The Bachelor of Arts* and a farce the second—and I went to see the performances, which went off capitally, and were, as far as I can remember, eminently successful.

The point gained was that it had not been interfered with by the authorities, and so formed a precedent.

On that very night a member of the Athenæum, George Lennox Conyngham, and a certain medical practitioner who had received a foreign diploma, and who shall be nameless here except as "The Doctor" (for he had nothing at all to do with the University, and was not recognised professionally by the tutors), met at the former's room for supper, and to criticise the whole performance, which we considered could have been vastly improved in various ways. I was annoyed at their having, as I considered, seized on my theatrical idea, and at my having been excluded from active participation in their performance, and so I determined to start something really

" big," as the Americans say, to which the Athenians should have to pay for admission, and that only as a favour.

I was not going to have my idea baulked. I proposed a Theatrical Club.

Conyngham jumped at the notion. It would be a slap in the face for the Athenæum. The Doctor naturally jumped at it, as he would have jumped at anything that gave him a chance of securing a footing among University men, and getting together a good outside practice. I did not see his motive then. I was only interested in the success of my scheme.

I proposed a permanent theatre. Where?

Old Litchfield—gathered to his ancestors long ago—who used to keep a well known *restauration* at Cambridge, whence issued the desserts for wines and dinners, and at whose shop the free-and-easy undergraduate took his dinner when he was either too late, or disinclined for " Hall,"—old Litchfield informed us, as an authority, that *he* remembered a theatre at what was now Death and Dyson's livery stable in Jesus Lane, and he described it as fitted up with boxes, and pit, and gallery, and how it was patronised by the town and county people—and how the University authorities sat on it, and how it collapsed. Then he told us of another abortive attempt in Swan's auction rooms: and of another at the Hoop.

" The Hoop!" we exclaimed; " are there rooms at the Hoop?"

" Of course—the Union (*i. e.*, the Debating Club) had them at one time, and now they're turned into billiard rooms."

Very evidently the proprietor, whoever it might be, would never consent to forego such a profitable concern as billiard rooms, to turn them into such a very speculative and uncertain affair as a theatre supported by undergraduates.

So after a dinner at Litchfield's we decided to look about.

Our looking about cost us several dinners at the Hoop itself, where, at length, we found two unused rooms apart from the billiard rooms, from which they were separated by a strong partition, and a securely fastened door.

I forget why these were never used. The objection was that they were over a stable : but the stable was empty, and was used for stowage of beer and wine casks. Another objection might have been that access to the rooms could only be obtained by going through the Hoop itself, or through the side gate of the Hoop Brewery, in Jesus Lane, and so across a badly paved and dimly lighted yard, whence we mounted up some dirty wooden steps to these rooms.

The larger of the two rooms was lighted by three big windows giving on to some leads, and the lesser by a skylight.

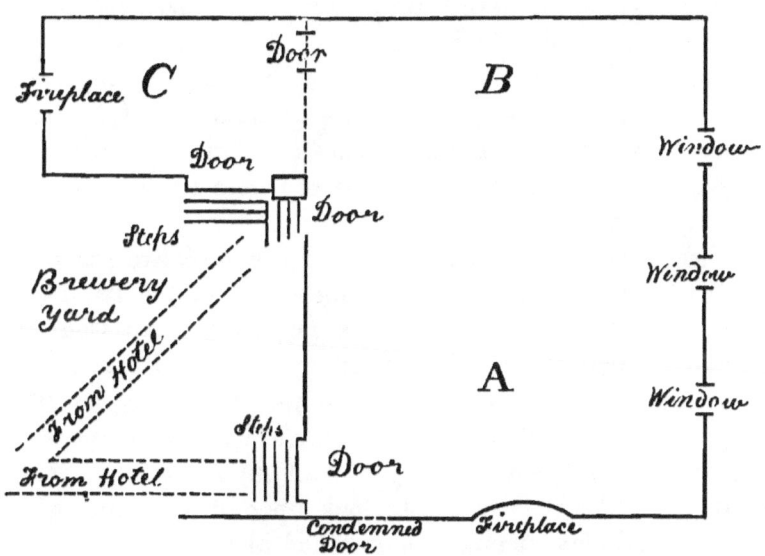

This is an exact plan of the room. The dimensions originally were :—33′ 10″ × 22′ 2″ and 14 ft. high.

In less than a quarter of an hour we had parcelled it out.

A. Auditorium with its door of entrance for the audience.
B. The stage with its door for the orchestra.
C. The green-room, to be used as dressing-room, &c., for the "artists," with their own private stage door

What could be more perfect ?

It was not large, but it was large enough to begin with.

The next thing was to ask about the lease, which the Doctor undertook to do, as neither Conyngham nor myself—certainly I less than anyone—knew very much about it.

However, the landlord—Mr. Ekin—would only treat with a member of the University. He did not want to know what it was intended for : enough for his purpose that it should be taken by responsible undergraduates as a Club.

The rooms were almost useless, and he was very glad to let them at a reasonable rent.

I suppose by this time (twenty-four years after) now that the Club possesses the entire suite, he is not sorry he entertained the original—the very original proposition.

The end of the Lent Term was fast approaching, and something had to be settled before we went away for Easter vacation, so that during our absence a commencement might be made, and something like a list of members obtained as a security for our expenses.

With a dash which was worthy of a speculative promoter of these modern times of companies .and limited liability I went in for the premises, I think in conjunction with Conyngham, and took them by the quarter; at least, I think such were the terms of our lease. We had something to sign which was easy, and something to pay which was not so easy, but which, being paid, not only gave an impulse to our undertaking, but also induced us to look upon it in a somewhat more business-like manner than we had hitherto done.

It was, I think, about the first matter of business into which—that is, signing and paying and taking a receipt—I have ever entered.

I looked upon it as a form, except the payment, and then I felt we were committed beyond hope of return.

The next step was to plan out the stage. For this work we were recommended to a capital carpenter, one Lovett, a tall handsome intelligent man, with a big beard, and a way of understanding what you meant before you had uttered half a sentence that saved a heap of trouble.

I fancy that Lovett, as upright and honest a tradesman as ever stept, wished like the Doctor, to make a University connection, and therefore went to work for us with a will, trying to do everything as reasonably as possible.

He was theatrically inclined too, and was, I fancy, himself a member of some town *Corps dramatique* that had its occasional performances, out of Term time, at the Barnwell Theatre.

Once, and once only, while I was staying up to read, did I witness a portion of one of these representations.

The piece was I think *The Field of Forty Footsteps*, but I am not certain. Anyhow it dealt with a Virtue much rouged in distress, who being at her wits' end in a wood alone with a villain of the deepest dye in awe-inspiring boots, cried frantically,

" 'Elp ! 'elp !! 'elp !!! "

" Aye," cynically replied the scowling ruffian, drawing his dagger—the point of which nearly reached his boots—" Aye ! 'elp ! but 'ow ? "

Whereupon the hero rushed in, polished off the double-dyed one in two-twos, and everybody lived very happily ever afterwards except the wicked nobleman who had employed the villain in the capacity of " a creature," and who vanished through a trap in the flames of a burning castle.

This by the way.

Lovett undertook to make us a stage, proscenium, and all appliances and means to boot.

What the amount of the contract was I forget. It may now be in the archives of the Club. But it has been with great difficulty that I have got at any archives at all. The early history of all great institutions is generally enveloped in mystery, and fact and fable are closely intermingled. Fortunately from almost the very commencement we had some sort of record kept, and this, with our oldest programmes,

I have by me. The date of the private amateur performance in the rooms shared by J. H. Norman, Glyn Vivian and myself, over the grocer's opposite Trinity, was November, 1854.

The date of the Athenæum performance at the Red Lion was about the middle of Lent Term, 1855, and it was immediately after this that we went to work.

So earnest were Conyngham and myself in the matter, that after receiving our exeat for the vacation, we " stayed up "—contrary to all college rules and regulations—for some days at the Eagle Hotel, in order to see Lovett well started, and then fearing lest we should suddenly be interviewed by the proctors, we went to town, where we used to meet either at Limmer's, in Conduit Street, or at Long's in Bond Street, to draw up rules for the Club, which henceforth was to be known as the Amateur Dramatic Club, or " A. D. C."

The rules were drawn up at Limmer's, and all our correspondence proceeded from these head-quarters. We had already several adherents, but not one, except Conyngham, from among the members of the aristocratic Athenæum Club, which, it was supposed, viewed our proceedings with disfavour.

Our original members were not undergraduates who had come up from Eton or Harrow with any particular prestige, but,—with two or three exceptions, who set up for possessing a certain intimacy with life in London,—our first members were law-abiding, quiet, well-conducted members of the University, and came from Trinity, Caius, St. John's, King's and Magdalene.

From Limmer's we issued notices of a meeting to be convened at the Hoop Hotel, where the objects of the Club would be stated, the rules finally settled, the amount of entrance fee and subscription fixed, and a date settled for our first public performance.

Conyngham and myself returned as early as possible to Cambridge in the ensuing May Term, and were delighted to find that Lovett had made good progress with the stage, and the rooms began to assume a habitable, or rather a clubbable appearance.

Then came our first public meeting at the Hoop, money was subscribed, the carpenter was refreshed, the landlord was satisfied, and we looked forward to such a sale of tickets for our first performance, as would more than reimburse us for our outlay.

CHAPTER III.

AFTER several preliminary meetings of those who were the chief promoters of the future Club, we managed to obtain a sufficient following to warrant our calling a public meeting at the Hoop Hotel early in the May Term, 1855.

The original members of the "A. D. C." who attended this first public meeting, and without whose hearty concurrence no start could have been effected, were—

Lennox Conyngham	Trin.
T. R. Polwhele	John's.
T. White	Trin.
Gerald FitzGerald	Trin.
F. C. Wilson	Trin.
"The Doctor"	Unattached.
G. Harvey	Magdalene.
Reginald Kelly	Trin. Hall.
— Wood	
— Collins	John's or Trinity.
— Whitley	Trin.
G. Lampson . . . . . }	Trin.
H. Lampson . . . . . }	
Tyrrel	Trin.
H. Snow	John's.
Peere Williams Freeman	Trin.
F. C. Burnand	Trin.

Of these, five besides myself were Etonians, and three Harrovians. We had only one sporting man among us, T. White—who was brought by Gerald FitzGerald on the ground, I believe, of his being an excellent subscriber to anything, and of his not being in the slightest degree interested in theatricals, which qualities, combined, would make him a most useful and most unobjectionable member of the "A. D. C." I remember the readiness with which, at the very first call, he produced five pound notes, and frightened all the quiet and moderate men by the force of his language, the energy of his character, and the amount of money at his command.

He was one of the best gentlemen riders of the University, and had the reputation among us of being excessively wealthy.

I am almost sure that over and above his entrance fee and subscription, he insisted on making the Club funds a very handsome present to assist us at starting.

Whether subsequently he ever witnessed a performance, or knew that he was a member, I cannot precisely say. I remember his appearance in the reserved seats once only during an *entr'acte*, when, having come in late after a long day's hunting and a heavy dinner, he fell asleep, and was only awoke by the man coming to lock up for the night.

Demand creates supply. I wanted a "stage manager"— whose duties should be to see to all the mechanism of the stage, the carpentering, the gas, the curtain, the trap—we had a trap—and so forth, but who had nothing to do with the acting.

I was the "acting manager," which in our phraseology meant ' a manager of the acting,' but did not imply what I now know to be the sole duties of a professional acting manager, *i.e.* to see to the advertisements, to the accounts, and the correspondence, the box office, the engagements, &c., &c.

At the "A. D. C." the 'Acting Manager' was equivalent to a professional stage manager, while our stage manager was a sort of head superintendent of scene-painters, carpenters and gasmen ; a good deal more than a "master carpenter" or even than the scenic artist at any ordinary theatre, his duties corresponding more nearly to those of Mr. Beverley's at

Drury Lane, though, at first, it included those of the property master and the machinist.

Subsequently, of course, these functions were divided and
properly apportioned, but this is how we began, and the
gentleman who took the place was Mr. T. R. Polwhele, of St.
John's, who was in every way the very man for the office.

He was ingenious, which was excellent to begin with; he
was practical, which was first-rate to go on with; and he was
economical, which was capital to finish with.

If it had not been for Polwhele's care from the first, we
should have run further into debt than we actually did.

For my own part, I had not my equal for ordering everything
we wanted, and everything else that we didn't want; but
fortunately, as a safeguard, I had agreed that no orders should
be valid unless countersigned "T. R. Polwhele." This saved
us pounds.

It is also due to his care that the early records, now before
me, are so clear, and so well kept.

I fancy our first secretary was Mr. Sheppard Harvey of
Magdalene, but I cannot find his name attached to any docu-
ment or notes, so if they were made by him, they were
afterwards copied into our book by other hands—in one
instance my own —but his signature was omitted.

Our landlord, Mr. Ekin, was inclined, from the first, when
he really saw we meant business, to afford us any assistance
in his power, and did not object to bear part of our expenses
in improving the rooms, though as they were ' improved '
mainly for our special purpose, the alterations could hardly
have appeared at the time as likely to be of any permanent
use to him.

The next point was to settle the first programme with
which we were to appeal to the sympathies of the University public, represented to us, chiefly of course, by undergraduates.

About the Vice-Chancellor and the Heads none of us ever
again troubled ourselves. They had winked—that is, if such

Heads could be guilty of so indecorous a proceeding—they had winked, and wisely winked, at the performances of the Aristocratic Athenæum, and it would be marvellously unjust to stop *us*, because we didn't happen to represent the swelldom of the University.

It is true that Gerald FitzGerald had commenced his career as a Fellow-commoner, but as, after a time, he had resigned the insignia of his position, his blue and silver gown, and had become a simple plebeian undergraduate, *he* didn't carry much weight.

Some few croakers there were who prophesied dire things about the interference of proctors and the dissolution of the Club, but the majority asked what could be done by any authorities if we kept our own counsel, if we told no one except a few privileged friends who would be willing to pay five shillings for a ticket, which would be *given* him, under seal of secresy, and in much the same mysterious way as the rendezvous, and ticket for the train and inner ring at a prize fight used to be confided to the initiated at the " Pugs " bars in the good old days of Ben Caunt, Bendigo, and Tom Sayers.

It was impressed on every one that the very meaning of the initials " A. D. C." was to remain a mystery : they were to be the masonic " B—z and J—n " of our craft, not to be revealed to a soul. This would excite curiosity, and induce earnest inquirers to join our little community, whose aim and object was the attainment of the most rational enjoyment by the employment of the least harmless and most beneficial means at the disposition of a secret guild of Dramatic Art, which after all did not deserve persecution because it could not bear the light, but which, if encouraged, might one day have its professors in the chairs of the University. What is this but an initiative of *Comédie Anglaise*? All the members had an equal interest in success, and were only inspired by their love of art, by their predilection for this form of amusement, and not by any sort of greed of gain ?

Yet we were in the catacombs. We kept our place of meeting a secret. Our records were confided to safe hands—our "writings," with which we wouldn't have parted even under the pressure of a Neronic persecution from The Heads, and we actually took such precautions at first that to ensure our safety by flight in case of a raid of Proctors, we had a speaking tube run through from the Hoop bar to our green-room, by which " the office could be given " in an emergency, and outside the windows of the stage we had a ladder placed, by which the performers could have descended into a yard below, and so out into the street, dressed in our caps and gowns, which would hide the theatrical costume under-neath.

This never happened, but we were prepared.

At one time we thought of having a pass-word and a sign of membership, and that there should be a change of sign and pass-word every night of performance for the admission of non-members, who would then not have paid five shillings for a ticket, but for a pass-word, without which, entrance would be as impossible as into a masonic lodge without the grip and sign.

However, tickets were adopted.

We had no idea that we were contravening any act of Parliament made and provided, and no one at any time thought it worth while to inform us that we required a license for a dramatic performance where money was taken from visitors, and we were in delightful ignorance of any such duty on the goods we used as ' fees to authors.'

If we knew of the existence of the Dramatic Authors' Society at all, we thought of it only as a Club, perhaps, something like ours at Cambridge, where, perhaps, there were rooms for the authors to write in, where probably Maddison Morton had a study to himself as a reward for having written *Box and Cox*, or that it was a sort of Garrick Club, and that was all we knew about it.

Now (1879) all this is changed. The performances themselves are under the Vice-Chancellor's rule, and the Club pays its fees regularly to the Secretary of the D. A. S. *This* is as it should be : *that* was as it shouldn't have been, but as, unfortunately, it *was.* But then we were in our infancy, some of us were still legal infants—I mean legally ' infants '— and we couldn't be expected to know everything.

We had to learn. Ignorance was bliss. It was a very happy time—one of the happiest—as ' So say all of us ' who remember those days.

We were seventeen members, and every one of us could easily get rid of from seven to ten tickets at the least. If we took a hundred and seventy at five shillings a piece, we should do very well. Our " Auditorium "—this name was not invented in those primitive days—would not hold more than sixty, comfortably, exclusive of the row in front reserved for members, which had to, be set considerably back in order to allow for our orchestra, and so it was absolutely necessary for us to give two performances, the expense for which would be but a very slight increase on that of one alone.

If the first night were a success we might give three performances, and announce the extra performance on the second night.

This actually happened. Our first performance was such a decided success, the novelty was so great, the whole thing so fresh, the fun so spontaneous and hearty, and so much to the taste of the undergraduates, that we did give three nights, and though the extra night was, on account of the short notice, not so good as we might have expected, yet on the whole we recouped ourselves for the expenses, and put by a small sum into our reserve fund. But at the same time, despite all the precautions of our thrifty stage manager, we had expended a great deal more than was necessary, and this outlay was not on our properties, or on our stage carpentering, or on our band, of which more anon,—but, on our scenery.

Naturally our scenery had presented a real difficulty.

Amateurs, such as the Athenæum Amateurs, playing for one or two nights only and there an end, had ordered a stage from London with scenery to hand, costumes, &c. It was paid for and done with. But we wished to make a store of scenery. The stage was our own : and we were determined to have the scenery painted for us.

By whom ?

Not one amongst us knew anything whatever of the professional stage. Nobody knew an actor. What an important personage would he have been considered who could have boasted of such an acquaintance ! no one knew a scenic artist.

Fortunately I had *heard* of one.

A gentleman, who, years before, had worked for Madame Vestris at the Olympic, and had painted pictures for Charles Mathews, had also done some work for a relative of mine, who had recommended him to my father as a good man to paint a likeness of me when a boy of fourteen. He did it. I have it now. Alas poor Jones !—that was his name. I daresay it is like what I was—I hope it isn't. . . . However—*passons.* When I recommended Jones I had not seen my own portrait for years; I did not remember *it*, which was lucky, but I remembered who painted it, which was still more lucky—for Jones.

Jones was his name. We knew him as " Old Jones." An eminently respectable, elderly artist, with grey hair and whiskers, satin stock, low waistcoat, tail coat (in the day time), and double eyeglasses suspended round his neck by a broad black riband. Quite a character; like a father in a farce, who objects to everything up to ten minutes to eleven and then gives in and blesses the young couple.

He had a number of anecdotes about Macready, and Kemble, and personal reminiscences of Mathews, Madame Vestris, and other theatrical celebrities, on the strength of which he asked us, while at work, three pounds per diem, exclusive of his board and lodging, which, as his introducer, and considering him as in some sort of way related to my family, on the portrait side,—I undertook to provide.

We found everything for the Great Jones, who, I am bound to say, gave us on this occasion three most effective scenes, which served the Club for the first ten years or more.

They were a Cottage Interior, "which," Jones observed with all the sagacity of an old stager, "will always be useful."

And an Exterior—a wood landscape, "which," observed our experienced and intelligent artist, "will serve for a gentleman's park, or a wood, or a garden, or for any out-of-doors scene in the country anywhere."

He painted an Act Drop, and with this concluded his labours, which extended over five days, and took the gilt off our gingerbread to the tune of eighteen pounds.

I have heard subsequent members begrudge this outlay. I never did. The scenes were capital and lasted admirably, besides serving as a model for our future amateur artists.

The Exterior, with four tree wings to match, was to be used for the wood where Bombastes encounters Artaxominous ; the Interior, with two wings to match, was to represent Distaffina's cottage. For we had settled upon *Bombastes Furioso* as our afterpiece at my instance, seeing that I had a very pleasurable remembrance of having played in it at Eton three years before, and I knew most of it by heart. My part was Artaxominous.

In order to put the authorities off the scent, we invented *noms de fantaisie* under which we were to appear in the programme.

As there is no longer any necessity for preserving our *incognitos* I will give both the real and assumed names in placing our first programme, entire, before our readers. It was on good, white foolscap paper, or rather what is known at Cambridge as "scribbling paper" size, clearly printed without any sort of ornamentation whatever, and the name of the printer does not appear, and there is no date to it. Here it is :—

A. D. C.

THIS EVENING WILL BE PRESENTED

A FAST TRAIN!   HIGH PRESSURE!! EXPRESS!!!

Colonel Jack Delaware	Mr. G. SEYMOUR.
Griffin	Mr. TOM PIERCE.
Biffin	Mr. A. HERBERT.

TO BE FOLLOWED BY

DID YOU EVER SEND YOUR WIFE TO CAMBERWELL?

Chesterfield Honeybun	Mr. TOM PIERCE.
Crank	Mr. W. SMITH.
Mrs. Houghton	Mr. C. DIGBY.
Mrs. Crank	Mr. T. KING.
Mrs. Jewell	Mr. R. JOHNSON.

TO CONCLUDE WITH THE BURLESQUE TRAGIC OPERA

BOMBASTES FURIOSO.

Artaxominous (*King of Utopia*) . . .	Mr. TOM PIERCE.
Fusbos	Mr. T. KING.
General Bombastes	Mr. JAS. BEALE.
Distaffina	Mr. C. DIGBY.

ARMY, COURTIERS, &c., &c.

Acting Manager—TOM PIERCE, *Esq.*   *Stage Manager*—N. YATES, *Esq.*
Prompter—J. SHEPHERD, *Esq.*
Scenery and Appointments by S. J. E. JONES, Esq.

That was our first night's bill.

Mr. G. Seymour was G. Lennox Conyngham; *Mr. A. Herbert* was Gerald FitzGerald; *Mr. W. Smith*, J. M. Wilson; *Mr. C. Digby*, F. C. Wilson; *Mr. T. King*, L. Evans; *Mr. R. Johnson*, R. Kelly; *Mr. Jas. Beale*, R. Snow; *N. Yates, Esq.*, T. R. Polwhele; *J. Shepherd, Esq.*, Sheppard

Harvey; and S. J. E. Jones, Esq. *was* himself, Tom Pierce being myself.

Why all the actors were "Misters," when the acting manager, stage manager, and even "prompter" were "Esquires," I don't know.

This invidious distinction disappeared from our bills after this first term.

The *lever du rideau* was chosen by Conyngham who "saw himself" in the part of Jack Delaware originally played by Charles Mathews.

I say "G. Seymour" *saw* himself, for it was more than the audience did, the stage being so dark—the action is supposed to be at night in an interior—that no one could see anything at all.

For some time it was a mystery play, and to the end the plot was on the first night very intricate, chiefly owing to the nervousness of the performers, and the insufficiency of the rehearsal of this piece, all our time having been bestowed on the two important pieces of the evening, the middle farce, and the burlesque tragic opera.

Two out of the three actors in this first trifle bustled about a good deal, and tried to find out the plot for themselves as they went on, while the third, who was supposed to be the hero of the story, rushed on and off in an excited manner, loudly declaring, in what he imagined to be a correct imitation of the American twang, that he was "A fast train, high pressure express!" that, consequently, he wouldn't wait for anybody to do anything. As *Griffin* I had to be an old man in a night-cap, perpetually lighting a candle, and tumbling across *Biffin*, whose *rôle* consisted in coming on and yawning. Whatever the author might have given him to say, he had reduced to yawning. The difficulty was to get him off the stage when he had once entered. There he stood and yawned, without reference to anybody. Once only he ventured on a "gag" consisting of a single word not ordinarily mentionable to ears polite, which so flabergasted us that we hustled him off, and

very soon afterwards the curtain was dropped on what we felt
to be a hopeless muddle. " A. Herbert " only played in that
piece, and his peculiar style on this occasion was due to his
having considered it necessary to support his pluck for a
public appearance by dining rather too late and too freely, so
that all he recollected of his part was the "business" of
yawning which, as I have said, he once varied with an
exceptional " gag:"

Let me say that when we repeated so as to do it justice,
this piece on the third night, we had carefully rehearsed it ;
all three dined together early, and it "went" capitally.
Entre nous I never thought much of *Griffin*, but it was a
" one part piece," and that part wasn't *Griffin*.

The farce of *Did you ever send your Wife to Camberwell* we
played for three nights, and it took amazingly. It was one
of those broad, old Adelphi farces in which Messrs. Wright,
Paul Bedford, and O. Smith were constantly playing, though
in this there was no part for " little Paul," Wright's part fell
to me (by my own choice it need hardly be said), and the part
of *Crank* was given to " W. Smith," who was nearly equal to
the original " O. Smith " in the gravity and earnestness of his
manner.

Unfortunately " W. Smith " (J. M. Wilson) was very near-
sighted ; indeed, " near-sighted," is hardly the word, as, unless
a book were touching the tip of his nose, he could not distinguish the print, and, when out walking, he was as likely as
not to bow to a lamp-post under the impression that it was
a tall Don of his College, or to follow a Proctor in full
academical costume, with his Master of Arts gown strings
flying, thinking that he was on the track of a pretty girl, and
would only discover his mistake on the Proctor's turning
round sharply, and coming right up against him to ask " his
name and College."

J. M. Wilson had invariably rehearsed in the daytime
when there was plenty of light, but he had never attempted
to walk on any stage at night.

Now J. M. Wilson as *Crank* had to appear at a door at the back of the stage—had to walk slowly forward, and addressing the other character, Honeybun, who is on the opposite side, and taking no notice of his entry, had to ask him,—

" Sir, would you oblige me with the loan of a bellows ? "

The stage directions at rehearsal were that he was to repeat " Sir " several times in order to attract Honeybun's attention. This was done : and the third repetition of the word " Sir " was to bring Wilson down to the flote, *i. e.*, the footlights, which, of course, were unlighted in the daytime.

At the last moment, outside the door of the scene by which he had to enter, it struck Wilson that he shouldn't be able to see his way down the stage.

The scene was, necessarily, partially dark, and the gas was not very brilliant; the flote threw a clear and decided light on the toes and up as far as the knees, but the remainder was in shadow. This was rectified during the burlesque when all the wings were open, and the side-lights were added, but the farce was played in a close, screened-in scene.

Poor Wilson appealed to the stage manager.

" I say, I shan't be able to see."

" You *must* go on," replied the inexorable Polwhele, who never played himself. " They're waiting for you."

" Which way does the confounded door open ?" asked Wilson in an agony.

" Inwards," replied Polwhele, giving it a shove, and at the same time whispering to the unhappy man who was blindly, or shortsightedly, rushing on his fate, " Go straight on, there's nothing in your way."

On came Wilson, like the street blind man without his dog, groping along, dazed by the peculiar glimmer he encountered, and just able to pull himself together sufficiently to recollect that he had to say " Sir" three times, and that the third " Sir" would land him in his proper place. Unfortunately he forgot that his first " Sir" ought to have been said at the door, in which case his calculation would have been exact—

for he was an excellent mathematician, and would have been a wrangler—and the consequence of the omission was that as he gave his first "Sir" three paces in advance of the place where he ought to have started from, so it followed that his last "Sir" would be also three places in advance of the place where he ought to have finished, and as this position was just one pace within the flote, so the two extra paces would have been two paces beyond the flote, *i.e.* in the orchestra.

Slowly he came down, his back was turned—"Sir!" I heard him saying gravely once. This was not my cue to turn.

"Sir!" he repeated, and as I was waiting for the third, I suddenly heard a crash, a shout, and a "Hullo! look out," and saw Wilson's heels above the lamps on the stage, while the rest of him, uninjured, was in the arms of the fiddler and the cornet player below. Luckily our orchestra were watching the piece, and in their anxiety to catch every word, had caught the speaker tripping.

J. M. Wilson was set on his legs again, provided with his spectacles, which had been fetched for him from the green room, the gas was turned up, and the piece went on as if nothing had happened, the audience being in a most excellent humour.

But our greatest cause for congratulation was the real *bonâ fide* unqualified success of *Bombastes*, which it is still my honest belief, was, if roughly, at all events earnestly played, with a true sense of the dignity of burlesque and with a genuine and intelligent appreciation of the fun of the piece, that won the most thorough approval of our audience.

The great success of *Bombastes Furioso*, however, was unquestionably due to Mr. C. Digby's (F. C. Wilson's) performance of *Distaffina*, which fairly took the audience by storm. Had F. C. Wilson been the most piquante burlesque actress within remembrance, the triumph could not have been greater. It surprised us all. So rapidly did the news of this impersonation get about, that the next night "the house" was crammed, the tickets went like wildfire, and we then decided on an " extra night."

On the second performance of *Bombastes*, which was then placed in the middle of the bill, all the Maudlin men—I mean the Magdalene men—came with bouquets of lilies of the valley, which they showered on the representative of Distaffina at the end of the Burlesque. Evans (of King's) was an excellent Fusbos, while our Bombastes, though very good, was just a trifle too noisy.

Before we rang up for the burlesque there was an alarm, not of Proctors but of fire. Something had gone wrong with the gas. With inimitable presence of mind, I, as manager, addressed the audience, informed them that " there was no ground for alarm, that it was only a gaspipe gone wrong which could be mended in a second,"—I used to think anything could be done ' in a second '—and finally wound up by asking them to be good enough to step into the Hoop hotel during the interval that must necessarily elapse before we recommenced, which they could advantageously occupy in *consommations*, "at," I generously added, "the expense of the Club."

This was received with cheers. The audience went out, refreshed itself at our expense, and returned in the most intense good humour, evincing - the heartiest desire to be satisfied with anything, and to be generally pleased with everything. Consequently, when the something good really did arrive—as it did in Bombastes—their enthusiasm was unbounded.

There was one other notable feature on this first night, namely, an introduction of a parody on " The Ratcatcher's Daughter "—at that time a very popular song at Evans's, when Evans's *was* Evans's, when Messrs. Sharpe and Sam Cowell sung and acted there, while Ross was giving us ' Sam Hall ' at the Old Cider Cellars in Maiden Lane, immortalised by Doyle in his illustrations to Percival Leigh's *Pips's Diary* in *Punch*—which was sung by Artaxominous, and, as I find in the authentic record of the A. D. C., "*created a great furore.*"

The same record states that on the first night "*the receipts were scanty, but a start was effected.*"

On the second night we played as a *lever du rideau*, a farce written by myself, my third attempt, entitled *Romance under Difficulties*, which, by the way, still 'holds the stage,' provincially, and among second-rate amateurs, as I have long since parted with my property in it, and the fees for its performance are very trifling, while the opportunities for tom-foolery are great. It was just the sort of farce that a novice fresh from a course of Maddison Morton dialogue, and from seeing Wright, Keeley, and Buckstone, in various farces, might have been expected to write.

One of our *dramatis personæ* sends me the following *souvenir* :—

"I remember," he writes to me, "the rehearsal of your farce *Romance under Difficulties*, in which you did not originally intend to play yourself, but in which you *did* play, owing to the incapacity of some one whose name I have forgotten. My conscience does not altogether acquit me of having failed to satisfy you on that occasion, but there was one worse than I,—I was kept in the cast and the more incapable one excluded. However, I remember the frightful ordeal of the rehearsal with the author sitting in front, and his being too evidently dissatisfied with his interpreters. A change was made directly after the rehearsal, and I have no doubt the improvement was very decided."

What a martinet I must have been! and in those early days too! evidently I didn't mince matters and was no respecter of persons where the success of a play, and that my own, was concerned.

The cast for *Romance Under Difficulties* was—

Benjamin Newbury	Mr. T. KING.
Frederick Markham	Mr. JAS. BEALE.
Timothy Diggles	Mr. TOM PIERCE.
Miss Fanny Newbury	Mr. C. RIGBY.

Then followed

Number One Round the Corner.

Flipper	Mr. JAMES BEALE.
Nobbler	Mr. RICH. JOHNSON.
Second Floor Lodger	Mr. COURTNEY.

Mr. James Beale was cast for this part *vice* Mr. George Seymour, who found the *Fast Train* quite enough for him, and ' Mr. Richard Johnson,' (Reginald Kelly of Trinity Hall) who had only appeared as Mrs. Jewell, quite a subordinate character, on the previous night, made what may really be called his first appearance in the role of *Nobbler*, and from that moment was marked as the most original and the most dryly humorous actor that ever appeared on the boards of the A. D. C. Kelly was of the Harley and Keeley school, but so slight was his acquaintance with the London stage that his *beau idéal* of a comic actor, after Buckstone, was ' Clarke of the Haymarket,' who used to play valets, waiters, innkeepers, comic clerks, and such like parts that fall to the share of the third low comedian—where three are kept.

Kelly preferred not acting in burlesque, he did not care for it; his line was comedy, or farce. I think Clarke of the Haymarket was not great in burlesque—*his* line also was comedy, or farce. Later on, in the history of the A. D. C., his performance of Potter in *Still Waters* (by Tom Taylor) was masterly. In *Number One Round the Corner* the back scene suddenly fell on the two actors, who had to support it until the carpenters set it right. The audience were delighted.

After this performance the popularity of the Club commenced, and we looked confidently forward to the next term when, with an accession of members, we should astonish the world with another performance which should be very far in advance of our first.

I have no news of anything until the following term, the October term; but as I then find, among the proposers and seconders, names not in the original list, I conclude that immediately after the first performance several members were elected.

Among them was Mr. Gibson, who was afterwards our President, and Mr. Charles Donne, son of the eminent scholar, Mr. William Bodham Donne, who for many years held the responsible position of Licenser of Plays in the Lord Chamberlain's office.

Mr. Nathan of Castle Street was at this time our costumier, and his charges were certainly moderate. It should be added that our requirements were not great. But "they grew and they grew" like the trees in the ballad of Lord Lovel.

Now came an important time when my friend Conyngham quitted his rooms in Trinity Street to take up his abode in Green Street, whither I very soon after followed him. He was a second-year man when I had only just commenced residence, and having passed his Little Go, was now going in hard for reading for his degree. He practically withdrew from the Club, and I never remember him as playing any other part on the boards than the one already mentioned.

He was on our committee, and interested himself more or less in the administration of our Club affairs up to the time of his taking his degree, which was in 1856, when with him disappeared from the University the last of a set, which, I believe, has never again reappeared there, I mean the old Fighting set, who could boast of such amateur pugilists as Jack Sheffield and Ferguson Davie, who, between them, had instituted the "Republic of Upware," to which admission as a member could only be obtained by *fighting the champion!*

It was a Fishing republic, and bargees belonged to it on the same terms as gentlemen. The landlord of the Fishing Hostelrie, where they met after their day's sport, was bound to let them have their beer at a certain reduction—I suppose on taking a quantity.

Nat Langham and Professor Harrison were frequent

visitors at Conyngham's rooms in Trinity Street, accompanied by professional performers on the banjo, and many a queer evening have I seen there, boxing in one corner, quarter-staff in another, a lesson on the banjo from a professor being given to the proprietor of the rooms himself in another part, "The Doctor" amusing a guest with card tricks and conjuring, at which he was an adept, somebody playing on the piano (regardless of the banjo) and myself in a corner by the fire, with some member of the "A. D. C.," books in hand, and cigars or pipes in mouth, rehearsing our "scene," and occasionally refreshing ourselves from the silver tankards on the table. It was very Bohemian, but very pleasant. We were the Bohemian Boys.

The mention of "The Doctor" brings to my mind the "tremendous situation" with which, I may say, the second act of our "A. D. C." drama terminated, and which very nearly "brought down the house."

Nothing succeeds like success, and after our first triumph a sudden accession of members—rich ones among them too—produced a considerable increase to our funds and to our real property, as most of the members gave presents to the Club from time to time, according to their means. Presents of books, chairs, and various articles, both of luxury and necessity, and before we separated for the vacation, it was decided unanimously that a treasurer was indispensable. The offices of treasurer and secretary were united, but they had hitherto been a sinecure, for the gentleman who held both, had to pay out the money as soon as he received it, and the minutes were kept in a very loose, fly-leafy sort of way.

Now, however, we found ourselves in possession of something like thirty-seven or forty pounds to the good, besides our club property.

The summer vacation would last a good four months—what a pleasant absurdity by the way!—and during our absence, who would attend to the rooms? and, what was still more important, who would take care of the money?

E

We wanted a responsible person to see that our stage was not used, that the damp did not injure our scenes, that our small collection of books was not diminished, and, of course, we wanted a responsible person to hold the stakes.

From the post of treasurer everybody shrank. It is odd that we never thought of depositing our funds in the bank, but we were inexperienced, and this never entered into our heads.

Our simple method was to buy a cash-box, with a good lock, and therein keep the money. But in whose charge were we to leave the cash-box? That was the question.

There were three of our members staying up for a part of the "Long" to read for their degree, and each of these positively refused in turn to have anything to do with the cash-box.

Now, about this time, there had been some scandal in diplomatic circles, about the defalcations of a certain Foreign Office clerk, and a great many jokes were made on the subject, and dark hints as to the uncertain future of our cash-box if trusted to any one of our members.

At last Conyngham proposed "The Doctor" as treasurer, pointing out that as he was a resident, he would be able to give an eye to the rooms, and look after our interests in our absence, while some one else proposed Gerald FitzGerald for the office.

The Doctor was much liked as a *bon camarade*, but he did not inspire general confidence, while FitzGerald had already refused, on the ground that he should only stay up a short time, but added good-naturedly, that, *faute de mieux*, he would undertake the responsibility if we absolutely insisted on it.

On this occasion several very witty lines were passed round the table, *à propos* of the scandal above mentioned, and the probability of our treasurer decamping, and, at our final meeting Peere Williams Freeman handed me a copy of verses, which in the free-and-easy and 'chaffy' spirit of our very pleasant society, I read aloud to the assembled company.

I regret I can do no more than call to mind one couplet with which, after humorously hinting that it really didn't much matter to which of the two candidates we entrusted our coin, it finished—

> "One word to the Doctor before he departs,
> We'd as soon lose our money by *Fitz* as by starts."

However it was decided that the Doctor, for the reasons given by his proposer, would be the safer man, and so he became *pro tem.*, our treasurer.

This was our last meeting in the May Term and then we broke up. The Doctor accepted the position, gave his receipt for the money, and we all went our various ways.

End of Act First. Curtain. The Entr'acte is the long vacation, when audience and actors are refreshing themselves.

The bell rings, or hammer knocks, and we re-enter for the Second Act, which you are already aware, is to have a startling *dénoûment.*

CHAPTER IV.

THIS began with a financial statement.

It was a very simple one.

The Doctor had disappeared.

Or, if he had not absolutely disappeared, his whereabouts was uncertain, his most intimate friends looked gloomy, and —our cash-box had gone.

On referring to the records of the exact sum for which our treasurer had been responsible, I find it differently stated at twenty-eight or thirty-two pounds. The entry is mild, and merely to this effect—I copy it *verbatim*—

" —— *injured the Club by spending its finances with which he had been intrusted ; this was a heavy blow to a young club. (Loss of £28).*"

But as there is no date to this, I fancy it was made some time afterwards, from memory. And it strikes me that the amount lost is here either not exactly stated, or is put at a less figure, or that the cash received in the May Term was reduced to this by payments, made perhaps, on account, to Lovett our carpenter, to whom we were still in debt, and if so, then this would represent the actual sum of which " The Doctor " relieved his patients.

We were all very sorry for him, and regretted that he had not confided his difficulties to his friends in the Club. He wrote us a letter acknowledging his fault, pleading his necessities, and promising re-payment. I, for one, never saw him again

—to speak to. He was an amusing man, many years older than any one of his very young friends (as may be imagined), had seen a great deal of life (as may be also imagined), and could do conjuring tricks as well as any amateur professor of legerdemain I have ever met. He had a talent for making things disappear, but hitherto we had always been permitted to recover them. But this final trick with the twenty-eight or thirty-two sovereigns admitted of no return, and he vanished from the scene.

This is what I have called end of Act the Second.

Act the Third began with a whip all round, which brought our finances up to the right mark, and then we sat down to arrange our performances for the term.

I now copy from the minutes. October, 1855.

"*At a General Meeting held, the prospects of the Club were discussed.*

"*Mr. Kelly was elected Treasurer and Secretary.*"

And we couldn't have chosen a better man than Reginald Kelly of Kelly, then undergraduate of Trinity Hall.

The following gentlemen were then elected :—

	Proposed by	*Seconded by*
Mr. Thomas Thornhill .	Mr. Harvey . .	Mr. Gibson.
Mr. Murray . . .	Mr. Kelly . . .	Mr. Donne.
Mr. Salter . . .	Mr. Burnand . .	Mr. Harvey.
Mr. Ernwin . . .	do. . .	do.
Mr. Woodmas . . .	do. .	Mr. Donne.
Mr. Dalton . . .	Mr. Herssel . .	Mr. Burnand.

And it was then decided that the second performances of the " A. D. C." should be given on the 6th and 7th November, when " were performed " (according to the brief entry written by two distinct hands, and filled in with blue ink), "*Delicate Ground.*—Characters by Donne, Wilson, FitzGerald. *Two in the Morning.*—Burnand and Donne. *Villikins and his Dinah.*—A burlesque by Mr. Burnand, acting manager. Room full."

" *Room Full* " speaks volumes for the then growing popularity of the Club, but the success was so great that on November 8th, 1855—the day following our second performance—I find a minute recorded thus—

" *Nov. 8, 1855. In consequence of the numerous applications for tickets, the same pieces were performed again, and were received with great applause by a numerous audience.*"

But not content with this, we thirsted for more blood, and at a meeting on November 12th, it was decided " *to have three more performances at the end of Term.*"

Two performances of three days each in one term ! And this after a three days' performance in the May Term.

An " A. D. C." enthusiast, in our day, could not go in for much else—specially if he were reading—except out of door exercise ; and if he were reading, he would even give up the " A. D. C." for that term, or would only play in one piece. Of course, I am prepared to admit that in its infancy the " A. D. C." was, necessarily, a secret society, rather Bohemian than aristocratic in its sentiments, rather jovial than ascetic in its tendencies.

The rehearsals were the occasions of delightful little dinners and suppers in each other's rooms, and in these we were not luxurious, nor were our " spreads " anything like so expensive, or so pretentious, as what were called the " Athenæum Teas."

Our games of loo, among those of us who played, were for moderate stakes ; and, as we were not a Dining Club, we had no reason for entering into any sort of competition with such ancient University Institutions as the Beefsteak Club or the True Blue, whose glory is in their " potations pottle-deep," and their ' chippiness ' in the morning. Oh ! how the Heads of the University that had been to the 'Steak on Saturday night used to ache at Sunday morning Chapel !

The active members of the " A. D. C." went in for small sociable gatherings, the bond of union among them being the similarity of tastes, and the one object in view, *i.e.*, the success of our performance.

As to what the Dons thought of it at this stage of our existence, I had a very good opportunity of judging.

Some malicious person had spread the report that our meetings in our Club rooms were orgies of the worst description.

The Proctors determined to assure themselves of the truth: and applied to me to show one of them over the "A. D. C."

I met him at the door of the Hoop Hotel, capped him most respectfully, expressed myself extremely pleased at the oppotunity thus afforded me of making his acquaintance, and walked him up the stairs to our little auditorium.

To his surprise there were no tables, no chairs, no signs of revelry or drinking.

The room was uncommonly like a lecture room without desks, until his eye rested on our proscenium.

Now I must here observe, that, if from the very commencement of my University career, I entertained a morbid dislike of Dons, I, on the other hand, felt an intense sympathy for the Proctors, who seemed to me to be doing the dirty work of the University.

I had always considered the Proctors as a sort of ecclesiastical police, parsons in white ties and bands, paid to do the work of common constables, making domiciliary visits, running risks of being grossly insulted by outsiders, and sure of getting more kicks than halfpence in a Town and Gown scrimmage, or in any other disorderly proceeding where they were bound to interfere. They must be accompanied—are now I suppose—by two men generally good 'on their pins' and not bad with their fists, who were styled "bull dogs."

The Proctors being unable to run, the bull dogs would have to chase the game, and once on the track of an offending undergraduate, their duty is to 'run him in.'

They were also spies—these bull dogs—and detectives;

very useful to an officious, over-zealous Dogberry, but obnoxious to a quiet gentlemanly Proctor, who happened to be in office because he couldn't help himself, or who was inclined to do no more than what was within the strict letter of the law.

Now from one such Proctor as this last mentioned, I had received signal kindness in my first term. I never forgot it. I was always civil and courteous to Proctors, and when fined for being without my cap and gown, I paid my money cheerfully, in the hope that out of it a worthy class of men might get some little percentage for performing so unpleasant a duty as theirs was in the University. It pleased me to think I was contributing a small sum for the support of the Proctors. That their bull dogs should get anything out of it, even a half pint of beer, annoyed me.

So it happened that instead of being in antagonism to this Proctor who paid the "A. D. C." a visit, I was on the contrary quite affectionately disposed towards him.

I was frankness itself. There was nothing to be concealed. There was nothing we were ashamed of. All was open and above board, except under the stage, which was below board; but there was not much of this—the elevation from the floor being only four feet (we couldn't get more) so that any unfortunate person who had to disappear down our trap had to lower himself—the only occasion when any member of the "A. D. C." was required to lower himself—and go on all fours in order to disappear altogether. For instance, when Faust and Mephistopheles went *ad inferos* together, it had to be done in that way. When in *Used Up*, Sir Charles had to go down into the cellar and meet the blacksmith—that is how it had to be done, and that was the space they had to do it in.

I explained all this to the Proctor, without the illustrations, as we had not at that time played either *Faust* or *Used Up*, —and pointed out our many ingenious contrivances in this, the merest nursery of art.

He was much interested, considerably amused, owned that our object was laudable, and our efforts, not only harmless, but absolutely beneficial. And I daresay he recounted to several Dons in Hall, or in the common room that evening, his visit to the " A. D. C.," and expressed his wish to see, unofficially, one of our performances. At all events, before we parted, he gave me his positive assurance that, as long as we continued in the path of virtue, as long as we stuck to our professed object of amusing the undergraduate public with our theatrical entertainments, and did not permit orgies, or suppers, or Bacchanalian gatherings in our Club rooms, so long we might be quite certain of not being interfered with by the authorities, that is, as far as *he* could speak for them. *He* at all events did not expect Cox and Box to be Fellows of Trinity, and did not wish us to be performing musty old Greek and Latin plays like the Westminster scholars.

His report must have been good, as during the whole three years and a-half of my University career we were never once molested, or warned, nor, I am bound say, did we, as a Club, ever once in any way give occasion for reprimand.

Gradually and unofficially the Dons came to us : dropping in, here a couple, and there a couple, saying no more about it to their stricter clerical brethren, than they would now-a-days had they paid an evening visit to the Aquarium, or if they had gone to see such a naughty French play as *Les Dominos Roses* at the Criterion.

There was no harm in a Don coming to witness our performances. He went away, not one whit the worse, but rather the better, as he had generally seen something to amuse him, and had also witnessed the spectacle of a number of young men enjoying a hearty laugh instead of losing more than they could afford at loo, or at billiards, drinking at wines, giving the Proctors trouble in the questionable environs, or steadily over-muddling their brains, while exhausting the midnight oil.

I have known, as time went on, plenty of reading men who made a point of taking our performances as their one exceptional evening recreation in the course of the term. The "Coaches" were always there.

We didn't at first attempt any union with the Musical Society at Cambridge, though I now think that this might have been done with advantage. I believe some such amalgamation was tried, but musicians are such uncommonly difficult people to deal with,—when, that is, theatrical people are dealing with them. On which side the fault lies I cannot say, but this I know that musicians invariably want to have it all their own way, and it is a most difficult task, requiring great tact, courtesy, and patience, to keep the conductor of a theatrical orchestra, or a composer, in his proper place. They begin by apparently yielding everything, they would end by assuming the entire control.

We commenced with a magnificent band of four musicians at the "A. D. C." under the leadership of "White-headed Bob," who played the violin. He was supported by an Italian looking person, of a sulky temperament, who played the cornet with a settled air of disgust, and another man with greasy hair and no shirt collar, who was very cruel to a violoncello, and who was perpetually being remonstrated with by his conductor, *sotto voce*, and making apologies for wrong notes, or wrong time, in an undertone. There was another musicianer who went about the town tied to a harp, as if he were a public example of the retribution that a man brought on his own shoulders by being a musical nuisance. The violoncello was not one of Bob's regular 'merry men,' but the harpist—a sad and seedy-looking man with ringlets peculiar to the gipsy tribe—was one of the three celebrities who played at all our 'wines,' at all our after-dinners, and who were paid by the hat going round for every-one to put a shilling in. The host on these occasions generally gave something extra, and, not unfrequently, as a patron of art, I used to give half-a-sovereign between the three, when

my party was small, and the *convives* unwilling to go beyond
' bobs up.'

As Bob and his merry men would visit several parties in a
night, commencing with wines soon after five in the afternoon,
I have no doubt they made an excellent thing of it. The
report was, years ago, that these three eminent musicianers
had purchased large freehold plots in the neighbourhood of
Cambridge, were considerable landholders, were really, besides
this, immensely wealthy—' *immensely*,' of course—and that
it was supposed by those who know something about them,
that the harpist would perhaps stand for the county at the
next election.

What has become of the harpist and the sulky cornet-
player I do not know, but to my astonishment and delight, on
revisiting the glimpses of the moon, in order to witness an
" A. D. C." performance in 1878—twenty-three years since
the foundation of the Club—I saw the white head of White-
headed Bob bending over the music score, and his right hand
that had lost none of its cunning fiddling away with all its old
might and main.

We had not an opportunity of speaking, but he beamed at me
behind his dark blue, or green, spectacles, and I returned the
beam that was in his eye with something like a mote in my
own, which prevented me from seeing quite distinctly, and a
gulp in my throat which hindered me from doing more than
murmuring " How d'ye do, Bob ?" from a distance, as all the
old scenes, all the old days, all the old companions, seemed
to crowd up before me, and I thought of myself twenty-three
years before, without a care, without a thought much beyond
the enjoyment of the moment—I was only in the beginning
of my nineteenth year—and as happy as the day, including
the night and plenty of it, was long.

Ah ! we were a very happy lot in my time at Trinity. No
doubt there are just as happy lots now, and have been since,
and will be to the end ; but taking *our* taste for what it was,
seeing what we enjoyed most, seeing what liberty we had for

social enjoyment,—a liberty which now-a-days, I observe, is considerably curtailed,—and comparing what we wanted to do, and did, with what our successors would like to do, and don't, I reaffirm, that, according to my unchanged notions on this subject, *ours* were very very happy days at Cambridge—I mean no pun by the italics though those happy *days* passed like *hours*—because there was far more opportunity of enjoyment, far more liberty, far more freedom than there has been since.

We saw the last and the best of it.

Some after us took advantage of the liberty, made it license, and brought on themselves and their successors the consequence of their foolishness.

We went right up to the limit of our bounds which were elastic enough, but we never overstrained the band.

Our active " A. D. C." members were, heart and soul, in our theatre, and we were bound together by the fraternal bonds of good fellowship, hospitality, and conviviality. Like Freemasons, we "proceeded from labour to refreshment," giving each its proper place in our daily arrangements, for the benefit of the " A. D. C."

All our dinners and suppers took place at each other's rooms, and consequently I was able to assure the Proctor, that we never had any Club dinners at the Hotel, or in the rooms, that the most ever done was, in the course of rehearsal, to send for a chop, or a glass of sherry, or a pint of beer, to refresh exhausted nature.

We didn't even allow smoking *on the stage* during rehearsal.

The scene painter had his fixed hours for work, and the actors had theirs, and the great difficulty was to settle some common time, when all, without sacrificing other more important occupations, or open air necessary exercise, could meet together for rehearsal. But this difficulty we met by mutual concession.

I will now give the full bill of the performances for Nov. 6th, 7th, and 8th. At the head of one bill marked

" Nov. 8th, 1855," I find this note evidently made at the time :—

> " *Wednesday.—Full. £15.*"
> " *Thursday.—Crowded—many members present. £16.*"
> " *Friday.—Crowded up to the footlights—no standing-room—only six members present. £18.*"

Evidently on the last night visitors were admitted into the seats reserved for members.

The form of the programme is the same as that used in the preceding term, but there are signs of greater care in drawing it up. All the "Esquires" are omitted except one, and the initials "A. D. C." are in ornamental lettering.

A. D. C.

THIS EVENING WILL BE PERFORMED, THE PETITE COMEDY,

A DELICATE GROUND;
OR, PARIS IN 1793.

Citizen Sangfroid	Mr. C. J. ALGERNON.
Alphonse de Grandier . . .	Mr. R. JOHNSON.
Pauline (*Citizen Sangfroid's wife*) .	Mr. C. DIGBY.

AFTER WHICH, A COMIC INTERLUDE, ENTITLED

TWO IN THE MORNING.

Mr. Benjamin Newpenny . . .	Mr. TOM PIERCE.
Stranger	Mr. C. J. ALGERNON.

To conclude with the Serio-Comic Burlesque (written expressly for the "A. D. C." by TOM PIERCE, *Esq.), bearing the heart-rending and well-known title of*

VILLIKINS AND HIS DINAH!

Master Grumbleton Gruffin (*a rich soap merchant of London, the original Parient*) .	Mr. TOM PIERCE.
Baron Boski Bumble (*ancestor of the celebrated Beadle—the original Lovier, so galliant and gay*)	Mr. F. HOUGHTON.
William Willikins (*socially and convivially known as "Villikins"*), in love with .	Mr. L. COURTNEY.
Dinah Gruffin (*sole feminine female offspring of the above-mentioned soap merchant*) .	Mr. C. DIGBY.

SERVANTS, &c., &c.

ACT I.—FRONT GARDEN AT GRUFFIN'S VILLA, CLAPHAM.
ACT II.—THE BACK GARDEN AT GRUFFIN'S VILLA, WITH A VIEW OF THE VEGETABLES.

Books of the new Burlesque may be had in the rooms, price One Shilling each.

Acting Manager—Mr. TOM PIERCE. *Stage Manager—Mr.* N. YATES.
Scenery by Mr. S. J. E. JONES.

The MS. notes on this bill are that the first piece was " *Capital.*"

That the second was "*A great hit on the third night,*" which doesn't imply much for its two first representations.

That " *All the books of the burlesque were sold,*" which must have been satisfactory to the author's printer.

And that " *the dresses were by Nathan of Castle Street, the wigs by Wilson, Strand.*"

Messrs. Nathan, the well-known costumiers for amateurs, had supplied the Athenæum performance, and had probably introduced Wilson, and we very naturally went to them.   The band was still by ' *White-headed Bob and talented assistants,*' and against " Villikins " and " Dinah " is written " *capital.*"

It is to be noticed here that, for some reason or other, there was a change in the assumed names.

" Mr. R. Johnson " no longer stood for Reginald Kelly, but for Gerald FitzGerald, while the latter appeared in the burlesque under the name of " Mr. L. Courtney," and R. Kelly as " Mr. F. Houghton."

" Mr. C. J. Algernon " meant Charles Edward Donne. " Mr. C. Digby " meant F. C. Wilson.   " Mr. Tom Pierce " —myself ; and the servants were taken by Messrs. Hassall and Murray, two new members, both got up most grotesquely.

Our artistic friend Jones was invited to pay us another visit at the same terms ; but it is clear that he had begun to be like ' poor Dog Tray,' of whom it was written by his affectionate master that—

> " Ten shillings in a year
> For his company was dear,
> So I put an end to Old Dog Tray."

And though we didn't put an end to Old Dog Tray—yet we proposed *cur-tailing* him considerably, as the committee held a meeting on the subject of " Jones," and it was decided that we were to dine him in turn, but that he was to stay with one of the committee.   I forget now who put him up on his second visit, but I rather think it was Conyngham who had moved to Green Street, and had a room at his disposal.

Jones—bless him—fed very well. He deserved it, for he worked hard, and our connection with him did not cease for nearly a year, and until he had painted for us.

1. *A wood scene, wings, and borders.*

(We noted the borders as " flies "—I thought the word looked technical and sounded well, and we were nothing at that time if not theatrical.)

2. *Palace scene and wings.*
3. *Lake landscape.   Drop.*
4. *Cottage interior and wings.*
5. *Dockyard scene.*

I recollect this last one. It really was an admirable example of scene painting on a small scale, and was most effective. We used it in *'Twould puzzle a Conjuror* (played here in 1856).

6. *Items.   Numerous set pieces " for a prison scene, a street, a cottage (exterior), a garden and fountain, a view from window, and,"* says the note in the records, *"very many other useful pieces."*

The ' *view from the window* ' was ' the backing' used in *Two in the Morning*, showing in perspective the opposite side of the street, with a transparent blind down, behind which are seen two figures embracing. The figures never could be got to appear at the right moment at rehearsal, but I have no doubt they did so on that third night representation, when this farce made such ' *a great hit.*'

We were successful, we were increasing in popularity, and we might have fairly considered ourselves as permanently established, that is, as permanently as any University Club which aims at being something beyond a mere reading room can be.

Each term brought us new members from among our seniors, our contemporaries, and our juniors.

On Nov. 12 we held a committee meeting at Mr. Donne's rooms which were at the further end of Jesus Lane, near the corner of Malcolm Street.

Mr. C. E. Donne, who had scarcely one more year of 'residence' at the University, came to us with a considerable histrionic reputation. It was whispered, that, "once upon a time," he and Alfred Thompson, who had taken his degree two or three years before my arrival—after getting up some theatricals at Cambridge, had actually gone to Norwich, or Yarmouth, and had performed on the real stage, in a real drama, with real, live actors, and that Charles Donne was absolutely on speaking terms with one Mr. Sidney, the manager, and Mrs. Sidney the manageress of the Norwich Theatre, and with a Mr. Billington, who, being on the stage himself, had strongly recommended Charles Donne to choose any profession but that.

For Charles Donne had entertained strong ideas on the subject, and so it appeared had Alfred Thompson, and on the occasion of their Norwich, or Yarmouth, visit, the former, whose voice and manner eminently fitted him for a tragedian, had, with great success, taken the part of Beverley in *The Gamester*. Heavens! What Mr. Alfred Thompson had performed on that occasion we were not then informed, and none of 'our year' up at Cambridge had ever seen the gentleman in question, and very few, of our generation, had even heard of him. And yet he had got up two performances at some rooms —Swan's auction rooms—and he has since informed me, that, three years before I came up, he had most successfully produced *The Rivals* in the very rooms subsequently taken by the " A. D. C."

This our landlord, Mr. Ekin, never mentioned to us, though perhaps it accounts for his unwillingness to hear any details from me as to what use we proposed to put his rooms.

Had we commenced with *The Rivals*, I do not think the " A. D. C." would ever have reached its second, much less its twenty-fifth year. We aimed low, and hit the mark exactly. Our selection of pieces does not show any great ambition. We only wanted to amuse, and—be amused.

Charles Donne who had succeeded so well in the *rôle* of Beverley at Norwich (or Yarmouth), and who might have been expected to propose himself for The Stranger in Kotzebue's drama, was cheerfully contented to be cast for the part of The Stranger—the comic stranger, I mean, in Charles Mathews' version of some French duologue, entitled *Two in the Morning.*

The piece had been popular in London, at the Lyceum, I think, with Charles Mathews as The Stranger, and Keeley as Newpenny.

I have never seen it, but the two must have been inimitable in it. I fancy we were inimitable too.

Charles Donne took great interest in the Club, and he was a first-rate rehearser, and went at it as in thorough earnest. What was worth doing at all, was worth doing well, and this was the opinion of the three who played in *Delicate Ground* when F. C. Wilson astonished us all as Pauline, and when Alphonso de Grandier's pistol wouldn't go off at the time when it ought to have gone off, but, choosing its own moment, nearly set fire to Citizen Sangfroid's white wig— which as a Citizen of 1793 he ought not to have been wearing.

So it came about—not through the pistol shot, but through Charles Donne's becoming so interested in Club matters—that he was soon on our committee, and that on the 12th of November, 1855, the committee met in his rooms as I have just mentioned.

On the brief minutes of that meeting I find it recorded that

" *Mr. R. L. Lomax was admitted as Honorary Member.*"

Mr. R. L. Lomax was a B.A., and had left the University.

" *The Laws were drawn up for the Club.*"

(So they had been rather vague up till now).

F

" It was decided to have three more performances at the end of Term."

On Nov. 22, 1855, same term, I find this entry :—

" At a General Meeting the Laws were passed with a few amendments."

The first rule shows the deep veneration—for it was more than respect—in which we held the celebrated Garrick Club, of which I—speaking for myself—had only heard, barely knew where it was situated, except that it was somewhere within the (to me) hallowed precincts of Covent Garden, and could not boast of any personal friends among its members : but, on the other hand, I *imagined* how it consisted of *all* the wits, and *all* the literary and dramatic celebrities of the time,—"All the talents " in fact—I was sure that Thackeray was a member of it—how I used to envy anyone who had the inestimable privilege of ' knowing Thackeray at home ! '—and I fancied that at night its smoking room sparkled with repartee and witticisms ; that actors came in to sup and to tell droll stories of ' behind the scenes '—that Albert Smith sat in a corner— like an entertaining Jack Horner—eating some sort of pie after his hard night's work at the Egyptian Hall, or whatever he might have been doing then,—and that a few—a very select few ' men about town,'—such as Andrew Arcedeckne, whom I only knew by sight at the Cider Cellars, Lord Exmouth and Sir Henry Webb, with both of whom I was on the mildest possible speaking terms, when I sat near them in a stall next my father's at the opera, Covent Garden,—lounged about in evening dress, addressing eminent men by their Christian names, or by familiar abbreviations ; I imagined how they drowned care, if they had any, these Olympians, in the flowing bowl, how smoke from fragrant havannas ascended—how everyone was jovial, convivial, chaffy, gay, and brilliant, in the Old Garrick Club, and, when we drew up our rules for the " A. D. C." I recommended a clause which should make membership at the Garrick a qualification for membership at the " A. D. C.," putting thereby the Garrick on a par, in this respect, with the two Universities; and rule 1 stood thus :—

I.

" *That this Club consist of Members and Honorary Members, the former to be Resident Members in the University, the latter to have had their names on the boards of one of the Colleges, or to have been elected* ad eundem *Members of the University, or be Members of the University of Oxford, or of the Garrick Club in London.*"

I take this from a copy of rules as at a latter date revised, but our first rule was substantially the same, and, as a proof of the estimation in which the Drama was held by us, it remains on our " A. D. C." rules that membership at the Garrick is equivalent to an *ad eundem* degree.

The Garrick Club has never returned the compliment, and has not yet considered membership at the " A. D. C." a sufficient qualification for election as an honorary member.

The next entry is,

" *Mr. Watt Gibson (of Magdalene) was elected President.*"

" *Mr. Donne was elected Treasurer and Secretary, Mr. Kelly having resigned.*"

I fancy the cares of a prospective Little-Go were weighing on Mr. Kelly's mind, but from the first he had disliked the office of " Secretary and Treasurer,"—which official position was destined to be the cause of considerable trouble to him at a future time, whereof more anon,—though on the defalcation of " The Doctor " he had kindly accepted the post of trust.

" *Mr. Baillie was elected Prompter.*"

This *was* a responsible position with a vengeance. It was not easily filled, as those who cared to be on the stage at all in any capacity, wished at least to be seen, if only occasionally heard by the audience.   Now a prompter's duty requires that he should be *never* seen by the audience, and heard *only* by the actors ; moreover, that he should attend *all* the rehearsals, make notes of all the changes and alterations in the stage directions, write out all the "calls," regulate the lights, ring up, ring down, give the cues to the carpenters and the orchestra, and, in the stage-manager's absence, preserve order behind the scenes.

Mr. Baillie, by accepting this post, to which he was unanimously elected—any one was sure of being unanimously elected to be prompter, as everyone dreaded being nominated for it—evinced his strong *penchant* for theatricals, and his deep interest in the welfare of a club, which henceforth would demand of him a considerable amount of self-denial in regard to the time he had hitherto allotted to such absorbing field sports as racing at Newmarket, hunting, and the drag.

He was a capital prompter, and generally came to rehearsal dressed in cords and tops, and with a formidable hunting crop in his hand, which being waved energetically during his stage directions, gave him the air of a refined slave driver.

He was very hardly used.   All our prompters were.   Whenever he renounced the drag to attend rehearsal, only two or three of the performers came ; and then, after trying to do something useful, they would all leave together—protesting.

' Protesting '—is *not* the word.

Not being a ' hunting man,' and never having been rash enough to attempt the drag,—though I witnessed it, once, in a boldly critical spirit, from the road—and not being a regular attendant at " Newmarket " — nor racket-player — nor a frequenter of the fives courts—nor given to billiards—nor much on the river—I was always ready for rehearsal at any time.   My riding exercise I fitted in to my times for rehearsal.

Well, Mr. Baillie was elected prompter, in which capacity he contrived to distinguish himself considerably.

At the same meeting

"*The prospects of the Club were discussed, and found to be in a flourishing condition.*"

"*A rehearsal was fixed for the 28th to try new members for the next performance.*"

There is a sporting, training sort of air about this resolution that seems to betoken our new prompter's influence on the board of direction. The prompter was always a committee-man.

The Committee consisted of the President, who had the privilege of giving the committee a dinner on the day of meeting, the Acting Manager, the Stage Manager, the Secretary and Treasurer, the Prompter.

The next performances, recorded as "*very successful,*" took place on Dec. 5th, 6th, and 8th, when the programme was

---

A. B. C.

THIS EVENING WILL BE PRESENTED

A FARCE IN REALITY;

Or, THE MANAGER IN DISTRESS.

Manager (*by himself*)	.	Mr. YATES.
Mr. Easy ⎱ (*friends of the Manager*) ⎰		Mr. E. DAVIS.
Mr. Bustleton ⎰		Mr. A. JONES.
Prompter (*by himself*)	.	Mr. G. LINDSAY.

It wasn't long before the new prompter appeared in public. I remember this piece well. We wanted to fill up the bill without repeating one of our former pieces. We got hold of the farce of *The Manager in Distress,* in which actors appear among the audience, and founded this piece on it.

"Mr. Yates" (Polwhele) appeared as himself, and "Mr. Davis" (R. Kelly), and "Mr. A. Jones" (myself) arrived as his friends to take dessert with him in his managerial room, and to help him out of the difficulties, which were announced by the prompter as having arisen from the non-appearance of the principal performers. We dispensed with any actors

among the audience, merely giving him a taste of our quality
as to what we each could do to assist him; my part I recollect
being to clear the dessert table of all the fruit as rapidly
as possible (though I don't quite see how this would have
helped any Theatrical performance), while my friend Mr. Easy
went in for the wine and biscuits.   The prompter re-appeared
just at the moment when we had reduced the manager to
distraction, and had made him feel very sore in consequence
of having pointed all our remarks by the very practical ' business' of digging him in the ribs, and slapping him on the
back.   In fact his part—unwritten but perfectly natural—
was limited towards the latter portion of the performance to
saying " Oh don't," and " Come! I say," then coughing
violently, and subsequently begging for mercy.   This was very
much to the taste of the audience, up to a certain point, when
they began to grow a little tired of the repetition of this
pantomimic exhibition, and Mr. G. Lindsay entered to
announce the arrival of the principals, when the manager
thanked *us*, apologised to the much enduring audience, and
the curtain descended, to rise again on—

BINKS THE BAGMAN.

Binks (*a commercial traveller*) . . .	Mr. Tom Pierce.
Kit Crimmins (*landlord of the "Benbow Inn"*)	Mr. R. Johnson.
Jack Robinson . . . , . . .	Mr. S. Vane.
Boots	Mr. E. Courtney.
Mrs. Crimmins	Mr. G. Foster.
Mrs. Robinson	Mr. R. Neete.
Mary Moggs (*housemaid to the "Benbow"*) .	Mr. S. Edwards.
The Bear (*Jack Robinson's*) . . .	Mr. G. Rece.

TO CONCLUDE WITH THE ROMANCE OF REAL LIFE, ENTITLED

BOX AND COX.

Box (*a journeyman printer*) . . .	Mr. Tom Pierce.
Cox (*a journeyman hatter*)	Mr. R. Johnson.
Mrs. Bouncer (*a landlady*) . . .	Mr. F. Millsom.

Stage Manager--Mr. N. YATES.   Acting Manager—Mr. TOM PIERCE.
Prompter—Mr. LINDSAY.
Scenery and Appointments by Messrs. JONES and CLARKSON.

In this bill, several new names occur. 'Mr. S. Vane" was R. Salter of Trinity Hall. Gerald FitzGerald changed his name again and took "E. Courtney. "Mr. R. Neete" was Dalton, "Mr. Edwards" E. Smith, of John's, and "G. Rece" (grease), who played the bear in the farce, was A. Hassall. In the last piece Salter appeared as "Mr. F. Millsom."

The absence from the bill of Charles Donne, "Mr. C. Digby," and F. C. Wilson, is one of the most noticeable features. The former, "Mr. Algernon," had only recently made his first appearance, and was already "a star;" while the other was recognized as the "Leading Lady," without whose assistance it had been considered impossible to have a performance which should prove sufficiently attractive.

"Mr. C. Digby" was already beginning to read for his degree of January '57, while "Mr. Algernon" was actually on the eve of his degree of January '56, so both gentlemen retired into private life, and, deprived of their valuable assistance, we determined to rely on the piece of nonsense already described, a slight farce, and the ever popular *Box and Cox*—not Fellows of Trinity.

Without Mr. C. Digby we dared not venture on a burlesque, and without Mr. Algernon we had no one on whom we could rely to support even a vaudeville of any serious interest.

But our remaining difficulty was our ladies !

With the demand came the supply, and "Mr. Neete"—the name was chosen to indicate his nattiness and *petite*-ness—came to the rescue and appeared as "Mrs. Crimmins,"—which was exactly the sort of part that would not have suited Mr. C. Digby, and indeed one which no one would have thought of offering him.

I call to mind how Dalton, in the smart landlady's dress, took us all utterly by surprise ; so much so indeed, that coming up the stairs of the "A. D. C." to the green room—which served us as dressing room as well—our ascetic prompter mistook him for a chambermaid from the hotel, and indignantly complained of such a *rara avis* having been permitted to appear within our jealously guarded, because still jealously watched, precincts.

I have said that our green room served us also for a common dressing room, and indeed for a property room, at first; and its appearance during our performances, when the performers were in full swing of painting, dressing, undressing, washing, going over their words, and hunting for properties, was not unlike Hogarth's 'Strolling Players' in a barn—only, of course, a gentlemanly and very much Bowdlerised version of that celebrated work.

This extra performance was for the benefit of the Club funds, and it was expected to pay on the strength of the reputation of the previous performances. No Jones was invited to paint, no Nathan was employed, only Clarkson the perruquier, who brought everything with him, including such costumes as were wanted for the farce, and we were saved the expense of band rehearsals, as we had no burlesque.

The performances would have passed without a hitch, but for the bear, who would *not* come to rehearsals, and who, at the last moment, was inclined to be recalcitrant. But it being pointed out to him, that, though this was only his second appearance on the stage (he had been a servant in *Villikins*) yet the opportunities for distinguishing himself were so numerous and so easily available to a man of his talent and capabilities, that as an ambitious and rising young actor, he would grievously injure his own prospects, if he did not avail himself of the goods with which the Gods had provided him in such a brilliant opening.

"But," he objected, "what can I do in a bear's skin?"

"Everything," was the impulsive answer.

It was shown him how he could see—and breathe too!—through a hole under the head, and how his master, Jack Robinson, played by a capital actor, "Mr. S. Vane" (R. Salter), was most anxious that he should share the honours of the evening with him; and he was also earnestly assured that whatever he, in the character of the bear, would like to do, he would find himself ably seconded—it was put in this flattering way—by Mr. S. Vane as Jack Robinson. "G. Rece" consented, a trusty member of the *Corps* was told off to bring him to the "A. D. C." on the night of performance, and when he presented himself, still faintly remonstrating and wishing to cry off, if he could have done so with honour, even at the very last moment, we got him into his bear's skin and fastened him up so tightly, that he certainly couldn't get out of it without assistance.

He waited at the wing for Jack Robinson, who soon appeared dressed as a sailor.

Now Mr. S. Vane was a conscientious actor, and, in thinking out the part of Jack Robinson, he had calculated thoroughly on the Dancing Bear.

"Of course," he had argued, "no sailor would go about with a bear, unless he had either a good stout stick or a whip to larrup him with."

He considered the stick as most appropriate to a sailor ashore, and with this 'hand-property' he had taken good care to provide himself. But, alas, for the unhappy bear! the stick was not a property sawdust-stuffed staff, such as is used on the stage by pantomimists, but it was a good, stout, substantial, undeniable cudgel. It was realism with a vengeance.

Mr. S. Vane before coming up to the University, had, like the celebrated T. P. Cooke, really been in the navy, at least, so it was said. He had a bluff, honest, hearty, rolling sort of way with him, and was a first-rate fellow on and off the stage —as even the unhappy G. Rece would have willingly owned, —up till this minute.

The farce went on: so did the sailor, and with him the bear led by a chain. No chance of escape. At first the bear tried to be funny—and he *was* funny—he stood up and danced. Alas! his fun was but short-lived, for at the first sign of any repetition of such a burst of humour, down came

Jack Robinson's thick cudgel on the bear's head and shoulders, who, thereupon, swore audibly. It was not a growl, it was an oath accompanied by a remonstrance which went entirely unheeded by the jolly tar, who, seeing the audience highly amused at his use of the stick, thought he couldn't give them, or the bear, too much of a good thing. He was right as to the audience, he was wrong as to the bear's view of the matter.

"I quite forgot," said the representative of 'Jack ashore,' earnestly explaining the matter, afterwards, to somebody, "I quite forgot it might hurt; and I really didn't think he could feel it through that bear-skin."

In vain the bear attempted to ward off the blows with much the same action of the paws as the bear in the illustrated fable-book attempts to get rid of the bees. He kept up the character as long as he could. He even pretended to have been taught some sort of dance by Jack Robinson, which necessitated his putting up his fore-paws in order to guard his head, and taking advantage of the attitude, he was just about to whisper behind his hand a real 'aside' requesting Jack Robinson to have a little more consideration for his feelings, when the sailor, being in the full swing of his part, and thinking that the bear was playing up to him in first-rate style, angrily exclaimed, "Ah! would you?" and down came a crack from the cudgel, and out came another and a louder oath from the bear.

At last the bear could stand it no longer—he made a rush at his tormentor, and there was a man and bear fight for the space of about half a minute, during which the audience shouted and applauded vigorously. But the unfortunate bear was heavily handicapped in his dress, and without it he would not have been a match for his antagonist, who, entering into the spirit of the scene, pretended to defend his life from the bear's deadly attack, and inserting his hand in the bear's leather collar, half strangled poor 'G. Reee,' while at the same time he caught him such cracks over the head, as but for the padding, would most certainly have incapacitated the representative of the bear from ever appearing on any stage again —at least for a very long time.

There was nothing for the unhappy bear but entire submission; so, sinking down, he lay as if completely vanquished, panting on the ground, while S. Vane gave him one or two playful taps on the skull, just to finish with, then struck an attitude like a victorious lion tamer, and having dismissed the bear with a parting kick, he resumed the business of the scene. There was immense applause. ' S. Vane ' bowed his acknowledgments, but the bear had availed himself of this respite to sneak quietly out by the door in the scene—and nothing could induce him to return. In fact, I think from that moment he retired from the Club and never paid any further subscription. His name does not occur again in the bills. He had had enough of it. His histrionic ambition had received a violent blow—several very violent blows—he had paid his halfpence, he had received all the kicks, and if he felt himself aggrieved, I must say I think he was more than justified.

Those who witnessed the scene, will never forget it, and many among the audience who afterwards became members, have since narrated the story to me from their point of view, and told me how admirably they thought the unhappy bear was acting his part !

We had a great many unrehearsed comic scenes in the olden time of the " A. D. C.," and this was one of them.

CHAPTER V.

AFTER this performance, and before we separated for the Christmas vacation, we held a meeting on Dec. 12th, 1855, when we decided to

" Furnish rooms and make them more comfortable."

The estimate for this was £40.

We were getting on.

This expenditure was advocated by the cautious stage manager, T. R. Polwhele, and by our secretary, C. E. Donne.

Then these two energetic gentlemen, rising to the occasion, and evidently exhilarated by their success, proposed *" The alteration of the passage."*

The expense for this was to be £10, part of which was guaranteed by Mr. Ekin our landlord.

This also was carried unanimously.

Somebody ' an Honourable Member ' whose name has not been handed down to posterity in our records, proposed that there should be

" No smoking in the dining room."

Which was carried unanimously.

But what was our dining room ?

It was the auditorium, when, instead of benches, and a red-baize partition, and reserved seats, it was occupied by a couple of property tables, and some kitchen chairs.

The " dinner " was an occasional " chop and potatoes,"

cooked over at the Hoop, and sent across the yard by the Boots, for whose services and those of his wife—" Mrs. Boots " —as charwoman, we allowed so much a term. But even these property tables had only been introduced since the friendly Proctor's visit, and I am glad they were not there on that occasion.

Then the two practical members abovementioned moved and seconded another resolution.

1st. *That Costume dresses be paid by the Club.*

2ndly. *That Farce dresses be provided and paid for by the actors themselves.*

3rdly. *That half the expense of female dresses should be borne by the Club.*
Carried unanimously.

When we did " agree on the stage about anything, our unanimity was wonderful ! "

Then the stage manager requested that "*he might have an assistant who should take charge of the property department.*"

Our " Property room " was a mere cupboard somewhere off the passage, and I think Mr. Ekin gave us an unused, loose box in the brewery stable.

The stage manager's request was granted, and

" *Mr. Ernwin was elected Assistant Stage Manager.*"

Then it was settled that "*All complaints be made to the Secretary, and in his absence, to any member of the Committee.*

The Committee were then re-elected.

Mr. R. Kelly (Trinity Hall)	.	President.
Mr. C. E. Donne (Trin.) .	.	Secretary and Treasurer.
Mr. Burnand (Trin.) .	. .	Acting Manager.
Mr. Polwhele (John's)	.	Stage Manager.
Mr. Baillie (Trin.)	. .	Prompter.
Mr. Ernwin (Trin.)	.	Assistant Stage Manager.

At a subsequent private committee meeting (Dec. 17), Mr. Cator . . . was elected as *Hon. Mem.*

At the general meeting on the 12th Dec., a bye-law was passed to this effect :

> "*That the Committee be held at the Committee Members' rooms in rotation, beginning with the President. And that the Member in whose rooms the Meeting is held shall give a dinner to the Committee only.*"

Up to this time the President, as I have already stated, always gave the dinners, and invited outsiders, This was found to be a check on business conversation and dinner discussion, and also the frequent meetings made the charge a heavy one on the President. Hence the above rule.

Minute at same meeting ; "*Agreed with Mr. Ekin to pay £40 per annum, with coals.*" This was our rent. As some one has remarked in our records, "what with coals, and other concessions we are *Ekin*' out our existence."

"*The sanction of the Members was given to the Committee to incur a debt of £50 for furniture, and to alter the staircase and smoking room.*"

The 'smoking room' was the apartment with a skylight, which served us for our green room and dressing room.

Our furniture, exclusive of 'property' chairs and tables, at present consisted of 'lockers' round the room, used as settees.

The alterations proposed included a small lavatory. But in those days the luxury of modern lavatories was comparatively unknown, and a basin under a tap, with a jack-towel on a roller behind a door, sufficed for our wants.

Thus ended the second year of the " A. D. C.'s " existence."

It had been successful beyond all anticipation ; it had tided over a considerable pecuniary loss, and it had paid its way fairly.

As far as the Dons knew anything about it, they were indifferent, or favourably inclined towards it.

We were on excellent terms with the Athenæum Club, which always mustered strongly at our performances—several of its new members joining the " A. D. C."

CHAPTER VI.

THE next term, Lent, 1856, we commenced with a Committee Meeting in my rooms.

Conyngham and myself were now located in Green Street, and very pleasant quarters they were. We were not particular to a shade at midnight, if we only knew our guests were safe men.

At this meeting I acted as secretary, in consequence of the resignation of C. E. Donne, who had already taken his degree.

About this time the Jones question arose again. He had painted well, but he had charged too much. Then it was asked why should we pay his travelling expenses as well as three guineas a-day for his work? And why should any member have the highly-respected Jones's company forced upon him at his own lodgings?

It was clear that we were tired of Jones. We had heard all his stories of Mathews and Vestris, we had never come across anything he had ever done at a theatre—his name was unknown to *us* as an artist. "Who was Jones?"

I had introduced him : *I* was answerable for him. I gave up Jones as a companion, but stuck by him as an artist. "Could any one, "I wanted to know," supply us with a better?"

There had been offers. A wheezy little man in the town, a house decorator I think, of a theatrical turn, had proposed to paint anything, for a quarter of what poor Jones would have received. Of course if it did not turn out to be 'anything we liked,' we should have to take it all the same.

Our excellent stage manager split the difference. And an arrangement was come to with Jones which was to be taken as applying to this term only—(alas! poor Jones! it was the beginning of the end!)—to the effect that

"*In addition to his travelling exs he should receive two guâs per diem*"—a drop of one guinea per day for Jones, and not to be made up in the time he took over it, we were too sharp for that—"*And he was to dine with each of the Committee in rotation, and that he should lodge at 27, Green Street, at the rate of twelve shillings per week.*"

That settled Jones.

He arrived and worked harder than ever : but a gloom had come over him. No one would listen to his stories. They watched him at work, took him to dinner, and saw him at lunch. But he was a broken man. Had poor Jones played his cards better, he might have taken up his abode at the University, and made a handsome income as a professor of drawing and painting ; there was no one there who knew more about it than he did, few so much. His mistake was that he would patronise the sharp-sighted young men. Then, he never had any new stories, which was a fault, and he repeated the old ones, which was a crime.

To this day I am sorry for the worthy and estimable Jones. He did some excellent work for the "A. D. C.," which has, by this time, been all painted out.

Heu prisca fides ! We did, for one term at least, believe in Jones.

    *   *   *   *   *   *

About this date we began to be strict. Feb. 5, 1856.

"*R. Kelly fined five shillings for being absent.*"

He was occasionally very absent. I hope he paid the fines.

Then there was a general meeting on Feb. 7 at 6.30, which meant, for Trinity men at least, immediately after Chapel. We were very careful not to clash with collegiate regulations. There was plenty of room in the University for both Colleges and Clubs. The University Governing Body 'with power to add to its number' ought to have constituted us into a Dramatic College. It is not too late now. Celibacy would have to be a qualification for the majority of Fellowships. The master could be a married man. Who should be the first to hold the important office? Say Mr. Henry Neville. It would look well 'in the bills,' Mr. H. Neville, Master of Roscius College, Cambridge; Senior Dean, J. L. Toole. But this is only by the way. *À nos moutons.*

Then, Feb. 7, we elected as honorary members—

> W. L. B. Cator . . Trin. Coll. (*mentioned previously,*
> *and election confirmed*).
> J. Wilkinson . . . St. Peter's.
> A. Thompson . (late of) Trin. Coll.

Here for the first time, Mr. Alfred Thompson's name appeared on our minutes.

As I have before said, some of us had often heard of him from C. E. Donne, his old friend, and there being a part in my new burlesque of *St. George and the Dragon* which we found it difficult to fill, it was suggested by Charles Donne that Mr. Alfred Thompson should be invited to join our theatricals.

This led to his being elected unanimously, and welcomed gladly as an honorary member.

His reputation, which had grown since he had first been mentioned, began to frighten us all, and I was afraid lest I should find some one who knew more about my own burlesque than I did myself, and who would be for putting us all to rights. However, he accepted our invitation,—writing to Donne from Canterbury, I think, where his depôt was quartered—he was in a cavalry regiment—and consented to take the *rôle* of

King Lollipop in my burlesque of *St. George and the Dragon*, which, I confess, I thought a great condescension on his part.

I anticipated his arrival with considerable anxiety. It was the first time a comparative stranger to all of us had played at the " A. D. C."

I well remember our first meeting.

It was at a dress rehearsal in the evening, a few days before the performance, a very few days—not more than two, I fancy.

He was cast for a part in *Sent to the Tower*, which he was to play with Reginald Kelly.

He soon showed us that he meant business, and that he had his own original ideas of the character of King Lollipop. It was a mad scene, and he came on imitating somebody as King Lear. It was not at all what I had intended, but the idea in execution was so much better, dramatically, than mine, that I watched it closely, adopted his suggestions, and only made one, which was that " the kneeling was ineffective."

" I'll do it as you wish, you know," he said, kindly, and I did not like to press the matter further.

Our new honorary member attracted a good deal of attention that evening, and we were looking forward to a first rate performance, when suddenly a message arrived post haste, informing him that he must at once join his regiment, which was ordered off to the Crimea.

He left us then and there, and I don't remember our meeting again until he had finally given up soldiering and was on the high road to that position he now holds in the literary and artistic world.

It is with great pleasure that I have to refer to Mr. Alfred Thompson—as an honorary member of the Cambridge " A. D. C.," though his first and last appearance on our classic boards, was at the above-mentioned dress rehearsal of *St. George and the Dragon*.

His departure, happening as it did on the very eve of our performance, left us in a difficulty. Alfred Thompson was to have played Perkyn Puddifoot in Maddison Morton's *Sent to the Tower*—we all had an intense reverence for the name of Maddison Morton, and also for that of the author, who, as the late Mr. Charles Mathews said in one of his after-dinner speeches, "cunningly contrived to have himself familiarly christened ' Tom ' ' "—I mean Mr. Tom Taylor—but this by the way—and the other parts, for which Mr. Alfred Thompson was cast, were, King Lollipop in my *St. George and the Dragon*, a burlesque, which I am sure was inspired by a picture in the *Illustrated News* of Paul Bedford, of the Adelphi, in the dress of a dragon—and the part of Mr. Aubrey in the opening piece, a little drama in two acts, adapted, I believe, from some French piece by Charles Mathews, and called *A Curious Case*.

Three parts to be filled !   It must be owned that having a star, we had determined to take the shine out of him considerably. A star ! He was a meteor—brilliant, flashing, and away !

There was no time for further rehearsal, so at once assembling a council of war, we accepted Evelyn Ashley's offer of playing Mr. Aubrey, while I undertook to be perfect in Perkyn Puddifoot. · Evidently we were both ' quick studies ' in those days.

How I got up my part, I remember perfectly—as though it were only yesterday.

Reginald Kelly was Launcelot Banks, and as the piece is a sort of *Box and Cox*, the entire business, except two or three scenes with the gaoler (played by Ernwin) was in our hands. I studied hard all the morning, and between three and four my *confrère* came to a light repast in my room—we dined early, professionally—when, instead of chattering over our meal our conversation was limited entirely to Morton's dialogue, and at night we played it without reference to the prompter.

Years afterwards I had to play it on the new boards of the " A. D. C.," and trusted to my memory. Mr. Charles Hall—our second Charles—who, as the Prince of Wales's Attorney-General for the Duchy of Cornwall, wears a very different wig from the one he used as "Launcelot Banks" —played in it with me on this last occasion, when my trust in my memory was as vain as Macbeth's in the juggling spirits; and if it be equally true, as on the first occasion, that we played it without reference to the prompter, it is only because, *had we stopped to listen to him*, there would have been a fearful *hiatus* between the speeches, as all we could do was to remember a few "cues" here and there, guiding ourselves to the conclusion by a general idea of the action of the piece, and entirely giving ourselves up to the inspiration of the moment. We were both of us in excellent spirits, and the audience did not detect the imposition. The prompter, after vainly endeavouring to find the place, closed his book in despair, regarding us vacantly as a couple of hopeless lunatics, and wondering, not how we should 'go on,' but how on earth we should ever 'get off.' We got right—somehow. Poor Maddison Morton! had he been there! I speak now as a dramatic author, with an intense horror of 'gag!' But more of this anon—in its place. I record it here for future reference.

On Wednesday, February 21st, 1856, after all our trouble, we were "all right at night," as the actors say, when they are all wrong in the morning.

Evelyn Ashley played the part of Aubrey in *A Curious Case*; Tom Thornhill the part of King Lollipop in the burlesque; and for Perkyn Puddifoot, Alfred Thompson's other vacancy, I have already accounted. Here is the programme, which was an innovation, as to size and details, on what we had hitherto adopted.

A. D. C.

THIS EVENING WILL BE PRESENTED, THE COMIC DRAMA
ENTITLED

A CURIOUS CASE.

Mr. Aubrey :	Mr. HUMPHREY DUKE.
Charles Stanton	Mr. E. COURTNEY.
Twiggleton	Mr. TOM PIERCE.
Edward	Mr. R. JOHNSON.
Mrs. Aubrey	Mr. C. DIGBY.

AFTER WHICH,

SENT TO THE TOWER!

Perkyn Puddifoot	Mr. TOM PIERCE.
Launcelot Banks	Mr. R. JOHNSON.
Gaoler	Mr. J. FARNHAM.

To Conclude with an Entirely New Historical, Comical, but still
slightly Mythical, Burlesque, in Three Acts,
by TOM PIERCE, Esq., entitled

ST. GEORGE AND THE DRAGON!!

King Lollipop (*King of Sugar Candia, from whom are descended the Royal Line of Bonbons*)	Mr. HUMPHREY DUKE.
St. George (*no relation to George St., Hanover Square—an undecided character, by Historian*) . . .	Mr. E. COURTNEY.
Toadee (*a Courtier at the Court of Sugar Candia, holding a fine old Government appointment*) . .	Mr. R. JOHNSON.
Tuftee (*a ditto, ditto*)	Mr. A. HERBERT.
Princess Zara (*the Sugar Candian reading of the English Sarah, sole remaining child of King Lollipop—a Damsel Coy*)	Mr. C. DIGBY.
The Dragon (*who is the Lion of the place of whom* BEN SHAKESPEARE *has written the memorable description,* "Monstrum informe ingens cui, regular rum 'un to look at;" *with whom the* HEIR *of the place seems to agree—since he has swallowed him at the opening of the piece —or, rather, at the opening of the mouth-piece—and who has* CAPTIVATED *the Princess by his* CHARMS)	Mr. TOM PIERCE.

Courtiers and Attendants (who will, and indeed must, be seen
to be appreciated,) by Messrs. H. WALKER, GAMMON, E.
HOOK, and SELL.

*For Description of Scenery, References, &c., see Books of Burlesque,
which can be had in the Room, price One Shilling.*

Stage Manager—*Mr. N. YATES.*   *Acting Manager*—*Mr. TOM PIERCE.*
Prompter—*Mr. G. LINDSAY.*   *Scenery by Mr. S. J. E. JONES.*
*Dresses and Appointments by Messrs. NATHAN and G. W. CLARKSON
of Drury Lane.*

The names when translated are as follows :—

Mr. Humphrey Duke *	. Mr. Tom Thornhill.
Mr. Humphrey Duke * ⎰	
Mr. A. Herbert . ⎱	. . . Hon. Evelyn Ashley.
Mr. E. Courtney . . .	. Mr. Gerald Fitzgerald.
Mr. Tom Pierce .	. . Mr. F. C. Burnand.
Mr. R. Johnson . . .	. Mr. Reginald Kelly.
Mr. C. Digby . . .	. . Mr. F. C. Wilson.
Mr. J. Farnham . . .	. Mr. J. Ernwin.
Mr. N. Yates	. . Mr. T. R. Polwhele.
Mr. G. Lindsay . .	. Mr. W. H. Baillie.

There is no record as to Messrs. H. Walker, Gammon, E. Hook, and Sell, but there is a note to the effect that Mr. J. Ernwin " made his first appearance on this occasion and was very successful."

St. George " went very well. Three songs, consecutively encored. The performance lasted three nights and the proceeds were £49 15s.," which at all events, after deducting expenses, would have paid half our yearly rent.

In the cast of *St. George* appears the name of Mr. R. Johnson, *i.e.* Mr. Reginald Kelly. It was his second and last appearance in burlesque, a class of entertainment against which he had all along decidedly set his face. As I have before remarked, Reginald Kelly was one of our best and most original actors, but he had generally excused himself from playing in burlesque on the ground of his not having ' a singing face,' of his not appreciating puns and doggerel, and finally of his not being a dancer.

In vain it had been pointed out to him that " Clarke of the Haymarket " had played in extravaganzas, that Harley, Compton and Keeley had all appeared in burlesque and extravaganza, but he still maintained that in doing so they

* The name assumed by Mr. Alfred Thompson, whose parts these two gentlemen took.

had gone out of their legitimate line. Kelly, could he have had his own way, would have exercised us in standard comedies, and a few modern (now old-fashioned) farces. But, thank goodness! for the future of the "A. D. C.," we, its originators, as a body, had no such daring ambition. Had we attempted *The Rivals,* or *The School for Scandal,* or *Every Man in his Humour,* or *The Heir-at-Law*—and Kelly would have been an admirable Dr. Pangloss—I doubt whether the Club would have lasted a term. Such things were too high for us, a very great deal too high—and in fact, fortunately out of our reach and out of our sight.

But in *St. George* I had modelled two characters on Noodle and Doodle in Fielding's *Tom Thumb*—their names Tuftee and Toadee—they were two courtiers—being evidently adaptations from Thackeray's creations.

Toadee is described in the bill as "A courtier at the Court of Sugar Candia, holding a fine old government appointment," and my *beau-idéal* of the character would have been Compton, and failing him 'our Mr. Kelly,' who, at my earnest solicitation, kindly undertook the part, on condition of dancing and singing not being expected of him.

The doggerel lines he had to speak were full of wretched puns, and Kelly gave them out at rehearsal, stolidly, in his Comptonian style, without a smile. I was in raptures. He would play it splendidly. As the rehearsals proceeded it was noticed that the more familiar Toadee became with his part, the less glibly he delivered it. He seemed to be lost in meditation before each line, which he would then repeat deliberately with a puzzled expression of countenance, and a side inquiring glance at me as much as to say, "Look here, you're the author, what do you mean by *this?*" but he never stopped to make any observation, until, at the fourth rehearsal, when he was slowly going over his first long speech—a miserable set of lines at the best, though I say it who shouldn't — now — though *then* I thought them uncommonly fine, and in answer to Tuftee was saying—

> "The son and heir of our great king, he went
> To take the sun and air——"

When he suddenly broke off, gave a short but emphatic "ha! ha!" repeated the "ha! ha!" and seemed so utterly unable to proceed with the rehearsal, that I asked anxiously if anything was the matter with him?

"No," he replied, still laughing jerkily. "Only I didn't see it before."

"What?" I asked.

"What?" he returned, staring at me. "Why, sun and air—son and heir. You mean it for a pun—don't you? Ha! ha!"

I admitted that my intention had certainly been to perpetrate a *jeu de mots,* which I owned did not seem to me absolutely novel.

"Well," he replied, "it mayn't be *here*—ha! ha!—but *I* never saw it before. Ha! ha! Son and heir—ha! ha!—very good. Why, I've said it over a hundred times without seeing it. But," he finished, by way of consoling me, "I *see it now —and I shan't laugh at it again.*"

Gradually, by fits and starts, all the puns in his own part broke on him. And each time he exploded in short laughs, like a cracker. When they came very close together—when, as modern critics on burlesque say, "the lines bristled with puns"—then he stopped short, repeated the lines slowly, examined them carefully, as though he were a schoolboy picking plums out of a cake, and not until he was quite certain of having mastered them all, did he proceed with his speech.

> "His heart within his breast,
> Began to *quaver,* while he took his *rest.*"

Here he paused, looked dubiously at me, then exclaimed—
"Oh, I see it—'*quaver*'—'*rest*'—terms in music—ha!

ha ! "—explaining the joke, as though he were a punster's dictionary.   Then he went on—

> "'Twas but an idle *crotchet* of the brain."

(*To himself*) "Crotchet—ha ! ha !—there's another" (*to me*) " I see it—

> "So *trebled* his pace to find his home again."

(*To himself*) " ' Trebled '—yes—that's another—ha ! ha !—"

And at last, when he reached the description of the Prince's meeting with the Dragon, who—

> "Looked at his *scales*, and thought 'twas *affaire finny*,"

he paused—thought it out, slapped his leg, and came out with a tremendous guffaw.

"I knew that was a pun," he cried, triumphantly.   "I told What's-his-name so, when he heard me my part this morning.   I told him you meant it for a pun—but he didn't see it."

Not until the night of performance did the full light of the puns *in the other parts* break on him, and, whether he were on the stage, or listening at the wing, the most appreciative audience for every point in the piece was Reginald Kelly, who, whenever any of the other characters came out with a punning line, gave his very audible laugh "Ha ! ha ! " adding, *sotto voce*, " Hang it ! there's another ! "—and at the first representation he undoubtedly led the laugh, for the undergraduate audience, quick to catch at such a peculiarity, took this as an original point in his part, and whenever he unconsciously directed their attention to a pun, which he had only just that minute discovered, and which had surprised him out of his ejaculation of " Oh, hang it ! there's another ! " they shouted and roared again, and applauded vociferously.

Certainly the success of *St. George and the Dragon* was largely due, on the first night, to Mr. Reginald Kelly as Toadee, and on the other nights to Messrs. F. C. Wilson and

Gerald FitzGerald, as the unhappy princess Zara and her lover St. George. For myself, I know that, while my dress for the Dragon was founded, as I have said, on a picture of Mr. Paul Bedford in a similar character, my embodiment of the part was a copy of Keeley as the Djin in the *Enchanted Horse*, an extravaganza in two acts, at, I think, the Haymarket, when Miss P. Horton played a Prince, and Mrs. Keeley a Peri, and I fancy that Alfred Wigan was also in the piece, but if not in that, he was in another—*Aladdin*—at the same house, when Mrs. Keeley played *Aladdin*, and her husband *Abanazar* the magician. How funny it was !! .

CHAPTER VII.

THE performances in the Lent Term, 1856, had brought us to the end of the first year of the "A. D. C.'s" existence, and at the close of the May Term—the first season of our A. D. C. year—we were aware of having some really serious changes.

Mr. Polwhele having taken his degree at the beginning of the year, had only been stopping up out of real liking for the "A. D. C." work, and in order to hand it over in the best possible state to his successor, whoever he might be.

Without Mr. Polwhele's careful management, the Club could never have made such progress as it did in its one year of life. He was an ingenious carpenter, and was never so happy as when looking after the mechanical appliances of the "A. D. C.," and making the best of them, such as they were. F. C. Wilson was reading, so also was Reginald Kelly. We might perhaps get their services once in the course of the forthcoming year, but we knew it would not be fair to press them.

Charles E. Donne and Gerald Fitzgerald were away. The past degree time, i.e., January, 1856, had taken away several of our "first members," active and inactive; the future degree time of 1857 was keeping others well occupied, and I was beginning to feel University age creeping upon me as a second-year man who had braved the Little-Go.

As for our financial position, we paid our way and our rent.

We were still in debt to our carpenter for his work in 1855, and had only paid him from time to time on account, while, I imagine, he was being called in to do all sorts of odd jobs about the place.

The subscriptions came in regularly, and our number was always up to the limit, with the names of candidates on the election board every term.

No club, with such expenses, could have done better ; and there was an *esprit de corps* which united in a common cause, as it were, a number of young men, of very different tastes, and in very different sets.

Our performances were invariably the occasion of the most jovial supper parties—not the least among the inducements to become an "acting member"—held at each other's rooms, when conscientious landlords and landladies, who had to make "the returns" of the hours kept by their lodgers, would allow their clocks and watches to get very much behind the time, when college porters would be less exact in noting down the precise moment of the undergraduates' *rentrée*, and when less scrupulous landlords took no notice whatever of the hours, except to ask their lodgers where they had been, who had seen them, and to trust to their honour for the truth.

A lodging-house keeper making a false return, or omitting his return, would be "discommoned" by the University, after, or without a warning ; and of course, as the lodging-house keeper was also a tradesman, this meant the loss of University custom, and something uncommonly near ruin—at all events a great loss for a time.

But the "A. D. C." performances came to be gradually accepted as a valid excuse for late hours—just once and away—that is during our three days' entertainment. Was it not evident that actors required refreshment after a performance lasting from eight till past eleven ? Was it not equally clear that the audience also stood in need of some refreshment ? Naturally. This was no "drinking for drinking" but "drinking for dry ;" and after all, none of our

"A. D. C." men had ever come across the police after midnight, nor had broken off bell-handles, and made night
hideous with their shrieks, as was the custom of the members of certain old-established, hard-drinking, port-wine University societies.

No; as a club, we were a quiet, orderly set—I mean we
must have had that reputation to have gradually won the
hearts of the Dons, who, after a while, granted leave and
license to acting members of the "A. D. C." to stay out till
one a.m. on the performance nights.

I say "after a while"—as I don't think it was a rule in my
time. Not that it mattered to me personally. I bore a
charmed life, as did the other men (only two) who "kept" in
my house.

I have said that "*as a club*" we were quiet and orderly;
but sectionally, so to put it, we were occasionally a trifle
frolicsome.

But of all the pleasant cheery evenings I ever remember to
have spent—noisy, I admit—sustained chiefly by the animal
spirits of youth, I allow—commend me to some of those
after-performance "A. D. C." suppers we used to have down
in Malcolm Street, especially when there was a goodly
number of our members congregated together, and when, at
a particular house, the fun was invariably at its fastest, at
its most furious, and at its latest.   One of our Irish members
was famed for his hospitality, and the flowing bowl—was it
a bowl of bishop?—never stood still in his room—not even
when it was empty—for then it was moved to be refilled.

Pleasant convivial evenings they were, when all the mistakes of the performance were good-humouredly reviewed, and
amusingly recounted; when "chaff" flew about, and rough-
and-ready repartee, more forcible than brilliant, knock-down
blows from a cudgel, rather than sharp, pointed thrusts from
flashing rapiers, were exchanged amid shouts of uproarious
merriment.

I recollect nothing like those supper-parties, except the late

Charles Lever's descriptions of similar festivities in the old days of Charles O'Malley at Trinity College, Dublin.

One of the strongest bonds of union among Freemasons is the banquet, when the brethren "proceed from labour to refreshment"; and though of less importance among the members of the "A. D. C." than among the "Sons of the Widow," yet our performances would have lost much of their zest, if, after strutting our brief hour on the stage, we had then been heard no more, and had sneaked off supperless to bed.

Old University men were our guests on these occasions, and were welcome to any "A. D. C." member's rooms where there happened to be an "After the Opera was over" supper.

Every old member of the Club—and our Retired List had already commenced in 1856—was free of the Club, and a guest at any of the feasts without invitation, though, as a matter of courtesy, the invitation was usually given. The "Entertainers," however, generally accompanied their written or verbal invitations with the expressed wish that you would "bring anyone you like"—which of course was only applicable to non-resident members of the University, or "strangers" on a visit.

Never were members of one society more thoroughly in earnest than were the first members of the "A. D. C." So entirely penetrated with the *esprit de corps* were we, that we were willing to take any parts for which we might happen to be cast; while, as for our beardless youths who played the women, so heartily did they "enter into the skin"—as the French say—of the feminine character, that I remember, on one occasion, when we played *Still Waters run Deep*, the representative of Mrs. Mildmay, thinking his "get up" insufficient, secreted the diamonds that Mrs. Sternhold ought to have worn. The latter was in the greatest distress. The costumier couldn't make out where they had been mislaid. Of course Mrs. Mildmay knew nothing about them, or, at least, baffled enquiry by returning, not the jewels, but the reply, "What should *I* know about Mrs. Sternhold's dia-

monds ?"   And imagine the latter's feelings when the first
thing that caught her eye in John Mildmay's drawing-room,
scene last, act 3rd, on the occasion of the dinner-party, was
her lost *parure* round meek Mrs. Mildmay's neck !

The piece was, however, just drawing to a close, and the
business of the scene did not permit of any irrelevant
remarks.

Before the tag, indeed, all was forgotten and forgiven, and
the amiable young Collegians, who played the two parts of
Mrs. Sternhold and Mrs. Mildmay, sunk their jealousies for
the public good, contributed largely to the success of the
drama, " forgave " each other,—but never " forgot,"—for the
incident was too absurd, and is well worth recording.

In the early days of the " A. D. C.," one of the patrons
among the Dons was the Rev. Dr. Donaldson, who was just
then very popular among undergraduates, on account of his
decidedly anti-donnish and liberal views. He highly approved
of the " A. D. C.," and asked me to show him over the
rooms. He stood on our little stage and gave us (Charles
E. Donne and myself) some account of his theatrical reminiscences.

À propos of Dr. Donaldson, and not at all of the " A. D. C."
—except that some members, who shall be nameless, as I am
not yet at liberty to divulge the secret, were mixed up in the
hoax—I remember how, one Sunday morning, the walls in
and about the University were placarded to the effect that
"*the Rev. Mr. Clayton*" — a well-known clergyman in the
town,—"*would burn Dr. Donaldson's heretical Book of
Jasher in front of Trinity College at* ——" then the hour in
the evening was specified. The bills were headed—

"Heresy !   Heresy ! !   Heresy ! ! ! "

which looked uncommonly attractive—especially on Sunday
morning, when there was nothing doing except church.

During the day, in spite of the police having torn down

most of the posters, the news spread far and wide, and by the time for evening chapel at Trinity, the whole of Trinity Street was in an uproar.

Mr. Clayton, coming out of Caius to go to his church, was followed by a mob of roughs and undergraduates—they were very much mixed on such occasions, until a strong line of demarcation was drawn by a positive Town and Gown row—hooting, shouting, and calling upon him to burn the heretical publication.

The air resounded with cries of "Jasher! Jasher! Clayton! Heresy!" raised, of course, by those who knew very little of either Dr. Donaldson or Mr. Clayton, and nothing at all of the Book of Jasher.

The police were called out in full force; Sergeant Robinson—"Bill Robinson"—being at their head, who, if any municipal official could have quelled the riot, would have been the man to do it, as he was immensely popular among undergraduates.

The gates of Trinity College were closed against all comers, and the porters were resolved to do, or die, in defending their post, should the fortress be besieged.

But a new difficulty arose from the men within, who, coming from chapel, wished to get out. Egress and ingress were alike forbidden.

"Force the gates!" was the cry from within and without, and the *émeute* would have assumed a most serious aspect, had not some quick-witted junior Don been inspired to sacrifice an old Euclid—supposed to represent the Book of Jasher—to the fury of the mob, which was about as orthodox as that in the Gordon riots, which shouted "No Property," as synonymous with "No Popery!"

In answer to the vociferous cries of "Burn the Book!" the junior Don above-mentioned issued forth from the porter's lodge gate at the side, with the flaming Euclid in his hand.

In a few moments the book was reduced to ashes, the crowd

H

cheered and broke up, the gates were opened, Bill Robinson went about cheerily assuring everybody that there was nothing more to be done or seen, and in another half-hour Town and Gown were quiet.

"Dr. Jasher," as we used to call him, was always a very good friend to us of the "A. D. C.," and besides attending several performances, used invariably to plead our cause, whenever the necessity arose, in those University Common Rooms from which his authorship of Jasher had not banished him.

To resume.

Since the commencement of the Club in the May Term, 1855, we had had about, as far as I can make out, four performances; and as our University year consisted of only three terms, we must count these as representing the first year of the "A. D. C.'s" existence as a Club.

FIRST YEAR OF "A. D. C."

May Term, 1855	One performance.
October Term, 1855	Two performances.
Lent Term, 1856	One performance.

1855.

PIECES PLAYED.

A Fast Train! High Pressure!! Express!!!	
Did you ever send your Wife to Camberwell?	
Bombastes Furioso	} May Term.
Romance under Difficulties . . .	
Number One Round the Corner . . .	
Delicate Ground	} 1st performance,
Two in the Morning	October Term.
Villikins and his Dinah	
A Farce in Reality	} 2nd performance,
Binks the Bagman	October Term.
Box and Cox	

1856.

A Curious Case	}
Sent to the Tower	Lent Term.
St. George and the Dragon	}

This represents the first year of the "A. D. C.'s" existence.

Of these fourteen pieces, three—one farce and two burlesques—were original works, of which two are still played in
the provinces and by amateurs.

Our new members elected previous to the Lent Term performance were—

February 18, 1856—

Mr. Arbouin	. . . . .	Trinity.
G. Feilden	. . . . .	do.
E. Ashley	. . . . .	do.

And

February 20, 1856—

Mr. Cresswell	. . . . .	St. John's.
Mr. Foster	. . . .	Christ's.
Mr. Graham	. . . . .	do.

But this second entry has been partially erased in the book,
and their election is not confirmed until Feb. 28th, after the
performance.

On the 10th March the following members were elected :—

Oliphant	. . . . .	Trinity Hall.
A. C. Lee	. . . .	Trinity.
W. P. Lysaght	. . . .	do.
Robert O'Hara	. . . .	Caius.
C. R. Lutwidge	. . . . .	Trinity.
R. Wharton	. . . . .	do.
Simpson	. . . . .	St. John's.

This batch proves the cosmopolitan character and the extended popularity of the Club. We had by this time
representatives from Trinity, John's, Christ's, Caius, Trinity
Hall, King's, and Magdalene—sporting men, serious men—
not *too* serious, but with ecclesiastical tastes—reading men,
lounging men, political debaters at the Union, as were
Messrs. O'Hara and Ashley—both of whom, I daresay, have
found that their public appearance on the boards of the
" A. D. C." was not the least part of the advantages of their
University experience, for both were excellent actors, and as
an exponent of one type of Irish character, Robert O'Hara

(now a distinguished counsel in the Committee Rooms at Westminster) had only one rival among us, viz., Mr. Rowley Hill, the present Bishop of Sodor and Man, whose name appears as a candidate on the " A. D. C." list, the 16th April, 1856.

The list of members for our first year, 1855-56, included—

T. R. Polwhele	J. F. M. Wilson
G. Sheppard Harvey	C. E. Donne
G. Lenox Conyngham	G. Tyrrell
G. H. Evans	T. Utton
G. Fitzgerald	W. Lysaght
W. R. Snow	Hon. A. E. M. Ashley
G. R. Hassall	W. H. Evans
G. C. Lampson	Alfred Thompson (honorary)
H. Lampson	A. C. Lee
J. C. Wood	G. Feilden
F. C. Wilson	J. Graham
W. H. Baillie	E. Cresswell
J. Watt Gibson	J. H. Simpson
H. J. Whitley	R. Wharton
R. Kelly	C. R. F. Lutwidge
W. E. Smith	R. O'Hara
P. W. Freeman	Rowley Hill
C. Grant	Thos. Thornhill
Arthur C. Cumberlege	R. Tennent.
M. N. R. Fitzgerald	

There was always a difficulty about our secretary. That office involved a large amount of trouble without any adequate recompense. A member in his ignorance generally accepted the post with avidity, eager to show how he could set everything straight, and what an example *he* would give to his predecessors of what their stewardship *ought* to have been.

But alas! he invariably found that on his devoted head fell all the blame. He had all the writing to do, all the accounts to audit—for the office of treasurer was combined with that of secretary—he was fined, in earnest, if he failed to attend a meeting—he had to yield an account of tickets sold, of bills printed, &c., &c., and, finally, as an unpaid and overworked official, he generally seized the first opportunity of resigning the situation.

But in doing this he was very careful to conceal the real nature of his grievance. He would generally plead "reading" as a valid excuse, and he would add that nothing but this would have induced him to resign, so delightful was the work, so congenial and so pleasant.

Had he not *said* this, we should have experienced some difficulty in finding a successor. It was like the simple countryman who having been inveigled into a show by the glowing description of what is to be seen within, is passed out by a side door, after seeing positively nothing, and implored not to say a word to the public without, but let them all be taken in as he had been. The victim at once becomes a party to the hoax, chuckling over the sell, which has already cost him sixpence.

We had had up to this time several secretaries, and the record shows how they had incurred fines of five shillings for absence, and had then so to speak, 'chucked it up.'

The fate of Mr. W. H. Baillie was as that of the others before him in this chair. He was fined on the 7th February, 1856, and resigned on the 28th of the same month.

This might be the epitaph on all our secretaries in the early days of the "A. D. C."—

Being fined,
He resigned !

And then they sat at the board and took their turn at worrying 'the new man.'

But, strange to say, so much was this official post sought after, that on this occasion there were two candidates—

G. M. Wilson (of Caius), proposed by F. C. Burnand,
seconded by Mr. W. Arbouin,
and
Honble. E. Ashley (Trin.), proposed by T. R. Polwhele,
seconded by G. S. Feilden.

The latter was elected by a majority of eight to two, where-upon the resigned secretary, Mr. W. H. Baillie, was unanimously elected prompter—and I am not certain whether he was much the better for the change.

However, he was the right man in the right place—when he *was* in the right place—and when he did prompt, it is a tradition among the "A. D. C." men, that he was *facile princeps*, and without a rival in this difficult department of dramatic art.

If anyone thinks I am wrong in classing it under the head of "Art"—let him try it himself. The prompter, like the stage manager, should be able to enter into the spirit of every individual part; should acquire a consummate knowledge of all the words and all the business of the play; should possess sufficient imitative power to enable him to pitch the word he has to give in the same key as the actor, to whom he has to give it, is speaking in; and, on occasion, to assume any character in the piece.

On the professional stage one frequently meets with these qualities combined, and such a one must have been a perfect Godsend at the Vaudeville during the run of *Our Boys*, when the prompter played Mr. David James's part whenever this gentleman was indisposed, or while he was "on the continong," touring with his partner, Mr. Thomas Thorne. The prompter could only of course have taken one part at a time, so I suppose that, at this theatre, there was somebody who formerly was an institution at Covent Garden and Drury Lane, viz., the "under-prompter," who possessed talents of the same order.

At the "A. D. C." the prompter was seldom called upon to appear in public, but we required him to be with us for every rehearsal, when W. H. Baillie used to appear booted and spurred, with a whip in one hand, and a 'Lacy's edition' in the other, requesting us to 'get on,' as he wanted to 'get off,' and 'get on' too — his horse being at the door.

Our prompter was immensely popular, and no one more thoroughly enjoyed the " A. D. C." work than he did. His election as prompter is facetiously entered thus—

> " *Baillie the Great, as prompter, proposed by F. C. Burnand, seconded by W. H. Evans, and unanimously elected.*"

Then our careful stage manager, Polwhele, moved—

> " *That members should buy their own performance books.*" (*Carried*).

We arrived at this through the negligence of our members, who were perpetually losing their playbooks, with which they had been supplied at the Club's expense, and then pleading their loss as an excuse for their imperfection.

The next resolution to be adopted as a bye law was also carried *nem. con., i.e.*—

> " *That no dogs be admitted;*" proposed by T. R. Polwhele, seconded by R. Kelly.

The proposer and seconder were the two most cautious and careful men in the Club ; and it must be remembered that in December, 1855, the Club had authorised the committee to spend fifty pounds in furniture, alteration, and ornamentation.

The Club was not going to the dogs, nor were the dogs allowed to come to the Club.

Against this resolution, and in a hand I think I recognise as that of the newly-elected secretary's, is appended the remark in brackets, " *Sad dogs !*"

Finally it was now decided that the Club should be limited to forty members.

This was " *Proposed by W. H. Baillie (Magnus), and seconded by T. R. Polwhele (sub-member), carried by a majority of iii.*"

Why " sub-member " was added I don't know, except as antithetically to " Magnus."

From this bill Mr. C. E. Donne, who had just taken his degree, disappeared ; but he was coming up again. " He would return, we knew him well."

Reading-men, who were acting members, never found that the performances at the " A. D. C." interfered with their studies : on the contrary, while they dropped all other amusements, all parties and convivialities, the rehearsals and the performances came as a refreshing recreation.

The best evidence on such a point would come from Mr. E. Gorst, and Mr. Grove, who were active members of the " A. D. C." while reading hard, and their interest in the Club did not prevent them from coming out, the one as Senior Wrangler, or at all events high up among the Wranglers, and the other a first Classic.

Some of our acting members, however, within two terms of their dreaded degree examination, retired into their cells not to emerge again until they could write B.A. after their names. To this circumstance it was owing that we were once more deprived of the services of F. C. Wilson, on whose representation of female characters so much had hitherto depended, and who now felt himself compelled *se reculer pour mieux sauter*, and to put himself in training for the *grand coup* which was to come off at the commencement of 1857.

CHAPTER VIII.

MAY TERM, 1856.—SECOND YEAR OF "A. D. C."

WE were emerging from the catacombs. We were no longer a secret society. We were not officially recognised, only tolerated. Our accommodation being limited, we had no difficulty in disposing of tickets. Dons—junior Dons of course —visited us and reported favourably in Common Rooms.

Whether the excellent Master of Caius, after relinquishing his Vice-Chancellorship, ever thought any more about us, I do not know. I think not—or he would have inquired after "Box and Cox Fellows of Trinity," and have asked us to get up some light trifle by Æschylus or Sophocles for his own personal delectation.

It would have been an attractive bill.

ANTIGONE, in the original Greek, for one night only! By special desire. Under the immediate patronage of The Vice-Chancellor and The Heads of the Colleges!!

To conclude with the laughable after-piece, Boξ καὶ Koξ, adapted from the classic work by T. Μαδδισον Μορτον.

*   *   *   *   *

About this time the financial accounts were not, I fancy, very clearly kept. We were in debt for one lump sum, but as to current expenses, we paid as we went, and we went very well.

In our records there is no very clear statement as to how the "A. D. C.," sharing the fate of clubs, nations, states,

and individuals, got into debt, but there is very precise information as to how we got out of it.

Such bills as I have as yet been able to discover, simply
relate to the performances, and not to their cost.

Internal evidence shows we were becoming more careful.
The scenery was still by Old Jones, "his last appearance."
The costumes were still by Messrs. Nathan of Castle Street,
Leicester Square, and our perruquier was now Mr. Clarkson
of Drury Lane, *vice* Wilson of the Strand.

Our next meeting was on April 8, 1856, when Mr. Polwhele's motion that "the present system of issuing tickets
be improved, and that all members receive forms, certifying
that Mr. So-and-so is a member of the University, which they
shall give to any gentleman, who may then obtain tickets at
the 'A. D. C.' rooms on application, or presentation," was
carried by a majority of twelve.

Its a funnily-worded resolution, but on that day some one
with rather a cramped hand directing a steel pen was at work
with the minutes, and the next entry is—

"*Proposed by Polwhele*"—he was always proposing something—"*that a voluntary subscription*"—there was no
seconder to this—"*be set on foot for a new proscenium.*"

"(*Rejected by an enlightened and excited audience by a
majority of two*)."

We wanted a new proscenium badly. It was only a can-
vassed frame, over which was pasted some very ordinary cheap
room-papering. However, the members thought it 'good
enough' for them.

Then the brave but partially unsuccessful Polwhele made
another proposition for "*a voluntary subscription*"—he was
as fond of voluntaries as an organist,—"*to provide a mirror
to be placed over the mantel-piece in smoking room*"—and
this was carried by a majority of ten.

Then it was arranged that, henceforth, the stage manager

should be also treasurer, which was carried by a majority of eight, evidently a tribute to the care, caution, and energy in all matters affecting the "A. D. C." displayed by T. R. Polwhele, who was now thoroughly in his element.

At a Committee Meeting held after the General Meeting, Mr. R. Preston, of Trinity, was elected, and on April 16th were elected—

L. T. Baines	.	.	.	.	.	Trin. Coll.
R. O. Lamb	.	.	.	.	.	Trin. Hall.
Rowley Hill	.	.	.	.	.	Trin. Coll.

On the 17th April, 1856, our performance consisted of the following bill, for two nights only.

A. D. C.

This Evening will be presented a new Farce, by TOM PIERCE, Esq.
(author of "Romance under Difficulties," "Villikins,"
"St. George," &c.), entitled

A   REGULAR   SELL!

Augustus Stanhope, Esq.	.	.	.	.	Mr. B. Norton.
Hon. Tom Lester	.	.	.	.	Mr. J. SEYMOUR.
Benjamin Twozzle	.	.	.	.	Mr. R. O. PAISLEY.
Miss Twozzle	.	.	.	.	Mr. C. DIGBY.

This was our *lever du rideau,* and it was simply put in to eke out our bill.

It might have been described as "A piece of impertinence" —as no such piece existed, either in MS. or in print, and was invented entirely on the spur of the moment by the actors.

Of course we had arranged a scheme, a sort of *charpente* as it were, but each one was left to fill up the sketch of character with his own business and dialogue.

As part of the "regular sell" we had included in the cast the name of "Mr. C. Digby," (*i.e.* F. C. Wilson) who, owing to academical engagements elsewhere, was unable to appear this term, much to our loss, as the record will show.

The account of *A Regular Sell* in our minutes is as follows :—

"*A piece not written but gagged throughout by O'Hara and Burnand on the stage, and Lee and Arbouin in the audience.*"

The two latter had to hiss and make themselves objectionable, and then to be called on to the stage in order to show what they could do themselves. This, of course, was founded on *The Manager in Distress*, and is the same as the business of *My Wife's Bonnet, Le Chapeau de ma Femme,* and many other pieces where the actors mix with the audience.

Unfortunately for Messrs. Lee and Arbouin, they made themselves so energetically obnoxious, that the audience began to cry "Order, order," and hush them down.

It had been arranged that I should ask the dissentients "if they could provide a better entertainment than we were giving," that to this they should reply "yes," whereupon I was to invite them to step up on to the stage ; but seeing the fun in front, I delayed to do so, and O'Hara and myself went on with our impromptu dialogue, while our confederates, in order to attract our attention to their position, which was becoming more and more unpleasant every minute, increased their interruptions in frequency and noise, until some muscular undergraduates sitting on the benches just behind our two *dramatis personæ*, threatened to bonnet and kick them out if they didn't there and then " hold their confounded row."

This settled our confederates, for the undergraduates would have been as good as their word.

Taking our cue from this unpremeditated and genuine interruption, we entered into a *pourparler* with Messrs. Lee and

Arbouin, who were only too glad to avail themselves of our invitation, to avoid the dangers with which they were threatened by the infuriated undergraduates.

The piece was not repeated a second night, as it was impossible to find any members bold enough to encounter the danger from which our two friends—who thought they were going to have *such* fun among the audience—had escaped on the first representation.

" On the whole," says the record of this performance, " the piece was just enough to put the audience in a good humour, and prepare them for the great piece of the evening, viz., 'Twould puzzle a Conjuror," described on the bill as—

" An Historical Comic Drama in two acts, by the author of ' Paul Pry.' "

This was our first attempt at anything at all elaborate. All our previous pieces had been one-act Vaudevilles, or farces,—the *Curious Case* was merely a farce in two acts,— and burlesques.

But there is this to be remarked as something commendable in amateurs, we played original burlesques and farces, where everyone had to " create " his *rôle*, or we played pieces that we had never seen performed on the stage, and therefore, our impersonations, if not entirely original, were certainly not slavish copies of any professional interpretation, though some of us, well acquainted with the peculiarities of established London favourites, might attempt to reproduce them.

The one exception to the above was myself, as I had been a theatre-goer since I was about eight years of age, and had acted in *Box and Cox* when I was about fourteen Still, even as far as I am concerned, I had never seen *Bombastes*, or *A Fast Train*, or *Number One round the Corner*, or *Delicate Ground*, or *Two in the Morning*, or *Sent to the Tower*.

To return to our first May Term programme for the 17th April, 1856. The cast was as follows, for

'TWOULD PUZZLE A CONJUROR!

Peter (*Czar of Muscovy, working under the name of Peter Michloff*) . .	Mr. M. CAXTON.
Admiral Varensloff (*Russian Ambassador*)	Mr. DESMOND BLAKE.
Count de Marville (*French Ambassador*)	Mr. J. RAINGER.
Baron Von Clump (*attached to the German Embassy*)	Mr. MILES HALL.
Van Dunder (*Burgomaster of Saardam*)	Mr. TOM PIERCE.
Van Block (*Master of the Dockyard of Saardam*)	Mr. HUMPHREY DUKE.
Peter Staunitz (*head workman in the dockyard*)	Mr. R. JOHNSON.
Officer	Mr. E. GAAUL.
Bertha (*Burgomaster's niece—betrothed to Peter Staunitz*)	Mr. F. HUMBY.

Workmen, Guards, &c., Messrs. H. SMITH, BROWN, WALKER, and E. HOOK.

For this piece the ever-faithful S. J. E. Jones—"none but himself could be his parallel"—painted a new scene representing the dockyard, and an admirable one it was. This was his last work for us, and we became aware of rising talent among ourselves, while there were rumours about a mysterious man "in the town"—as mysterious as the man in the moon,—who, for a consideration, less by far than what we had given to our eminent professional friend—our now ex-associate Jones—would be willing to paint, or assist in painting, whatever scenery we might require.

At present, however, we had a very fair stock of scenery in hand, and we wished to be economical.

The key to the *noms de théâtre* is here :—

Mr. M. Caxton   represents   { Hon. E. Ashley.
                                 { — Simpson.

The latter playing the part of Peter at short notice on account of Evelyn Ashley's being suddenly unable to play.

Mr. Desmond Blake	represents	"	— O'Hara.
Mr. J. Rainger	.	"	— Arbouin.
Mr. Miles Hall	. .	"	— Murray.
Mr. Tom Pierce	.	"	— Burnand.
Mr. Humphrey Duke		"	— Thornhill.
Mr. R. Johnson	.	"	— Kelly.
Mr. E. Gaaul	. .	"	— Erhwin.
Mr. F. Humby	.	"	{ — Simpson. { — Fielden.

And

Messrs. Smith, Brown, Walker, and E. Hook stood for R. Preston, A. C. Lee, W. Lysaght, Lutwidge, and Evans, &c.

Mr. Feilden, who had never played before, and was quite a novice—it was only his second term at the University—played and "looked" Bertha to general admiration. Kelly's Peter Staumitz is briefly and emphatically recorded as "*capital*," and the others all more or less satisfactory. Of "*the officer*" it is recorded that "*he was of the arms army.*"

I should here observe that the "notices" are in various handwritings, and were generally the concoction of three or four of the members, who, meeting together after the performance, each in turn acted as secretary, while tobacco and "modest quenchers" refreshed us during our labours of composition.

They were generally written in Evelyn Ashley's room, or in Tom Thornhill's.

In '*Twould puzzle a Conjuror*, our "supers," the soldiers and workmen, had been very irregular in their attendance at rehearsal, and caused a good deal of trouble on the night of performance, by invariably coming on at the wrong times, and then positively refusing to be moved off, except at the command of their legitimate superior, the Master of the Dockyard. As to the prompter, they ignored him entirely, and W. H. Baillie used to be seen waving his hands in utter despair at the wing—which they, the workmen, took either as signs of encouragement generally, or indica-

tions that they ought to cheer, on which latter understanding the word was ˙passed, and a seriously interesting
scene between Peter and the ambassadors was suddenly interrupted by an outburst of misapplied loyalty on the part of
the workmen of Saardam. They were immediately repri-
manded, in a forcible aside, by one of the ambassadors in
disguise, whereupon they retired sulkily, and it was with
difficulty they could be induced to make their re-appearance
at the right moment. Strikes were not so common twenty-
four years ago as now, or their conduct might have been
easily accounted for.

As it is the "A. D. C." record ironically states that " *The
soldiers and workmen* OUGHT TO HAVE BEEN SEEN *to have been
appreciated.*"

Then came the farce of

WHO DO THEY TAKE ME FOR?

Colonel Templeton	Mr. MILES HALL.
Terence O'Reilly (*travelling artist*) .	Mr. DESMOND BLAKE.
Isaac Pickings (*steward of the Hard-acre Estate*)	Mr. R. JOHNSON.
Posset (*landlord of the "Hardacre Arms"*)	Mr. TOM PIERCE.
Mrs. Dorrington (*a rich widow*) . .	Mr. M. CAXTON.
Miss Prudena Pickings . . .	Mr. C. REEPER.

The new name that appears here is Mr. C. Reeper (Mr.
Wharton), who, I think, was coxswain to the Third Trinity
— the Eton Boating Club, and who had come up from
Eton with the *sobriquet* of " Creeper Wharton,"—why, the
boys only knew, I never did. Hence the name, Mr. C.
Reeper.

Mr. O'Hara was very original as the Irish hero. He was
remonstrated with as to the force of some of the language
which was not that of the author, as we had heard, that for
the first time since the commencement of the "A. D. C.," some
Dons were to be among our audience, and as these Dons were
clergymen, we were afraid that our institution would be

endangered by Terence O'Reilly's impulsive vivacity. In compliance with a very general request, Terence toned himself down considerably on the second night; "but," as he explained to us, "you must throw some little dash into the part,"—to which it was at once replied that "no one objected to a little 'dash,' but only to a good deal of d——."

Robert O'Hara afterwards observed that "he had been told of how great Power had been in this part, and as we couldn't get the great Power, we must put up with a little force."

The performance, whether loud or modified, was an excellent one, and its charm was its unconventionality. Terence was magnificently arrayed in bright check trowsers, a very white waistcoat, a light dustcoat, and glossy white hat. This wasn't the sort of 'Terence' whose classical works Vice-Chancellor Guest would have had on our boards.

Then we played, as a revival, with a new cast, the evergreen *Bombastes*, with Kelly as *Fusbos*, A. C. Lee as *The General*, myself as the King, Simpson as Distaffina, and "Mr. C. Reeper" as the fifer, in which character he was very droll, and the General had the greatest difficulty in stopping his music and getting him off the stage. In this, Artaxominus had to sing a parody on a song—then in vogue at the Cider Cellars or Evans's — called *The Dark Arches*, which used to be encored three times every night.

We were very simple in our tastes. Nowadays, in 1879, one of the "A. D. C." actors would as soon think of tying a squib to the Vice-Chancellor's gown as of singing such a song on the boards of the "A. D. C"— whence all burlesque has been *pro. tem.* banished. Our fun was a trifle rough, perhaps, but it was hearty, spontaneous, and was throughly enjoyed both by audience and actors.

On this occasion the record of the Club says:

" *Distaffina—very good, not equal to Wilson.*"

So that even within one year after our start we had already begun to be *laudatores temporis acti*. However, F. C. Wilson was to re-join our *troupe* when his academical studies should permit him. There was a demand for young undergraduates to fill these beardless parts—such a demand as must have been occasionally experienced in Shakespeare's time when he was looking everywhere for an Ophelia, a Rosalind, a Desdemona, or an Awdrey—and the demand created the supply.

We had another performance in this term, quite an exceptional case, and a very risky thing to attempt in a May Term, when so many men would be engaged in out-of-door amusements up to a late hour of the evening. However, in spite of the enforced absence of some of our 'leading artists,' we still had a powerful and energetic company, and, of all pieces, we selected the old Adelphi burlesque *Norma*.

I don't suppose that such a burlesque as *Norma*, written by J. Oxberry, and played by Paul Bedford as the *prima donna*, Wright as *Adalgisa*, and Miss Woolgar (afterwards Mrs. Mellon) as *Pollio* would be possible now, either on professional or amateur boards. The above-mentioned low comedians in petticoats were extravagantly absurd, and intensely vulgar,—far beyond anything I ever remember to have seen since. Miss Woolgar was, of course, always elegant; she, Miss P. Horton (Mrs. German Reed) and Miss Julia St. George were, as far back as I can recollect, the princes of burlesque and extravaganza.

We " saw ourselves " in *Norma*. Its fun was of the very broadest, the music popular, and, the cast being small, and the whole burlesque, too, being in one scene, it was a great boon to amateurs.

The following is the bill for May 13, 1856 :—

THIS EVENING WILL BE PRESENTED A FARCE, IN ONE ACT,
BY MR. CHARLES MATHEWS, ENTITLED

THE RINGDOVES!

Sir Harry Ringdove	Mr. TOM PIERCE.
Harry Ringdove	Mr. HUMPHREY DUKE.
Morny	Mr. GORMAN BOURKE.
Hobnail	Mr. A. M. SANDWICH.
Miss Longclachit	Mr. M. CAXTON.
Cecilia	Mr. L. A. VENDAR.

AFTER WHICH, FOR THE FIRST TIME AT THIS THEATRE,

THE ETHIOPIAN SERENADERS,

Messrs. C. N. E. GREEN and BLACK, H. MOORE, P. RETTY,
and E. HOOK,

*Who will give some of the most beautiful and popular Melodies
of their own Native Land !*

TO BE FOLLOWED BY THE OPERATIC BURLESQUE OF

"NORMA."

Polio (*a Roman consul*)	Mr. M. CAXTON.
Flavius (*a Roman centurion*)	Mr. L. A. VENDAR.
Oroveso (*the Arch Druid, no relation to the "Dark Arches"*)	Mr. U. GLYCOVE.
Norma (*a Druidess*)	Mr. HUMPHREY DUKE.
Adalgisa (*a ditto*)	Mr. TOM PIERCE.
Clotilda (*a nurse*)	Mr. T. WINKLE.
Two Children (*Norma's "pair of kids"*)	Masters SQUALL and BRAT.
The Moon (*who has condescended to descend for this occasion only by*)	The MAN IN IT.

Druids, Warriors, &c., by Messrs. HEER, T. HARE, EVERY,
and WARE.

TO CONCLUDE WITH THE SCREAMING FARCE ENTITLED

SLASHER AND CRASHER!

Mr. Benjamin Blowhard	Mr. MILES HALL.
Sampson Slasher	Mr. TOM PIERCE.
Christopher Crasher	Mr. GORMAN BOURKE.
Lieutenant Brown (*of the Marines*)	Mr. HUMPHREY DUKE.
John	Mr. E. GAAUL.
Miss Dinah Blowhard	Mr. L. A. VENDAR.
Rosa	Mr. M. CAXTON.

The key to the above is,—*Humphrey Duke*, Hon. Evelyn Ashley, who still retained the name that Alfred Thompson was to have appeared under in the previous term; *Tom Pierce*, myself; *Mr. Gorman Bourke*, Rowley Hill; *Mr. A. M. Sandwich*, L.T.Baines; *Mr. M. Caxton*, R. Simpson; *Mr. L. A. Vendar*, Arthur Cumberlege.

The serenaders were E. Ashley, Rowley Hill, A. C. Lee, Ernwin, and myself.

We all blacked our faces severely, and thought we should never get it off again. The audience, who had not been particularly pleased with the Serenaders—it was one of our failures,—clamoured for the commencement of *Norma*. We didn't try the Serenaders—or rather the Serenaders didn't try the audience, again. Washing the nigger white was found too arduous a task.

The *Ringdoves* went very well indeed. The notice recorded is to the effect that—

" *Sir Harry was very good generally, but not made up old enough.*"

" *Harry, doubly good—his make up as the real Sir Harry, capital.*"

" *Mooney, Mr. Hill's début, excellent.*"

" *Hobnail, Mr. Baines' ditto, short and sweet.*"

" *Miss Longclackit, first-rate in everything.*"

" *Cecilia, rather too old.*"

" *Norma.*"—The special success of this piece seems to have been achieved by the nurse Clotilda, and the two children, played by a chorister and Wharton, the latter " doubling " as " The Man in the Moon."

We were very proud of this Moon, as it was the genuine article—I mean the real property moon used at the Adelphi, lent to us for the occasion by Mr. Benjamin Webster.

Of the chorus, by Messrs. Lee, Preston, Lysaght, Evans, Ernwin, Lutwidge, Hill, it is recorded, " *All equally good, specially Lutwidge.*"

The chorus were very well trained, and had worked hard, I know, for three weeks with White-headed Bob and his band, for whom I had had printed a paper of "cues for music."

Our band, as a rule, had to "vamp" considerably, but in this instance we insisted—Mr. Ashley and myself, who were chiefly concerned in the success of the burlesque—on a proper score being made for the fiddle, cornet and violoncello; we had stipulated that White-headed Bob and his Merry Men should come regularly to rehearsals, for which I think they were at first remunerated by shillings all round—"Bobs up," as it used to be called—from everyone in the room. This Bohemian and irregular plan was soon dropped, and a fixed charge was made for their attendance.

The chorus were immensely imposing in their grey beards and white Druidical robes, their action energetic, and their march—*the* march—superb. As they complained of not having enough to do, they were brought in on every possible occasion, and plenty of business was invented in order to keep them quiet, as while on the stage they were in very good order, though a trifle uncertain about their notes; but had they been allowed to remain off for any length of time, we should have heard more than we wanted of them, as, from our experience at rehearsal, they, being a large party, were safe to indulge in a performance of their own in the green room, where every word would be audible to the audience. As it was, over and over again, our anxious stage manager, Polwhele, used to rush into the green-room, shutting the door carefully and exclaiming in an agonized stage whisper, "I say, for goodness' sake don't make such a row. They can hear every word in front."

But it must be remembered that our green room served us for dressing rooms and temporary property room as well.

Slasher and Crasher, another old Adelphi farce, and just the thing for that audience. Murray played Old Blowhard, and could not remember his part. Rowley Hill was very funny and very noisy as Crasher.

Towards the end of the piece, when the fun becomes fast and furious, and Crasher has to draw a sword and pursue Old Blowhard round the stage, off at one wing and on at another, and then chase him round again, we heard a loud cry of agony, and we attributed it to the excellent acting of Old Blowhard, who was keeping up his character of being frightened by Crasher, even when off the stage. It turned out, however, to be a very real expression of pain, from a carpenter, who accidentally getting in Mr. Hill's way, while he was in full cry after Old Blowhard with a drawn sword, was forcibly reminded of the fact by the energetic Crasher, who wouldn't keep the stage waiting and let the excitement drop, for all the carpenters in the world.

After the performance the injured carpenter was comforted with a different sort of 'tip' to that which had so disturbed him, behind the scenes, during *Slasher and Crasher*.

" The idiot wouldn't get out of the way," was Crasher's subsequent explanation, and when the O'Crasher's Celtic blood was up, he couldn't stand a Saxon obstructionist.

The prompter had plenty to do the first night of this farce, for our " *Norma* " had occupied most of our time and attention; the ladies were " elderly and respectable " and " good as usual," and our orchestra, in spite of all the rehearsals, were so nervous in approaching their work, that taking advantage of the twenty minutes' rest afforded by our Serenaders, they so attuned themselves at a neighbouring public—perhaps at the bar of The Hoop—as to give a very uncertain sound when called upon.

For myself as Adalgisa, having been absolutely perfect in the second of the duet at the last rehearsal, I was so nervous when the time came, that I sang all Norma's music and got off anyhow. The second night we were all quite at home in it, but on the whole, as far as the principals were concerned, I don't think " *Norma* " proved a favourite.

At the end of this notice, which is signed by two names, E. Ashley and F. C. Burnand, comes the following eulogy—

evidently written on the departure of our stage manager, who was now leaving the University, having stopped up two terms after taking his degree in January, 1856 :—

" But we have forgotten our great duty to the members of the ' A. D. C.' as well as to the enlightened audiences that have patronised our performances, as having omitted all mention of that energetic gentleman, truly loyal, yet-not-the-less-on-that-account-wonderfully talented stage manager, who, though he has but once attempted the histrionic line, and ' strutted his short hour on the stage,' has deserved the united and cordial thanks of the ' A. D. C.' in general, and the acting members in particular, and who by his comity of expression, his sauvity of temper, his financial acumen, and invariable, and therefore-for-that-reason-not-like-the-weathercock-changeable deportment, has left the name of—(shall we breathe it)—' Polwhele '—to be handed down to all future members as an object of affectionate regard."

It was a true word spoken in jest, and though the Club has been most fortunate in its stage managers, yet none have had so difficult a time of it, none have ever had so much to do, as our first stage-manager, whose undoubted " financial acumen " prevented us ' running a muck ' at the outset.

At a General Meeting held May 31, 1856—

1. *Mr. W. Lysaght (Trin. Coll.) was elected Stage Manager, vice Polwhele resigned.*

(And now the records are in a new hand, the first, very neatly written, being signed " E. Ashley.")

2. *It was agreed that there should be an auditor on the Committee, who shall audit the accounts at the end of every term.*

J. M. Wilson of Caius was elected unanimously to this office.

3. *The previous rule respecting the Treasurer and Stage-manager being merged into one was cancelled.*

(So that Mr. Polwhele's offices were now divided.)

4. *F. C. Burnand, Acting Manager, E. Ashley, Secretary and Treasurer, were re-elected. Evans as Prompter.*

(This was *vice* Mr. W. H. Baillie resigned. I think *Norma* and *Slasher* finished *him*.)

5. *Mr. W. H. Baillie elected President, vice Kelly resigned.*

(Mr. R. Kelly had commenced serious reading for his degree. Mr. F. C. Wilson was also similarly engaged. Two of our best men 'out of it.' Mr. C. E. Donne, and Mr. Gerald Fitzgerald down, and Mr. O'Hara had left the University; at all events, he never reappeared on the A. D. C. boards.)

Then we made a rule—

6. *That the Prompter be present at one undressed rehearsal of each piece, and one dresser.*

(Evidently the Prompter had complained of his onerous duties, and, as evidently, the actors had represented that they couldn't get on without him.)

7. *Mr. Lutwidge appointed Assistant Stage Manager, vice Ernwin resigned.*

(The Stage Manager objected to the entire responsibility being on *his* shoulders.)

8. *That smoking be allowed on rehearsal nights in the large room, but never on the stage itself.*

This last rule speaks well for the discipline of the Club.
In fact we were becoming very orderly and gradually set-

tling down, and before the end of the term, at a Committee Meeting, June 7, 1856, we decided that—

1. *" The second and last Monday in term be fixed days for Committee Meetings, and that the days of performance be settled finally at least ten days before the first night of performance."*

Henceforth " extra nights in consequence of a great success " were doomed.

2. *Immediately on such settlement each gentleman cast for any character shall* provide himself *with a book, as also the Stage Manager, Prompter, and Acting Manager.*

3. *After the settlement of day and pieces the Secretary shall send printed circulars at least a week beforehand, specifying the pieces and days of performance to every member.*

(This was to further the sale of tickets.)

4. *That the performances be always, if possible, on a Wednesday, Thursday, and Friday.*

(Saturdays were excluded principally because a performance on that night might clash with a Beefsteak Club dinner.)

5. *That the whole number of tickets be distributed equally among the members of the Committee, who shall on payment for the same issue them to members for distribution, or to others.*

(" No credit " system.)

6. *That there be a fine of 2s. 6d. for being half an hour late for rehearsal, and 5s. for being absent altogether, the only excuse taken being positive illness. Any member throwing up his part after once accepting it to be liable to a fine of one guinea.*

(We had suffered from insufficient rehearsals during this May Term.)

7. *Of Rehearsals. That one time especially be set apart for Rehearsal every day after the settlement.*

(This made ten days certain. This term we had had three weeks, but though the rehearsals were frequent the attendance was irregular.)

That only one piece be rehearsed at each rehearsal.

(We had done ' bits ' of *Norma*, ' bits ' of *Slasher*, just as it happened to suit those present.)

And that notice be put up before four o'clock on the previous day in the rooms, the acting members determining the time by ballot.

(At four o'clock most of us were absent, as at that hour we went to get "marked" in Hall. We were 'marked' if we attended, and we were 'marked men' if we didn't. Four was then the dining hour at Trinity. *Now* there are three dinner hours. Early for athletes, medium time for reading men, and seven for those who would otherwise prefer dining in their rooms—as most of us, in our time, used to do ordinarily, for " Hall " at Trinity was then a very uncivilised affair.)

Finally. *That the Dressed Rehearsal be the only night Rehearsal of a piece, and it shall commence at 6.30 p.m.*

(That is, immediately after chapel, before the men separated.)

This allowed for taking an early snack at " Litchfield's," the Restaurant—or even something short, and as sweet as possible, in Hall—or a cut off a cold joint in our own rooms,— there was always this luxury *chez nous* in Green Street—then " keeping chapel," so as to be on the windy side of the law, and then going all together to rehearsal, finishing at about nine, when we betook ourselves to the pleasantest meal of our day, supper, or an "Athenæum Tea," which was the same thing, but only open to members of the Athenæum, and to those specially invited. The undergraduates' day generally finished with Loo, varying from eighteenpence and three shillings, to three and nine up to half-sovereigns and Club force, and so to unlimited. But these card parties had, of course, nothing whatever to do with the "A. D. C.," most of the acting members preferring to sup together quietly, and talk over the business of the performances.

The Club's acceptance of these rules brings the first season of our "A. D. C." new year to a close. Then came the Long Vacation.

CHAPTER IX.

WE had already made a good start for our second year. Charles E. Donne, B.A. and myself, had commenced an ambitious drama, in two acts, called *The Husband*, specially written for the cast we could get at the "A. D. C." in the following term.

It was a wonderfully 'original' drama. All the originality came from other original works, from *Robert Macaire*, from *Still Waters Run Deep*, from the acted version of *The Battle of Life*, business from farces, and a hero as gloomy as The Stranger, as tragic as Beverley, and as dashing as Robert Macaire.

How it fell through I don't know, but somehow or other, though we had it printed, and though the cast is down as "for the A. D. C., November, 1856," yet as far as I can remember, it was never read to the company and never rehearsed.

I fancy that in consequence of F. C. Wilson being unable to play, we gave up *The Husband* and settled on *The Jacobite*, a comic drama, in two acts, suggested by Reginald Kelly, with four parts in it for all our principals.

The first move this term was to elect Mr. A. C. Lee, of Trinity, Prompter, vice Mr. Evans, absent.

The next to elect Mr. Whitley Assistant Stage Manager, vice Lutwidge, absent.

Then in a very business-like way we "resolved—

> "*That the Prompter be requested to provide himself with books of the pieces.*"

What trouble we had with those prompters! and this in spite of all the recent rules so carefully drawn up the previous term!

> "—— *That he should attend every rehearsal.*"

This was more stringent than the latest rule on the subject.

> "—— And *keep an inventory of the properties.*"

This was italicised. It was in consequence of the gradual accumulation of "properties," which were made for us and seldom hired, that, at length, the Stage Manager complained of being unable to get on without an assistant, who should be responsible for these troublesome articles.

Then we resolved "*That all stage accounts (i.e.,* as separate from Club accounts) *should pass through the Stage Manager's hands to the treasurer and be paid by him.*"

The Treasurer was never to pay without the bills being signed by the Stage Manager. After a while the signature of the Assistant Stage Manager was also requisite.

Hitherto the orders had been signed by the secretary only.

Then, in accordance with the statute 'made and provided' in the May Term, we settled that the days of performance should be the 18th, 19th, 20th and 21st of November, *i.e.*, Tuesday, Wednesday, Thursday and Friday.

There were elected:

Mr. Charles Hall (Trin.); Mr. A. F. Sealy (Caius); Mr. Julius Rowley (Magd.); Mr. P. P. Gwynne (St. John's); Mr. R. Tennant (Trin.); Mr. H. W. Hoffmann (Trin.).

After vain endeavours to restrict the smoking to one room, we gave it up as hopeless, and on October 27, passed a resolution to permit smoking in both rooms. Performance days of course, excepted.

Our next elections were 29th October, Mr. F. V. Wright (Trin.), and Mr. R. Hobart (Trin. Hall), and on November 8th, Mr. Frank Smith (Trin.).

A great change had come over the spirit of the Club since May Term, 1855, and many of our members belonged also to the Athenæum, which had never again attempted a performance.

The ancient Jones having been respectfully *congédié*,

> "When he who had painted
> Had left but the name,"

which we still retained in the bill, as our stock scenery was the work of his hands,—we accepted the services of one E. Gage, a townsman, the precise nature of whose trade I forget—if I ever knew—as he is associated in my mind only with Chinese lanterns, fireworks, transparencies, paint pots, a state of chronic perspiration, and a small shop where there was a muddle of everything.

He was an ingenious man up to a certain point, and was certainly at first far from an expensive one. Personally, I was never so struck by the excellence of his scenery as he was himself.

It was ' not a patch ' on what the discarded Jones would have done, but then the discarded Jones had to be, traditionally, entertained by one committee man, who had to feed him, and listen to his old stories, and Jones's work cost the Club two guineas, or more, per diem, while Gage was at our beck and call, and delighted at the opportunity thus afforded him of extending his connection among the undergraduates.

Gage—who was a fussy, funny little fat man, always " hot and hot," no matter what time of year it might be—was persistently worried at his work by Rowley Hill, who after inspecting some *chef d'œuvre* of scene painting, intended to represent a window, would ask in the most undeniable brogue —which he could accentuate considerably when it suited his humour—

"Gage, come here! What's this at all? Is it a cow ye've been painting? Sure then there's no cow in *The Jacobite,* unless ye think a Jacobite's a cow."

Of course the listeners kept their countenances, for Gage was a very fair butt, and a very all round one too, besides being exceptionally good tempered with *us,* as a matter of business.

"No, Mr. Hill," he would explain, eyeing his questioner's serious face to find out whether he was really being chaffed or not, "No, sir, don't you see it's a window?"

"A window!" Rowley Hill would exclaim, "*That* a window!! now ask anyone—and they'd swear it's a cow. Why, look here, Gage," and he would point to a branch intended to belong to a tree in the landscape outside, as seen through the window, "isn't this the cow's tail? A window! get out with ye! 'tis a cow, and there's its tail!"

Gage would then commence an apologetic explanation with the view of proving to us that the scene was not yet finished, and that it was not fair to judge of it in its present state, when, perhaps, he was ready to admit, what was meant for a window *might* bear some resemblance to a cow : but we had all got the cue, and one after the other informed him that there was no cow in *The Jacobite* and he must paint it out.

Next day he triumphed. He had painted an extraordinary piece of drapery partly hiding the window. "There," he said to us, "That's not a cow, now, is it, Mr. Hill?"

"No, Gage, ye've made a bull of it now," returned Rowley Hill. "But it's about as much like a window as he'll ever get it."

The result was a Gothic chamber of a bright reddish brown colour, with impossible lights and shades, and quite a curiosity in perspective. "I'm not a nartist," said Mr. Gage complacently, "but I don't think as you've got anythink 'ere to beat *that*." We hadn't, and we never had.

The theatrical work commenced with the arrival of a distinguished character, Mr. W. G. Clarkson, the well-known Perruquier (*then* of 15, Little Russell Street, Covent Garden), who had undertaken to provide the dresses, and as these came from Mr. May's, the Costumier of Bow Street, it was with the latter that for some time to come the Club regularly dealt. The name of Messrs. Nathan at this time disappears from our programmes, and up to the October term of 1858, W. G. Clarkson is always advertised at the foot of the bill as "providing the costumes and appointments." What the latter word implies I do not know, except that we were thoroughly satisfied, and that Clarkson brought with him no *dis*-appointments.

The amount of our Costumier's luggage made a formidable show in our small rooms, and some contemporary wag has written in the A. D. C. Book that "as the Club only possesses a pit and stalls, Mr. Clarkson has brought down with him some private boxes."

I treat this *jeu de mot* as Mr. Clarkson did his box on leaving, and *re-cord* it.

Our amiable costumier and perruquier—two single gentlemen rolled into one Clarkson—preferred coming down on Sunday early as it gave him ' an outing.' He was most willing and obliging, and a great favourite with the members, whose cigar cases were placed at his disposal in the most generous fashion. Where he slept was always a mystery; but it was supposed that when all the members had retired, he " set " a cottage interior on the stage, and took his rest on a property bed. Except on a Sunday, he was never seen out of doors, but always among pomatum pots, dressed in a white apron, like a man-cook, and with a large comb stuck in his hair over his right ear. So rare was it for him ever to be seen out of the Club, that, when, on one of the above-mentioned Sundays, some member of the " A. D. C." came up to another's rooms with the startling information that Clarkson was 'wandering about the backs of the Colleges,' it was immediately feared that either our informant was hoaxing us, or that there must be something wrong with Clarkson. Several members were at once got together, and this impromptu commission of inquiry immediately sallied forth, in a great state of anxiety, to learn the truth of the extraordinary statement they had just heard.

Yes, there he was. He had been listening to the afternoon anthem in King's College and admiring the 'make-ups' of the Dons, as they issued forth in their academicals.

We followed him at a cautious distance, as though we were dogging an escaped lunatic, or a rare bird that had escaped from its cage, and which we were only awaiting the first opportunity to capture. He gradually found his way back to the green-room of the "A. D. C." where we found him, all among the grease-pots, slumbering in an arm chair, his head falling forward, and his hands clasped over his well rounded form, and so we left him, happy, undisturbed, playing his own Sunday anthem on his own nasal organ.

Clarkson once accompanied a party out partridge shooting. He confided to one of us that 'Though he'd often eaten the birds he'd never seen 'em *undressed.*'

No one ever saw Clarkson arrive—no one ever saw him leave. He was summoned to attend, and lo! one morning we went to the "A. D. C." and found he was there.

His mode of living was remarkably unostentatious on these occasions, but his presence was invariably notified in the afternoon by a mixed smell of frizzling fat, and hair-grease, arising, I fancy, from the fact that the curling-tongs were being heated between the lower bars of the fire, where at the top his chop was cooking.

After the performance he often used to receive an invitation to our supper parties, but when he came, though highly appreciating the compliment, he seemed rather scared, and subsequently 'declined with thanks,' preferring to sit—like

K

Marius among the ruins—surrounded by the muddle of a green-room after a performance, and take his quiet meal on one of his boxes, while he chatted with " Mr. and Mrs. Boots "—*i.e.* Boots and his wife—who belonged to the Hoop Hotel, and were told off for the special service of the " A. D. C."

On Monday we rehearsed my new burlesque, *Lord Lovel and Lady Nancy Bell; or the Bounding Brigand of Bakumboilum.* And on Tuesday we played it as a last piece, preceded by *The Jacobite,* to commence with, and a new farce of mine, *In for a Holiday,* in the middle of the bill.

The house consisted of sixty-three audience, exclusive of members. This gave us fifteen guineas. It doesn't sound much; but this for two nights, with an increase on the two last produced about eighty guineas, which gave us a considerable profit, and is recorded in the Annals as " pleasing to the Club."

" *C. E. Donne,*" says the jocular notice, " *as Sir Richard Wrighton. His acting, though the author only wrote thirty-six pages, spoke volumes.*

E. M. Ashley. Major Murray—acted evidently as Major Murray would have done in similar circumstances—very good.

R. Kelly. His John Duck inimitable. Even Clarke of the Haymarket could have done it no better. ' We ne'er shall look upon his like again.' "

In the margin, in a different hand, is a query to ' Clarke,' intimating that Buckstone was meant. Another hand has scribbled below this, " *It's a joke, stoopid!* " The joke being, that Mr. Kelly's *beau idéal* on the stage was Clarke of the Haymarket.

The quotation ' never look upon his like again,' applies to

the fact of it being probably his last appearance, it being his last term at the University.

" *Gerald Fitzgerald . . . took the part of Widow Pottle. His*
   ' *make up' was wonderful; his voice carefully altered,*
   and his acting so clever as to make a real part of a cha-
   racter which in the hands of an inferior artist would have
   been nothing at all."

[I have an old faded photograph of him now, as I have of all the characters in this piece, except myself, with Clarkson about to try on John Duck's wig.]

" *Patty Pottle, by F. C. Burnand, his first appearance as a*
   young woman. His acting added much to the success of
   the piece.
" *Lady Somerfield. R. Hobart. Looked pretty, and acted*
   very nicely.
   " *Great praise is due to the officers and soldiers who so*
   nobly did their duty in the cause they had espoused for
   four nights only."
   The Officer.—Mr. Julius Rowley.
   The Soldiers.—Messrs. Wright and Hall.
   " *Some people were weak enough to say the soldiers must*
necessarily have been HALL WRIGHT !
   " *We write this,*" the record continues, " *to prevent any*
young wag when reading this from perpetrating the bad joke
which every one makes on seeing these two names in conjunc-
tion."
   " *The piece was very successful.*"

The next night, instead of *The Jacobite,* we played *Used
Up,* and the final notice is :—

   " THE JACOBITE *and* USED UP *were two of the most*
perfect pieces of amateur acting. This remark must espe-
cially apply to USED UP. *There was not a shaky man in the*

cast, Donne, Fitzgerald, Kelly, Burnand, Ev. M. Ashley,
C. Hall, Rowley, R. Hobart.

"*There were four nights, and the first was almost as well
filled as the last.*

"*The performances never improved from the first night
(except, perhaps, in a few minor details), but the first night's
performance was as smooth and as good as the last.*

"*This was the effect of careful and timely rehearsals.   We
had nearly three weeks of daily rehearsal.*"

(So that the sad experience of the previous term and the
new rules had effected some good.)

"*There was no one who did not enter into these two pieces
with all his energy.*"

The fact is that at this time all our principals were indefatigable rehearsers, and had no counter attraction out of the
"A. D. C."   We were prepared to give our undivided attention to the stage business, and we undoubtedly did.

Charles Donne's *Sir Charles Coldstream* was a really good
performance.   I find I played Lady Clutterbuck, and against
it is scored "*good.*"   I hope so.

The burlesque was also successful, but not equal to either
Villikins, Bombastes, or *St. George.*   All our burlesques were
more or less successful.   The singing, dancing, and costumes
were new to our audience in those happy Thespian and un-
critical days.

Evelyn Ashley played Lord Lovel, Preston and Rowley two
Brigands, and Tom Thornhill the Baron Bell.

Here is the Bill *in extenso.*

A. D. C.

THIS EVENING (FRIDAY) WILL BE PERFORMED THE PETITE
COMEDY, IN TWO ACTS, BY DION BOUCICAULT,
ESQ., ENTITLED,

USED UP!

Sir Charles Coldstream	Mr. C. J. ALGERNON.
Sir Adonis Leech	Mr. HUMPHREY DUKE.
Mr. Tom Saville	Mr. HAWLEY CHARLES.
Wurzel (*a farmer*)	Mr. R. JOHNSON.
John Ironbrace (*a blacksmith*) . .	Mr. A. HERBERT.
Mr. Fennel (*a lawyer*)	Mr. POLER.
James (*a servant*)	Mr. FEATHERSTONE.
Mary (*Wurzel's daughter*) . . .	H. AUDLEY.
Lady Clutterbuck	F. MAYDEN.

ACT. I.—Saloon in Sir Charles Coldstream's House.

ACT. II.—Interior of Wurzel's Farm House.

AFTER WHICH, AN ENTIRELY NEW FARCE, BY F. C.
BURNAND, ESQ., ENTITLED

IN FOR A HOLIDAY!

Gustavus Popple (*a young gentleman retained, between ten and three, by Government*)	Mr. TOM PIERCE.
Rory O'Bobster (*a gentleman retained by a commercial house for his persuasive powers*)	Mr. GORMAN BOURKE.
Mrs. Amelia Waggles (*a young widow*)	Mr. H. AUDLEY.
Mrs. O'Bobster	Mr. S. GILBERT.
Mrs. Comfit	Mr. B. STUART.

---

*After which, will be presented for the first time, an entirely new
Burlesque, written expressly for the "A.D.C.," by the author
of St. George, Villikins, &c., and bearing the aristocratic
but not-the-less-on-that-account-exceedingly pathetic title of*

LORD LOVEL AND LADY NANCY BELL;
OR,
THE BOUNDING BRIGAND OF BAKUMBOILUM.

Lord Lovel (*a swell betrothed to Lady Nancy Bell*)	Mr. HUMPHREY DUKE.
Baron Billy Bell (*no joke can be made on such a BARREN subject, so that we will simply state that he is the parent of Lady Nancy*) . .	Mr. FEATHERSTONE.

Rumtifoozle (*formerly Duc di Rumti-*
foozle, now living in exile under the
title of "The Bounding Brigand"). Mr. Tom Pierce.
First Brigand ⎱ (*making in all two* ⎰ Messrs. V. Glycove and
Second Brigand ⎰ *Brigands*). . ⎱ Poler.
  (*belonging to Lord*
First Retainer ⎱ *Lovel who may not* ⎰ Messrs. J. Norton and
Second Retainer ⎰ *for this reason be* ⎱ F. Roper.
  (*called a Law Lord*)
Lady Nancy Bell (*daughter of the*
Baron — beloved by Rumtifoozle —
married to Lovel—and—and—oh !
a lot of things !) . . . . Mr. E. Bishop.

Guests, Servants, and Bloated Aristocrats by Messrs. Heer, T. Hare, Avery, Ware, and a host of talent.

ACT I.

"I'm going, my Lady Nancy Bell, foreign countries for to see "—words of Lord Lovel, extracted from old song. To show the why and wherefore of his saying these words, the Curtain being drawn up, will show—

Scene 1st.—A Dark Wood in the Bakumboilum Country. (Painted by S. J. E. Jones.)

Scene 2nd.—Baronial Hall in Baron Billy's Castle. (Painted by S. J. E. Jones.)

ACT II.

" He rode and he rode (home) on his milk-white steed—
After having been absent a year and a day—
'Now who is defunct !' quoth he (Lord Lovel).
'A lady is dead—and they call her the Lady Nancy.'"

Extracted from the MS. in possession of Mr. Samuel Cowell, Antiquarian and Lushington Professor, at Evans's Grand College, Covent Garden.

Scene 1st. — Lady Nancy's Boudoir. (Painted by S. E. Gage.) *How she took poison and died !!!*

Scene 2nd.—Tomb of the Billy Bells—*Night.* (Painted by Charles Lester, Esq.)

Arrival of Love ! Defeat of Rumtifoozle !! Exhuma-
tion !!! Exclamation !!!! Perturbation !!!!! Con-
glomeration !!!!!! and something of everything-else-
ation !!!!!!! an

IMPRESSIVE DENOÛMENT !!

Concluding the Piece with (we hope) approbation.

Books of the Burlesque may be had in the room, price One Shilling.

Manager—Mr. G. LESLIE. Acting Manager—Mr. TOM PIERCE.
Assistant Stage Manager—Mr. V. Glycove.
Prompter—Mr. CHARLIE CHUCKLER.
Scenery by Messrs. S. J. E. JONES, E. GAGE, and C. LESTER, Esq.
Costumes by J. W. CLARKSON (of Drury Lane).
Decorations by E. GAGE.

" Mr. G. Leslie " was our new stage manager, W. Lysaght, Trin. Coll.; R. Preston was his assistant. The Prompter was A. C. Lee.

The peculiarity of this bill is that no " Mr." was pre-fixed to the names of those who played the women in the comedy.

Used Up was the best played piece ever produced at the " A. D. C." Besides having a really admirable Sir Charles Coldstream in Charles E. Donne, we had in Evelyn Ashley, as Sir Adonis Leech, an old beau whose make up and per-formance could only have been surpassed in later days by Mr. Hare in *School*—where Tom Robertson had given him an imitation of " Cousin Feenix " in *Dombey & Son*. And then there was Charles Hall (our *first* Charles Hall, Charles the First, who entered the army, while our Charles the Second went to the bar), who, as Honourable Tom Saville, could not have found his equal, for this small part, among amateurs or professionals. Kelly's Wurzel was excellent. Gerald Fitz-gerald's Ironbrace was energetic and made an excellent foil to the languid Sir Charles, but though a strong character in the play, it was the weakest in performance, yet not so weak as to impair the general excellence. Julius Rowley—called of course " Polee " in the bill—as the lawyer, was another excel-lent bit of character acting, and anyone looking at a photo-graph of R. Hobart as *Mary Wurzel*, would probably say " What a pretty girl ! and how exactly she looks her part." Yes, certainly, *Used Up*—as, apart from the written record, I am reminded by old members of the Club, and as I well remember it myself—was, without exception, the very best played two-act drama ever represented on the " A. D. C." boards.

Recent performances may perhaps challenge comparison with it, but good as was their *Ticket of Leave Man* in October Term, 1878, it was too ambitious an attempt, and though Mr. Brookfield's Jem Dalton was exceptionally good, yet it had not the advantages of such a perfect and experienced cast all round, and of such close careful rehearsals for three weeks, as we had, twenty-two years before, for *Used Up*.

Notice the author's idea of Government employment, as instanced in the description of Gustavus Popple in *In for a Holiday*.

This farce went immensely, Rowley Hill as Rory O'Bobster being wonderfully amusing, both on and off the stage. On the second night the stage manager had set the scene wrong, and Rory O'Bobster's entrance door was omitted.

"B'dad, then, how'm I to get in at all?" screamed the representative of Rory O'Bobster, as, dressed in red check trousers, with a white waistcoat, a blue coat and brass buttons, he executed a wild war dance of enraged disappointment at the part of the scene where his door ought to have been.

The prompter, who will be found in the bill as "Mr. Charlie Chuckler"—an irritating name when you want a person who *won't* chuckle—recommended him to go on anywhere.

"Anywhere!" shouted the unfortunate Rory. "But *where*, man alive? Where's anywhere?"

It seemed to be nowhere.

But the cue came, and inspired by desperation, Rowley Hill, with a furious energy that would well have suited the character he had to play, if he hadn't had to assume a demeanour all smiles and heartiness immediately he appeared, burst on to the scene through a bedroom door, which puzzled the audience considerably, as they couldn't for the life of them make out why Rory O'Bobster should have been hiding in the bedroom, and why he should appear without any explanation being given or demanded.

Prompter, stage manager, and assistant stage manager, would have got it hot from Rory O'Bobster that night, for he was armed with a real shillelagh, which he flourished wildly, accompanying the war-dance, all round the stage behind the scenes in search of the offenders who had fled, with "strange guttural noises" that, as our record of this episode states,

" were successfully imitated by Mr. Lee "—the " Charlie Chuckler " above mentioned—and " must have been heard," —as they were by two favoured individuals—" to have been appreciated."

Tom Thornhill, made up and dressed like a carrotty-headed ostler, appeared as the man with the bonnet-box. His business was limited to scratching his wig dubiously. This was received with rounds of applause, and the more he was applauded the more he scratched. His conduct on this occasion would have qualified him as a member of a " scratch " company.

Reginald Kelly, having devoted himself heart and soul to *Old Wurzel* and the *Jacobite*, had undertaken, at short notice and in the kindest way possible, to master the difficulties of Mrs. Comfit, the landlady, and on the first night he read his part from a tea-tray which he was carrying; but on the second night, having found this proceeding highly embarrassing, he did away with all the difficulty that might arise from reading and acting at the same time, by coming on, without his book and without his tea-tray, and forgetting his part altogether.

In our records, Evelyn Ashley has remarked of this piece that "it went without a *hitch*, except what was apparent when Mr. Thornhill *scratched.*" Also

" *The dialogue ran smoothly, and the author, contrary to his usual custom, seemed very much pleased.*"

"H. Audley," in the farce, stands for R. Hobart; " S. Gilbert," for Gwynne; and " B. Stuart," for R. Kelly.

As to the burlesque, I am sure that at this time I knew nothing of Victor Hugo's *Hernani*, or the character of Rum- tifoozle,—the exiled Duke living as a bandit—might have been taken as a burlesque upon that absurd personage. Perhaps I had seen the opera *Ernani*. I do recollect it well, with Mdlle. Bosio as the heroine.

Our two scenes, "*painted by S. J. E. Jones,*" were old ones. The first was the wood scene, which had been his work in 1855 for *Bombastes;* and the second had been painted for *St. George and the Dragon.* We made a flourish about them, because " Mr. E. Gage " had requested that he might have his own name in the bill, and because we had a new amateur scenic artist, whose work had cost us only the price of the paint and canvas. The last was Mr. C. Lutwidge, who, both before and after he became a pupil of O'Connor's, painted several things for the " A. D. C."

The reference, in the bill, to Sam Cowell, who used to sing Lord Lovel, will be recognised by all who remember Evans's in " the old days " of Paddy Green, when the room was a quarter of its present size, and only men were admitted.

After this performance, we had a general meeting in December, whereat were elected

W. H. Baillie . . .	President.
Ernwin	Stage Manager,

Vice Lysaght resigned.

F. C. Burnand . . .	Acting Manager.
A. C. Lee	Prompter.
E. Ashley . . .	Secretary and Treasurer.
J. M. Wilson (Caius) . .	Auditor.

This arrangement was almost immediately upset by Mr. Ernwin's suddenly quitting the University at Christmas; and during the next term—when, after our brilliant exploits there was, for reasons which will presently appear, a lull in our little theatrical circle—the post of stage manager remained vacant, or as good, or as bad, as vacant, the holder being thus named in the bills for the Lent Term—

Stage Manager . . .	Mr. St. Ewpid.

CHAPTER X.

FINANCIAL CRISIS—DEBT—DOUBTS AND DIFFICULTY—WRITTED
—NOT ARRESTED—WE RISE LIKE A PHŒNIX FROM THE
ASHES OF THE PAID ACCOUNTS.

THE Lent Term of 1856 must be ever memorable in the
annals of the Club, as it was then that we first had to borrow
money to meet our liabilities.   It was our 'Money Lent
Term.'

We were brought face to face with our difficulties with
a startling suddenness.

In the January of 1857, Reginald Kelly having taken his
degree, stayed up all jubilant for 'The Bachelors' Ball,'
which was given either just at the very commencement of the
Term, or at the close of the Christmas vacation before the
men came up.

Be that as it may, very few members of the "A. D. C."
were in Cambridge for this festivity, and Reginald Kelly
with his blushing honours thick upon him, appeared on the
red-baized steps of the brilliantly lighted hotel, resplendent
in the lemonest of lemon-tinted gloves and the whitest of
white ties, and had just requested the ladies of his party to
wait for one moment while he handed his cap and new
stringed Bachelor gown to a polite official who was stepping
forward to receive them, when the demeanour of the polite
official suddenly changed, his aspect became less polite and
more official, and just as the gay young Bachelor was about
to ask why he didn't take the proffered cap and gown, the

man produced a neatly folded slip of paper which turned out to be a writ.

Reginald Kelly couldn't believe his eyes. He had heard something of this sort of proceeding in farces on the stage, when the bailiff generally got the worst of it, and when the low-comedian who had to escape from him, was shut up in a jam cupboard, whence he issued with his mouth and fingers daubed all over, or in a cupboard with a bottle of brandy, when, of course, he reappeared very much the worse for liquor, in which case he usually smashed the bailiff's hat over his eyes, and then effected his escape from an open window, which was immediately the signal for the prompter to let fall a basket of broken crockery, supposed to represent "a crash," and some one would cry out "he's gone through the conservatory"—whereupon the "minion of the law" would follow his victim as speedily as possible, and of course, had far and away the worst of it.

But in real life, it was evidently quite another affair altogether. Here was the bailiff, here was Reginald Kelly, there was no jam cupboard at hand for either to hide in, and no window for either to escape out of with a crash. The crash had come with a vengeance, but how? Was he arrested, if so, at whose suit? He owed nothing in the University? If he had already taken his degree, the consequences were not so serious as if the ceremony were still to come, as the Bachelor is supposed to be free of debt. If he *had* taken his degree, then clearly it was the creditor's intention to catch him before quitting the University for ever.

At whose suit?

Our unfortunate carpenter's, or that of *his* creditors, for *he*, poor man, had failed, and we owed him about two hundred pounds. Somehow he had got hold of Reginald Kelly's name as a prominent member, as President, and also Secretary and Treasurer, in which latter capacity he had signed the orders, had probably given receipts, and paid money on account.

However, so it was.

Kelly explained that it was all right, but the server—being anything but a *time*-server—was inexorable.

Reginald Kelly pointed out to him that he was engaged for the next half-a-dozen dances, and couldn't come. The bailiff simply replied that he couldn't hear of his dancing with anybody but him (the bailiff) and that he had been instructed not to lose sight of him until some settlement should be arrived at.

The upshot of it was, that, with great presence of mind, the gay young Bachelor excused himself for a few minutes, returned to his College with the man and the writ, interviewed his tutor, the matter was there and then arranged, and apparently free and unfettered Reginald Kelly returned to the mazy dance, cherishing vindictive thoughts against the " A. D. C." committee, who, by their want of prevision, had placed one of their leading members in, so to speak, " a hole."

Precisely the same situation occurred the same night or very soon afterwards at Evelyn Ashley's rooms, where the server was so astonished by his warm reception, that he was for proceeding with a summons on his own account, had it not been shown that the writ was itself illegal, in fact a writ of error—and the bailiff a trespasser.

Ashley had also been our secretary, and so his name had been given to some of the orders for work.

Before the Committee came up, however, both our secretaries had forgiven us, while Kelly, who had been actually out of pocket by the transaction, only wished to be recouped as quickly as possible, for the advance which he had been compelled to make in order to appear at that Bachelor's Ball as gay and light-hearted as the gallant young waterman.

Before a committee, specially called, Reginald Kelly told his grievance. His narrative was so highly amusing that the board were in fits of irrepressible laughter. But then *he* had been the sufferer, not we.   Therein lay the point of the joke, as far as it was a joke at all.

As for Evelyn Ashley, he could join in the laugh most heartily, as *he* had dismissed the bailiff summarily, and had paid nothing for the amusement.

He reminded us particularly, that when, so far back as the October Term of '55, he had been elected secretary and treasurer, he had begged to be excused, and had very soon resigned the post after being fined five shillings for being absent from a meeting.   He had, he said, never wished to be secretary and treasurer, he didn't care about writing, and was no hand at accounts, and look! hadn't it turned out just as he had expected?   Hadn't he, in his official capacity, been compelled to sign everything, and hadn't he now been held responsible for his rashness?   Yes.

We all agreed that this was the case, and that in fact there could be no argument nor two opinions about it.   Good. " Then what was to be done?" that was what he, Reginald Kelly, as a practical man and a B.A., who was not going to stop up at the University any longer, wanted to know?

This brought us to book, or rather to books, and to business.

It was very plain and simple.   We owed about two hundred pounds or more, and we hadn't got it.

Kelly had advanced so much in payment on account to Lovett's creditors.   He must be reimbursed at once.   Carried *nem. con.*, much to the satisfaction of Kelly, who thereupon declared that he had rather enjoyed the farcical situation of the ' Bailiff at the Ball' than otherwise, but at the same time he was careful not to treat it as too good a jest, lest we should also take that view, and consider him well recouped for his outlay by having been the sole member privileged to enjoy this bit of fun all to himself.

First of all we got a whip all round from the committee. The next step was to appeal to the Club.   We were a little afraid of this, as the possible result might be a whip *for* the

committee. However we started with a donation from one of
our honorary members, Mr. Lomax, and five guineas from Mr.
Watt Gibson, an ex-president of the Club.

What the exact amount was, it is difficult to ascertain,
but it was nearer three than two hundred, and, I think, it
approached close on four.

However, be that as it may, unexpected aid was afforded us
by a gentleman who had been elected a member in Oct.
'56, but of whom we had not seen much at the Club. This
was Mr. A. F. Sealy of Caius. He sent us word, through
J. M. Wilson of the same college, our auditor, that he would
be willing to lend the Club the money at a small per-centage,
and I need hardly say his offer was accepted with thanks, the
bond was signed, sealed—or Sealy'd—and the money
delivered—which was a deliverance indeed!

Mr. Sealy also consented to take a portion of his principal
back from time to time, and so reduce our debt.

Nothing could be more satisfactory. Every member gave
one, two and three guineas to our fund. New members were
elected, and we were "on velvet." Feb. 7th, 1857, were
elected—

> Mr. Partridge, of Trin. Coll. proposed by F. V. Wright,
> seconded by R. S. Preston.
> Mr. Gorst, of St. John's, proposed by J. H. Simpson,
> seconded by L. T. Baines.
> Mr. G. Hawes, of Trin. Hall, proposed by ——, seconded
> by ——. (*No names recorded.*)

Then, on February 21st were elected—

> F. Davy, Trin. Hall, proposed by ——, seconded by ——.
> (*No names recorded.*)
> J. H. Cochrane, Caius, proposed by C. R. Lutwidge,
> seconded by H. W. Hoffman.
> J. H. Robinson, Magd. Coll., proposed by A. C. Lee,
> seconded by W. P. Lysaght.

There did not seem to be much chance of a performance

this term. Kelly was going down, Fitzgerald the same, Charles Donne reading for his voluntary,—which to any but a Cantab suggests the notion of going in for an examination on the church organ. The 'voluntary' was the theological examination for intending clerics. Other men were reading for little-go.

Just at this time I had somehow, at Long's Hotel, and through Lacy the publisher, made the acquaintance of a certain theatrical amateur—a captain who has since taken to the stage professionally, I believe—who proposed a short tour in the provinces, if I could get away from Cambridge and bring two friends. Out of seven or eight weeks of the Term, four counted as 'residence,' and so armed with an "exeat," I went with Reginald Kelly and Gerald Fitzgerald, both now "Bachelors" and free, and the aforesaid captain, to play at Leamington, Bath and Plymouth. These were my first appearances on the regular stage. We had a very pleasant time of it, and performed *Villikins and his Dinah* among other things, and then I returned to Cambridge in time to save my Term.

On my return we had a meeting, and decided that to allow a term to pass without a performance of some sort would be a dangerous precedent.

Only Evelyn Ashley, Cresswell, and myself were free. F. C. Wilson consented to play in two pieces, if the part in the first was not too long, and if the second were a revival of a burlesque.

We chose *The Victor Vanquished*, by Charles Dance, in which there are only four characters, and *Villikins and his Dinah.*

We had all the scenery. Cresswell took a servant in the first piece, and confessed himself unequal to the Baron Boski Bumble in the second. Our original Baron (Kelly) was away, as also our original Villikins (Fitzgerald).

As unexpectedly as the pecuniary aid from Mr. A. F. Sealy, came the help we needed from Mr. W. H. Baillie, who having hitherto confined his services entirely to prompting, now wished to be seen as well as heard, and volunteered for the part of the Baron. This settled the question.

On the 26th and 27th of March we played the following bill :—

A. D. C.

THIS EVENING WILL BE PRESENTED, A COMEDY, IN ONE ACT, (BY CHARLES DANCE, ESQ.), ENTITLED

THE VICTOR VANQUISHED!

Charles the XIIth (*King of Sweden, surnamed "The Lion of the North," under the assumed title of Count d'Oltren*)	Mr. HUMPHREY DUKE.
Baron Gortz (*his secretary*) . . .	Mr. TOM PIERCE.
Olfortz (*servant to Baron*) . . .	Mr. C. REESWELL.
Stela (*niece to the Baron—a Tartar princess*)	Mr. C. DIGBY.

Scene is laid in the Baron's House at Stralsund.

~~~~~~~~~~

AFTER WHICH, THE AWFULLY TRAGIC, SLIGHTLY PATHETIC, BUT-NOT-THE-LESS-ON-THAT-ACCOUNT DELIGHTFULLY COMIC VERSION (BY MR. F. C. BURNAND) OF THE STORY WHICH EVERYBODY KNOWS AS

VILLIKINS AND HIS DINAH!

Grumbleton Gruffin (*a rich Soap Merchant—the original "parient"*) .	Mr. TOM PIERCE.
Baron Roski Bumble (*ancestor of the celebrated Beadle — the lover "so galliant and gay"*) . . .	Mr. H. BALEE.
William Wilkins (*socially and convivially known as Villikins*) . .	Mr. HUMPHREY DUKE.
IN LOVE WITH	
Dinah Gruffin ("*An unkinmon fine young gal* "—*sole daughter of the abovementioned merchant*) . .	Mr. C. DIGBY.

Acting Manager—Mr. TOM PIERCE. Stage Manager—Mr. St EWPID. Prompter--Mr. CHARLIE CHUCKLER. Scenery and Appointments by Messrs. S. J. E. JONES and G. W. CLARKSON.

L

Our "A. D. C." record says—

"*This performance was for two nights only. Various circumstances prevented the usual strength of the company coming forward. Mr. Baillie kindly volunteered and did his best as the Baron. Mr. Ashley played Fitzgerald's old part of Villikins. There was hardly any expense. Clarkson not coming down, and no new scenery required. So it gave the club a little assistance, and the term was not allowed to pass without a performance of some sort. Ashley played the King excellently. So for F. C. Wilson as Ikla, and Burnand as the Baron. The servant was very amusing. F. C. Wilson lost none of his ancient glory as the original Dinah.*"

At a meeting held March 28, same term, it was

"*Proposed by J. M. Wilson, seconded by W. Lysaght, that after next term eighteen donors of three guineas shall pay half subscriptions for two terms certain, or three if the funds of the club admit.*"

This was carried by a majority of seven.
Then

"*Proposed by O'Hara, seconded by F. C. Burnand, that a Judge and Jury be held in the large roon for three times in the term and the club defray expenses up to two pounds. Members allowed to bring two friends.*"

The idea of this was that we were to establish a sort of debating society, under the form of Judge and Jury, within the "A. D. C." that the cases should be regularly got up, the briefs drawn up, the rules of a court of law, civil or criminal ascertained and carried out exactly. It was a capital notion, but it was dangerous, as an innovation to the "A. D. C." However, we had one meeting, when O'Hara showed great skill as a Q. C. engaged for the defence, and several of us figured as witnesses in various dresses. The witnesses were obstreperous, and the stately trial threatened to degenerate into an irregular free fight, as the judge wanted to come down and assist the police, who, in the execution of their duty, had to remove the refractory witnesses, or bring in the prisoners. There was also a difficulty in getting any one to represent the prisoner. True that, on the model of the celebrated Judge and Jury Society of "Baron" Nicholson's time at the Coal Hole, the prisoner was allowed a cigar and what he liked to drink, on the condition of paying for it himself, and the utmost rigour of the law, if he were found guilty, only condemned him to a heavy fine of glasses round, and to be transported—with joy, at the issue of the trial. Everyone wanted to be the counsel, everyone wanted to speak, and no one *would* stop to listen to the judge's summing up. In fact what with the comic witnesses, the police, and Robert O'Hara as counsel, we never got as far as even half-way to a verdict.

After three trials the Judge and Jury was dropped, and we heard no more of it. O'Hara devoted himself entirely to the Union Debating Club, and was very rarely seen at the " A. D. C." Certainly he never played again on the stage, where, henceforth, there was but one Irish star, Rowley Hill, under the name of " Mr. Gorman Bourke."

This brings us to the close of the Lent Term, 1857, and consequently to the end of the second year of the " A.D.C.'s" existence.

A. D. C., YEAR 1856—1857.

May Term, 1856	.	One performance.
October Term, 1856	.	One performance.
Lent Term, 1857	.	One performance.

Pieces played.—*The Ringdoves, Norma* (burlesque), *Slasher and Crasher, The Jacobite, In for a Holiday, Lord Lovel* (burlesque), *Used Up, Dearest Elizabeth, Victor Vanquished, Villikins* (revived).

CHAPTER XI.

On May 11th there was a Committee Meeting, when were elected—

Merthyr Guest .	. Trinity College.
— Saunderson . .	do.

And on the 18th—

H. Snow	. John's.
Lord Richard Grosvenor . .	Trinity.
E. C. Clark	. Peterhouse.

The performances commenced on Wednesday, May 20, when we played *A Blighted Being*, characters by R. Preston, R. Hill, J. Thornhill, F. C. Burnand, and R. H. Hobart.

After which *An Unwarrantable Intrusion*, Nathaniel Snozzle by Mr. Gorst, and the Intruder by Mr. Burnand.

Concluding with, for the first time, a new burlesque, by the author of *Villikins*, *St. George*, *Romance under Difficulties*, &c., entitled *Alonzo the Brave, or Faust and the Fair Imogene*.

Of Rowley Hill, as O'Rafferty in the farce of *A Blighted Being*, it is recorded that—

" *He played it well on both nights, but better on the second than either of them.*"

" *As Job Wort,*" says the record, " *Burnand made a poor Job of it the first night. Friday it was very good.*"

In R. Hobart for our female characters we were most fortunate, and of his Susan Spanker in this farce it is said that " *he never looked or played better*" than in this character.

But there was a scarcity of heroines—the singing and dancing heroines—in burlesque, and we should have been hard put to it for an *Imogene* in *Alonzo the Brave*, had not F. C. Wilson ' kindly obliged the company ' by coming from town to play this character.

I copy verbatim from the records a sort of apology for the comparative failure of our first night's performance :—

" *We must here give a short account of Wednesday's proceedings, and show cause why the performances upon this night were not so good as they might have been :—At the beginning of the day everyone was fairly tired out by the dress rehearsal (8 p.m. till 1) of the burlesque on the previous evening.*"

(I wonder how that one o'clock was managed ? Undergraduates had to be in by midnight.)

" *A new piece as a makeshift was settled upon on Tuesday afternoon (The Unwarrantable Intrusion) and Messrs. Gorst and Burnand learnt it from one book, and rehearsed it twice Wednesday afternoon, from one till two, and from five till six, and this piece was played without needing a prompter. The last rehearsal of A Blighted Being took place on Wednesday*

*afternoon, as also several of the songs and some of the
'hitching' business of the burlesque; so that from twelve till
six the time was taken up with rehearsal, and everyone came
to the performance fagged and out of spirits.*

*"The Unwarrantable Intrusion went very well.   Mr.
Gorst made his début very successfully, and by his universal
willingness and good nature on and off the stage, proved himself to be several degrees removed from a wrangler."*

This alluded to Mr. Gorst's being if not 'a noble
lord' at least 'of high degree.'   He only played here
once.

As for the burlesque I find that—

"Mr. Rowley played Faust in Faust-rate style."

This joke is signed "T. T." so I suppose it was perpe-
tuated by Tom Thornhill.

Julius Rowley got all the part in his head except two lines,
which he never could master.   These were—

> (*Aside.*) Well, of two evils, I the least must choose;
> (*Aloud to Dame.*) As you're so pressing, I can't well refuse.
> Accept my hand.

Which he invariably gave thus,—

> Of two evils, I the least must choose,
> As you're so pressing, here's my hand.

On which, one record has this note, signed "A."—(Evelyn
Ashley ?)

"This STANZA *as it* STANDS, SIR, *does not seem to come out
with a very harmonious* ROLL, EH ? (*Rowl-ey*)."

Here is the fac-simile of a pen and ink sketch of Mephisto-

pheles, done by a very constant attendant at our performances, Mr. Johnston of Trinity, who, during our under-
graduateship, illustrated an absurd poem of mine called
" Croke."

Johnston, fecit.

F. C. BURNAND AS MEPHISTOPHELES.

SCENE I.—(*Thunder—Lightning. Enter Mephistopheles through window.*)
" Good evening, Doctor !"

" The account of this piece in our book is interspersed with all sorts of absurd remarks signed by different people, into whose hands the book fell, for of course it was open to any member to read. Here is an example, copied exactly :—

" *Sybel.   Mr. Thornhill made a good deal of nothing (vide business with jam pots).*
" *Note by Mr. Ashley—He played this part as if it had been written for him.*"
(*So it was, stupid.   The author.*)

Then of *Imogene* it is said—

F. C. Wilson kindly came from town to play this part, and played it admirably.   The success of his performance was " the Cachuca" accompanied by Mephistopheles on the casta-nets, and Faust on the tambourine.   This was nightly encored.

Then is added in another hand—

" *In fact Mr. Wilson did take steps to delight his audience.*"

Mr. A. C. Lee is praised for his efficient prompting, and Messrs. Lutwidge and Hoffman, to whom was entrusted the duty of looking after the thunder and lightning for the entrance of Mephistopheles in the first scene—which was a faithful imitation of Charles Kean's arrangement at the Princess's—are memorable in the " A. D. C." annals as " The Boanerges, or Sons of Thunder."

Of Mr. Hoffman separately it is said that he *lightened* the heavy business, and of Mr. Lutwidge that he might have been appointed by Sir Robert *Peel* as Master of the *Rolls.*

Thursday evening we played, with the following cast, Tom

Taylor's capital dramatic version of Charles de Bernard's novelette *Le Gendre.*

STILL WATERS RUN DEEP.

Mr. Potter	Mr. R. Johnson.
Captain Hawksley	Mr. Hawley Charles.
John Mildmay	Mr. Humphrey Duke.
Dunbilk	Mr. Gorman Bourke.
Langford	Mr. D'Uleymer.
Markham	Mr. K. Phipps.
Gimlet	Mr. P. Heeler.
Jessop	Mr. Cresswell.
Mrs. Mildmay . . .	Mr. C. Digby.
Mrs. Hector Sternhold	Mr. L. Fynne.

This, being a three act comedy-drama of considerable serious interest, would have been rather too much of an undertaking for us, had it not been that, besides several who had played in *Used Up* and *The Jacobite*—the most successful programme we had as yet put forward—we had an excellent representative of Mrs. Mildmay in Mr. C. Digby. All the other parts fitted the men like a glove.

On this occasion a very serious incident occurred. The last scene represents the drawing-room of Mildmay's house during the *mauvais quart d'heure* preceding dinner, when old Potter—excellently played by R. Kelly—has to receive the visitors. In order to give importance to the finish of the drama, we had increased the number of guests, and anyone who wanted to come on and say a few words as one of "old Potter's guests," had been invited by the stage-manager to do so. We had several volunteers, who all came to a rehearsal. One gentleman—Mr. D'Uleymer—was most anxious about his part. He had three lines to speak, I think, and having consulted me as to his dress, decided on a bran new suit, a flower in his button-hole, and a good half-hour at the hair-dresser's before appearing at old Potter's party. He was to be "Captain Langford," and was so announced in the bill. Unfortunately, the only rehearsal he attended was without scene or properties. He was satisfied with being perfect in his words, which were, I think, " How are you, Potter ? " and then, in reply to Potter, " Deuced cold," or something of that sort; and, as he saw no door and no scene at all, it never occurred to him to inquire where he was to enter. He knew nothing of any other stage, and very little of ours. We were so hard up for space, that Mildmay's drawing-room had to be set right up to the back wall, where a conservatory was represented, about two inches deep, widening towards the left, *i.e.*, prompt side, by about two inches or so more, just to enable anyone, not very portly, to squeeze himself in between the scene and the wall, and then gradually to screw himself out, expanding as he stepped in sight of the audience, and throwing open his dress-coat, as though he had lounged at his ease, into the drawing-room, through the conservatory. Mildmay, who had to enter at back by the conservatory, was crushed up in this manner for a second before the curtain rose, as, the scene being one composed of screen pieces, it was so arranged that all the characters had to be at these entrances on the left hand side, *before* the curtain went up, *or they couldn't come on at all.*

This is a ground-plan of the scene—

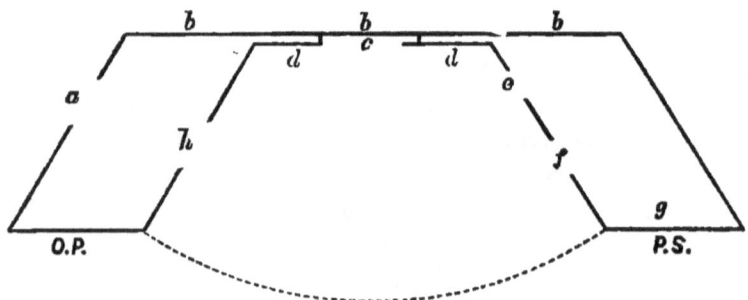

a. Entrance from Green-room on to Stage on O. P. (Opposite Prompt) —*i.e.*, R. H. side. *b. b. b.* The back wall of the building itself. *c.* The Conservatory—where Mildmay was hiding previous to receiving his cue. *d. d.* The walls of scene. *e.* Door of entrance for guests. *f.* Door of entrance for Mrs. Mildmay, &c. *g.* The Prompter. *h.*, on O. P. side, a fire-place.

So it will be at once apparent that there was no passage at the back for the guests, and all the entrances were *on the prompt side, farthest from the green room.*

Now our screens did double duty; one side would be painted as an attic and the other as a drawing-room, the openings being filled up either with doors, windows, or fire place as the scene might require.

It so happened that " *h.*" the opening where the fire-place was, represented on the side *away from the audience*, a door.

Everyone was in his place for the rising of the curtain, except D'Uleymer, who was still beautifying, and who hadn't the slightest idea of the difficulties to be encountered.

Up went the curtain; on went the scene. Reginald Kelly received his guests, fidgeted, wondered where on earth Captain Langford was, looked round, saw no one, went on talking about the weather to the other guests, every now and then casting an appealing look first to the door, and then to the prompter, who was energetically making signs to D'Uleymer, whom he could just see at the opposite corner, and shouting in a hoarse whisper " Come on!" which sounded like an invitation to a pugilistic encounter.

Kelly, aware of some hitch, contrived to go on with an impromptu vapid conversation, quite in keeping with old Potter's part, and, in the meantime, the unhappy D'Uleymer was on the stage on the wrong side, *i.e.*, O. P. instead of P. S., utterly helpless, incapable of squeezing round by the back, or as far as he saw, of getting on at all.

The prompter gave it up as hopeless, and struck with a brilliant idea, he sent on Jessop, the servant, to say to Potter, " Captain Langford's compliments, sir, but he's very unwell, and can't come."

" Hey? very unwell—can't come—dear me, how very sad," exclaimed Potter, heartily glad that the difficulty was got over, and expecting Mrs. Sternhold to enter, and the piece to proceed.

But D'Uleymer was not going to be done out of his appearance on the stage in a speaking part after all his trouble with the tailor and the hairdresser. If a brilliant idea had occurred to our prompter for cutting him out of the piece, an equally brilliant idea had occurred to D'Uleymer of putting himself back again.

Before him, on the O. P. side, was a door. Evidently a door. He was in happy ignorance of the fact that what was a door to him, was, on the other side, a chimney-piece and fire-place to the audience. To D'Uleymer it was a simple door, and "nothing more." He had only got to PULL it towards him, and he was on the scene. "What could it possibly matter," he argued with himself, "whether Captain Langford came in right or left?" So acting on the impulse, and, just as Kelly was standing on the hearth-rug rubbing his hands, with his back to the fire, saying—

"Dear me! I'm very sorry Langford can't come," he heard a strange noise behind him, and turning round, he saw, to his utter dismay, the looking glass over the mantel-piece suddenly disappearing, mantel-piece and all, and in its place appeared Langford's head and shoulders in all the glory of a white tie, open front, and flower in his button-hole, while through the chimney came his legs, thus revealing the entire gentleman himself.

Kelly literally staggered to the centre of the stage as if he had seen a ghost, and uttered so strong an expression in good old Saxon as to make the audience shout with laughter. But D'Uleymer never lost his presence of mind, in fact he was not aware, till afterwards, *that he had come down the chimney* to the dinner-party. So there he stood smiling and undismayed, the welcome but unexpected guest.

"How are you, Potter?" he said, quite coolly, extending his hand. "Couldn't come before, I lost my way."

"Lost your way!" gasped Kelly, who hadn't yet recovered, "you must have—with a vengeance—why you've come down the chimney!"

D'Uleymer turned, and for the first time became aware that

he had not made his entry through the door. He had no reply ready, except " Well, yes—you see—it's a very fine day," as though the state of the weather would satisfactorily account for his preferring to come down the chimney, instead of in at the door. Then he simpered, twiddled his watch-chain, and fell into his place among the other guests, as though he really had no further explanation to offer, and considered it rather ill-bred of Potter to have made any remark on the mode of his guest's arrival.

The reason for his coming down the chimney, subsequently given, at supper, was that "he wanted to show his new *soot*."

It was hard work for the piece to recover this shock. But it went on well to the end, and was repeated on Saturday night with the burlesque. It was on this occasion that the representative of Mrs. Mildmay secreted Mrs. Sternhold's jewels and wore them herself, as I have already mentioned.

We were now getting on with what we called the ' Lovett-Sealy fund,' and the book shows a fair list of subscriptions, signed by "E. Ashley, Hon. Sec."

On the 29th May, Committee dinner at Merthyr Guest's, when we found our expenses for performance had been thirty pounds, and our subscriptions forty. And on June 4th we had a general meeting and an anniversary supper, when Evelyn Ashley announced that we were only £130 in debt, and that everything was satisfactory. I resigned my office as Acting Manager, giving an account of all the performances from the commencement, and Rowley Hill was elected to occupy my post.

The Committee were—

A. C. Lee . . .	President.
R. Hill	Acting Manager.
M. Guest . . .	Stage Manager.
W. Lysaght . .	Treasurer and Sec.
— Evans . . .	Prompter.
H. Snow	Auditor.

I find in a note that the exact amount owing at this moment

was £200, so that our retiring secretary took a cheerful view of the matter. Perhaps he calculated on the new subscriptions for the next term, which would reduce it by about that sum, or he took into account the Sealy-Lovett fund. But beyond these notes there is no financial statement, and we evidently got on well enough without it.

As to the supper, I have tried to obtain particulars of it from members who were present on that occasion, but no one can recollect anything about it, everyone having a generally vague impression that it was 'great fun.'

> "'Ah that I cannot tell,' said he,
> But t'was a glorious victory."

Somebody wrote to me to say that he thought he remembered having a fight *under the table* with another man who would squeeze lemons and empty powdered sugar on his head, under the delusion that he was making some sort of cup; but my informant is far from certain as to facts. Somebody else asked me if I didn't remember one of the party, unable to find his way back to college, passing the night among the beer barrels which were stored up in the yard of the Hoop Brewery. But if these things happened, I do not remember them; I can only find an incomplete record of the names of members and visitors, commenced unsteadily, and abruptly terminated. Was it attempted by our secretary at the table itself? This could scarcely have been, or it would not be in my possession now.

With this festivity the May Term, 1857, as far as the "A. D. C." was concerned, ended.

CHAPTER XII.

DURING " the Long " I had been introduced at Beaumaris
Castle to Mr. Quintin Twiss by Lord Richard Grosvenor,
who thereby did a signal service to the " A. D. C.," for
Quintin Twiss, being an Oxford Man, was eligible as a member
of the " A. D. C.," and I promised to propose him next term,
when he hoped to be able to act for us. He had already
a great reputation as an amateur actor, and the " A. D. C."
of Cambridge has since been greatly indebted to him for his
kindly assistance on many occasions.

Of course Quintin Twiss was duly proposed, seconded, and
elected as early as possible in the October Term, during
which our numbers were increased by the accession of

Cresswell Tayleur .	. Emmanuel Coll.
W. C. Streatfield	. . Trin. Coll.
T. G. Pearse . .	. Caius.
F. A. Hudson . .	. . Trin. Coll.
H. Arkwright	. do.
Honble. J. Leigh .	. . do.
Honble. Lionel Ashley .	. . do.
R. Wingfield Digby .	. do.

The ' Theatrical Week,' as it was now termed, began Nov.
18th, first performance, and the last performance was on the
21st. Four nights.

The occasion was memorable as the *début* of Quintin
Twiss on our boards, and as the first appearance of

Rowley Hill as the author of an original burlesque which was performed every night.

Here is the programme of the first nights of this series.

A. D. C.

THIS EVENING (WEDNESDAY), WILL BE PRESENTED THE FARCE ENTITLED

MY FRIEND IN THE STRAPS.

Mr. Nupkins	Mr. JIMBOLY.
Major Capsicum	Mr. U. GLYCOVE.
Frederick	Mr. HUDDAUGHTER.
O'Blarney	Mr. GORMAN BOURKE.
Grumpy	Mr. NIX.
Caroline	Mr. F. HOOLISH.
Mrs. Capsicum	Mr. B. AGPIPE.

AFTER WHICH, WILL BE PERFORMED

TO PARIS AND BACK.

(A FARCE, IN ONE ACT.)

Mr. Samuel Snozzle	Mr. OLIVER TWIST.
Mr. Spriggius	Mr. NIX.
Mr. C. Markham	Mr. HUMPHREY DUKE.
Lieut. Spike	Mr. GORMAN BOURKE.
Pounce (*a detective officer*) . . .	Mr. U. GLYCOVE.
Joseph (*a waiter*)	Mr. CASTON.
Superintendent	Mr. K. ARROTS.
Telegraphic Clerk	Mr. F. HOOLISH.
Guard	Mr. JIMBOLY.
Miss Fanny Spriggins	Mr. B. AGPIPE.

Scene — *TUNBRIDGE.*

TO CONCLUDE WITH THE SERIO-COMIC BURLESQUE, IN TWO ACTS, ENTITLED

TURKISH WATERS,

A *TAIL* OF *COARSE-HAIR;*

OR, MEDORA'S PRIVATE TEAR.

Redschid Seyd (*the Sultan's Prime Minister—"a Great Gun," Conrad wished to fire*)	Mr. NIX.
Conrad (*a Roving Pirate, who hauled off other's property; in fact, "he was a man"—take him for haulin'-all— you'll never look upon his like again*)	Mr. R. POLEE.

Jumbo (*a Plotting Lieutenant, one of those warlike characters who like following their "Mars" at home*) . Mr. Tom Pierce.

Medora (*the girl Conrad left behind him*) . . . . . . Mr. R. Krong.

Gulnare (*the Harem Queen, who showed her sense in not liking to be the wife of a "Seed"*) . . . . Mr. L. Etterby.

Chorus, Turks, Guests, Pirates, etcætera —especially etcætera.

ACT I.

Scene I.—The Island Home of the Corsair.

Scene II.—Apartments in the house of Jumbo.

Scene III.—Seyd's Palace during the Turkish Festival of the Muzzymuzzum.

Invasion of the Pirates !—Abduction of Gulnare ! ! TERRIFIC COMBAT ! ! ! CAPTURE OF THE CORSAIR ! ! ! ! ! !

ACT II.

Scene I.—Prison in Seyd's Palace.

Scene II.—Island Home of the Corsair,—a run with the Drag, and

GRAND FINALE.

Scenery by Messrs. BROWN, JONES, and ROBINSON.
Costumes by Mr. W. CLARKSON, 10, Great Russell Street, Covent Garden.
Decorations by Mr. GAGE. Acting Manager—Mr. GORMAN BOURKE.
Stage Manager—Mr. M. HOST. Prompter—Mr. A. ZURESKY.

Key to the names is—

Mr. Jimboly is Hon. J. Leigh ; *Mr. U. Glycove,* R. Preston ; *Mr. Huddaughter,* Hudson ; *Mr. Gorman Bourke,* Rowley Hill ; *Mr. Nix,* H. Snow ; *Mr. F. Hoolish,* Cresswell Tayleur ; *Mr. B. Agpipe,* R. H. Hobart ; *Mr. Oliver Twist,* Quintin Twiss ; *Mr. Humphrey Duke,* Hon. Evelyn Ashley ; *Mr. Caston,* Mr. Digby ; *Mr. K. Arrots,* Streatfield ; *Mr. R. Krong,* H. Arkwright ; *Mr. L. Etterby,* Hon. Lionel Ashley.

The first night *My Friend in Straps* signally failed, owing to want of rehearsal. In the emphatic words of the record—

" *The performers, with the exception of Mr. Snow, came on the stage with very vague ideas about their exits and entrances,*

M

*&c., (especially the etcætera)—which circumstance, added to a
very complicated scene, caused a complete mucker."*

The last word ' mucker ' is very expressive.

For the next three nights, as the *lever du rideau*, was
played *The Practical Man*, the rest of the bill being the
same.

The failure of *My Friend in Straps* was redeemed by the
great success of *To Paris and Back for Five Pounds;* and
after the report of the first night had got about, the fame
of our new honorary member Quintin Twiss attracted the
largest audiences ever known at that time in our very small
auditorium.

The note here is copied *verbatim* from the records :—

*" N.B.—Snozzle, who had come down from town on pur-
pose to take the part, did it to perfection, and by his great
humour and originality, brought down unbounded applause !
He has particularly requested that it should be made known
for the benefit of posterity that his shirt front was not painted
on this occasion. (Vide picture)."*

This allusion is to the studs, which were very large, and
Preston had suggested that to avoid losing them, it would be
safer to *paint* them on the shirt front.   It was supposed that
Quintin Twiss had adopted this suggestion ; and it was gradually circulated, and generally believed, that in private life,
Mr. Twiss was in the habit of painting studs on his shirt
front, in which art it was said he had arrived at such perfection as to defy the most severe scrutiny.

Everyone was examining the effect closely ; some even
brought opera glasses to see ' the man who painted studs on
his shirt front.'   Extra tickets at increased prices, it was
stated, were sold every night in order to gratify the curiosity
of numbers who were compelled to come early, and submit
to be squashed, in order to get a sight of the celebrated
painted studs.

Members of the "A. D. C." came round into the green room to ask him if they really *were* painted, and if so, to show them how he did it. At about the hundredth repetition of the question, " I say, Twiss, do you paint your studs?" our new Star began to think he had had enough of the joke, and proclaimed aloud to all assembled in the green room, that, in order to avoid further unnecessary trouble, he wished it publicly known that he did *not* paint his studs, that he never *had* painted his studs, and did not intend to.

This was received with acclamation.

The noise attracted the attention of the audience, who were awaiting the commencement of the burlesque, and some among them knocked at our stage door to ask for an explanation. The opportunity was too good to be lost, and some one stepping forward, announced in a loud voice at the door of the auditorium that " Mr. Twiss did not paint his studs as a rule, but that perhaps *to-morrow night he might do so, to oblige.*"

This was inaudible to the Star in the green room, who, the following evening, was not a little astonished to see that the number of *lorgnettes* was increased, and was again bothered by several members, strangers to him hitherto, who were waiting about the green room most anxious to be introduced to Quintin Twiss, who, accustomed by this time to reiterated offers of hospitality—he could have dined and supped out six times in an evening had he been so inclined, not to mention luncheons and breakfasts—merely thought that each of them was coming with some fresh invitation, which he regretted his inability to accept. But now the form generally was put dramatically in this way—

Smith (inactive member of " A. D. C." to stage manager or some one in authority)—I say, introduce me to Twiss, there's a good fellow.

Stage Manager (hurriedly).—All right. Here, come on! I say, Twiss! (*approaching him*).

Twiss (pausing in the process of making up for Snozzle).—Yes ; what is it ?

Stage Manager.—Here, I want to introduce Smith to you—(*Twiss smiles, and bows, and says that as Twiss he is delighted, but as Snozzle he must proceed with his " make-up"*).

Smith (apologetically).—Oh, I won't interrupt you. I'm sure we have to thank you immensely—(*Twiss as Snozzle smiles, and deprecates further compliment*). Can you come to supper this evening ?

Twiss (pleasantly).—Thanks—I'm afraid I can't—I'm going to Hill's (*continues Snozzling*).

Smith (who is not going to Hill's).—Ah ! I wish you'd been able to manage it—(*Twiss, intent on finishing himself as Snozzle, expresses, in pantomime, his despair at being previously engaged, wondering to himself who the deuce Smith is*)—but—I want to ask you something—(*Twiss assumes an affable expression, and pauses with a hare's-foot in his hand, and one cheek rouged, ready to afford any information in his power, and Smith continues hesitatingly*)—um—ah—do you—do you paint your studs ?

Whereat there would be a roar from the listeners, in which our Star couldn't help joining.

He thought he had heard the last of it when he went down after playing on Saturday, Nov. 21st, but immediately he had left, it was carefully entered into our record book by a hand that I do not recognise ; and here I find this joke embedded—a joke which ranks among those that are " so funny at the time," and depend for their success so entirely on the circumstances and the situation—a joke which, as the record says, is preserved for the sake of " posterity,"—and no doubt some amongst us will remember the pertinacity of the members, and the long-suffering of our honorary member twenty-three years ago.

Another incident was that on his entering the " A. D. C."

rooms, where I took him immediately on his arrival, Preston was the first to be introduced to him, and being a trifle dazzled by the theatrical reputation of our visitor, he became confused, and beyond some remark about it being a fine day, when it happened to be raining heavily, was unable to start any subject of conversation, and fidgeted about nervously until a brilliant idea seemed to occur to him, which, beaming all over as at a triumph of genius, he formulated in this question—

" Will you have some soup ? "

Twiss was quite taken aback by the sudden politeness, and for a second was puzzled how to reply. As this was his first visit to the University, he was a little uncertain whether this offer of soup were, like the presentation of the loving cup at a civic banquet, or the *vin d'honneur* in France, a custom peculiar to Cambridge, which it would be a breach of good manners to decline, or whether it was only an impulse of spontaneous hospitality which a prior engagement prevented him from accepting.

Preston, however, would take no denial ; he seemed to think that soup would act in some magic manner on Quintin Twiss's constitution, and ordered a basin of some thick stuff from the Hoop ; but, as we were compelled to leave before the soup was ready, Dick Preston had to stay and eat it himself. The story of the soup got about, and in reviewing Preston as *Joli Cœur* in *Blue Beard* in the Lent Term of '58, I find this remark, which concludes a long critique on what appears to have been a first-rate performance, " *His mad scene, his defiance of Abomelique—his pathetic maniacal verse—his hoop-de-dooden-doo tag—were all hits,—he wanted but one thing—' More Soup !'* "

A joke soon became traditional at the " A. D. C." when it had been once started—and for years standing jokes were never allowed to drop. When worn out by use, they are still to be found in our Museum of Curiosities, or Record Book, though who the various recording angels were, I am at a loss to discover, except when I recognise the handwriting, or come across a signature.

The "chaff" is rough but good-natured, and there are hardly any severe criticisms.

Mr. Digby in *To Paris and Back* so distinguished himself as the Waiter, that it was pronounced to be henceforth his peculiar line, and, henceforth, any waiter's or page's part should fall as of right to Mr. Digby. He had his photograph taken in this character.

Our collection of photographs was fast increasing, but, twenty-four years ago, photography, at Cambridge at least, had not been brought to anything like its present perfection, the consequence being that many of our earliest photographs are partially faded, and some so completely as to be unrecognisable.

Even now a collection could be easily made, as many of our first photographs have been preserved in portfolios by individual members. In the hope that the "A. D. C." at Cambridge will become a permanent institution, with its examination and prizes, as "an extra" duly authorised by the governing body, former members would be glad to contribute duplicates of the photos in their possession for the sake of compiling an historical "A. D. C." album.

To return to the performance of this term, Rowley Hill's burlesque was a great success.

"*As 'Conrad' Mr. Julius Rowley,*" says the faithful record, "*sang very well; but, as he says himself, 'acting is not his forte.' In reciting poetry, too, he has a singular habit of making such words as 'pudding' and 'crocodile' rhyme, which gives the audience a very peculiar idea of what the author intended to say.*"

I wonder if the author himself penned this remark? I think so.

Unfortunately there is no further notice of this burlesque.

The opposite page was, it appears from its heading, intended to be devoted to a *critique* on the *Practical Man* (characters by Tom Pierce, Huddaughter, Nix, U. Glycove, C. Reeper, Pickles, and R. King), but the intention came to nothing, and there is only a blank where the notice ought to have been.

The summary of performances for 1857, however, says—

" *This was one of the Club's most successful performances. Everything went capitally, with the solitary exception of ' My Friend in the Straps.' On the Friday night there were 120 in the house, including members, and nearly fifty were turned away from the door.*"

This extra attraction is attributable to the curiosity about the ",painted studs."

" *An extra night was given, when the ' Practical Man,' ' To Paris,' and the Burlesque were played. Mr. Twiss made a great hit. The ' Practical' was another. The acting of all the members was a great improvement upon former occasions ; yet, ' meliora speramus.' We regretted the absence of some of our old and valued members, F. C. Wilson, Kelly, Donne, Fitzgerald ; but even the ' Used Up' and ' Jacobite' time did not equal this.*"

In spite of this contemporary criticism, I still adhere to my expressed opinion as to the superior excellence of *Used up* and *The Jacobite*.

There was certainly a great enthusiasm about this performance, which introduced Quintin Twiss, and, with him, the " star system " to our boards, which continued for many years afterwards, until later on it was found, that, to depend upon the exertions of the non-resident and honorary members for the performances, was injurious to the club and unfair to the rising talent—or, as we used to call it, " local talent "—among the resident members, and so, recently, the star system

has been abolished, the " A. D. C." relying solely and only
on ' local talent.' *

This brought the theatrical week to a close. It had
inaugurated a new era in our history.

The remainder of the Term was devoted to business meetings and elections.

Dec. 7.—"*Proposed by Sealy, seconded by Preston, that the
Club elect members, and that one black ball in five excludes.
Carried by a majority of six.*

" *That any member of the Committee shall have the power
to enforce fines.*"

Record of debt, £130. Signed by W. P. Lysaght, Sec. and
Treasurer.

So we were about ' as we were ' in the previous Term.

Then we passed another rule as to rehearsals, which were
always our difficulty :

" *That no acting member, or the prompter, be allowed to miss
a rehearsal in the last week previous to the performance on any consideration whatever.*"

This is severe. No excuse ! But notice how " or the
prompter " is introduced. He had inadvertently congratulated
himself on not being an " acting member," and therefore not
amenable to the fine. But this didn't serve him, and the
amendment settled him—

—— " *Unless notice be given to the Acting Manager
three days previously. Fine for total absence, one
guinea.*"

This was severe on the Total Abstainer.

---

* Perhaps an exception might be made in favour of a " Quarter-centenary
Anniversary," which would be in the May Term of 1880. A very strong
team might be got together for the occasion.

We then went into the question of Club voting, and decided that the ballot was to be open for three days. After this we settled that the subscriptions should be increased to enable us to take rooms, as a club, apart from theatrical purposes, to include reading and writing rooms, &c.

We were expanding.

Hitherto the subscription had been one guinea per term, now it was doubled. But the difficulty was to find the rooms. The large one was still devoted to billiards, and of course we didn't wish to move our stage and our stock of scenery and properties from our present homely quarters.

Our old friend Jones had long since disappeared, but his name, coupled with "Brown" and "Robinson," appears for the last time in this term's bill, in connection with the scenery.

Mr. Gage was the paid local artistic talent, but in the year 1857 C. Lutwidge, of Trin. Coll., painted a proscenium for us, representing the figures of Tragedy and Comedy standing in niches under the busts of Shakespeare and Molière. A scroll ran along the width of the proscenium with the motto "All the world's a stage," and the club initials, "A. D. C.," in the centre. The same amateur artist also painted for us "thé conservatory flat" in *Still Waters*—a very effective set-piece —and some other set pieces for the burlesque of *Turkish Waters* and *Lord Lovel.* He had also commenced a design for an act-drop.

The painting-room at the "A. D. C.," which was of course the stage itself, might have been, and may yet be converted, into a school of art.

As we came to depend more on our members for everything, stage carpentry, stage mechanism, painting, &c., so we dispensed with all extraneous help, and Lutwidge and Merthyr Guest—a worthy successor of our first manager, Polwhele—might be seen, in paper caps and aprons, hard at real work on the stage, thus saving the Club great expense, while adding to the interest of the performance, and strengthening their own personal attachment to the society itself.

These traditions remain, and the offices of stage manager, and assistant stage manager, and scenic artist have never been sinecures at the "A. D. C."

CHAPTER XIII.

LENT TERM, 1858.

I HAD now taken my degree, and this was to be my last term as a resident member of the "A. D. C."

We began by annulling, at a general meeting, the rule of the former term about the ballot, and we returned to election by committee.

Whereupon we elected :

> H. Dent (Trin. Coll.) Proposed by W. P. Lysaght, Trin., seconded by Rowley Hill, Trin.
>
> C. Weguelin (Trin. Coll.). Proposed by Hon. L. Ashley, Trin., seconded, by Hon. J. Leigh, Trin.
>
> Barnett, (Trin.). Proposed by Hon. J. Leigh, Trin., seconded by Rowley Hill, Trin.
>
> Knapp (Emmanuel). Proposed by Cresswell Tayleur, Trin., seconded by W. H. Evans, Trin.

And H. Robinson of Magdalen, was elected prompter, our former prompter, Mr. H. Baillie, seconding the nomination.

The minutes now appear in a clear running hand, kept in a most orderly manner, and signed " W. P. Lysaght."

Feb. 24.—F. C. Burnand proposed as President, vice Evans resigned.

> *Merthyr Guest as stage manager.*
> *Both elected unanimously.*

Feb. 25.—*Committee meeting at the President's rooms.*
Were elected—

> Lord Pelham (Trin. Coll.). Proposed by W. P. Lysaght,
> seconded by Hon. J. W. Leigh.
> Hon. E. O'Brien. Proposed by Hon. L. Ashley, seconded
> by W. H. Baillie.
> Lord Brecknock. Proposed by Hon. J. W. Leigh, seconded
> by W. P. Lysaght.

Then we passed seven resolutions as to non-payment of
subscriptions and posting defaulters, and determined that no
member of the Committee should be either a proposer or
seconder.

Our theatrical week commenced on Tuesday, March 9th,
with the comedietta of *A Loan of a Lover*, the farce of *Two
Heads are Better than One*, and the burlesque.

Here is the bill of the second night—

A. D. C.

On Wednesday, March 10th, 1858, will be performed
THE FARCE, ENTITLED

TWO HEADS ARE BETTER THAN ONE.

Mr. Strange	Mr. K. Arrots.
Mr. Maxwelton	Mr. U. Glycove.
Master Samuel (*his Son*) . . .	Mr. Jim Boly.
Charles Conquest	Mr. Huddaughter.
Miss Strange	Mr. T. Huckegs.

AFTER WHICH, A FARCE, IN ONE ACT, ENTITLED

BETSY BAKER.

Mr. Marmaduke Mouser . . .	Mr. Tom Pierce.
Mr. Christopher Crummy . . .	Mr. Gorman Bourke.
Mrs. Mouser	Mr. Kickensnau.
Betsy Baker (*a laundress*) . . .	Mr. B. Agpipes.

AFTER WHICH THE NURSERY-KNOWN, CHILD-DELIGHTING,
BABY-THRILLING, ADULT-TICKLING, BLAZING EXTRAVA-
GANZA, WITH ORIGINAL SONGS, ENTITLED

BLUE BEARD.

Baron Abomelique (*the celebrated Lady-killer, surnamed Blue-Beard*	Mr. Tom Pierce.
Joli Cœur (*a nice young man in love with Fleurette*)	Mr. U. Glycove.

O'Shack O'Back (*groom of the Blue Chamber and "Head" Valet to the Baron*)	Mr. GORMAN BOURKE.
Bras de Fer and Longue Epée (*Fleurette's two brothers, very sharp blades*)	Messrs. TOPPY & POPPY.
Fleurette (*a vewy poothy keathur*) . .	Mr. T. HUCKEGS.
Anne ('*Sister' Anne*) . . .	Mr. B. AGPIPES.
Dame Perroquet (*Mother of the above young ladies*)	Mr. JIM BOLY.
Margot (*A waiting maid*) . . .	Mr. KICKENSNAU.
A Page (*one unread in history*) . .	Mr. D'HUMMI.

Officers and Gentlemen of Blue Beard's Household, &c., forming a Procession, and Chorus unequalled in anything of a similar character (on this occasion only) by Messrs. W. Barlow, S. Hall, Reuben Wright, and the Ratcatcher's Daughter.

SCENE I.—"A COTTAGE NEAR A WOOD."
(*Jones and Gage.*)
"Call me early, mother dear"—Arrival of Blue Beard—The momentous question—Who's afraid?—And the scene changes to

SCENE II.—"CORRIDOR IN BLUE BEARD'S CASTLE."
(*Gage.*)
The forlorn maiden—Reviving effects from a blow on the nose—"Tink a tink"—Return of the marriage party, who will be found collected in

SCENE III.—"STATE CHAMBER IN THE CASTLE."
(*Jones.*)
The happiest day of his life—Urgent private affairs—Departure of Abomclique—

SCENE IV.—"THE BLUE CHAMBER."—(*Gage.*)
A h(eadifying sight) !—Awful disclosure ! ! !

SCENE V.—"ANTICHAMBER."
Fleurette and Anne on the key vive !—What can the matter be ?—The maniac—The conspiracy—

SCENE VI. AND LAST.—"CASTLE TERRACE."
Return of Blue Beard—Fleurette seized with terrors (terrace) wishes she could *slope* — Investigation ! — Accusation ! ! — Refutation ! ! ! — Deputation ! ! ! ! — Agonization ! ! ! ! !—Fraternization ! ! ! ! ! — Fight in which (A) shone ! ! ! ! ! ! — Flumbustification ! ! ! ! ! ! ! ! — Ending in a general congratulation ! ! ! ! ! ! ! !

Stage Manager—Mr. M. HOST. Acting Manager—Mr. G. BOURKE. Property Manager—Mr. A. PENNIE. Prompter—Mr. E. CRUSOE. Scenery by E. GAGE, of Sidney Street, and talented assistants. Costumes and Appointments by C. W. CLARKSON, of 16, Little Russell Street, Covent Garden. Music by Messrs. SWANBOROUGH. Decorations by Messrs. GREEN and GAGE.

Books of the Incidental Songs, Choruses, Music, &c., in the Extravaganza, may be had at the door.

N.B.—*On Friday will be performed* "THE PRACTICAL MAN," *by particular request.*

It will be noticed that the scenery is now announced by E. Gage, and the name of Jones has disappeared. "Alas! poor Yorick!" The Messrs. Swanborough simply meant "White-headed Bob" and talented assistants.

In the *Loan of a Lover*, C. Weguelin, under the name of "Mr. T. Wiggling," made his first appearance. He took the place left vacant by Charles E. Donne, his line being the same, but his style lighter, as he also played and sang in burlesque; but we still held to Robsonian tradition as to burlesque, and whether it was *Alonzo, Lord Lovel, Blue Beard,* or *Turkish Waters,* there were always two principal characters playing extravagant parts with serious intensity, which seems to me to be of the very essence of true burlesque.

In *The Loan of a Lover,* the greatest praise in our record is given to R. Hobart for his impersonation of *Gertrude;* it says,

"*Too much credit cannot be given to Hobart for the literally wonderful manner in which he made up for the part. His reading of the character was most careful. His acting especially clever. F. C. Wilson could play the fine lady in a manner not to be surpassed, but Hobart has taken a different line than that of the soubrette.*"

By "fine lady" I fancy the writer meant in his ignorance of technical terms, "leading lady," as I never remember to have seen F. C. Wilson play any "fine lady," unless *Mrs. Mildmay* came under that description.

Another new member, Partridge, acting under the name of "Mr. Peter Perdix," appeared as *Delve,* and, says our chronicler,

"*Made it a part to be remembered by those who saw it. His very original 'beer' and 'wheelbarrow' business were great hits. ... Delve never will, and we venture to say never has, found a better representative.*"

"*But,*" adds the faithful Chronicler, "*the whole piece was flat.*"

The Chronicler was then down on *Betsy Baker* played by Hobart, Hill, Burnand, Knapp, and Digby as a page.
This didn't "go."

"*The fault lies with Burnand, Hobart, and Hill. Of the first Mouser is not in his line, being neither light comedy nor burlesque . . . his acting is too exaggerated . . . while Hill was too hurried and not sufficiently distinct as Crummy.*"

The Chronicler's praise is given solely to Digby as the page, who is pronounced "*Excellent.*"
Blue Beard by Messrs. Planché and Dance, with new songs and choruses by Messrs. Burnand and Hill, was, like almost all our burlesques, a success; Lionel Ashley obtaining great praise for his singing as *Fleurette*, while Hobart was a capital *Sister Anne*, with whom the only fault found was, that she was rather too jovial when her sister's head was in imminent danger of being cut off. Of ' Jimbo' Leigh, it is recorded that—

"*His careful playing of this small part (Dame Perroquet) materially aided the success of the first scene. The stoop, the voice, and walk, were all perfect, whilst the decrepit jig with which Mr. Leigh made his exit in the procession was delightfully funny.*"

Preston as *Joli Cœur*—"his songs were all good."
Rowley Hill as O'Shack O'Back, "*very funny—O'Shack never found a more humorous representative than in Mr. Rowley Hill.*"
He introduced a line about " what Demosthenes said when he was sent for by his tutor," which turned out to be " Rum tum tiddly um," or some such idiotic chorus as the finale

to the piece, which took amazingly with our Undergraduate audience.

The Page was played, of course, by Mr. Digby, on whose performance a high encomium — evidently in chaff — is passed.

"The Page is," says the Chronicler, "one of those small parts, pigmies to ordinary men, which in Mr. Digby's hands become giants of his creative genius."

The summary says—

> "*The secret of the success of the Extravaganza was that we had nearly three weeks' rehearsal, and the rehearsals had been well attended by the Band, Principals, and those who had little, and those who had very little to do in the piece . . . It was one of the greatest successes we ever had at the 'A. D. C.' We benefited much from the properties having been a present from Mr. Pearse, Caius Coll., while Mr. Norman had given five pounds for decorations. The last night was very good, but no one house has come up to our third night of last term's performance which was a bumper.*"

The hit of *Two Heads are Better than One*, a very slight farce, was made by J. Leigh as the idiot Sammy Maxwelton, ordinarily a very subordinate part, while the success of Cresswell Tayleur as *Strange* is recorded as a "*triumph of dramatic art.*"

On the last night Reginald Kelly and Evelyn Ashley were present, for the first time, as non-resident members, and heartily congratulated the Club on its continued success. Ashley had played last term, but Kelly had not been in the Club since the May Term of '57.

We now managed to reduce our debt to ninety-three pounds, and our Secretary and Stage Manager interviewed the landlord in order to come to some arrangement as to the larger rooms *en bloc*. But in this they appear to have exceeded their commission, as the Club only required one extra room to be used in reading and writing, so that the Theatrical part would be quite separate. It was inconvenient to have members necessarily present during rehearsal, and as to stroll in during rehearsal was one of the privileges of membership, it was impossible to confine them to our small green-room with its skylight and settees, and so shut them off from the stage. The papers were taken in, and there was a writing table. But these matters were of secondary consideration, and the worst place in Cambridge for seeing a daily paper was the " A. D. C." room. However, it was all coming in due course.

And now for the first time the rules were published. A new committee was elected, the peculiarity of entry in the book is the addition of " Esq." to each name.

A. C. Lee, Esq.	President for the May term, 1858.
M. Guest, Esq.	Stage Manager.
W. Lysaght, Esq.	Secretary and Treasurer.
H. W. Hoffman, Esq.	Auditor.
F. Smith, Esq.	Property Manager.
— Robinson, Esq.	Prompter.

Then it was finally announced that should any arrangement be made with Mr. Ekin for an additional room, the double subscription would commence from next term, and on the 25th March, 1858, a considerable payment on account was made of our debt and interest to Mr. Sealy, who had so kindly assisted us in the Lovett difficulty.

The Club's prospects were flourishing at the end of the Lent Term, 1858, which brought us to the close of the third year of its existence, and me to the time of my departure from the University. With the Easter Vacation of '58 I ceased to be any longer a resident member of the Club, which I hoped often to revisit, and in which I continued to take as lively an interest as I had from the very commencement of its career. Of course I could not help looking upon it as my child, though but for helping hands and timely assistance in

N

its infancy, it could never have been reared, far less have been able to run alone, though, as it still relied on "Stars," it did not succeed in doing this for some time to come.

PIECES PLAYED IN THE THIRD YEAR OF THE "A. D. C."

May Term, 1857.
(Four Nights.)
- *A Blighted Being.* (*Farce.*)
- *A Most Unwarrantable Intrusion.* (*Do.*)
- *Alonzo the Brave.* (*Burlesque*).
- *Still Waters Run Deep.* (*Comedy.*)

October Term, 1857.
(Four Nights.)
- *A Practical Man.* (*Farce.*)
- *To Paris and Back.* (*Do.*)
- *Turkish Waters.* (*Burlesque.*)
- *My Friend in the Straps.* (*Farce.*)

Lent Term, 1858.
(Four Nights.)
- *Betsy Baker.* (*Farce.*)
- *Loan of a Lover.* (*Vaudeville.*)
- *Two Heads Better than One.* (*Farce.*)
- *Blue Beard.* (*Extravaganza.*)

On the last night of performance this Term there was a supper at, I think, Mr. Rowley Hill's rooms, where the Club presented me with a silver inkstand, on which was engraved under the initials "A. D. C." an inscription recording the occasion and date of presentation to me as "Founder of the Club; on leaving the University."

This gift was perfectly unexpected by me. I had not heard a single word about it, and was quite unprepared for this unrehearsed effect, when, after supper, which had been simply one of the ordinary jovial gatherings, perhaps more crowded than usual—" the more the merrier"—my old friend A. C. Lee, placed something before me wrapped up in tissue paper, and then, after a kind and humorous speech from Rowley Hill, proceeded to "unveil" the testimonial.

I need hardly say how delighted I was at this token of affectionate regard from my friends and companions. To quote the notorious swearer, who explained to the friend who had asked him how it was he did not rap out an oath when his new umbrella fell into the mud, " It was impossible to find words equal to the occasion." I was poor in the expression of my thanks, but it was indeed from my heart I thanked them, and not without emotion did I tell them how I should always treasure the memory of a time I can now look back to as the pleasantest, sunniest, and happiest three years of my life.

CHAPTER XIV.

THE Star system had now set in at the "A. D. C.," and
Mr. Oliver Twist was always ready to give the Club the benefit
of his services.

In burlesque Rowley Hill seems to have been the leading
spirit; though for the next two terms after my departure
only one burlesque, Frank Talfourd's *Macbeth* (which he
wrote when a boy at Eton), was played, and that, as far as I
can make out, for only two nights out of the four in the May
Term performance. The record of it is chiefly confined to
an enumeration of the advantages of playing burlesque, " a
form of entertainment," it says, "which has so many attractions for our audience."

But a Domestic Drama was more to the taste of all concerned in the management except Mr. R. Hill, and the result
was the following bill for two nights out of the four, and on
the other evenings the burlesque was played instead of the
two farces. It was the first time that burlesque had not been
the feature of the series.

For my part, personally, I strongly incline to burlesque
for good amateurs, but never at the expense of true comedy.
In the particular case of the "A. D. C.," the peculiar
character of the University audience, mainly composed of
undergraduates, ought to be fairly considered before sentence
of absolute banishment be pronounced against burlesque.
On this subject I shall have more to say later on.

This is the first bill in which the name of " Mr. Tom Pierce " does not appear :—

A. D. C.

On Friday, May 21st, 1858, will be represented the
Farcical Interlude, in One Act, entitled

THE FEARFUL TRAGEDY IN THE 7 DIALS.

Mr. Slumpington (*a retired butterman*)	Mr. Gorman Bourke.
Mr. Mulligatawney (*cook & confectioner*)	Mr. U. Glycove.
Mr. Twigley	Mr. K. Arrots.
Jacob	Mr. Jimboli.
Mrs. Slumpington	Mr. B. Agpipes.

After which the Domestic Drama, in Two Acts,
entitled

THE HELPING HANDS.

(BY TOM TAYLOR.)

Lord Quaverly	Mr. Huddaughter.
The Hon. Calverly Hautbois . .	Mr. Gorman Bourke.
Lorentz Hartmann	Mr. Darting.
John Merton	Mr. K. Arrots.
Isaac Wolff	Mr. U. Glycove.
William Rufus, alias Vinkin, alias Shockey (*one of the shoe black brigade*)	Mr. Oliver Twist.
Lazarus Solomon (*appraiser & valuer*)	Mr. Raptap.
Margaret Hartmann	Mr. T. Huckegs.
'Tilda	Mr. Jimboli.
Mrs. Booty	Mr. Kickensnau.

To conclude with the Screaming Farce, in One Act,
entitled

THE TWO BONNYCASTLES.

Mr. Bonnycastle (*alias Jeremiah Jorum*)	Mr. Oliver Twist.
Mr. John James Johnson . . .	Mr. Jimboli.
Mr. Snuggins	Mr. Darting.
Mrs. Bonnycastle	Mr. R. Krong.
Helen	Mr. T. Huckegs.
Patty	Mr. B. Agpipes.

*The Drop-Scene, which is entirely new, was painted and
presented to the Club by Mr. Lutwidge.*

Stage Manager—*Mr. M. HOST.*   Acting Manager—*Mr. JIMBOLI.*
Property Manager—*Mr. A. PENNIE.* Prompter—*Mr. R. CRUSOE.*
Scenery by *E. GAGE*, of Sidney Street, and talented assistants.
Costumes and Appointments by *C. W. CLARKSON*, of 16, Little Russell
Street, Covent Garden.   Music by Messrs. SWANBOROUGH.
Decorations by Messrs. *GREEN* and *GAGE.*

" Mr. B. Agpipes " was R. H. Hobart, and the others will
be recognised by reference to previous bills.

The Chronicle which dismisses this piece as *"rayther
flat"*, records the great success of *Helping Hands* in these
words:—

" *Would that our much lamented and never-to-be-forgotten
founder, supporter, and actor, F. C. Burnand, had been here
to witness this performance, as I am sure it would have
pleased him much.   It was an entirely new style of piece at
the 'A. D. C.,' and many were the doubts whether it would
succeed or not; but these doubts were speedily removed when
it appeared before the delighted audience : its success was
complete.*"

C. Weguelin, under the name of " Mr. Darting," instead
of as formerly " T. Wiggling," was, says the record— ·

" *Thoroughly good.   The acclamation and applause of the
house, long and loud, showed how it was appreciated.   We
very much wish F. C. B. had been here to see it.   In a word,
it was wonderful.*"

Equal praise is meted out to Quintin Twiss as *Vinkin*,
the *'Tilda* of Jimbo Leigh, and the *Hon. C. Hautbois* of
Rowley Hill.   *Isaac Wolff* and *Solomon*, the two Jews,
respectively played by R. Preston and Lord Brecknock are
spoken of as " capitally played "—the accent and appearance
of the former being "*perfect,*" while of the latter it is recorded
that he " *looked an unmistakable Jew.*"

And now the old Chronicle begins to drop off.   Here a
page and there a page.   A few blanks, and then all criticisms
cease.

The last entries are—of a committee meeting held at the
Hon. J. Leigh's rooms in the October Term (Oct. 21st, 1858),
when the following gentlemen were unanimously elected.—

Beecher, F. Lee, Rowley, Augustus Guest, Alec. Baillie—of a general meeting Oct. 22, "*Nothing done but to receive subscriptions*," and of another meeting Nov. 3rd, when Ion Trant Hamilton, Moncrieff, D. Powell, S. A. Hankey, were elected, and Evans (of King's), an original member who had taken his name off when he went down, was re-elected on his coming up to reside.

The pieces performed were *Thumping Legacy, Tit for Tat, The Victims*, and *The Irish Tutor*.

On Friday, November the 26th, the performances were in aid of the Royal Dramatic Fund. This was the first public act of the "A. D. C."

I came up for this night only, and delivered an address which has been copied into the book without any mention of the author's name.

A. D. C.

On Tuesday, November 23rd, 1858,
WILL BE PREFORMED AN ORIGINAL COMEDY, IN THREE ACTS,
BY TOM TAYLOR, Esq.,
ENTITLED

VICTIMS.

Mr. Merryweather (*a Stock broker*) .	Mr. Huddaughter.
Mr. Rowley (*an Indian Merchant*) .	Mr. U. Glycove.
Mr. Herbert Fitzherbert (*a Literary Gentleman*)	Mr. Darting.
Mr. Joshua Butterby (*his friend and humble Admirer*)	Mr. O. Twist.
Mr. Curdle (*an Economist and Statist*)	Mr. S. Mc Mias.
Mr. Muddlemist (*a Metaphysician*) .	Mr. Potille.
Mr. Hornblower (*Editor of the 'Weekly Beacon'*). . . .	Mr. A. Host.
Carfuffle (*Butler to Mr. Merryweather*	Mr. Gorman Bourke.
Skimmer (*Footman to Mr. Merryweather*)	Mr. E. Kartz.
Mrs. Merryweather	Mr. T. Huckeggs.
Mrs. Fitzherbert	Mr. Sylva.
Miss Crane (*a strong-minded woman*)	Mr. Jimboli.
Mrs. Sharp	Mr. Ochre.

To conclude with a Farce, by J. MORTON, Esq.,
CALLED

A THUMPING LEGACY.

Fillippo Geronimo	Mr. Darting.
Jerry Ominous	Mr. O. Twist.
Bambogetti	Mr. M. Host.
Leoni	Mr. Jimboli.
Brigadier of Carbineers . .	Mr. A. Host.
First Carbineer	Mr. Bullock.
Second Carbineer	Mr. N. Inepins.
Rosetta (*daughter of Fillippo*) . .	Mr. T. Huckeggs.

Scene,—CORSICA.

On Friday, November 26th, there will be a
Performance in aid of

THE ROYAL DRAMATIC FUND,

When the following Pieces will be played—

IRISH TUTOR.

TIT FOR TAT.

A THUMPING LEGACY.

New Scenes by Messrs. LUTWIDGE and POWELL.

Stage Manager—Mr. M. HOST.   Acting Manager—Mr. JIMBOLI.
Prompter—Mr. K. LARKE.   Artists—Messrs. POTILLE and N. GAGE.
Properties by Mr. A. PENNIE.   Dresses by Mr. S. MAY.
Perruquier—Mr. CLARKSON. Leader of Band—Mr. SWANBOROUGH.
[VIVAT REGINA.]

The Club had now two scenic artists among their own members, *i.e.*, Lutwidge and D. Powell.

The "Properties" had become a separate department. Clarkson was no longer answerable for costumes, which were provided by Mr. S. May of Bow Street. "White-Headed Bob" was now announced as "Leader of the Band."

The proceeds of the performance in aid of the Dramatic College amounted to £22, which was paid into the hands of the treasurers of that institution by Quintin Twiss.

The address contained these lines :—

> " We youthful vot'ries of the Thespian art
> Are called to play a very easy part :
> Our acting pleasure—'tis for your delight—
> Kind friends to greet us—future prospects bright !
> Change we the scene—a sterner lesson read
> In the poor player's life, whose cause we plead."

And then followed a very grim contrast, representing the poor player in the depths of starvation, concealing an aching heart under the motley garb, &c., &c.

The author doubtless thought it was perfectly true, and, for myself, I'm sure I believed it, my general impressions of the actor off the stage being founded on Charles Dickens's " Dying Clown," and on certain theatrical sketches by Albert Smith. The address went on to say, that, for once and away, we were playing with a serious purpose, *i.e.*, the benefit of a professional charity, concluding with this couplet—

> " And for ourselves who labour for this end,
> Pardon our faults, and what is worth commend." *[Exit.*

Here finishes the Ancient Chronicle.

There is an entry farther on, under date 1860, to which I shall presently have to refer, when the " A. D. C." joined with the Quidnunc Cricket Club to give an annual performance during the " Sussex week," at Brighton.

The new Chronicle commences with a record of a meeting Dec. 4, 1858, when the election of committee for the ensuing term took place.

Lord Brecknock (Trin. Coll.) . .	President.
Hon. J. W. Leigh	Acting Manager.
D. Powell	Stage Manager.
J. T. Hamilton	Secretary and Treasurer.
F. Lee	Property Manager.
Alec. Baillie	Prompter.
Hon. L. Ashley	Auditor and Assistant Acting Manager.

As to the prompter, it seems to have been hereditary.   W. H. Baillie had been *par excellence* our prompter, and now his brother was elected.   "Not Amurath an Amurath succeeds, but Baillie Baillie."

The original mistake—mine—of calling the stage manager "acting manager" was still retained, and was not dropped for a long time, not indeed until some time after the Club had employed a professional to "coach" them, when the name of the member who happened to be the stage manager was omitted entirely (as in the bills now before me as recently as 1877 and 1878) and that of "Assistant Stage Manager, Mr. Coe" (with his town address by way of not losing the chance of advertisement), or "Assistant Stage Manager, Mr. Horace Wigan," with *his* town address.

The professional coach is, sometimes, as necessary for amateur actors as the professional drill sergeant for volunteers. But it is not in this perfunctory manner that I would have the art taught at the university "A. D. C."

In Feb., 1859 (Lent Term), were elected Henry Thornhill (Magdalene Coll.), A. G. Knox, G. de Robeck, — Walford, and G. Buxton, all of Trinity.   "Mr. Oliver Twist" came up as the star, and Weguelin, R. Hill, and J. Leigh were still on the scene.

A. D. C.

ON TUESDAY, MARCH 15TH, 1859, WILL BE PERFORMED A FARCE, BY G. DANCE, ESQ., CALLED

PETTICOAT GOVERNMENT.

Hectic (*an old bachelor*) . . .	Mr. JIMBOLI.
Clover (*his friend*)	Mr. U. GLYCOVE.
Stump (*servant to Hectic*) . .	Mr. MURAL FOORD.
Bridoon (*Serjeant of Dragoons*) . .	Mr. GORMAN BOURKE.
Mrs. Carney (*housekeeper to Hectic*) .	Mr. ION TRANT.
Anabella (*housekeeper to Clover*) .	Mr. KNIGHT.

ON THURSDAY AND FRIDAY WILL BE PERFORMED THE
SCREAMING FARCE, ENTITLED

TICKLISH TIMES.

When Mr. O. TWIST will appear in the Character of

LAUNCELOT GRIGGS.

AFTER WHICH WILL BE PERFORMED A COMIC DRAMA, IN
TWO ACTS, BY J. R. PLANCHÉ, ESQ., ENTITLED

NOT A BAD JUDGE.

Marquis de Treval	MR. GORMAN BOURKE.
Count de Steinberg	Mr. S. MC MIAS.
John Caspar Lavater	Mr. DARTING.
Christian	Mr. HUDDAUGHTER.
Betman	Mr. U. GLYCOVE.
Zug	Mr. A. HOST.
Rutly	Mr. PRETTYMAN.
Notary	Mr. K. NOTCH.
Servant	Mr. OCHRE.
Louise	Mr. T. HUCKEGGS.
Madam Betman	Mr. KNIGHT.

*Soldiers, Peasantry, &c., Messrs. Bullock, Piercemount, Lucas,
Raptap, A. Zuresley, &c., &c.*

TO CONCLUDE WITH A FARCE, BY JOHN POOLE,
ENTITLED

DEAF AS A POST.

Mr. Walton	Mr. K. ARROTS.
Tristram Sappy	Mr. JIMBOLI.
Captain Templeton	Mr. DARTING.
Crupper (*an Ostler*)	Mr. GORMAN BOURKE.
Gallop	Mr. A. HOST.
Waiter	Mr. KNOTCH.
Sophy Walton	Mr. T. HUCKEGGS.
Amy Templeton	Mr. OCHRE.
Mrs. Plumply	Mr. KNIGHT.
Sally Mags	Mr. SYLVA.

*Stage Manager—Mr. POTILLE. Acting Manager—Mr. JIMBOLI.
Prompter—Mr. N. INEPINS. Artists—Mr. POTILLE & N. GAGE.
Properties by Mr. C. UTTIT. Dresses by Mr. S. WAY.
Perruquier—Mr. CLARKSON. Leader of Band—Mr. SWANSBOURNE.*

The form of the programme is as different from our old
ones of '57, as is the elegant and over-perfumed programme of
to-day from the old flimsy, dirty, inky "bill of the play" with

which one spoilt one's gloves and dirtied one's fingers at all our theatres twenty years ago.

Observe that White-headed Bob had protested against being called "Mr. Swanborough." His real name was "Swansbourne."

Not a Bad Judge was specially successful, owing to the playing of Rowley Hill, R. Preston (who came up to play Betman), and C. Weguelin as Lavater.

The Two Bonnycastles was revived for the sake of Twiss's Jeremiah Jorum, which had delighted everyone in May Term, 1858.

The difficulty of getting suitable representatives of the female parts seems to have been got over by Lionel Ashley as Louise, and G. Knox as Madame Betman.

The *Thumping Legacy,* a great hit in October, 1858, was also revived. So that there was not much novelty. The star of Oliver Twist was in the ascendant at the close of the fourth year of the "A. D. C.," ending Lent Term, 1859.

CHAPTER XV.

For the first time in the history of the Club there were no performances to record in the May Term, " *as* " says the record, " *the only week when they could have taken place was the week of the boat races.*"

As if boat races would have mattered to *us* in 1856, when we had two sets of performances in the May Term. The elections were :—"*Powys and Aug. Campbell of Trin. Coll., and R. Doyne of Magdalene. Hon. J. Leigh resigned his stage managership.*" Here, in the record, the office is called by its right name, but not so in the bill. "*And Mr. Weguelin was elected in his place.*"

By this time A. C. Lee, R. Hill, W. P. Lysaght, &c., had all disappeared from the scene, and the names with which we first commenced are no longer found, such as R. Kelly, Donne, F. C. Wilson, J. M. Wilson, &c.

The Club was prosperous, and the tickets were no longer distributed in secresy. It had become a recognised form of recreation both for members of the Club and their visitors.

Already the tutors had given " leave till one," to *acting* members of the Club during the " A. D. C." week. This meant that the time of being in in college, or in lodgings, was extended beyond midnight, on the clear understanding that none should avail themselves of this licence except *genuine acting members of the Club*. This concession was almost equivalent to a formal recognition by authority, and was certainly something more than mere "toleration," unless the brotherhood of freemasonry with its Royal Grand Master is considered as merely "tolerated" in this country—for the Club, as regards the University authorities, was in much the same position as is freemasonry with regard to the government, which, when closing the lodges of the secret societies, specially exempts, on certain conditions, the masonic lodges. The "A. D. C." was in a similar position.

In October, 1859, they woke up again. Another term couldn't be allowed to pass without a performance. During the vacation Quintin Twiss had been invited, and, happening to meet him, we talked over a new edition of *Alonzo*, in which he was to play—first time in burlesque—Alonzo, and a popular air with chorus, "Sally come up the middle," was to be introduced.

With delight I went up to Cambridge, having been as an "active member" absent from the "A. D. C." since the Lent Term, 1858—for the merely going up to deliver an address does not count as acting—and attended a Club meeting, Oct. 22, when it was decided that the performances should commence on Tuesday, Nov. 29, and that the pieces should be,—

> *My new version of Alonzo*, now ready for rehearsal.
> *In for a Holiday* (my farce).
> *Curious Case*, a revival.
> *Helping Hands*, also a revival.

Then were elected E. Hambro', Percy Lee, A. E. Guest, — Newton, Hon. H. Bourke, — Plowden, F. W. Hudson, all of Trinity.

Being once more in harness, Richard was himself again, and went to work with a will, the rehearsals of *Alonzo the*

Brave, or Faust and the Fair Imogene, commencing on *Oct.* 24, of course without Quintin Twiss, who could not attend until the last two rehearsals, but who was always a safe man, sure to know his part, and be up in all his music.

Nov. 25 were elected members, The Duke of St. Albans, Hon. A. Strutt, N. M. de Rothschild, all of Trinity.

A great success was anticipated, and the Chronicle shows that expectation was not disappointed.

" So large an audience as that which attended on Tuesday had never been seen on the first night of representation. This, as well as the unequalled success of the latter performances, is doubtless to be attributed to the combined attraction of Messrs. Twiss and Burnand, the return of which latter gentleman to the ' A. D. C.' boards was hailed with great delight."

For myself I remember how remarkably "rusty" I felt, and what a signal failure was my performance in what had been one of my great successes. Here is the critique :—

" On Mr. Burnand rested the whole onus of the piece's success, and in this, especially the second night, he perfectly succeeded, as far as the piece in our opinion is capable of going ; a lighter rendering would have been better, and Mr. Burnand spoke too low, but through want of practice he has somewhat forgotten that light and funny style which was so well depicted in ' the Practical Man.' "

This was perfectly true. I was no longer a light-hearted undergraduate, and in the time intervening between my last appearance on the boards and this present one, much had happened to make me take a far more serious view of life in 1859, than I had in the beginning of 1858.

I remember Weguelin's performance of Laurence Hartmann, " de old Hartmann," in *Helping Hands.* It was really admirable, as was also Twiss's *Vinkin,* and J. Leigh's *Tilda.*

Here is the bill of the last night's performance:—

A. D. C.

ON SATURDAY EVENING, DECEMBER 3, 1859,
WILL BE PERFORMED,
A FARCE, BY J. MORTON, Esq.,
CALLED

A THUMPING LEGACY.

Fillippo Geronimo	Mr. J. DARTING.
Bambogetti	Mr. M. HOST.
Leoni	Mr. JIMBOLI.
Brigadier	Mr. G. HOST.
Jerry Ominous	Mr. O. TWIST.
Rosetta	Mr. T. HUCKEGGS.

To conclude with a Tragical, Comical, Demoniacal, and What-ever-you-like-to-call-it-iacal Extravaganza, uniting in its construction the romantic pathos of the well-known Ballad "Alonzo and Imogene," with the thrilling horrors of Goethe's Tragic Poem "Faust," by F. C. Burnand, Esq., entitled

ALONZO THE BRAVE;

OR, FAUST AND THE FAIR IMOGENE.

Alonzo (*pupil to Faust—who steals time from his studies to join the rifle corps*)	Mr. O. TWIST.
Dr. Faust (*ABC, XYZ, etc., etc., Professor in Muddleberg University—well read in black letter*) . . .	Mr. J. DARTING.
Mephistopheles (*a character—without one*)	Mr. TOM PIERCE.
Sybel (*a simple youth, the current of whose thoughts flow in the direction of* raspber.y *jam*)	Mr. E. CARTS.
Gyppo (*Faust's servant-of-all-work, who is too busy to appear more than once this evening*)	Mr. H. OCHRE.
Bandini (*a gentleman in an official capacity at Muddleberg University*) .	Mr. G. HOST.
Barco } (*his attendants — belonging* Byto } *to the* K9 *division*) . .	M. A. L. HAMBRA. M. T. ILLCAVE.
Pipo de Clayo (*a sergeant in Alonzo's company*)	Mr. E. PAULETT.
Imogene (*the Fair par excellence since the one at Greenwich has been stopped*)	Mr. T. HUCKEGS.

Dame Martha (*Imogene's nurse and guardian—a good specimen of an "Ugly"*) . . . . . Mr. JIMBOLI.

Sailors, Students, Aristocrats, talented Individuals, distinguished Foreigners, Soldiers, Stokers, Ladies, Guests, Umbrellas, Thunder, Lightning, and a splendidly appointed and Victorious ARMY (*including a drummer*), by

Messrs. TIP, TOP, PETER, PIPER and PECKER,

who have been engaged for Four Nights only, at an enormous expense.

SCENE I.—FAUST'S LABORATORY.
(*Painted by Mr. POWELL.*)
The Wish! The Tempter!! The Compact!!!

SCENE II.—ROOM IN IMOGENE'S HOUSE.
(*Mr. E. GAGE.*)
The Cake—The Nurse—*The Vow!!*—The Review (*not the "Saturday"*)—Departure of Alonzo—

SCENE III.—A GARDEN.—(*Mr. Powell.*)
The meeting—'Take now this ring'—Unpleasant position of Sybel—Triumph of Mephistopheles.

SCENE IV.—A WOOD.—(*Jones.*)
Halt of *maimed* Soldiers—Scenes of my childhood—The plot.

SCENE V.—BANQUET HALL IN FAUST'S CASTLE.
(*Mr. POWELL and ASSISTANTS.*)
The apparition!—Glorious and astounding denouement!!

Books of "Alonzo" may be had in the room, price One Shilling, and of the other Pieces at Mr. T. H. Lacy's, 89, Strand.

Acting Manager—Mr. J. DARTING.   Stage Manager—Mr. POTILLE.
Chorus Master—Mr. K. ROTCHIT.   Property Man—Mr. E. F. LEA.
Dresses by S. MAY, Bow Street, Covent Garden.
Perruquier, Mr. CLARKSON, Little Russell Street, Covent Garden.

The success of the burlesque was unquestionable; it went better than when it was first produced in 1857. Twiss was first-rate as *Alonzo*, and "Sally come up" was encored twice; but the hit of the evening was an *ad captandum* introduction in the first scene, of Mr. Augustus Guest, dressed as a proctor, accompanied by his two bulldogs, represented by E. Hambro, six feet four, and F. Plowden, five feet eight. They were inimitable.

The situation is this, Dr. Faust in his study hears a noise of students without, and sends for the proctor to know what

o

is going on. The proctor and his two followers arrive, inform Dr. Faust that Alonzo the student is giving a farewell supper to his companions, and then, on being further questioned by Dr. Faust, exclaims :—

Proctor (excitedly). Excuse me, Sir, I can no longer stay. (*Rushes to window, to which his attention has been already directed by the bulldogs.*) A man without his cap and gown ! Away ! !

TRIO.

(AIR.—"*Begone dull care.*")

Six shil-*lings*, a fourpence, a fourpenny piece,
By these things our revenues increase.

SOLO.—*Proctor. Second part.*

Oh, while he laughs and while he sings,
    We can no longer stay,
Oh, if he likes to do such things,
    Of course he'll have to pay.

TRIO AND DANCE.

Six shil-*lings*, &c.

      [*Exeunt Proctor and bulldogs dancing.*

This was encored six times at least—the Proctor and attendants becoming wilder and wilder in their antics. It was without exception the funniest thing, of its kind, I ever saw on the " A. D. C." stage, and, considering its appropriateness, I am not prepared to say that it was not the most genuine spontaneously funny thing I have ever seen on any stage. The point would perhaps be lost on a mixed audience, and when we played *Alonzo* away from the " A. D. C." Theatre, we invariably cut out the Proctor and Co.

Now-a-days, on the same principle that caused the Lord Chamberlain to interdict the performance of *The Happy Land* at the Court Theatre when the actors made up as Messrs. Gladstone, Ayrton and Bob Lowe, and to issue the order that

Mr. Corri should alter his make-up as the Shah in my piece of *Kissi-Kissi*, so now the Proctor and his bulldogs would not be permitted to appear on the "A. D. C." stage, out of respect to the authorities. I don't think it did any harm to a single undergraduate, and the proctors, unofficially, came themselves to witness the performance.

In the Lent Term, 1860, H. W. Hoffman was elected President, vice Lord Brecknock, and Augustus Guest, Auditor, vice Hon. L. Ashley. And N. M. de Rothschild was elected "assistant stage manager" at the request of the stage manager, who found he had too much work to do.

The first important step this term was to discharge the debt to Mr. Sealy, which was forthwith done, and the next was to conclude arrangements with Mr. Ekin for the larger set of rooms at a rent of £75 per annum.

A subscription-list was opened to defray the expenses consequent on the change, the subscriptions were increased to £1 10s., not doubled as they were to have been by a former resolution. The Club was increased to sixty members, and Messrs. Everett, Smith, Marryat, Osborne, Featherstonehaugh, Evans, Heathcote, Gurdon, Leigh, and C. Barclay, all of Trinity, and Willis, of King's, were elected.

No wonder that Mr. David Powell wanted an assistant stage manager, as he had devoted himself entirely to the scenery, and had painted the whole of what was required for the burlesque in the previous term.

The subscription-list soon mounted up to well over a hundred pounds, and on March 6, 1860, took place the first performance on the new stage. Here is the bill, which in shape and texture was a return to the old original style.

Barefaced Impostors was played instead of a burlesque, and I regretted that I was unable to be present on this occasion. At all events, I had played in the first and last performance on the old stage, and it was due to the "fitness of things" that a new generation should now appear on an entirely new stage.

A. D. C.
NEW THEATRE.

On Tuesday, March 6th, will be Performed the celebrated Comedy, by TOM TAYLOR, Esq., entitled

STILL WATERS RUN DEEP.

Mr. Potter	Mr. Mural Foord.
Captain Hawksley	Mr. Sylva.
John Mildmay	Mr. Darting.
Dunbilk	Mr. Hare.
Langford	Mr. Ochre.
Markham	Mr. H. Usband.
Jessop	Mr. Hawk.
Gimlet	Mr. O. Twist.
Mrs. Mildmay	Mr. F. Huddaughter.
Mrs. Hector Sternhold	Mr. Ion Trant.

After which will be performed the grand
Zoological absurdity of

BAREFACED IMPOSTORS.

Schahabaham (*a pacha of 3 tails*)	Mr. H. Usband.
Mustapha (*his Vizier*)	Mr. R. Acoon.
Bill Stumps } (*quondam proprietors of*	Mr. O. Twist.
Jack Hocus } *the original united*	Mr. A. Host.
Happy Family)	
Ali	Mr. Ochre.
Osman Khan (*chief executioner*)	Mr. A. L. Hambra.
Achmet Aga (*an officer of the Sultan*)	Mr. E. Mergency.
Mirza Hadji Baba (*chief keeper of the*	
monkeys)	Mr. S. Mc Mias.
First Ferash } (*thrashers of the*	Mr. Hare.
Second ditto } *people*)	Mr. Ion Trant.
Barikallah (*keeper of the Harem*)	Mr. Oldpound.
Jacko (*a blue-nosed baboon*)	Mr. Mural Foord.
Sambo (*an ourang outang*)	Mr. J. A. Huddaughter
Ayesha (*formerly Jemima Stumps,*	
now first favourite of the Pasha)	Mr. T. Illcove.
Fatimer (*second favourite of the*	
Pasha)	Mr. Aldershot Big Ben.

*Various Choice specimens of Zoology, Guards, Slaves, and
Attendants.*

The programme is wanting in details. No officials are
mentioned.

An address was written by G. O. Trevelyan, which was delivered by Mr. Weguelin as acting manager. The somewhat ironical allusion to "Dido's great author" refers to my having produced my first piece at the St. James's under the management of Messrs. Willott and Chatterton in the early part of the year. The Drum-major was Mr. Hambro, six feet four in his stockings, who was so effective as a bulldog on our stage.

"Monday week" alludes perspectively to the "little go," and the "clotted gravy and bleeding beef," to the execrable dinners then given in the Hall of Trinity College.

AN ADDRESS

By G. O. TREVELYAN, Esq.

ON THE OCCASION OF THE OPENING OF THE NEW "A. D. C." STAG
MARCH 6, 1860.

SPOKEN BY C. WEGUELIN, ESQ., *Acting-Manager.*

BRING them in, Prompter ; all of them.   Why, bless us !
What a vast heap of Prologues and Addresses.
Is't for my own or for my parent's crime
That I must wade through all this mass of rhyme ?
I'll read 'em out, and you shall help me choose.
'Gad ! here's an invocation to the muse.
" Descend, Thalia, from yon heaven descend :
" The inauguration of your shrine attend ;
" Melodious goddess."   No, not if I know him ;
It's too much like a Chancellor's prize poem.
Here's one in Latin, all about Cothurnum,
And Sophocleum ; take 'em off and burn 'em.
This seems the best.   Kind gentles, one and all,
Whether from Jesus Lane, or Humphry's Hall,
On Magdalen's jovial towers, or pleasant Clare,
Or the lone waste of distant Downing's air ;
We'll give each one in our several parts,
A brave house-warming that shall cheer your hearts.

Compare this spacious area with the floor
Where once you jostled, laughed, perspired, and swore ;
Fitter for some old unwashed Cynic's tub
Than for the home of our Dramatic Club.
How can our actors now they've grown so tall
Within such puny limits strut and bawl ?
At the Queen's rifle levée I'll engage her
To see no sight so fine as our Drum-major ;
Yet not without one fond and loving sigh
We bid our ancient stage a long good-bye.
For there full oft, marred by no envious hiss,
Loud swelled the laugh that hailed each tone of Twiss.
There he whose name we proudly cherish still
Dido's great author fleshed his maiden quill.
Is there one here whose brains with Paley reek ?
Who shudders at the thought of Monday week ?
Let him to-night, while laughing till he hoarse is,
Forget the parallelogram of forces.
Ye sons of Trinity, lay by your grief,
The clotted gravy and the bleeding beef,
The greasy female waiters, hideous vision,
And the precarious fate of our petition.
Enjoy the passing moment as it flies,
We'll do our best to feast your ears and eyes :
Forgive our faults and recognize with glee,
In a new dress, your old friend, "A. D. C."

I was considerably astonished when on going up in the following term I found the new rooms, of which I have given a ground plan.

The green-room was where we, the original founders of the Club, had been contented to play, and the space "B" beyond, which had served for our old green-room, was now blocked up, or used for storeage.

Beyond the auditorium, and not shown in the plan, is a club-room and lavatory. The club-room walls are now covered with photographs, chiefly coloured, of all the characters and tableaux in the pieces performed from the commencement ; but our old ones are beginning to look very shady, and represent a period which, to most of the present generation, must be more or less mythical.

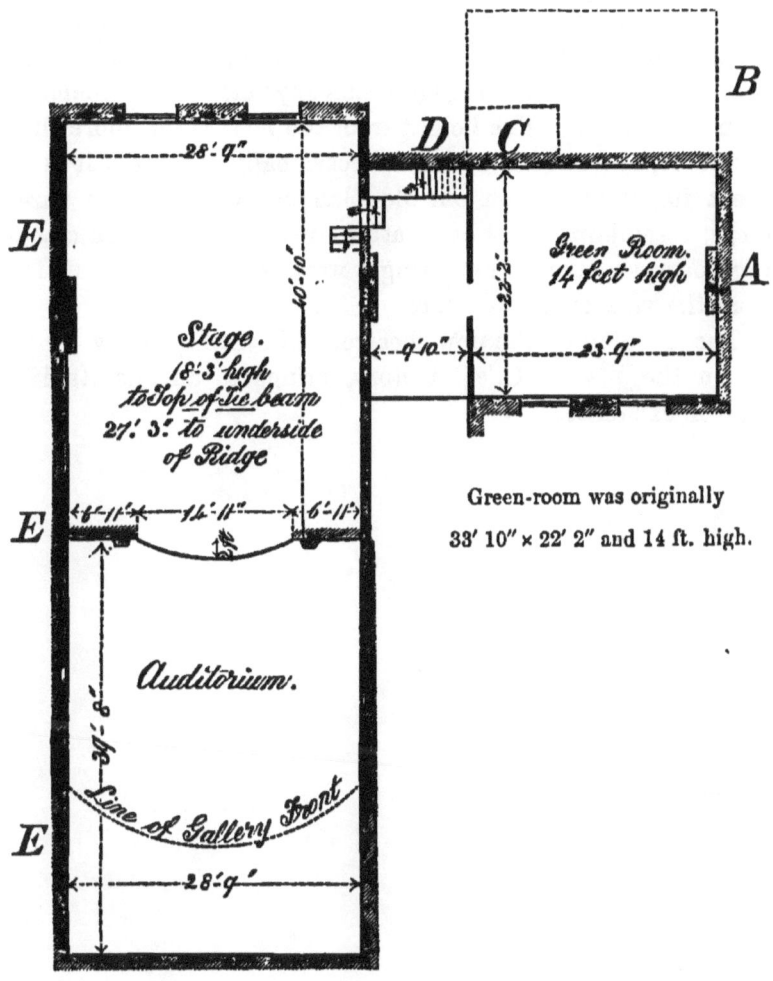

Green-room was originally
33' 10" × 22' 2" and 14 ft. high.

PRESENT PLAN OF "A. D. C." CAMBRIDGE, JUNE 12, 1879.

A.   This was the room where the first stage was erected.

B.   Was our Green-room, which no longer exists.

C.   Door into Hoop Yard (down a stair-case).

D.   Door opening into Auditorium.

E. E. E.   These were the old Hoop Billiard Rooms after. The Union Debating Club had given them up.

The stage is excellent, but unfortunately not on an incline, and while the depth is sufficient for any scenic effect of distance, the narrowness of the opening cramps the acting, and the small space at the wings prevents any perfect stage management of crowds. The height from the floor is not more than four feet, and though a trap is occasionally managed, it is no great improvement on our old plan of walking down three steps, resembling those of a bathing-machine, and then stooping down, as though expecting a wave, until we were hidden from the view of the audience.

The opening of the new theatre, while commencing a new era in the "A. D. C.'s" history, brings to an end its fifth year of existence.

CHAPTER XVI.

MR. WEGUELIN was succeeded by Mr. Grove as stage-manager, and Mr. Hambro took the place of assistant, vacated by Mr. Rothschild.

The price of seats was fixed all round at five shillings. The three-shilling back-row being abolished.

So little did the once almost secret society of the "A.D.C." now dread publicity, that the question was discussed as to whether they should begin to play in their own names. The result, however, was to leave this as they found it, and the old *noms de théâtre* were still retained.

Elected Messrs. Hervey, N. A. Langham, and Scholefield.

This term I went up to play *B.B.*, a farce that Montagu Williams and myself had written for Robson on the occasion of the *Benicia Boy's* (Heenan) visiting England to contest the championship with Tom Sayers. Twiss was to take Robson's part of Benjamin Bobbin. But there was more than this to be done. It had been decided that a testimonial should be presented by the Club to Mr. Quintin Twiss, in recognition of his signal services to the Club, always coming at their call, and putting aside other engagements to assist them at the " A. D. C."

" *On June the seventh,*" Mr. J. T. Hamilton, the secretary, mentions, in his farewell chronicle, "*an illigant entertainment was given to Q. Twiss, Esq., in the audience part of the theatre. About forty-three gentlemen were present; many of whom were guests. The chair was ably filled by the President, Mr. Hoffman, and the testimonial, a beautifully chased silver claret jug, was presented to our very active member. The company broke up shortly after twelve."*

The performances of this term, which were over before the dinner was given, had not been so successful as usual. *The Wonderful Woman, B. B.*, and *The Omnibus* were comparatively failures, though Mr. Bourke distinguished himself as Pat Rooney in the second piece—we were always fortunate in our Irish representatives—and we once more discovered an excellent impersonator of female character in Mr. Hoffman. Benjamin Bobbin was pronounced to be not in Quintin Twiss's line, and Mr. Grove was blamed for lacking that energy and spirit which had "characterized his three first terms' performance." Perhaps his reading for honours was taking it out of him. He never omitted acting, and in 1861 came out in *First Class Pol.*

Lord Lovel was not to the taste of the present University audience, which had seen such a strong cast in the more modern version of *Alonzo* at the last performances. The only success here was Mr. D. Powell's scenery.

The orchestra was becoming a difficulty. White-headed Bob and talented assistants no longer sufficed; their "vamping" was not up to the growing requirements of the Club, and the services of Mr. Sippel had for some time past been brought into requisition. I think he became conductor, and that our white-headed friend and his merry men—the *Vamp*-ires—still remained under Sippel's direction.

I know burlesque singing had come to be a difficulty, and that when any one on the stage wanting assistance, looked towards Sippel to take up the cue, or to give him the note, or whatever it might be, he would either be met by a blank stare of astonishment, coming from over the rim of Sippel's spectacles, or Mr. Sippel would be in conversation with another member of the band, perhaps asking what the next cue might be, in which case he would look up, and seeing that something was wanted, would say audibly, "Oh, I beg your pardon—I didn't see." And then he would tap the footlights in front of him sharply and look round at his men, saying, " Now then !" as though the *hiatus* had been all their fault. He was very trying, especially at rehearsals ; but, with a few notable exceptions, he was generally "all right at night."

However, in the October Term of 1860 the Club expressed themselves of opinion that the music ought to be conducted properly, and elected the orchestra manager on to the committee, which was thus constituted:—

President	H. W. Hoffman.
Stage Manager	D. Powell.
Acting Manager	W. C. Grove.
Treasurer and Secretary . . .	T. F. Kirby.

One of the most active secretaries and best business men the Club ever had.

Prompter	(vacant).
Property Manager	F. Lee.
Assistant Acting Manager . .	A. F. Guest.
Ditto Stage ditto . . .	E. Hambro.
Orchestra Manager . . .	F. W. Hudson.

The proposition for retaining their own names in the bills had been negatived last term. The Hon. H. Bourke, with the true gallantry of his nationality, asked for a " Ladies' Night," when the county families should be admitted.

This was an inspiration from without.

But the secretary, Mr. Thomas Kirby, asserts, and signs it with his own hand, that at the time a strong party existed among the Dons unfavourable to the " A. D. C.," " as they are," he sarcastically writes, " to all harmless enjoyment." At the same time he very sensibly adds, that ladies would detect faults in the female characters to which the ordinary University audience was willingly.blind.

Finally, the Rev. W. G. Clark, Public Orator, was consulted, and, in consequence of his advice, the Club for the present decided not only against the Ladies' Night, but also that they would adhere most strictly to the old rule of not admitting to the performances any but members of the University, unless they came provided with a ticket signed by three members of the Committee.

The elections were—

R. C. Jebb . . . . Trin. Coll.
E. H. Wynne . . . . . do.
Hon. C. Lyttleton . . . . do. .
H. L. Wood . . . . . do.
J. W. Hawkesworth . . . do.
Hon. W. P. Bouverie . .. . . do.
Lord J. Hervey .. .. . ., do.
Hon. J. M. Henniker-Major . . do.
D. H. C. Henniker . . . . do.
J. Hamilton . . . . . do.
Hon. — Fitzwilliam . . . . do.
C. J. Fletcher . . . . do.

And

F. H. Whymper, M.A. . . . Trin. ⎫
C. T. Royds, B.A. . . . . Christ's ⎬ Honorary Members.
Hon. R. M. Harvey, B. A. . . Trin. ⎭

Then, on the proposition of D. Powell, they began to form a library. There was some slight opposition to this on account of the extra subscription, but it was decided in the affirmative by thirty to five.

The theatrical week commenced Nov. 20, and there were four fixed performances and one extra night—Saturday.

CHAPTER XVII.

1860. In the August of 1860 the "A. D. C." joined with the Quidnunc Cricket Club, and, after the Quidnunc *v.* Sussex match, gave a performance at the Theatre Royal, Brighton, then under the management of T. Nye Chart. The pieces were *Not a Bad Judge*, with Weguelin for *Lavater, Zug,* Augustus Guest, Evelyn Ashley as the *Marquis de Treval,* and myself as the *Burgomaster.* The *Thumping Legacy,* with Quintin Twiss, and Merthyr Guest as *Bambogetti.* The burlesque of *Alonzo* concluded the evening, with Twiss as *Alonzo,* Weguelin as *Faust,* myself as *Mephistopheles,* Hon. J. Leigh as *Dame Martha,* Miss R. Ranor as *Imogene,* and an army composed of W. H. and Alec Baillie, R. Fitzgerald, E. Drake, R. Forster, and Quidnuncs *ad lib.*

In 1861 the Club again played at Brighton. *The Bachelor of Arts,* with Weguelin, Balfour, Whymper (who had been elected an honorary member of the "A. D. C.") *Whitebait at Greenwich,* with Twiss, Weguelin, Hon. J. Leigh, Mrs. Daly, and Miss Marion Daly. *The Seventh Shot* burlesque by Messrs. Montagu Williams and F. C. Burnand, *Rodolph* (Twiss), *Caspar* (Burnand), *Agnes* (Miss R. Ranor), *Anne* (Miss Fanny Stirling), *Kilian* (Augustus Guest), *Prince Ottacar* (Miss Pauline Burette).

In 1862, at Brighton, *A Curious Case.* F. Whymper as *Aubrey,* Frank Marshall (Hon. Mem. of "A. D. C." as an Oxford man, *pro tem.) Charles Twiggleton,* Burnand, *Mrs.*

Aubrey, Miss Booth. Quintin Twiss, Weguelin, and the " Guest family " were absent. There was an interlude by the *corps de ballet* of the Theatre, and afterwards was played *Alonzo the Brave* (burlesque), with the following cast: *Alonzo*, Miss Marion Daly ; *Dame Martha*, Mrs. R. Soutar ; *Faust*, Miss Ruth ; *Imogene*, Miss Pauline Burette ; *Mephis- topheles*, F. C. Burnand ; *Sybil*, F. Marshall. The army by Robt. Fitzgerald, M. C. C. as sergeant, W. H. Baillie, Alec Baillie, Biron, E. Drake, Hoblyn (drummer) R. Forster. They were excellent, and " Sally come up ! " was loudly encored.

In 1863, August 22. Another performance to a crowded house. *Two Bonnycastles*, with Twiss in the principal *rôle*, and the burlesque of *Aladdin*, with Twiss as *Widow Twan- kay*, Hon. C. Carington as *Aladdin*, F. C. Burnand as *Abana- zar*, Miss R. Ranoe as *Pekoe*, and P. Finch as *Sultan*.

There was another performance in 1864, when we did the *Critic*, with Mr. Brandram as *Don Whiskerandos*, but, I think, in consequence of the difficulty of getting the team together, this was the last of the " A. D. C." and Quidnuncs at Brighton.

Mr. Brandram and Mr. F. A. Marshall, who kindly gave us their assistance, were never elected as regular honorary members of the Cambridge " A. D. C."; at least there is no record of their election in the Club books. As Oxonians they were eligible.

CHAPTER XVIII.

THE following extract comes from the Annals *pro tem.*, as kept by the Club's most conscientious and energetic Secretary, Mr. Kirby :—

"THEATRICAL WEEK, FEBRUARY 26TH, 27TH, 28TH,
MARCH 1ST, 2ND, 1861.

" The performances this term were prepared with great care and much cost, as it had been resolved that on Saturday, March 2nd, on which evening the Prince of Wales attended, ladies should be invited. It was a hazardous venture, and one which received deep consideration, but it was attended with great success. After reviewing the pieces which were then acted shortly, a more detailed account of it shall be given.

" The following plays were acted by the members :—

> *Not a Bad Judge,*
> *A Thumping Legacy,*
> *Taming of a Tiger,*
> *Retained for the Defence,* **and**
> *The Fair Maid of Wapping,*

a T.-P.-Cookical and romantical burlesque written for the 'A. D. C.' by Messrs. M. Williams and F. C. Burnand. For the first time since the foundation of the Club the actors played under their own names, and those ingenious sobriquets which reflected so much credit on the ingenuity of their inventors, and amused the audience while the scenes were being shifted, were now discarded. The reasons need not be particularised which led to the establishment of this time-honoured custom, as they no longer exist ; but we cannot help thinking that *this* custom, at any rate, might have been honoured by observance, in a Club which, generally speaking, adheres so closely to its old institutions."

The allusion is of course to our first state of existence as a secret society, afraid to let our names be known, and keeping our whereabouts concealed from all but the initiated.

The new state of affairs, so different to what we had been accustomed to only six years before, considerably astonished our friends. F. C. Wilson also reappeared, " by particular desire for this occasion only," to play in *Not a Bad Judge* and *A Thumping Legacy*.

Here is the Secretary's account of it :—

" Mr. Becker, with his usual kindness, undertook the servant's part.

" Few here now recollect Mr. F. C. Wilson's triumphs in *St. George and the Dragon*, *Still Waters*, &c. ; but that he has forgotten none of his old skill during an absence of several years was soon clear. The vivacity united with pathos displayed by him as Louise, proved such a true picture of woman's character as has not been seen since he last played here. Our other actors of female parts limit themselves to the beauty of repose, Mr. Wilson can delineate the finer feelings of a woman's nature. His hands and action in general are wonderfully correct, and his voice justly modulated.

" *Madame Betman* [Mr. D. Henniker] looked the gay matron all over, and played her part with some tact.

A THUMPING LEGACY

has been played twice before by the ' A. D. C.,' so needs

few remarks now; many of the performers now having played in it on the last occasion.

Filippo	Mr. WEGUELIN.
Leoni	Mr. HAWKESWORTH.
Bambogetti	Mr. STEWARD.
Brigadier	Mr. GUEST.
Jerry Ominous	Mr. TWISS.
Carbineers	LORD HERVEY and Mr. BANKES.
Rosetta	Mr. WILSON.

" The piece went well, better than any of the other pieces. Indeed on the Saturday night it went without a fault. Mr. Weguelin, Mr. Guest, and Mr. Twiss took the same characters as before, and played them very well.

" Mr. Hawkesworth as *Leoni* was spirited, especially in the quarrel with *Bambogetti*. His anger was most capitally assumed, and the gradual rise of his wrath when induced by *Jerry Ominous* to pick the quarrel with *Bambogetti*, was artistically depicted. Mr. Steward made his début as *Bambogetti*, and showed great power of comic acting. Indeed he shows as much promise as any who have lately appeared ; we only hope that he will continue to study his part as carefully as he has done.

" Rosetta [Mr. Wilson] added much to the success of this piece by her spirited way of showing that she had a way of her own. She drew the dagger as if she meant it, and we can understand poor Jerry's alarm.

TAMING THE TIGER.

Charles Beeswing	Mr. GROVE.
Mr. Chili Chutnee	Mr. WEGUELIN.
Jacob Mutter	Mr. STEWARD.

" A very tolerable ' first piece,' and that was all. Mr. Grove was, we must confess, not as good as he might have been in it. Mr. Weguelin, too, took the part of Chili Chutnee, at eight hours' notice, Mr. Usborne, our ' first old man,' having been seized by an attack of rheumatism. Under this

P

disadvantage all we can say is, that he played as well as we could expect. The only interest in the piece was centered in Jacob Mutter, who was in look, voice, and gesture most comic, and, we may say, saved the piece. What fun there was in the play could be heard by every one, for, unlike some whom we might name, all three actors spoke up throughout."

The following speaks well for the proficiency of the scenic artists, all Club members, and gives a fair account of the burlesque :—

" It was necessary to have the theatrical week early—delays also took place in printing the piece; consequently, when it at last came down, only *ten days* remained for rehearsing a piece of the most elaborate kind that has ever been 'put on' here. We were, however, lucky in five painters, Messrs. Powell, Bouverie, Hambro, Hoffman, and Woodroffe, who worked at the seven scenes with untiring energy, as well as several others whose ambition reached no higher than laying on the first coat of ground-colour. Attendance at rehearsals, we are sorry to say, was not kept with the same punctuality as during the last term. Performers should always recollect that the absence of one character for even ten minutes, keeps all the others waiting, and when this is repeated, others lose confidence and become also unpunctual. Therefore, on Tuesday night the piece dragged its weary way along until 12 o'clock, and it became evident that it must be compressed, and so we cut out. Then it improved nightly, and latterly was very good.

" The incidents are of a tolerably stirring sort throughout; no situations so strong as some in *The Seventh Shot*, but its end is far more powerful than the end of that play, which was quite weak.

" Scene 1st, Wapping, with a view of the Thames, extremely well painted by Powell. The imbecility of the watermen made the beginning lame : a roar of laughter followed,

when Billy rowed across the stage and danced in. He sings
a very good song ' Did you ever hear of a jolly young waterman,' and retires to prepare for the impending boat-race, for
which he is in strict training. *Polly* enters and is followed
by *Blackbrow,* who in set terms declares his love, but is
rejected. The duet—

> " ' Ah ; my ear, your wit's a
> > Decidedly
> > > high-deadly blow."

is a pretty one. Mr. Burnand was unable to sing in his
usually effective manner, having scarcely recovered from an
attack of bronchitis. Mr. Hudson sang it very fairly : it is
impossible to criticise a song like this where one of the performers was incapacitated from singing, except with great
efforts ; otherwise it would have been very well received.

" Act II. A Carpenter's Scene. *Blackbrow* and *Jonas*
concert measures for vengeance. It is curious how different
Mr. Augustus Guest is in different characters and situations.
Single words and half lines he always gives with great effect,
and quite as they should be given, but he really quite spoilt
this very comic speech by a kind of hesitation that never
ought to beset him."

The next scene would have been utterly impracticable on
our old stage in the small room.

" The shipwreck takes place.

" It was most ably arranged by Messrs. Powell and
Hoffman.

" Amid thunder and lightning the winged clouds, or clouds
from the wings, cover all the wretched victims, and a drop
painted by Mr. Hoffman is lowered, showing the crew on a
raft at sea.

" This was well done ; but as much had to be changed on
the first night, it was kept down twenty minutes, during
which thunder and lightning continued until, as one in the
audience was heard to say, ' flesh and blood could stand it

no longer.' On the subsequent nights, however, a species of bearfight or horseplay of savages was introduced, which served to amuse the audience (who could not in the least tell what it was all about), until the drop rising disclosed—

"Scene VI. 'The shores of Catchemalivica.' Too much cannot be said in praise of the painting of this scene. If any fault could be found, perhaps it was this, that the back drop was a little too distinct. Had it been less so, perhaps a still more effective illusion of distance might have been produced. A member had walked through the gauze-drop before the performance, which injured it slightly. But no doubt it was 'the' scene of the play—the savage dance was both novel and effective. Mr. Arthur Guest did his part exceeding well, and his make-up was irresistible."

The County Night, March 2, 1861, was a novelty with a vengeance : here is an account taken from a weekly journal, then existing, called the *Drawing Room* :—

"AMATEUR THEATRICALS AT CAMBRIDGE.

"The 'A. D. C.' Club, which, with the exception of one or two honorary members—old Cantabs—consists of under-graduates of the University, gave a series of performances last week, and their efforts met with an unusual amount of success. In addition to the resident undergraduates, Messrs. Weguelin, Twiss, and Burnand, honorary members, kindly lent their assistance on this occasion ; and a new burlesque from the joint pens of Messrs. Montagu Williams and F. C. Burnand, written expressly for the Club, was produced each evening during the week. The house was crowded nightly, but as the Prince of Wales had signified his intention of being present on Saturday evening, and the Heads of the University, for the first time since the formation of the 'A. D. C.' had consented to allow ladies to be admitted, that was of course 'the' evening of the week, and the entertainments passed off with the greatest possible *éclat*. As soon as the doors were opened, the theatre was at once filled with the members of the University, and ladies and gentlemen from the county, and several who had come expressly from London. Immediately after the arrival of H.R.H. the Prince of Wales, the curtain was raised, and the performance commenced with Planché's comic drama of *Not a Bad Judge*, the characters in which were sustained by Messrs. Weguelin, Grove, Hawkesworth, Burnand, A. Guest, Grant, Becher and Henricher. The *Lavater* of Mr. Weguelin, and the *Betman* of Mr. Burnand were admirable performances; the acting of the former reminding us very much of Mr. A. Wigan. Mr. Hawkesworth, as *Christian*, Mr. A. Guest, as *Zug*, and Mr. Wilson, as *Louise*, were all that the most fastidious could desire. After the drama, Maddison Morton's farce of *A Thumping Legacy*, was received with roars of laughter, and we are bound to say that the *Jerry Ominous* of Mr. Q. Twiss was the best piece of amateur acting we have ever witnessed. He was ably supported by Messrs. Hawkesworth and Steward, as *Leoni* and *Bambogetti*. The performances concluded with an original legitimately-nautical T.-P.-Cookical burlesque by Messrs. Montagu Williams and Burnand, entitled *The Fair Maid of Wapping, or The Tragical Tale of William Taylor*, in which Mr. Q. Twiss as *Billy Taylor*, Messrs. Burnand and Guest as *Blackbrow* and *Jonas*, and Mr. F. Hudson as *Polly* the Fair Maid of Wapping, fairly divided the honours. The jokes and puns were as burlesque jokes ought to be—painfully funny—and the music was well chosen, and admirably sung. An immense amount of praise was decidedly due to Messrs. Powell, Bouverie, and Hoffman, the principal scenic artists, for the very great taste they displayed in painting the scenery. The wreck of the ship, and the last scene, where the audience is introduced to the King of the Cannibal Islands, were as well done as any we have ever seen in any of the London theatres; in fact, no expense was spared to ensure success, and the Committee of the Club and their attentive Secretary, Mr. Kirby, may certainly congratulate themselves on having achieved it. The Prince of Wales, accompanied by the Duke of St. Alban's, Colonel Bruce, and suite, waited until the conclusion of the performances, and his Royal Highness expressed himself highly pleased with the evening's entertainment."

"Era," *March* 9, 1861.

"Amateur Theatricals at Cambridge.

"On Saturday evening, March 2, 1861, an amateur performance was given at the Hoop Hotel, Cambridge, by the members of the 'A. D. C.,' or Amateur Dramatic Club, before His Royal Highness the Prince of Wales, and a numerous assembly of ladies, and most of the distinguished luminaries of the various colleges. The pieces selected for representation were Mr. Planché's drama *Not a Bad Judge*, Mr. Maddison Morton's farce *A Thumping Legacy*, and a new burlesque extravaganza, called *The Fair Maid of Wapping, or The Tragical Tale of William Taylor*, written expressly for the occasion by Messrs. Montagu Williams and F. C. Burnand. It is to the exertions of the latter gentleman that this club owes its existence. The company consists entirely of members of the University, and the system of management is such as could only be attained after much practice by a body of gentlemen of education. The undergraduates not only act, but fill the menial offices—such for instance, as the posts of scene-shifters, property-men, and the like. The result is, as might be expected, a complete success. We do not propose to enlarge upon the acting of any particular individual on this occasion, it is rather our object to notice the admirable manner in which the pieces are put upon the stage. The credit of this is principally to be attributed to Mr. David Powell, the chief scenic artist, who, with consummate ingenuity, contrived to give a perfect representation of a ship in full motion, a storm at sea, and a wreck, terminating in the crew and passengers being cast on the shores of the Cannibal Islands; this last effort being a most exquisitely

painted tropical view, and almost worthy of Mr. William
Beverly himself. All this, it should be observed, is
accomplished upon a stage about half the size of the Strand
Theatre. Another distinguishing feature of this club is, that
the female characters are sustained by men, and considering
the difficulties with which they have to contend—such as
voice, figure, and the like—the effect is remarkably good.
The representative of *Polly* in the burlesque, both looked
and acted his (her) part admirably. We understand that, in
consequence of the Prince of Wales having signified his
intention of honouring these performances with his presence,
the authorities of the University called a meeting of the
Senate, for the purpose of taking into consideration the
subject of the existence of the Club being officially recognised.
As the performance took place, it is to be presumed that the
decision was given in its favour; and we cannot but congratulate the authorities upon their good sense in sanctioning
an amusement which, while it is harmless in itself, must,
from the time which must be consumed in arriving at any
pitch of perfection in it, to a great extent contribute towards
keeping its votaries out of harm's way. The principal
characters were sustained by Messrs. Weguelin, F. C.
Burnand, Arthur Guest, Augustus Guest, Grove, Jebb,
Hawkesworth, Steward, Wilson, Grant, F. W. Hudson, and
Quintin Twiss."

"ERA," *December* 8, 1861.

"CAMBRIDGE UNIVERSITY AMATEUR DRAMATIC CLUB.

"On Saturday, November 30th, His Royal Highness the
Prince of Wales honoured the performance given by the
'University Amateur Dramatic Club' (A.D.C.) with his
presence. The theatre (which is an entirely private one,
belonging to the Club) was most tastefully decorated,
the front of the house presenting a very brilliant appearance, crowded as it was by ladies, who had received
special invitations from the Committee—an exception to

the general rule, which prohibits the presence of the fair sex either before or behind the curtain,—all the female parts in the performance being enacted by members of the University. His Royal Highness, who is himself a member of the Dramatic Club, visited the green-room, where the principal performers were presented to him. The pieces played on this occasion were *Used-up;* a new burlesque, specially written for the occasion by Mr. F. C. Burnand, called *Alonzo the Brave, or Faust and the Fair Imogene;* and the farce of *To Paris and Back for Five Pounds;* in which Mr. Q. Twiss played the hero *Snozzle* in a most amusing manner. The scenery in the burlesque, which was admirably painted by Messrs. Powell and Bouverie, assisted by members of the Club, elicited great applause from the audience. The Prince quitted the rooms at the termination of the performance, and expressed himself much pleased with the entertainment, which seemed to have given general satisfaction."

" The following persons had the honour of receiving invitations to meet his Royal Highness :—

Master of Trinity, and Lady Affleck, The Portmans.
Master of Sidney and Miss Phelps.
Provost of King's and Mrs. Okes.
The Vice-Chancellor and Mrs. Neville.
Colonel and Mrs. Baker.
Rev. and Mrs. Girdlestone.
Duke of Leeds and Ladies Osborne (3).
St. Quentens (4).
Earl of Hardwicke and Ladies Yorke (3).
Bishop of Worcester and Mrs. Philpott.
Master of St. John's and Mrs. Bateson.
Master of Downing.
Desboroughs (3).
Master of Christ's and Mrs. Cartwell.
Professor Sedgwick.
Mr. and Lady E. Adeane.
Messrs. Burn, Bright, Clark, W. G. Gunson, Mathison, Blore,
    Lightfoot, Leapingwell.

" Some of these declined—there were actually present Lord F. Osborne and Ladies Osborne, Lady Affleck, Major-General and Mrs. Bruce, Herbert Fisher, St. Quentens (4), Master of Sidney and Mrs. Phelps, Rev. and Mrs. Girdlestone, Colonel Baker, Messrs. Burn, Bright, Blore, Clark, Leapingwell, Mathison, and sixty-seven friends of different members, who paid for their tickets 10s. 6d. each. Refreshments, tea, coffee, ices, &c., were provided by the 'Hoop,' and served by the servants of the members. The lavatory was made a ladies' cloak-room. The ordinary benches were removed from the daïs in the audience room, and their places supplied by settees covered with crimson baize. The room thus held 100 comfortably."

The Master of Trinity, Dr. William Whewell, did *not* come, but imagine his having been invited to meet His Royal Highness the Prince of Wales, the Master of Sidney, the Vice-Chancellor, and other "Heads," by that very society which had gradually developed itself out of the result of an unsatisfactory visit paid by an undergraduate, in his first year, to the Vice-Chancellor, in 1855, who would not sanction the proceedings of the unfortunate Box and Cox, *not* Fellows of Trinity.

The next entry after this is,—

" This day the extension of the stage was completed without any expense to the Club, the donation of £10 from H.R.H. the Prince of Wales being applied thereto, and the rest made up by the generosity of Mr. Hambro.

" Another committee meeting was held on May 17th, in Mr. Kirby's rooms, when

H.R.H. THE PRINCE OF WALES

was elected an honorary member of the Club. Also the following gentlemen :—

W. S. Sandes	Trin.
J. M. Wells	. . Trin.

were elected members.

"It was agreed that the performances should take place on Thursday, Friday and Saturday, the 23rd, 24th, 25th May, being first three days of the examinations for degrees."

I copy the above *verbatim*, but I have also seen the Prince's name at the head of a contemporary list as "Honorary President." At all events it is to his Royal Highness that the Club owes its open recognition by the highest university authorities.

CHAPTER XIX.

THE following is an extract from Mr. Kirby, the secretary's
notes :—

" THEATRICAL WEEK, MARCH 18, 19, 20, 21, 22, 1862.

" The ' A. D. C.' has passed through a severe trial, and
has triumphed. It has long been said that the Club depended
for its dramatic successes mainly on its founder, F. C.
Burnand, and old acting members, and that, should a time
come, as it must, when none of them could aid us, the Club
must inevitably fail to support its reputation. That these
opinions were unsound, has been amply shown by the present
performances. Not a single old member, except Mr. Preston,
took a part, and we did not fail. We may mention, however,
that the valuable assistance of Mr. J. Clarke, of the Strand
Theatre, was freely given, and in consequence the burlesque
was put on with more knowledge of the 'business' than the
actors generally show. A drop-scene by Calcott presented by
J. W. Clark, Trin. Coll., who became a member of the Club,
was greatly admired, and the lime-light introduced on our
stage for the first time increased the effect of *Zerlina's* bedroom scene considerably. The elections of new members have
introduced several good actors to the Club, who promise to
sustain its present reputation in after-years—a contrast to

some of our members who have never acted, sold tickets, or done anything to support the Club, except by subscribing one guinea, and occupying reserved seats at performances.

"In fine we have every reason to consider the Club in a state of peace and prosperity.

"The pieces played on this occasion were *On and Off, Poor Pillicoddy, Our Wife, Twice Killed, Fra Diavolo.*

ON AND OFF.

Mr. Peter Dunducketty . . .	Mr. W. EVERETT.
Mr. Chas. Langhton . . .	Mr. SAUMAREZ.
Mr. Alphonso de Pentonville . .	Mr. BIGWOOD.
Three Musicians	Messrs. HUMBERSTON, ACLAND, and ASHTON.
Letitia . . .	Mr. ARBUTHNOT.
Mrs. Muffit	Viscount POLLINGTON.
Servant	Viscount AMBERLEY.

"A slight but laughable farce—the interest of which was sustained throughout, Mr. W. Everett* playing with his usual vivacity. Mr. Saumarez wants more vigour in his style of playing—having been used to act female characters, he has not quite got over the mincing style he then employed with effect. Mr. Bigwood as *Alphonso* was in make-up inimitable, and his acting for the part good. He only wants a *little* more courage ; his part was a thorough success. The musicians were as good as any who earn a shilling a night on the London boards. *Letitia*—Arbuthnot—very successful, figure, dress, manner, and deportment all good. He will make an excellent first lady—one hint only—to speak a little louder. Viscount Pollington, as usual, thoroughly at home in his part, and played it with good spirit. He has improved immensely, simply from the great attention he pays to the *words* and *meaning* of the author.

" Son of the American Minister, and author of *On the Cam.*

POOR PILLICODDY.

Mr. Pillicoddy (*Nurseryman*)	.	Mr. Finch.
Capt. O'Scuttle . . .	. .	Mr. Aug. Guest.
Mrs. Pillicoddy . . .	.	Hon. C. Carington.
Mrs. O'Scuttle . . .	. .	Mr. Wells.
Sarah	. .	Viscount Pollington.

" Thoroughly successful and received with roars of laughter. Each actor had a part which suited him exactly. *Mr. Pillicoddy* is certainly one of Mr. Finch's happiest efforts. The jealous nurseryman contrasted well with *Capt. O'Scuttle.* Mr. Guest seldom shows that thorough knowledge of his part which a captious critic might require—in this, however, he was at home—the piece had been well rehearsed, which tended greatly to its success, though we think that Messrs. Finch and Guest between them, especially if aided by Mr. Carington, could carry off any farce to the satisfaction of our audiences. The latter gentleman was dressed with his usual good taste, and acted well—Lord Pollington also played the part of *Sarah* very well — the ' chambermaid' line is about his best, we think; he plays these characters with suitable vivacity, and attends to the *stage business* not the *audience*, a point in which so many might copy him. *Mrs. O'Scuttle* (Mr. Wells) was very fair, but still, as last term, shows some of that uneasiness which men acting women-characters often exhibit. He should also endeavour to *throw out* his voice more than he does.

OUR WIFE.

Marquis de Ligny . .	. .	Mr. Hope Grant.
Count de Brissac . .	. .	Hon. T. de Grey.
Pomaret . . .	. .	Mr. Preston.
Dumont . . .	.	Mr. Edwards.
First Officer .	. .	Mr. Acland.
Second Officer . .	. .	Mr. Longfield.
Messenger . . .	. .	Mr. Arbuthnot.
Rosine . - . .	. .	Hon. C. Carington.
Mariette . . .	. .	Mr. Sanderson.

" This piece was prepared at the request of Mr. Preston, who took the part of *Pomaret*.   As the stage manager had quite enough to do in preparing the four other pieces, and was not engaged in this, and as Mr. Preston was in town until the day before it was performed, the piece, though a regular two-act comedy, was only once rehearsed, and a miserable failure was the result.   Several of the actors did not know their parts at all.   The first Act was very fairly sustained, principally by Mr. Preston, who showed all his old vigour in acting, matured by several years of experience.   The second act was noticeable only for the exertions of Mr. Evans, our talented prompter, who sustained an animated mono-polylogue throughout. Hon. T. de Grey did not take the right view of the character of *Brissac*, he woefully overplayed it, making the poor Count seem a third-rate contortionist, rather than one of the ancient *noblesse*.   He has, however, clearly good powers, and a few lessons from some professional would make him a very effective actor.   We may add that Mr. Sanderson, unlike the rest, *did* know his part."

This hint as to the beneficial effect of a little professional coaching shows in what direction they were moving.   In the earlier days of the " A. D. C." such an idea would never have entered into our heads.   A professional would have overawed us, and our originality would have been " nipped in the bud."

I continue the Extract of Kirby:—

" A screaming farce was produced on the Saturday night.

TWICE KILLED.

Mr. Euclid Facile .	Mr. FINCH.
Mr. Ralph Reckless .	Mr. AUG. GUEST.
Tom	Mr. T. EDWARDS.
Mr. Holdfast .	Mr. SAUMANCEY.
Mr. Fergus Fable .	Mr. ARTHUR GUEST.
Robert	Viscount AMBERLEY.
Mrs. Facile .	Mr. SANDERSON.
Miss Julia Flighty	Mr. ARBUTHNOT.
Tawny Pepper	Viscount POLLINGTON.

"No one knew his part at all. Mr. Finch, whose character was that of a pedantic old fellow who carries a work on Hydrostatics about with him, very wisely carried a 'Lacy' instead. The others were not so fortunate. We watched it carefully, but could ascertain nothing from the progress of the piece, except that *Mr. Euclid Facile* thought that he had thrown *Reckless* out of the window (who was really hidden under the sofa). No other character but these two exhibited the least individuality. Still as the piece is one which depends mainly on the two low comedians, and leaves room for unlimited 'gag,' a luxury in which all largely indulged, it went very well. We must compliment the ladies in particular: Mr. Sanderson 'makes up' well, acts carefully, and promises to be a great acquisition to the Club, as does also Mr. Arbuthnot when he conquers his timidity, which, however, sat on him well. *Tom* seems a good actor, and deserved a better part."

Mr. Kirby was severe in his criticisms. When the members subsequently got hold of the book, and like the Admiral in the ballad of *Billy Taylor*, "came for to hear on it," they were not best pleased with the notices.

FRA DIAVOLO;
Or, THE BEAUTY AND THE BRIGANDS.

Lord Allcash	. . . . .	Mr. ARTHUR GUEST.
Fra Diavolo	. . . . .	A. DE ROTHSCHILD.
Matteo	. . . . .	Hon. T. DE GREY.
Lorenzo	. . . . .	Mr. AUG. GUEST.
Beppo } *Two Brigands* {		Mr. FINCH.
Giacomo } {		Mr. HOPE GRANT.
Francisco	. . . . .	Mr. BIGWOOD.
Antonio	. . . . .	Mr. ACLAND.
Zerlina	. . . . .	Hon. C. CARINGTON.
Lady Allcash	. . . .	Viscount POLLINGTON.

Carbineers, Villagers, Peasant Girls.

Here is the honest Secretary's opinion on this performance; he was evidently delighted at having secured the services of

"Johnny Clarke" as their professional coach. He seems to have succeeded in bringing the "supers" up to something above the usual happy-go-lucky-amateur super level.

"This burlesque owed its unqualified success to the exertions of Messrs Guest, Finch, &c., aided by Mr. J. Clarke of the Strand Theatre. This gentleman, who once played *Lorenzo* in the burlesque, came down three times, and gave his valuable assistance in rendering every song and every situation in the piece telling and effective. The scenery too, as superintended by Messrs. Powell and Howard, was far more magnificent than we have ever put on the stage. We never remember a better disciplined or more numerous body of ' supers.' The only objection to the burlesque that we have heard is, that it is deficient in plot. Besides which, if we remember that *Alonzo* has *two* distinct plots, we may argue that the Cambridge public is becoming hypercritical.

"The piece opened with a chorus of Carbineers, Messrs. Acland, Chapman, Humberston, Ashton, and Pullen, who were very well dressed by May—we may mention here that the supers in general knew when to come on, what to do when on the stage, and when to go off far better than usual. Mr. Guest acted the part of *Lorenzo* very well—we think it is his happiest character, except perhaps that of *Kilian*, in *The Seventh Shot*. His comic business in Scene 3, ' Lorenzo in a state of gin and water,' was particularly good, and showed that he had studied his own part carefully, as well as rehearsing the piece in general. His two songs were well received —' The Cork Leg,' and ' Nelly Gray '—the latter of which, though now out of date, was very funny, and the ' sensation tears ' was a capital bit of business. Both songs were encored nightly—Mr. Guest, though, is still not so perfect in the ' words' as he should be; he has also a bad habit of craning over the footlights, in order to see his audience, which throws his own face into the shade.

"The part of *Fra Diavolo*, generally so uninteresting (it

was played originally by Miss Swanborough), really became quite interesting in the hands of Mr. A. de Rothschild. He devoted great pains to dressing and rehearsing the words and songs, which, added to a natural talent for acting, a pleasing manner, and a good carriage on the stage, made his *début* perfectly successful. Though he has not a powerful voice, he sang well, and his song, ' I am a Simple Muleteer,' was encored. In fact, he was a most graceful Brigand, and thoroughly realized the character.

"*Matteo* (Hon. T. de Grey) slightly overacted his part. He promises well though, and has the stuff of a good actor in him ; all he wants is experience.

" *Beppo* (Mr. Finch), a most melodramatic scoundrel, was perfection in make-up and in acting. Some men act well by nature, others by careful study—he has clearly united both. The fight in Scene 2 was most cleverly done, and his duet with *Giacomo* took amazingly. ' It is hard to put the hand ' with appropriate action, being encored nightly. In all this he was ably supported by Mr. Hope Grant as *Giacomo*. All the scenes went so perfectly, that it was clear they had re-hearsed them long and carefully, a point which all amateurs should observe, as that only will or can make a scene ' go ' as it should.

" We were certainly surprised and pleased with Mr. Car-ington as *Zerlina*. We knew, of course, that he would make-up well, especially with Mr. Sutherland's aid, but we hardly thought he would prove as good in burlesque as he did last year in comedy, or, that he would so soon prove a worthy successor of Mr. F. Hudson. His songs were well sung, his acting neat, and seems always able to dispose of his hands— and in all his scenes, especially in Scene 3, that most difficult one, he was always at his ease—so very hard for a man in such a character to accomplish.

" Lord Pollington as *Lady Allcash* played with great animation. He made it one of the best characters in the piece. It was easy to see in his acting on this occasion what we have said before, that he always seems to have *thought over* the part more than the other actors, his actions and language being generally so appropriate. He was well supported by Mr. Arthur Guest, as *Lord Allcash,* who took the part at short notice, Mr. Currey being ill.

"*Francesco* (Mr. Bigwood) came on to be kicked off, and was kicked off accordingly. We hope to see him soon in a more important part, as his success in *On and Off* proves him an actor.

"*Antonio* (Mr Acland) played his unimportant part with skill and dexterity. From him we pass, by a very slight step, to the ' supers,' who were a good lot, upon the whole. Mr. Troyte gave valuable assistance on the stage. The changing of scenes is greatly impeded by the members who crowd on the stage during the performance. Some, it is true, offer assistance, but, as they are usually ignorant of the principles of the art of scene-shifting, they obstruct those whose business it is. Not only that, but members bring friends on the stage, even resident undergraduates. Surely it would be enough to show the *stage* after the performance instead of during it ? Visitors also flock into the dressing-room, often totally unacquainted with the actors, but brought by their friends to see what they can—a course which not only does away with scenic illusions, which it is our object to produce, but annoys the men who are dressing, several of whom have complained grievously about it. It is perhaps not too much to hope that members will prefer the good of the Club, and the wishes of some of its members, to the private pleasure of patronising a friend."

It is instructive to remark the eagerness of the uninitiated to take advantage of any opportunity of ' going behind the scenes,' even on the stage of an amateur club ; and the proud position of any one who had the *entrée.*

" The music was, upon the whole, better than usual. Sippel exerted himself greatly, thanks to Mr. Bigwood. The burlesque was improved by our hiring the original score copies from the Strand Theatre, while Mr. Charles led the choruses with great ability. Mr. T. Edwards deserves a corner to himself, he danced so well and so gracefully as to be encored every night, and his dance was not only the success of the scene, but one of the most admired points in the whole burlesque.

"At a committee meeting on May 11th,

C. A. Rycroft .	. . .	. Trin. Hall.
R. Heathcote	. . . .	. Trin. Coll.

were elected members of the Club.

"At the ordinary general meeting of the Club, held in the Rooms on June, 1862, the following gentlemen were duly elected by the Club to serve on the committee for the October Term :—

W. A. Bankes .	. Trin. Hall	.	President.
Hon. C. Carington	. Trin. .	. .	Stage-Manager.
G. Howard .	. . Trin.	.	Superintendent of Scenery.
T. F. Kirby .	. Trin. .	. .	Treasurer and Secretary.
E. H. Wynne .	. . Trin.	.	Prompter.
A. de Rothschild	. Trin. .	. .	Orchestra-Manager.
C. A. W. Troyte	. . Trin.	.	Director of Machinery.
W. Æ. Currey .	. Trin. .	. .	Assistant Stage-Manager."

Nothing could please the old members more than the continued prosperity of a Club for which, in their time, they had worked so hard, and to which they have all been so warmly attached.

The secretaries who have kept the annals, have recorded with what regret they have said farewell to the " old book," and strong bonds of good-fellowship still unite those, who, now separated from one another by the various duties of life, can look back to their earlier time, when, in their little world, they all put their shoulders to the same wheel, and went at it heart and soul.

CHAPTER XX.

AFTER this gratifying independent success, the Club commenced its eighth year by resting for a May Term,—which we never did, as we preferred one performance to none at all,—and the Secretary makes the following remarks and *résumé:*—

"This Term was so short that no performance could be given. A performance in the May Term is at best a losing concern, and would have been particularly so upon this occasion, as the degree examination succeeded the boat-races immediately.

" There were ten nights of performance in the year 1861-62, for which 1116 tickets were sold, producing an average audience of 111·6 per night. For the previous year, 1860-61, 1183 tickets were sold for eighteen nights, an average of 91 per night; but if we deduct as exceptional the three performances given in May 1861, it appears that the average in 1860-61 was only 100·5.

" Thus the audience have increased in the year by an average of 11·1 per night.

" The following persons not being members of the University have usually been invited to one performance by the Club:—

Mr. Metcalfe, our Printer, giver of " The Cambridge Memorials."
Mr. Hoppett, Marker at Trinity College.
Mr. Ekin, our Landlord.
Sergt.-Major Cox,* of the the University Volunteers.
Mr. Bulstrode, our Upholder, Carpenter, &c.
Mr. Todd, his managing Clerk.

---

* I am so glad to observe this name historic in the annals of the A. D. C. (*vide* Chapter I.—*The First Step*). But what has become of Box? Has he deserted? And where is General Bouncer?

" Tho tutors and deans of Trinity College are always invited, and Mr. Mathison, senior tutor, has the *entrée* to all the performances, in return for his kinduess to the Club on several occasions.

"Thos. T. Kirby, *Sec.*"

* * * * *

"About this time a new glass chandelier was presented to the Club by Messrs. Bankes and Troyte. A clock for the dressing-room, new fitted up, was given by Hon. C. Carington, stage-manager."

* * * * *

" Messrs. Bankes, Troyte, and Patrick deserve the thanks of the Club for their beautiful present of a book for containing photographs, in which members are invited to place their ' cartes de visite.' "

The Club at the commencement of its eighth year was amassing treasure. The library was growing, and the writing accommodation at this time really astonished me, when I remembered how difficult it was in our primitive days to get anything to write on, whether note-paper or table, and anything to write with, in the rooms which served us for stage, auditorium, green-room, dressing-room, and all. *On a changé tout cela.*

But the idea of the tutors and deans being always invited, and the senior tutor having the right conferred on him by the Club to wander at his own sweet will behind the scenes, all over the Club, just wherever he choose,—how gratifying this to the old original members, who met in fear and secrecy, who kept hidden the true meaning of the mystic initials " A. D. C.," and who had scouts placed, and a ladder ready for escape over the roof of the adjoining brewery ! At last the Club was recognized, and in those primitive days it was recognition that we carefully avoided.

By the request of H.R.H. the Prince of Wales, on this occasion a performance was given to which ladies were admitted, similar to, but even more successful than, that of March 2nd. The pieces performed were—

Used Up, Alonzo the Brave, and *To Paris and Back.*

All of which were well received. The hits in the burlesque all made as well as they had done on the ordinary nights, which was considered a great triumph. The room was crowded, but not to excess; we might have sold fifty more tickets had we been inclined to do so. The performances commenced at 7.30 and concluded by 11.30. The company, however, were not all clear of the rooms until twelve o'clock. Refreshments were provided by Miss Palmer and Litchfield. The Club invited the following guests :—

> Duke of Leeds, Lord and Ladies Osborne (3).
> Earl of Hardwicke and Countess, Lady Agnes Gorst.
> Mr. and Lady E. Adeane.
> Mr., Mrs., and Miss Portman.
> Mr., Mrs., and Miss St. Quentens.
> Mr. and Mrs. G. Newton (of Croxton).
> Mr. and Mrs. Newton (of The Downs).
> Mr., Mrs., and Miss Daynell.
> Lady Affleck and party (3).
> Master of Magdalene, Mrs. Neville and party (3).
> Provost of King's and Miss Okes (2).
> Master of Sidney and Mrs. Phelps.
> Professor Kingsley and Mrs. Kingsley.
> Colonel and Mrs. Baker.
> Mr. and Mrs. Girdlestone.
> Mr., Mrs., and Miss Pemberton (of Newton).
> Mr. Pemberton (of Trumpington).
> Mr. Birbeck and the Greek Professor.
> Messrs. Blue, Burn, Bright, Clark, W. G. Gunson, Mathison.
> Mr. G. Sutherland (who painted the drop).

And seventy-eight friends of members were paid for. The seats were arranged very well by Mr. Hambro, and the company, we have reason to believe, were generally pleased with all the arrangements. H.R.H. the Prince of Wales arrived punctually with his suite.

THE "TIMES," *June 4th,* 1864.

"After a few hours of much needed rest last evening, their Royal Highnesses the Prince and Princess of Wales, and the Duke of Cambridge, honoured the Vice-Chancellor and Mrs. Cookson with their company at dinner in the hall of St. Peter's College. At half-past eight the royal visitors proceeded to the small private theatre in Jesus Lane, belonging to the Cambridge Amateur Dramatic Club, more generally, however, known by the abbreviated name of 'A. D. C.' The building itself is calculated to contain about 100 visitors; and as considerably more than that number obtained tickets of admission, the result was rather a packed audience. The performances consisted of the burlesque of *Aladdin, or the Wonderful Scamp*, and *Whitebait at Greenwich.* The talent displayed by the gentlemen forming the Club, and who took part in the performance, seemed to be highly appreciated by the select audience; and the Prince and Princess of Wales, with the Duke of Cambridge, were evidently as much delighted as the other visitors, for their royal highnesses remained during the performance of both pieces. A remarkable proof of the effects of perseverance under difficulties is shown by the present position of this Club. When founded it was necessary to have performances almost by stealth, in order to avoid the hostility of the proctors; but it has flourished, notwithstanding, under the protecting care of its founder, Mr. Burnand, and rejoices in having the Prince of Wales as hon. president."

THE "STANDARD," *June 4th.*

"At a few minutes before nine, the royal visitors, attended by their suite, went to the little theatre belonging to the Amateur Dramatic Club. This Club owns the 'Hoop Inn,' and has a room in it fitted up with a stage and scenery, a pit in front, and over all a gallery. The seats for the royal party were right under the face of the gallery, the front of which, as well as other parts of the room, were draped with the flags of the various colleges; and the orchestra was occupied by some members of the rifle band. The curtain rose to a well-filled house on the farce of *Whitebait at Greenwich*, wherein every one of the actors did so uncommonly well that it would be invidious to name any of them. The house was in roars all the time the farce lasted, and at its close the applause was unanimous, the Prince and the Duke of Cambridge expressing as loudly as anyone their satisfaction, the latter none the less that several. allusions in the piece to the commander-in-chief were pointed by the laughter of the audience.

" The second piece was Mr. Byron's burlesque, *Aladdin, or the Wonderful Scamp;* and here, as in the last piece, the female characters were sustained by young undergrads in such a way as left nothing to be desired, save, perhaps, a little slenderness in the ankles. The acting was so thoroughly good that the actors deserve to have their names in print. The following was the cast :—

The Sultan	Mr. FINCH.
The Vizier	Mr. C. HALL.
Pekoe	Hon. A. STRUTT.
Aladdin	Hon. C. CARINGTON.
Abanazar	Mr. F. C. BURNAND.
Te-to-tum	Mr. MICHELE.
The Slave of the Lamp . . .	Mr. BUCHANAN.
The Genius of the Ring . . .	Mr. FLOWER.
The Widow Twankey . . .	Mr. TWISS.
Princess Badroulboudour . .	Mr. SEYMOUR.

Maidens, mandarins, and the rest of the Chinese population by Messrs. Pellow, Tottenham, Swaine, France, Newman, Denman, Powlett, Lowry-Corry, Stevenson, Usborne, Macnaghten, Hood, and Willes.

" The scenery was admirably managed, and one scene in particular, showing the cave where the rubies and diamonds grew, was superb. The dresses were rich, and indeed everything was beyond criticism. It was emphatically. the best amateur performance we ever attended, and it reflected the utmost credit upon the president of the club, the Hon. A. Strutt, and upon the stage manager, Mr. Williamson."

"DAILY TELEGRAPH," *June 4th.*

"Who or what may be meant by the 'A. D. C.?' is possibly a question outside Cambridge; but there is no prevailing ignorance on the subject within the university. Everybody here knows that the company of amateur histrionics who last evening had the honour of entertaining the Prince and Princess of Wales, the Duke of Cambridge, and nearly three hundred ladies and gentlemen beside, were formed seven years ago by Mr. F. C. Burnand; that for a time the little troop played with closed doors, and in the fear of proctors; that they have now for their honorary president the Prince of Wales himself, whose name on the list of members, by-the-by, appears among the W's somewhat in this fashion,—Watson, Adolphus; Wales, Prince of; Walker, John: and that, in short, there is no sounder institution connected with the University of Cambridge than the 'A. D. C.' or Amateur Dramatic Company, whose performance on the occasion of the royal visit was a notable point of the entire programme. The members of the 'A. D. C.' speak of their old room, or theatre, as a small one, and it must have been very small indeed if by comparison they consider their present quarters large. The rooms which they now tenant once formed part of the 'Hoop Hotel,' from which they have been cut off. They were, in fact, the old Union Rooms; then they were turned into billiard rooms; and then they were taken in hand by the 'A. D. C.' who have made them what they are. And what they really are can only be known by those who saw them filled by such a company as that of last night. The auditorium is a square chamber, with a gallery at the back. The ground space between this gallery and the stage is occupied by four rows of chairs—no more : but there are several other rows at the back. The royal visitors last evening sat in the row just in front of the gallery. In a line with them were the Duke of Devonshire, the Duke and Duchess of Manchester, Lady Spencer, and Lady Morton. During the performance, which was relished exceedingly, the Prince recognized and shook hands with several old friends, and much hilarity was caused by frequent mention of the 'Commander-in-Chief,' on the part of one Glimmer, in the farce, who has continual business to transact with the Commander-in-Chief, and who opines that there are many things which cannot be done in a day—the Commander-in-Chief being one of them. Turning to the Duke of Cambridge, the Prince was heard to say—or else rumour was mistaken in the syllables—'You're catching ˙it.' The lady characters were played in a gentlemanly way; and it must have been remarked by nearly all present, that Mr. Seymour, who enacted the Princess Badroulboudour, looked wonderfully like his sister, Lady Spencer. The following is a copy of the programme, which was emblazoned on white satin, with a gold fringe, for the use of the royal party :—

"On Thursday evening, June 2, 1864, will be presented the screaming farce, by T. Maddison Morton, Esq., entitled *Whitebait at Greenwich.* 'John Small,' Mr. Twiss ; 'Mr. Buzzard,' Mr..Finch ; 'Mr. Glimmer,' Mr. C. Hall ; 'Lucretia Buzzard,' Mr. Pulleine ; 'Sally,' Mr. Flower. To conclude with a burlesque extravaganza, by H. J. Byron, Esq., entitled, *Aladdin ; or, The Wonderful Scamp.* 'The Sultan,' Mr. Finch ; 'The Vizier,' Mr. C. Hall ; 'Pekoe,' Hon. A. Strutt ; 'Aladdin,' Hon. C. Carington ; 'Abanazar' (a magician), Mr. F. C. Burnand ; 'Te-to-tum' (an attendant), Mr. de Michele ; 'The Slave of the Lamp,' Mr. Buchanan ; 'The Genius of the Ring,' Mr. Flower ; 'The Widow Twankay' (Aladdin's mother), Mr. Twiss ; 'Princess Badroulboudour,' Mr. Seymour. Maidens, mandarins, and the rest of the Chinese population, Messrs. Pellew, Tottenham, Swaine, France, Newman, Denman, Lowry-Corry, Stevenson, Usborne, Macnaghten, Hood, and Willes."

"The dons, who, with the single exception of the most unpopular man among them, countenance the pleasing labours of the 'A. D. C.,' are surely taking a sensible course, for there can be no more decided or mischievous folly than a systematic opposition to harmless amusements, in college, or anywhere else soever."

By this time I had become a member of the Dramatic Authors' Society, and the *argumentum ad pocketum* weighed as cogently with me as with the "Elder Brethren" at the office in King Street, Covent Garden, who now began to inquire into the nature of the performances at the "A. D. C.," Cambridge.

It was decided by the D. A. S. that the "A. D. C." was "in a parlous state," and I was deputed to act as intermediary between the two secretaries representing the two societies. Here is the result—

"The Dramatic Authors' Society" wrote through their secretary, J. Stirling Coyne, Esq., to F. C. Burnand, thus—

> "DRAMATIC AUTHORS' SOCIETY,
> "23, KING STREET, COVENT GARDEN, W.C.
> "*January 14th*, 1862.

"MY DEAR BURNAND,

"The Committee of this Society perceive that the Cambridge University A. D. C. have been (inadvertently I am sure) infringing on the rights of the Dramatic Authors by playing their pieces without permission or payment of the usual fee—viz., 10s. for each representation of a piece belonging to any of our authors—I have taken some pains to learn how these performances are conducted, and have no doubt that they come under the Act 3 & 4 Will. IV. cap. 15, and that we could recover penalties from the amateurs. We prefer, however, an amicable arrangement. I therefore write to you for the purpose of requesting you to make known to the society of the A. D. C. the claims of this society."

"Upon referring to the Act aforesaid, it appeared that we were clearly liable. The words "any place of dramatic entertainment" being most comprehensive. Some correspondence took place, and the secretary had an interview with Mr. Stirling Coyne, at 28, King Street, Covent Garden, ending in an agreement to pay the sum demanded. Montagu Williams, Esq., a member of the Dramatic Authors' Committee, wrote in the most handsome way giving us leave to play any of his pieces without charge."

A general meeting was held in the Rooms on February 14th. Mr. P. S. Trict was unanimously elected assistant stage-manager.

> Resolved—"*That the subscription for the Term be raised to £1 10s. to meet the unexpected claim of the Dramatic Authors' Society.*".

At a Committee meeting previously held in Mr. Powell's rooms,

F. C. B. Acland	Trin. Coll.
E. W. Chapman	do.
J. H. Humberston	Magd. Coll.
W. A. Longfield	Trin. Coll.
Lord Amberley . . .	.do.
E. A. Catt	do.
Hon. A. Strutt . . .	do.

were elected members of the "A. D. C."

CHAPTER XXI.

My last appearance, but one, on these boards. Here, too, ceases almost entirely the record of the acting. If another has been kept since, I have not seen it, and if it exists I leave to other hands its publication. *Aladdin* was as big a success as *Alonzo* had been. The difference in the style of the two burlesques—the latter being the outcome of the Robsonian tradition, and the former the child of what was then the new Strand company, with their dash-away, sparkling, dancing fashion—marks an era.

The "A.D.C." had poor little Johnny Clarke to coach them. Of this "coaching" I most thoroughly disapproved. The result, in my opinion, was not one whit more satisfactory than the form of *Alonzo, Villikins, Lord Lovel, Seventh Shot, Fair Maid of Wapping, Turkish Waters, Blue Beard*, or *Bombastes*, when we trusted to ourselves for stage management and for acting. To employ "a coach" seems to me to be a lazy proceeding, injurious to originality, both of conception and practical illustration. That lectures on the dramatic art giving general principles, with illustrations by historic examples, would be an excellent thing, I am the first to admit, and I would be among the first to propose and to assist in furthering such a scheme at the University; but that intelligent, well-educated young men should be made into mere puppets, repeating what perhaps a second-rate actor, or even a fair actor of limited resources, would tell them at secondhand, himself only copying originals, is a system that should at once be discouraged.

Let pupils in the dramatic school note the general principles of the art, and then apply them to particular instances. Let them study the character they have to portray, master it thoroughly, and then decide to the best of their ability how such a character would behave in certain given circumstances. Dramatic cause and effect would then be reasoned out, and fixed on a sure basis.

As a rule, the ordinary professional actor would be unable to give you the reason why he made an effect which, in ninety-eight cases out of a hundred, would not be original but traditional.

Unfortunately for the stage, the dramatic art has come to be considered as something that any one can acquire in any haphazard, rough-and-tumble way. It is called a " self-educating profession," and, judging by the slip-slop pronunciation, the poor elocution, the frequent absence of aspirates, the self-conscious attitudes, and the awkward bearing of so many, it is evident the theatrical profession, left to itself for education, is a very indifferent, if not an absolutely bad, school.

But to return to these performances of October Term, 1862.

PERFORMANCES NOV. 25TH, 26TH, 27TH, 28TH, 29TH.

" The performances, as usual in this Term, were very successful, and were remarkably so on this occasion, from the unrivalled ' cast ' which the stage manager was able to make of every piece.

" The following pieces were acted—

> *Samuel in Search of Himself,*
> *A Practical Man,*
> *Whitebait at Greenwich,*
> *Box and Cox,*
> *Aladdin (Burlesque).*

· "It is a curious proof of the excellence of the acting, that the house, which was thinner than usual on the Tuesday and Wednesday, was, on the latter nights, crowded to excess. The attendance on Friday night must have recalled to old members present the memorable performance of *Faust* in 1859, when thirty visitors never got past the door. The fiction of ' reserved seats ' can hardly have retained its credit.

"It is not to be wondered at that the room was so full, when we think of the attractions which the very names of Burnand, Finch, Twiss, and Weguelin have for the rising generation. But the acting on this occasion was not like that which we see in country theatres, which we *have* seen on our own stage in past times, when two or three ' stars' from London are feebly supported by the local talent : on the contrary, the acting of the resident members (though not such practised hands as our London friends) in spirit and evidence of careful study and innate power, fully equalled that of the older members. This is due to the care of the stage manager and his assistant Lord Pollington,, and to the rehearsal with Mr. J. Clarke, of the R. S. T., whose services were secured to ' coach ' the burlesque."

The fact is, they were allowing the office and work of a stage manager—or, as we used to call it, acting manager, meaning "manager of acting"—to become a mere sinecure.
· There is no more interesting department of dramatic art than that of stage manager.

The stage manager should be a host in himself; not a great actor, but the cause of great acting in others. He should be discriminating, appreciative, patient, forbearing, clear-sighted, cool, courteous, determined. What should be his qualifications can be best arrived at by an inquiry into his duties. Let us suppose the piece chosen independently of the stage manager.

The author should first of all read his piece to the stage manager, who should then master as many of the important points as might be necessary to guide him in his own private perusal, which would immediately follow the author's own reading.

The stage manager having studied the piece carefully, should then return to the author with his list of queries, objections, and suggestions for the consideration of the author, who might be less a practical dramatist than a good writer of poetic or prose dialogue.

A consultation ensues between stage manager and author. Dates are correctly ascertained, period of costumes settled, &c., &c., the speeches are curtailed, the entrances and exits are arranged, probabilities are discussed, and the best effects are in a fair way of being obtained.

Again the stage manager retires with it to his study, where he gradually masters the piece in the rough, makes his ground-plan of scenes, and then calls in the scenic artist alone, then with him the costumier, and these three should argue the effects of colour combination ; the stage manager's being, as it were, the casting vote, *pro tem.*, until at their next meeting, when the artist brings his perfect stage models (to scale) of all the scenery, and the costumier his characters of the piece (also to scale) coloured, the final decision can be arrived at.

The stage manager now knows what is to be done with the *mise-en-scène* of the piece on the stage.

He next sets to work with models and figures to play his game of chess, scene by scene, act by act, until he knows every movement of every character, and is prepared, without the slightest hesitation, to give a good and sufficient reason for every movement or change of position.

Then comes the consideration of properties, and here the scenic artist is again called in to deliberate. I assume throughout that authorities are consulted. Then, lastly, the *chef d'orchestre* is summoned, and he is consulted in his department by the stage manager, on whom the ultimate responsibility in all cases must rest.

Then the piece is ready for the stage, scene by scene. No time is lost by the actors in finding out where they come in, or what they are doing, or why they do it. They are at once told, and all they have to do is to hear, obey, and remember. The stage manager's command must not be disputed for a moment. Implicit obedience must be yielded to him by all the *troupe* from the highest to the lowest.

Suppose an act rehearsed in this way three times, and all having come nearly perfect in their words, are now perfect in their words and ordinary situations, the next step will be for the stage manager to invite the criticism of the principals on his work. This leads to conversations, to suggestions, and to trying and re-trying of effects, until the final decision is either for what the stage manager had originally designed, or for something much better; but, in any case, the casting vote is in his hands, the responsibility is on his shoulders, and in all probability, under these conditions, the very best result is pretty sure to be obtained.

Finally, when the stage manager's eye is accustomed to the piece as a whole, and the actors are thoroughly at home in their parts, then, for the last rehearsals, he must call in the author to stamp the result with his approval.

The author and stage manager may here differ, and the actors' opinions may be divided. Of two ways, when there are admittedly more than one of doing the same thing, let both be tried, and let the better survive. The author seeing his work before him for the first time, may make some invaluable suggestion, arising out of the novel effect, that may solve a doubtful or a difficult point: but as a rule, he will bow to the judgment of a skilful, well-trained, and experienced stage manager.

To my thinking, the stage manager should be the best man in the theatre. He should *never* be the manager, nor an actor in the company. His one duty should be to stage manage, and he should be exempt from ever being called upon to act. There should be an assistant stage manager to relieve him of some of his work at night, and to help him, where crowds have to be rehearsed during the day.

The stage manager should possess the power of " showing" practically, by a mere sketch, what the action he requires ought to be—a mere outline which the actor, whether of exceptional creative genius, or of ordinary dramatic talents with executive power, should be able to use as the design for the picture which it is *his* art to elaborate and carefully finish.

There are heaven-born editors and heaven-born statesmen, but I have never yet come across a heaven-born stage manager. Charles Dickens had this reputation, but he had few opportunities of showing us what he could do, and I believe him to have been too good an actor ever to have been excellent as a stage manager.

The actor who is also stage manager neglects the whole for the part, and the part is generally his own.

The manager-actor who is his own stage manager is guided unconsciously by the principle of *omne ignotum pro magnifico*—and again, the *magnifico* in question is himself.

If at the "A. D. C." one good piece were fixed two terms in advance, and studied, on the above lines, by their stage manager, the Club would soon be an invaluable school of art for painting, antiquities, music, and drama.

The Secretary's record for this term continues thus :—

A PRACTICAL MAN.

Cloudesley	Mr. BURNAND.
Horton (*a Merchant*) . . .	Mr. CHAPMAN.
Rockstone (*a Solicitor*) . . .	Hon. A. STRUTT.
Jennings } *Clerks* . .	{ Mr. HEATHCOTE.
Biggs }	{ Mr. PULLEINE.
Mrs. Mildmay	Mr. BUCHANAN.

"We always thought *Cloudesley* Mr. Burnand's best character ; he never acted better in it than on this occasion. He was the life of the piece throughout, and all his ' business,' the ' Andneto at Banco' of the Italian 'bus cad, &c., went swimmingly.

" Chapman played *Horton* quietly and well, and with a well-assumed voice. He made up as a middle-aged, well-to-do merchant.

" *Rockstone*, a tedious ' feeding ' part throughout, was well played by Hon. A. Strutt, at short notice. He acted it conscientiously, not attempting to get a ' bit of fat ' for himself, but simply playing up to *Cloudesley*.

" Mr. Heathcote suffered from timidity, and had hardly time in his short part to recover from it.

" Mr. Pulleine made the most of so small a part as that of *Biggs*.

" Mr. Buchanan as *Mrs. Mildmay* was too inclined to laugh for so romantic an elderly female as that lady. But we expect much of Mr. Buchanan in future performances.

WHITEBAIT AT GREENWICH.

" Though this piece was performed here in March, 1859, with Messrs. Twiss and Weguelin in the same characters as now, yet much cannot be gathered from Mr. Hamilton's somewhat fragmentary critique on page 51 of this book.

Mr. Benjamin Buzzard . . .	Mr. FINCH.
Mr. Glimmer	Mr. WEGUELIN.
John Small	Mr. TWISS.
Miss Lucretia Buzzard . . .	Lord POLLINGTON.
Sally	Hon. C. CARINGTON.

" Mr. Finch had a part which allowed full play to his comic humour.

" Mr. Weguelin played, as he usually does, with great spirit, and was as successful in the character now as on the former occasion of its production here.

" The same remark may be applied to *John Small*. It is one of the characters which first established his reputation on our stage.

" Lord Pollington made one of his greatest ' hits ' in the character of *Miss Buzzard*.

" The comically pathetic part of *Sally* was rendered with great effect by Hon. C. Carington.

BOX AND COX.

" This perennial Romance of Real Life, as it is touchingly styled by its author, Maddison Morton, was very successful. The characters were :—

Box	Mr. Q. Twiss.
Cox	Mr. Finch.
Mrs. Bouncer	Lord Amberley.

To *Box and Cox* no greater praise can be given than to say that each knew his part so well that they sat down, got up, came in and went out, as the journeymen hatters and printers of ordinary life may be supposed to do. The tossing (" where's my lucky sixpence ?") and the throwing of dice took well with the audience.

" Lord Amberley as *Mrs. Bouncer* might have acted the part with a little more fussiness and vivacity; and he errs, like almost all our young actors, in not speaking loud enough, —but considering this was his *début* in a speaking part, he succeeded very well, and we hope to see him establish a reputation in characters of this kind.

ALADDIN

Is certainly one of Byron's best burlesques. It is a curious fact that it was reproduced at the Strand Theatre on the 25th, the first day of our performance here. Our cast was a strong one throughout.

The Sultan . . .	Mr. Finch.
The Vizier . . .	Lord Pollington.
Pekoe	Mr. Hope Grant.
Aladdin	Hon. C. Carington.
Abanazar . . .	Mr. F. C. Burnand.
Te-to-tum . . .	Mr. Blake Humphrey.
The Slave of the Lamp . . .	Mr. Buchanan.
The Genius of the Ring . . .	Mr. Chapman.
The Widow Twankay . . .	Mr. Twiss.
Princess Badroulboudour . . .	Hon. A. Strutt.

" Mr. Finch, we need hardly say, was successful as the *Sultan*. He dressed it well, and throughout preserved that strong contrast to the *Vizier* which is so necessary to the success of his scenes. His dance at the end of the concluding trio of Scene 1 was encored nightly, and certainly was a fine bit of Terpsichorean display. Lovers of the Park Street ' Thalia,' will no doubt remember the *furore* which his dance as *Beppo* in *Fra Diavolo* created last March (1862).

"Lord Pollington as the *Vizier* was also a most satisfactory specimen of genuine acting. We are always glad to be able to compliment him on a success, from the conviction which we entertain that all his acting is the result of careful study, and that, unlike, alas ! many others, he never comes on the boards without a thorough and usually correct conception of his character.

" Mr. Grant as *Pekoe*, is rather an instance to the contrary. Possessed of great personal advantages, he yet seldom learns his part sufficiently, the result being that he does not seem quite at home on the stage. On this occasion, however, much could not be expected, as he was reading for his degree.

" *Aladdin*—Hon. C. Carington—was decidedly a very ' great success.' He looked the character all over. The careless young scapegrace, ' chivying his mamma about the stairs,' according to the widow's complaint, seemed a child of mischief, and quite realized the character. His natural and unaffected way of acting is highly to be commended. All his songs and dances took tremendously.

" The heavy and thankless part of ' *Abanazar* ' was played well by Mr. Burnand. We can hardly venture to comment on the style of so finished an actor as he undoubtedly is. *Abanazar* labours under the disadvantage of appearing very early in the piece—while his best scene is the last, in which the actor is usually too tired to do his best. He made the most of his part though throughout—his soliloquies, which ordinarily are somewhat tedious, were improved by a dexterous imitation of certain personages of note, such as Frikell. We can hardly say of him as Pope said of Macklin, ' This is the Jew, that Shakespeare drew ; ' but he was a good imitation of an ancient member of that once persecuted, but now popular race. His ' Cachucha,' in the poisoning scene, went famously, and was always applauded.

" *Widow Twankay*—Twiss—needs hardly any comment, as he has been uniformly successful in every character attempted by him on our stage. His voice, perhaps, was never in better order—and he was happily induced to sing the parody on ' My own, my guiding Star ' — which Mr. James Rogers always omits — a capital song, notwithstanding.

" Mr. Buchanan made his *début* as *Slave of the Lamp*. He was well dressed for the character, and spoke out distinctly and well.

" Mr. Chapman, as *Genius of the Ring*, was at first rather fidgety, and overacted his part. Dressed at first as a harlequin, a costume that hardly suited his brawny shoulders and breadth, after three nights' performance he came on as a prize-fighter. The anachronism of a prize-fighter appearing in a Chinese Palace perhaps injured the romance of a fairy tale like that of ' Aladdin '—but Mr. Chapman, perhaps from feeling more at home in the new costume, toned down his gesticulations, and made the part (a very difficult one) successful.

" *Te-to-tum* — Mr. Blake Humfrey — made his salaam nightly in a way that the most rigid of Mussulmen might envy.

" Hon. A. Strutt made his *début* on our stage as *Princess Badroulboudour*. He sang well, danced well, and spoke his words with unaffected ease, and, thanks to Clarkson, seemed a worthy object of *Aladdin's* somewhat hasty courtship.

" The Chorus went well enough, thanks to Pulleine in front of the scenes and Charles behind them.

" For the Scenery.—To this Messrs. Banks, Howard, Clark, Patrick, and Troyte had directed their united efforts. The ' North Western Gate of Pekin,' by Mr. Howard, was admired, and the cave by Mr. Clark was a *chef d'œuvre*. The novelty of the ' Willow Pattern ' as a background to the hall in the Emperor's Palace was remarked by all spectators ; and the sudden disappearance of the Palace in Scene 6 was well arranged by the mechanical skill of Mr. Troyte. The blank desolation of the ' Desert of Sahara,' as seen in the last scene, was depicted by the fertile pencil of our Superintendent of Scenery, Mr. Howard.

" In conclusion, the Club may, we think, congratulate itself upon a very successful performance. The acting was good throughout, and there was no breaks-down. There were few rehearsals ; indeed, many could not be had, from the absence of the chief actors ; but all went 'merry as a marriage bell ' from the first night until the fall of the curtain on Saturday. We atoned for our failures on the first night last March by a very scanty audience on Tuesday and Wednesday, while on Thursday and Friday more were in the house than have ever been before—showing the real merits of the pieces chosen most decisively. The expenses, however, increase each term ; and unless the present high character of the performances is maintained, unless actors are carefully selected, and pains taken by all engaged, the Club will some day collapse by its own weight. May that day be distant ! "

I give one more extract as to " Another Ladies' Night."—

" THE LADIES' NIGHT.

" Saturday, November 29th, 1862.

" The Ladies' Night seems to have become an established fact in every week of performance. We are sure that its arrival is looked forward to with some anxiety by many people in and around Cambridge. The arrangements under the supervision of Mr. Bankes, were exactly as they have hitherto been. Of those who received invitations from the Club, the following were present :—

Earl and Countess of Hardwicke and Lady Agneta Yorke.
Mr., Mrs. and Miss Wyndham Portman.
Mr., Mrs. and Misses (2) St. Quentens.
Mr., Mrs. and Miss Pemberton.
Mr. and Mrs. Townley.
Mr. and Mrs. Charles Townley.
Master of Magdalene and Mrs. Neville.
Provost of King's College and Misses (3) Okes.
Mr. and Mrs. Charles Webster.
Master of Sidney and Mrs. Phelps, Miss Phelps, and
    Miss Amy Thomas.
The Registrar and Mrs. Luard.
Colonel and Mrs. Baker.
Mr. and Mrs. Brooks Bumpstead.
Mr. and Mrs. Girdlestone.
Mr. and Mrs. Leapingwell.
Professor Birbeck.
Professor Thompson.
The Public Orator.
Professor Liveing.
Mr. Stephen.
Mr. T. P. Hudson ;

besides friends of members : the number of the audience being about 100.

"The room was not overcrowded, and general satisfaction was expressed by the visitors on leaving."

It is to be noted how strongly the artists had come out in the scenery. Alas! poor Jones! His name had vanished from the bills, and most of his scenes had been painted out.

CHAPTER XXII.

Extract from Annals, signed by Secretary Kirby :—

" The performances commenced this term on March 11th, and were continued on three following nights. The pieces performed were—

> *Ici on parle Français.*
> *The Pacha of Pimlico.*
> *A Turkish Bath.*
> *Romeo and Juliet (Travestie).*

" As in the corresponding term of 1862, all the parts, with one exception, were filled by native talent ; while, however, last year, the piece in which the talented Richard Preston appeared came to an unparalleled grief, on this occasion Mr. Arthur Guest, our sole visitor, gave great strength to the burlesque by his delineation of the apothecary. It is always satisfactory in one sense to have no old members down, as in these cases many new members come into notice, who might otherwise, as 'supers,' have 'wasted their sweetness on the desert air.' "

This seems a very natural observation. But the effect of the visits of the old members was to " let the performances down easy," and had contributed largely to the permanent success of the Club.

In proof of the demand creating the supply, I quote the following from the criticisms :—

" *Mr. Oliffe*, on the second night, read his part at six

hours' notice. We can say no more. On the two following nights his acting was extremely good; though his voice was not powerful, he made it tell, and, in fact, gave success to two or three trios and duets, which fell flat on the first night, when Mr. Carrington could not sing. But what we admired particularly is his extremely unaffected style of acting; he made such a very *lady-like Juliet*. We do not mind saying that his business of reading the ' supper ' and fainting off on the sofa, though simplicity itself, was the best bit of lady acting we have seen since F. C. Wilson's days."

The Club has never yet failed in this respect, but latterly adaptations of popular plays have been so ingeniously contrived as to omit the female characters. Mr. J. W. Clark, Fellow of Trinity, did a version of *Le Courrier de Lyon*, in which the *dramatis personæ* were men only. The only perfectly pardonable liberty of this sort that I ever took, was with *Mrs. Bouncer* in *Box and Cox*, whom I elevated to the ranks as Sergeant Bouncer. Had the piece been French, she might have been transformed into a vivandière, as Mdlle. Bouncer, *La Fille du Régiment*.

"*At a Committee meeting in Hon. C. Carington's rooms on April 26th, the following gentlemen were duly elected members of the Society*—

Mr. — Williamson	Jesus College
Mr. P. Candy	Magd. Coll.

" *The general meeting took place on April 27th.*

"Hon. C. Carington resigned his office of Stage Manager.

" A. Patrick, that of Superintendent of Scenery.

'· Mr. Pulleine was elected Stage Manager.

" Hon. A. Strutt was elected Assistant Stage Manager.

" The office of Orchestra Manager, thereby vacated, was filled by election of Mr. Oliffe.

" Mr. Troyte was elected to his old office of Superintendent of Scenery upon his return to College.

"Mr. Everett then addressed the meeting and moved—

"' *That the Critique Book, as kept by the Secretary, be abolished.'*
" Seconded by Lord John Hervey, and carried.

"Mr. Hope Grant then moved ' *That the critique on last Term's performances be erased.'* We did not catch the name of the seconder.

" The latter motion was lost.
"The meeting then dispersed."

This brought the eighth year to a conclusion.
The Committee after the election on April 27th—

W. A. Bankes, Esq. . .	Trin. Hall . .	President.
I. J. Pulleine, Esq. . .	Trin. Coll. . .	Stage Manager.
C. A. W. Troyte, Esq. . .	Trin. Hall . .	Supt. of Scenery.
T. F. Kirby, Esq. . . .	Sec. and Treas. . .	Trin. Coll.
I. F. Oliffe, Esq. . . .	Trin. Coll. . .	Orchestra.
J. T. M. Russell, Esq. .	Trin. Coll. . .	Director of Machinery.
E. H. Wynne, Esq. . .	Trin. Coll. . .	Prompter.
Hon. A. Strutt	Trin. Coll. . .	Assistant Stage Manager.

"A. D. C."—LIST OF MEMBERS FROM 1855 TO 1863.*

F. C. Burnand (Pres.,Feb. 24,1858).
T. White.
F. C. Wilson.
Reginald Kelly.
Collins.
G. Lampson.
Tyrrell.
P. W. Freeman.
Murray.
C. E. Donne.

Woodmass.
R. L. Lomax.
R. Kelly (Pres., Dec. 12, 1855).
W. L. B. Cator.
G. Feilden.
J. S. Oliphant.
W. P. Lysaght.
C. R. F. Lutwidge.
Simpson.
J. Graham.

* I am afraid this list is incomplete, and the spelling of some of the names is not absolutely correct ; but I have been unable to verify it by the original.

L. T. Baines.
R. Hill.
W. H. Baillie (Pres., Oct., 1856).
J. M. Wilson.
Lennox Conyngham.
T. R. Polwhele.
Gerald Fitzgerald.
G. Harvey.
T. C. Wood.
Whitley.
H. Lampson.
H. Snow.
T. Thornhill.
Salter.
Ernwin.
Dalton.
J. Watt Gibson (Pres., Nov. 22, 1855).
T. Wilkinson.
Arbouin.
E. Ashley.
R. O'Hara.
R. Wharton.
J. Foster.
R. Preston.
R. O. Lamb.
W. Evans.
G. R. Hassall.
C. Hall.
A. F. Scaly. ..
P. Gwynne.
H. W. Hoffman.
R. Hobart.
A. Cumberlege.
T. Utton.
P. Gorst.
F. Davy.
J. H. Robinson.
S. Saunderson.
Lord R. Grosvenor.
W. C. Streatfield.
T. A. Hudson.
Hon. J. Leigh.
R. Wingfield Digby.
C. Weguelin.
Knapp.
Lord Pelham.

Hamilton.
M. N. R. Fitzgerald.
Lord Brecknock (Pres.Dec.4,1858).
H. Thornhill.
G. de Robeck.
J. Rowley.
R. Tennant.
F. V. Wright.
F. Smith.
C. Grant.
H. Partridge.
G. Hawes.
G. H. Cockrane.
M. Guest.
H. Snow.
E. C. Clark.
Creswell Tayleur.
T. G. Pearse.
H. Arkwright.
Hon. L. Ashley.
H. Dent.
Barnett.

Hon. E. O'Brien.
A. C. Lee (Pres. May Term, 1858).
Moncrieff.
S. A. Hankey.
A. E. M. Ashley.
A. E. Knox.
G. Walford.
D. Powell (President, Dec., 1860, Oct., 1861).
N. Madan.
J. Hall.
J. Sankey.
Woodroffe.
J. B. Dyne.
H. M. G. Coore.
W. R. Phelips.
W. S. Sands.
Finch.
J. Chambers.
Hon. de Grey.
G. Howard.
C. Walsh.
L. D. Hall.
P. McNeile.
G. Charles.

E. W. Chapman.
W. A. Longfield.
E. A. Catt.
F. G. Arbuthnot.
S. T. Ashton.
T. J. Sanderson.
C. A. W. Troyte.
W. A. Bankes (Pres., Apr. 4, 1862).
C. A. W. Rycroft.
H. T. Russell.
J. Manners-Sutton.
E. C. R. Ross.
P. F. Stewartt.
W. A. Bankes.
J. Begwood.
S. V. Saumarez.
Viscount Pollington.
W. A. Currey.
T. M. Wells.
Marriott.
Hawner.
G. O. Trevelyan.
A. H. Baillie.

A. de Rothschild.
Lieut. Butts.
F. C. B. Acland.
P. H. Hamberston.
Lord Amberley.
Hon. A. Strutt.
F. Pullen.
T. Edwards.
H. G. M. Kirby.
J. W. Clark.
Wells.
R. Heathcote.
R. Patrick.
G. Buxton.
Grove.
Hon. — Powys.
Augustus Campbell.
Percy Lee.
Newton.
Plowden.
F. W. Hudson.
Hon. — Strutt.
Everett.*

* Mr. William Everett, author of a pleasant, chatty, little book, entitled *On the Cam*, a son of the famous American orator, Edward Everett, well known in England as the U.S. Minister in 1841. He was a clever Yankee, with a considerable amount of dry, caustic humour. A *jeu de mot* of his is worth recording. The young republican was watching a game of whist, in which the Duke of St. Albans, and a Cambridge man who had recently won the Bell Scholarship, were opponents. A discussion arose as to some nice point of the game, and the players, unable to settle it among themselves, appealed to the bystanders, when Everett, quietly interposing, said to the Duke : "My dear fellow, it's not worth dispute, as the difference between you is only a slight question of distinction." The disputants begged him to explain his oracular pronouncement, which had been delivered in the hardest American twang. With a sly twinkle in his eye, which prepared the listeners for something worth hearing, he replied : "Well, don't you see, there can't be much difference between you and St. Albans, as you're a *Bell Scholar* and he's a *Beau Clerk*." Equinamity was instantly restored ; the game proceeded amicably, and Mr. Everett, "having scored," subsided quietly into an arm-chair, and dozed. In his book *On the Cam*, he speaks of the "A. D. C." as giving "excellent stage performances, open to all the University, for a few nights in every term. It is fortunate in possessing some members of very superior dramatic talent, who, though they have long ceased to be members of the University, make a point of coming back to Cambridge to act, and to assist in developing the rising dramatic talent. The acting is generally extremely good, and the society an agreeable one."

Usborne.
Evans.
Heathcote.
Leigh.
F. C. Grant.
J. Kirby.
Lord John Hervey.
Scholefield.
R. C. Jebb.
Hon. C. Lyttelton.
J. W. Hawkesworth.
Lord J. Hervey.
C. C. Henniker.
Hon. Fitz William.
C. T. Royds.
R. M. Harvey.
H. Becher.
R. Doyne.
E. Hambro.
A. E. Guest.
Hon. H. Bourke.
S. Hoare.
Duke of St. Albans.
N. M. de Rothschild.
Smith Marryat.
Featherstonehaugh.
Willis.
Gurdon.
C. Barclay.
Wilmot.
F. Holland.
N. A. Langham.
H. W. Hoffman (Oct. Term, 1860).
E. H. Wynne.

H. L. Wood.
Hon. W. P. Bouverie.
Hon. J. M. Henniker.
J. Hamilton.
Hon. F. Whymper.
C. J. Fletcher.
Hon. H. Bourke.
G. Osborne.
E. Buchanan.
T. F. Oliffe.
Chapman.
E. F. Wayne
J. H. Elwes.
Hon. A. C. Stanley
A. J. Clay.
H. J. Mealycott.
H. C. Russell.
S. C. Allsopp.
Williamson.
R. Denman.
H. Blake-Humfrey.
J. J. Pulleine.
Hon. E. F. Kenyon.
C. Hall.
P. T. Ralli.
T. Melvill.
Lord Aberdon.
A. H. Harrison.
Ramsbotham.
S. E. Buxton.
Melvill.
Ashton.
P. Candy.   [1863).
Hon. C. Carington (Pres. June 3,

HONORARY PRESIDENT.
H.R.H. PRINCE OF WALES.

HONORARY MEMBERS.

Alfred Thompson   .   .   .   Trin. Coll.
Quintin Twiss .   .   .   .   .   Ch. Ch. Oxon.

CHAPTER XXIII.

Performance Week, May 26th, 27th, 28th, 29th.

" *The performances took place on the above days, but in
compliance with the resolution passed at the general meeting
last April 27th, no account of them is preserved.*"

This is rather a change. It was the Secretary's last flicker.
Then he gracefully retires.

" *The retiring secretary, after a service of three years, begs
to add his regret that he cannot longer remain on a committee in acting on which he has spent so many days of
amusement and satisfaction.*

"THOS. F. KIRBY, *Secretary.*"

" *At a general meeting held on Wednesday, October 21st,
1863, a motion was carried that a record of the performances
be written by the Stage Manager and revised by the Committee, be kept in the rooms.*

" E. W. CHAPMAN, *Hon. Sec.*"

MAY TERM, 1863.

" *The performances this Term took place May 26th, 27th,
28th, 29th.*

" *The first and third nights (Tuesday and Thursday) were ladies' nights, and were both well filled. Wednesday night also brought a crowded audience. On Friday the number of visitors was small.*"

" The pieces performed were—

> *A Nice Firm.*
> *Twice Killed.*
> *The Maid and the Magpie (Burlesque).*

" On the first night the programme consisted of—

> *A Nice Firm,*

and the burlesque.

" On Wednesday, Thursday, and Friday, all three pieces were performed."

A NICE FIRM.

By TOM TAYLOR, Esq.

Mr. Messiter	*of the firm of Messiter & Moon, Solicitors and Attorneys at Law*	Mr. F. C. BURNAND.
Mr. Moon		Mr. C. HALL.
Mr. John Ripton	. . . .	Mr. ELWES.
Mr. Richard Ripton	. . .	Mr. H. C. RUSSELL.
Mr. Duncuft Meazle .	. . .	Mr. BUXTON.
Mr. Mumps, M.R.C.S. .	. .	Mr. ALLSOPP.
Ryder .	. . . . .	Mr. MELVILL.
Tottie .	. . . . .	Mr. WILLIAMSON.
Miss Susannah Applejohn .	. .	Mr. ARBUTHNOT.

TWICE KILLED.

By J. MADDISON MORTON, Esq.

Euclid Facile .	. . . .	Mr. PULLEINE.
Reckless .	. . . .	Mr. C. HALL.
Tom (*Reckless's servant*) .	. .	Mr. ELWES.
Mr. Holdfast	. . . .	Mr. H. C. RUSSELL.
Mr. Furgus Fable .	. . .	Mr. CHAPMAN.
Robert .	. . . .	Mr. OSBORN.
Mrs. Facile .	. . . .	Hon. A. STANLEY.
Julia .	. . . . .	Mr. DENMAN.
Fanny .	. . . . .	Mr. OLIFFE.

THE MAID AND THE MAGPIE.

By H. J. BYRON, Esq.

Fabrizio . . '	Mr. CHAPMAN.
Granetto	Mr. C. HALL.
Pippo	Mr. WILLIAMSON.
Fernando Villabella	Mr. PULLEINE.
Isaac	Mr. F. C. BURNAND.
The Magistrate	Mr. CURREY.
Ninette	Mr. OLIFFE.
Dame Lucia	Mr. SANDERSON.
Elvira }	{ Mr. DENMAN.
Luisa }	{ Mr. ELWES.

I make this last extract from the book :

" *The usual critique on the performances was discontinued for some time, either on account of the excellence of the acting, or the inefficiency of the various secretaries, or the modesty of the actors.*"

The Mr. Melvill mentioned as playing the part of *Ryder* in *A Nice Firm* is the gallant officer whose loss we have so recently had to deplore, and who will ever be remembered by his countrymen as the Hero of Isandula.

Mr. H. C. Russell, who was cast for *Mr. Richard Ripton*, is now the Vicar of Doncaster, and Charles Hall is the Prince of Wales's Attorney-General for the Duchy of Cornwall.

The *Nice Firm* was what would nowadays be described as " a Genuine Success,"—" Charley" Hall being as good a *Mr. Moon* as could be named, after Frank Matthews and the others were all suited down to the ground. In the afterpiece *Twice Killed*, Melvill was to have played *Reckless*, but he had contrived to get himself " gated " by the authorities that very evening, and consequently was compelled to be back in college by nine or ten o'clock, which, of course, prevented him from appearing in the farce. In this difficulty Charley Hall " kindly undertook the part at a moment's notice," and the stage-manager went before the curtain, and by way of apology, told the plain unvarnished tale of Melvill's being " gated," which was received with great good-humour by a

ĸ

decidedly sympathetic audience. His substitute went on and read the part from the book, and as the piece depended mainly on the exertions of Messrs. Pulleine and Stanley, the result was eminently satisfactory.

On the second night, being quite at home in *A Nice Firm*, *Messiter* and *Moon* went in for an impromptu conversation, chiefly relating to the latter's health, his walking exercise, what he had for dinner, when he was vaccinated, his opinion on the topics of the day, and so forth ; which at last quite upset *Mr. Moon's* gravity, and it was only by feigning a violent fit of coughing—which produced further gratuitous advice and offers of various ingenious remedies from *Mr. Messiter*—that he managed to recover his characteristic gravity and resume the piece where he had left off.

We—Charles Hall and myself—had done this sort of thing, a very dangerous game by the way, before, on at least one important occasion. A piece to fill up the evening was wanted in consequence of some mishap somewhere, and Mr. C. Hall undertook to play *Sent to the Tower* with me. I was in town at the time, but on receiving his letter I at once set myself to work, studied *Launcelot*, but was unable to get down to Cambridge until the very evening of the performance, when Charles Hall met me at the station at five o'clock, and we rehearsed as we drove to his rooms, when we continued our rehearsal over the cutlets and claret. This was the second time I had got up this piece in a hurried manner, and I should not have consented had I not trusted to my memory of the former performance being better than in the event it turned out to be. I knew the chief situations, I knew the plot, such as it is, and a good deal of the dialogue, but not all. I knew that it was a sort of *Box and Cox*, only not so good, and that one man had 'Bacon and Beans' for dinner, and the other 'Beans and Bacon'—but which had which I hadn't time to get fixed in my head. So somehow when we had once fairly got into the very middle of the farce, like *Laertes* and *Hamlet* in the fencing scene changing rapiers, we suddenly changed parts. I was "not *Launcelot*—but another"—I took the words out of C. Hall's mouth, and he took my words out of mine. The Prompter looked first at one and then at the other, and vainly attempted to bring us back to the right paths. But how was he to manage it? He couldn't prompt *Perkyn Puddifoot* in the very speech which by right belonged to him, but which had just been uttered by *Launcelot Banks*, and it was clearly no use giving *Launcelot Banks* the next speech which he ought to say, but which was at that very moment issuing from the lips of *Perkyn Puddifoot.*

There never was such a muddle. The Prompter shook his head, whispered, pointed to the book, all to no purpose. He waited patiently, following the dialogue and wondering whether by accident we should each resume our original parts before the piece came to an end, and be once more "as we were before we were as we were."

No such luck. Finding that we were mistaken in our characters, we made a desperate attempt to try back to the point of departure. It was hopeless. The Prompter gasped. He too made a try back. Where *were* we going to? We heard the leaves rustle. We durst not stop, or we should have exposed our utter incapacity to the audience. A happy thought struck *Launcelot,* and in the hope that *Perkyn* would remember how and where to go on, if he only had time given him, *Launcelot* commenced an impromptu story. This utterly staggered the Prompter who shut up the book, and *Perkyn,* giving himself up for lost, quietly lighted a pipe, listened to the story, threw in a few remarks, and finally observed that when "*Launcelot* had *quite* done, it would be as well if they went on regularly." Whereupon *Launcelot,* at his wits' end, turned for the word to the Prompter. His book was closed on his knees, and he was half asleep. Hearing his name called, he roused himself, and to the hurriedly and anxiously whispered demand for "the word," he replied by suddenly handing the book to *Launcelot* and whispering, audibly, "Just let me know *what page you've got to.*"

Fortunately at that moment the "Gaoler" was inspired to come on, and as we had to take our cue from him we were once more fairly started, and, with the help of the Prompter, who had found the place by this time, we got safely to the finish of *Sent to the Tower.*

This brings me to the end of my personal recollections of the "A. D. C." as far as I was actively concerned.

Since my day they have played *She Stoops to Conquer*, *The Rivals*, and, I think, *The School for Scandal*. Of this last I am not so certain. We had one excellent performance of *The Critic*, of which we gave both Acts, but the bill is missing from my collection, and the exact cast from my recollection. Quintin Twiss played *Sir Walter Raleigh*, and C. Weguelin was, I fancy, *Sir Fretful Plagiary*. The undergraduate audience was much tickled by the absurdities, but in allusion to the premeditated mistakes of the sham Rehearsal, expressed its opinion very generally that "It was a pity the fellows didn't know their parts better," and "what a lot of trouble Burnand had to keep 'em straight." I was playing *Puff*. The undergraduate of that time was evidently not well up in his Sheridan.

Considering the secrecy of our commencement, it was amusing, within the last few years, to see the large handbills —*e.g.*, of November, 1876—serving for University advertisements, in which it stated that "Tickets 5s. each" could be had "at Hart's, Trinity Street, and at the 'A. D. C.,' Park Street." Park Street is a small turning out of Jesus Lane, where the door of the old Billiard Rooms at the back of the "Hoop" used to be.

In the previous year the Club had played *London Assurance*, and on its advertising handbill, publicly displayed, the public was informed that, "*Tuesday, November* 23, *and Thursday, November* 25, *would be University Nights, and Wednesday, November* 24, *would be the County Night. On*

Thursday the first four rows will be reserved for Ladies. Tickets 7s. 6d.''

The Tickets on University nights at this time were five shillings apiece, and on the County night half-a-sovereign, and '' were to be obtained '' (here was the old rule still in force) '' *by members of the University only* '' at Messrs. Metcalfe & Son's, Trinity Street, or at the ' A. D. C.' ''

In 1870 the Rules were revised, and remain as follows :—

𝕷𝖆𝖜𝖘 of the 𝕬. 𝕯. 𝕮.

REVISED BY THE COMMITTEE, JUNE, 1870.

I. THAT this Club consists of Members and Honorary Members, the former to be Resident Members in the University, the latter to have had their names on the boards of one of the Colleges, or to have been elected *ad eundem* Members of the University, or be Members of the University of Oxford, or Garrick Club in London. That the number of Resident Members be limited to 60.

II. That at the last meeting in each Term the Club shall elect a Committee of eight for the next Term, consisting of a President, Stage-Manager, Superintendent of Scenery, Treasurer and Secretary, Acting-Manager, Librarian, Director of Machinery, Assistant Stage-Manager, and at all meetings the President take the Chair, and have the casting vote.

III. That the Committee elect Members, at which Election not more than two of the Committee may be absent.

IV. That all Members and Honorary Members shall pay an entrance-fee of £2 2s., and shall pay a Subscription of £2 per term. All Members in residence who have paid their Subscriptions for the current Term shall have a right to vote at General Meetings.

V. That any Member having paid his Subscriptions for nine Terms shall become a Life Member, and, as such, be allowed free use of the Club.

VI. That any Member graduating or going out of residence, before nine Terms, shall be required, should he again enter into residence, to pay Subscriptions for the use of the Club.

VII. Any Member whose Subscription or Fine remains unpaid after it has been due a fortnight, Subscriptions being due on the first day of residence, shall be fined Five Shillings, after due notice given by the Secretary.

VIII.   There shall be a General Meeting at the end of every Term.

That any Member or Members can call a General Meeting provided they have the sanction of the President.

IX.   That due notice of Rehearsals shall be posted in the rooms : that any Member being more than ten minutes late for a Rehearsal, shall be fined 2s. 6d. ; or more than fifteen minutes, 5s.   That all excuses must be sent in to the Stage-Manager in a written form.

N.B.—Members half-an-hour late shall be considered to have missed the Rehearsal.

X.   That no Acting Member or the Prompter be allowed to miss a Rehearsal in the week previous to the Performances, on any consideration whatever, unless notice be given to the Stage-Manager three days previously.   The fine for total absence is Ten Shillings.

XI.   That none but Members perform on the A. D. C. stage, and that none but Members of the University be admitted as spectators of the performances, without the sanction of the Committee.

XII.   That no Member take any Club property out of the rooms, under a penalty of Five Shillings.

XIII.   That no Member throw about Club property, or in any way damage it, under a penalty of Five Shillings.

XIV.   That if necessary it be at the option of the Committee to fine any Member infringing Laws XII. and XIII. a sum not exceeding the value of the property.

XV.   That the Secretary and Treasurer shall keep minutes of the Meetings, and correct accounts of all moneys received and paid during the term of office.

XVI.   That the Committee have power to make Bye-Laws necessary for the good of the Club.

XVII.   Any Member breaking the Laws or Bye-Laws of the Club shall be fined Two Shillings and Sixpence per week, after notice having been given, until payment be made.

XVIII.   That no Dogs be permitted in the rooms, under a penalty of Five Shillings, which will be *strictly* enforced.

XIX.   That money received for tickets shall be paid to Members of the Committee from whom the tickets have been received, within a week after performances, under a penalty of Ten Shillings.

XX.   All Members during their first two terms in the Club shall take supers' parts, if required to do so, under a penalty of Two Guineas, unless they shall give a sufficient excuse to be approved as such by the Committee.

XXI.   That Strangers (not Members of this University) be allowed the use of the Club rooms and property, provided that their stay at Cambridge does not exceed a week, and that *their* names and the names of their introducers be entered in a book provided for the purpose.

XXII.   That any Member failing to pay his Subscription or Fines during the Term in which they become due, after notice given by the Secretary, shall cease to be a Member of the Club.

XXIII. That any Member of the Committee have the power of enforcing Fines.

A. D. C.

LIBRARY RULES.

REVISED FEBRUARY, 1872.

I. That every Member taking a Book out of the Library enter his own Name and that of the Book, with the date of its removal, and, on the returning it, the date of its return, in a Book provided for that purpose.

II. That Books may be kept out for any period not exceeding a fortnight; and that any Member keeping a Book out beyond the period allowed be fined One Shilling.

III. That notice be sent by the Librarian to any Member who infringes Rule II.; and if after such notice sent the Book be not returned at once, that an additional fine of Sixpence a day be imposed till the Book be returned.

IV. That no Book be taken out again by the same Member until one clear day has elapsed from the time of its return.

V. That no Member do take any of *Lacy's* Acting Plays from the Club Room without the written permission of the Stage-Manager, or Assistant Stage-Manager.

VI. That any Member who loses or injures a Book be required to replace it.

VII. That all Books be returned to the Library on or before a day at the end of each term, of which a week's notice be given by the Librarian.

VIII. That any Member removing a Newspaper or Periodical from the Club Rooms be fined Ten Shillings.

IX. That any Member transgressing Rules I. IV. V. VII. be fined Five Shillings.

X. That any Member of Committee have power to impose the above fines.

XI. That notice of any fine be posted in the Club Rooms, and that any Member refusing to pay a fine receive a notice from the Committee that if the fine be not paid within three days, he will be expelled from the Club.

In the Library there is a very valuable edition of Hogarth's works presented to the Club by Reginald Kelly of Kelly, Devonshire, whose name is in the first list of members.

The Club possesses a very fair Dramatic Library, and its walls are covered with photographs and sketches.

In 1871 the following Rules were accepted by the Club, acting, I believe, under the advice of Mr. J. W. Clark, of Trinity, who has on more than one occasion done the " A. D. C." excellent service, and who is sincerely interested in the Club's prosperity.

𝔄. 𝔅. ℭ.

RULES ACCEPTED FROM TUTORS BY THE CLUB, 1871, OCTOBER TERM.

I.   The performances are to take place in the Michaelmas Term only, and in one week, and on three nights only, of which Saturday shall not be one.

II.   The performances are not to take place during the time of the Previous, General, or Special B. A. Examinations.

III.   There is to be no Town night.

IV.   There is to be only one Ladies' night.

V.   There is to be no Burlesque.

VI.   The performances are not to begin earlier than 7.30, and are to close at 10.30 o'clock.

VII.   That those who take part in the performance undertake positively during that week to be in before 12 o'clock at night, and that all Members of the A. D. C. will, as far as possible, discourage supper parties after the performances.

VIII.   The plays to be performed shall previously be submitted to a Committee of Tutors of Colleges.

IX.   The Performers shall be Resident Members of the University only.

Remarks.

1. The performances are limited to the October term only. This rule ought to be of singular benefit to the Club, which could be carefully preparing its work from the beginning of the year. The scenery could be put in hand in the Lent

term : rehearsals could be got on with by easy stages : and all the details, all the *mise-en-scène*, could be most carefully and artistically considered.

2. The second rule is also good. Years ago we had, to a certain extent, adopted it.

3. This is decidedly right. The "A. D. C." was never instituted for the Town, only for the Gown. The Town had its own Dramatic Club and its own amusements.

4. The previous rule applies to the Gown, this to the petticoats.

5. I have no fault to find with this, if exceptions are permitted. Our old-fashioned friend *Bombastes*, then the burlesques of the Robsonian school, and certain extravagant musical pieces (where both music and drama are combined— as for instance, *Trial by Jury*, and the Triumviretta of *Cox and Box*, the latter so easily performed, and containing some of the best music ever written by Arthur Sullivan, *Mus. Doc.*), might be occasionally played. At present there is a tendency to heaviness in the "A. D. C." entertainments, which would be vastly relieved by a song and dance.

6. Excellent.

7. Why "*before* 12," why not "*at* 12 ?" and why discourage those cheery and social gatherings? Englishmen, as a rule, do not meet for any combined effort, without feeding together, either before or after the event. Parliament has its Greenwich dinner. The Royal Academy has its banquet. After an evening's hard work on the stage, some sort of supper is a necessity. Eating alone is bad for the digestion, and supping together is harmless. Besides, if the performance is over at 10.30 punctually—and if they begin punctually at 7.30 they could be finished by 10.15 or 10,—there are a couple of clear hours for a quiet supper, whereat, all the difficulties surmounted, all the behind-the-scenes *contre-temps* will be discussed, and the heroes will fight their battles over again, and finish by drinking a bumper at parting to the success of the "A. D. C."

8. No objection to this. But it would be still better were there a Dramatic Professor, who would lecture on the Art, and himself choose the plays for his students to perform. Why should there not be one French night a year out of the series of performances? And why should not encouragement be given to original dramatic and musical composition? The "A. D. C." stage could be written for by those who knew it best, and the pieces, whether purely dramatic, or also operatic, would form a perfect *répertoire* for amateurs everywhere. The pieces written specially for the "A. D. C." might be so ingeniously contrived as to omit the feminine element entirely.

9. This excludes the old members, unless—having nothing better to do—they choose to come up and go into residence. Still, on the whole, it is a good rule. A great festival—such as the celebration of the twenty-fifth year of the Club's existence—might be admitted as an exception.

There remains nothing to add, except that in 1878 I witnessed a capital performance of *The Ticket of Leave Man*. This class of drama (in five Acts!) is too long and too heavy for the place, and the farce was but small relief,—in fact on the next night the latter was omitted.

We went in for lightness and music. Above all a University audience wants a good hearty laugh. Such was the result of *To Paris and Back, Alonzo the Brave, A Thumping Legacy, The Goose with the Golden Eggs, Helping Hands, Aladdin, The Jacobite, Used-up, The Seventh Shot* —and, of all these, not one ever caused so much amusement, whenever it was played, as *Alonzo*. It was a burlesque of the old school, specially written for the "A. D. C." And none of the modern burlesques, not even *Aladdin*, ever suited actors and audience so well as this. I am convinced that some absurdity of this sort, *well and carefully done*, is an essential of success at the "A. D. C." The audience like it—*tout est là*.

The drama's laws the drama's patrons give,
And those who live to please, must please to live.

No matter how short the eccentric afterpiece, *if only half-an-hour*, so that it be full of sparkle, humour, practical fun, good situations, laughable songs, and well-executed duetts, trios, and concerted pieces, the audience, having to the full appreciated the high art of the first piece—but withal a trifle weary of it—will go away at the end of an Aristophanic extravaganza, tickled with the 'hits,' delighted with its brilliancy, and in the greatest good-humour with the songs, music, dances, and the scenery, which last should be a special feature. The Committee of Tutors would be the first to enjoy such an entertainment, and would amend the rule by " excepting exceptions."

So finishes my labour of love, which I trust will not be Love's labour lost.

Hæc olim meminisse juvabit. These are happy memories, and to paraphrase Lord Houghton's sparkling epilogue of fifty years ago, already quoted in the Preface—

> But, as the present chronicle expires,
> The writer asks one boon, and so retires ;
> That on some pleasant evenings, when you're freed
> From toil and care, and these brief records read,
> In thought you will the path of life retrace,
> And hear once more the voice, and see the face
> Of many an old companion, then so young,
> With whom you've acted, laughed, and danced, and sung.
> · Then, as you watch the fragrant cloud ascend,
> Distance enchantment to the view shall lend,
> While, as you close the book, and cease to read,
> You'll murmur, "Those were happy days indeed !"
> The coffee finished, sip your *Eau de vie*,
> And. from your heart, cry, " *Floreat ' A. D. C.!*'"

THE END.

193, *Piccadilly, London, W.*
November, 1879.

𝕮𝖍𝖆𝖕𝖒𝖆𝖓 𝖆𝖓𝖉 𝕳𝖆𝖑𝖑'𝖘

CATALOGUE OF BOOKS.

INCLUDING

DRAWING EXAMPLES, DIAGRAMS, MODELS, INSTRUMENTS, ETC.

ISSUED UNDER THE AUTHORITY OF

THE SCIENCE AND ART DEPARTMENT, SOUTH KENSINGTON,

FOR THE USE OF SCHOOLS AND ART AND SCIENCE CLASSES.

CHARLES DICKENS'S WORKS.

New Books.

The Cheapest and Handiest Edition of

THE WORKS OF CHARLES DICKENS.
The Pocket Volume Edition of Charles Dickens's Works. In 30 vols., small fcap. 8vo, £2 2s. [*In November.*

THE LETTERS OF CHARLES DICKENS.
Edited by his SISTER-IN-LAW and ELDEST DAUGHTER. 2 vols., demy 8vo. [*In November.*

LIFE AND CORRESPONDENCE OF RICHARD
COBDEN. By JOHN MORLEY. 2 vols., demy 8vo. [*In January.*

CRITICAL MISCELLANIES.
Second Series. By JOHN MORLEY, forming the new volume of the New and Uniform Edition of his Works. Large crown 8vo. [*In the Press.*

The New Volume in the Household Edition of Dickens's Works.

THE LIFE OF CHARLES DICKENS.
By JOHN FORSTER. With Illustrations by F. Barnard. [*In November.*

SKETCHES OF YOUNG COUPLES AND YOUNG
GENTLEMEN by "BOZ," and of YOUNG LADIES by "QUIZ." With Illustrations by "PHIZ." Small crown 8vo, 3s. 6d.

PRECIOUS STONES AND GEMS.
By EDWIN W. STREETER, F.R.G.S. Second Edition, demy 8vo, cloth, 18s., calf, 27s.

NEW VOLUMES OF THE SOUTH KENSINGTON
MUSEUM HANDBOOKS.

THE DYCE AND FORSTER COLLECTIONS.

[In the Press.

THE JAPANESE ART.

[In the Press.

THE "A. D. C.": being Personal Reminiscences of the
University Amateur Dramatic Club, Cambridge. By F. C. BURNAND,
B.A., Trinity College, Cambridge. Demy 8vo, 12s.

OUR HOME IN CYPRUS.

By ESME SCOTT-STEVENSON. With a Map and Illustrations.
Demy 8vo. *[In November.*

MY CHIEF AND I; or, Six Months in Natal after
the Langalibalele Outbreak. By ATHERTON WYLDE. With Portrait
of Colonel Durnford. Demy 8vo. *[In November.*

A YEAR IN PESHAWUR AND A LADY'S RIDE
INTO THE KYBER PASS. By E. F. TREVELYAN. Crown 8vo.
[In November.

CHRONICLES OF NO MAN'S LAND.

By F. BOYLE, Author of "Camp Notes." Large crown.
[In November.

THE CARLYLE BIRTHDAY BOOK.

Prepared by permission of Mr. Thomas Carlyle. Small crown 8vo, 3s.
[In November.

DIDEROT AND THE ENCYCLOPÆDISTS.

Forming new volume of the New and Uniform Edition of John Morley's Works. Large crown 8vo, 12s.

JACK'S EDUCATION ; or, How he Learnt Farming.

By PROFESSOR HENRY TANNER, F.C.S., Senior Member of the Royal Agricultural College, Examiner in the Principles of Agriculture under the Government Department of Science. Large crown 8vo, 4s.

FARMING FOR PLEASURE AND PROFIT.

By ARTHUR ROLAND. Edited by WILLIAM ABLETT.

VOL. I.—DAIRY FARMING, MANAGEMENT OF COWS, &c. Large crown 8vo, 5s.

VOL. II.—POULTRY-KEEPING. Large crown 8vo, 5s.

VOL. III.—TREE-PLANTING FOR ORNAMENTATION OR PROFIT. Suitable to every soil and situation. Large crown 8vo, 5s.

LESSONS IN HORSE JUDGING AND ON THE

SUMMERING OF HUNTERS. By W. FEARNLEY, late Principal of the Edinburgh Veterinary College. With Illustrations. Crown 8vo, 4s.

REPRESENTATIVE STATESMEN : Political Studies.

By ALEX. CHARLES EWALD, F.S.A. 2 vols., large crown 8vo, 24s.

THE REALITIES OF FREEMASONRY.

By MRS. BLAKE, Author of "Twelve Months in Southern Europe." Demy 8vo, 9s.

TEN LECTURES ON ART.

By E. J. POYNTER, R.A. Large crown 8vo, 9s.

New Novels.

TOM SINGLETON : Dragoon and Dramatist.
By W. W. FOLLETT SYNGE, Author of "Olivia Raleigh." 3 vols., crown 8vo.   *[In November.*

WAPPERMOUTH.
By W. THEODORE HICKMAN. 3 vols.   *[In November.*

THE BROWN HAND AND THE WHITE.
By MRS. COMPTON READE, Author of "Sidonie," &c. 3 vols.   *[In December.*

HER DIGNITY AND GRACE.
By H. C. 3 vols.   *[In November.*

GEORGE RAYNER : A Story.
By LEON BROOK. 2 vols.   *[In November.*

COUSIN HENRY.
By ANTHONY TROLLOPE. Crown 8vo, 2 vols.

BEATING THE AIR.
By ULICK RALPH BURKE. 3 vols.

COUSIN SIMON.
By the HON. MRS. ROBERT MARSHAM. 1 vol.

THE PARSON O' DUMFORD.
By GEORGE MANVILLE FENN. 3 vols.

GRACE ELWYN.
By the Author of "On the Banks of the Delaware." 2 vols.

BOOKS

PUBLISHED BY

CHAPMAN AND HALL.

ABBOTT (EDWIN)—*Formerly Head-Master of the Philological School—*

A CONCORDANCE OF THE ORIGINAL POETICAL WORKS OF ALEXANDER POPE. With an Introduction on the English of Pope, by EDWIN A. ABBOTT, D.D., Author of "A Shakespearian Grammar," &c. &c. Medium 8vo, price £1 1s.

ABBOTT (SAMUEL)—

ARDENMOHR: AMONG THE HILLS. A Record of Scenery and Sport in the Highlands of Scotland. With Sketches and Etching by the Author. Demy 8vo, 12s. 6d.

BARTLEY (G. C. T.)—

A HANDY BOOK FOR GUARDIANS OF THE POOR: being a Complete Manual of the Duties of the Office, the Treatment of Typical Cases, with Practical Examples, &c. Crown 8vo, cloth, 3s.

THE PARISH NET: HOW IT'S DRAGGED AND WHAT IT CATCHES. Crown 8vo, cloth, 7s. 6d.

THE SEVEN AGES OF A VILLAGE PAUPER. Crown 8vo, cloth, 5s.

BEESLY (EDWARD SPENCER)—*Professor of History in University College, London—*

CATILINE, CLODIUS, AND TIBERIUS. Large crown 8vo, 6s.

BENNETT (W. C.)—

SEA SONGS. Crown 8vo, 4s.

BENSON (W.)—

MANUAL OF THE SCIENCE OF COLOUR. Coloured Frontispiece and Illustrations. 12mo, cloth, 2s. 6d.

PRINCIPLES OF THE SCIENCE OF COLOUR. Small 4to, cloth, 15s.

BIDDLECOMBE (SIR GEORGE) C.B., Captain R.N.—

AUTOBIOGRAPHY OF SIR GEORGE BIDDLE-COMBE, C.B., Captain R.N. Large crown 8vo, 8s.

BLAKE (EDITH OSBORNE)—

TWELVE MONTHS IN SOUTHERN EUROPE. With Illustrations. Demy 8vo, 14s.

BLYTH (COLONEL)—

THE WHIST-PLAYER. With Coloured Plates of "Hands." Third Edition. Imp. 16mo, cloth, 5s.

A 2

BRADLEY (THOMAS)—of the Royal Military Academy, Woolwich—

ELEMENTS OF GEOMETRICAL DRAWING. In Two
Parts, with Sixty Plates. Oblong folio, half-bound, each Part 16s.

Selection (from the above) of Twenty Plates for the use of
the Royal Military Academy, Woolwich. Oblong folio, half-bound, 16s.

BUCKLAND (FRANK)—

LOG-BOOK OF A FISHERMAN AND ZOOLOGIST.
Second Edition. With numerous Illustrations. Large crown 8vo, 12s.

BURCHETT (R.)—

DEFINITIONS OF GEOMETRY. New Edition. 24mo,
cloth, 5d.

LINEAR PERSPECTIVE, for the Use of Schools of Art.
Twenty-first Thousand. With Illustrations. Post 8vo, cloth, 7s.

PRACTICAL GEOMETRY: The Course of Construction
of Plane Geometrical Figures. With 137 Diagrams. Eighteenth Edition. Post
8vo, cloth, 5s.

CADDY (MRS.)—

HOUSEHOLD ORGANIZATION. Crown 8vo, 4s.

CAITHNESS (COUNTESS)—

OLD TRUTHS IN A NEW LIGHT: or, an Earnest
Endeavour to Reconcile Material Science with Spiritual Science and Scripture
Demy 8vo, 15s.

CAMPION (J. S.), late Major, Staff, 1st Br. C.N.G., U.S.A.—

ON THE FRONTIER. Reminiscences of Wild Sport,
Personal Adventures, and Strange Scenes. With Illustrations. Demy 8vo, 16s.
Second Edition.

ON FOOT IN SPAIN. With Illustrations. Demy 8vo, 16s.
Second Edition.

CARLYLE (DR.)—

DANTE'S DIVINE COMEDY.—Literal Prose Transla-
tion of THE INFERNO, with Text and Notes. Second Edition. Post 8vo, 14s.

CARLYLE (THOMAS)—See pages 17 and 18.

CLINTON (R. H.)—

A COMPENDIUM OF ENGLISH HISTORY, from the
Earliest Times to A.D. 1872. With Copious Quotations on the Leading Events and
the Constitutional History, together with Appendices. Post 8vo, 7s. 6d.

CRAIK (GEORGE LILLIE)—

ENGLISH OF SHAKESPEARE. Illustrated in a Philo-
logical Commentary on his Julius Cæsar. Fifth Edition. Post 8vo, cloth, 5s.

OUTLINES OF THE HISTORY OF THE ENGLISH
LANGUAGE. Ninth Edition. Post 8vo, cloth, 2s. 6d.

DASENT (SIR G. W.)—

JEST AND EARNEST. A Collection of Reviews and
Essays. 2 vols. Post 8vo, cloth, £1 1s.

TALES FROM THE FJELD. A Second Series of
Popular Tales from the Norse of P. Ch. Asbjörnsen. Small 8vo, cloth, 10s. 6d.

DAUBOURG (E.)—

INTERIOR ARCHITECTURE. Doors, Vestibules, Stair-
cases, Anterooms, Drawing, Dining, and Bed Rooms, Libraries, Bank and Newspaper Offices, Shop Fronts and Interiors. With detailed Plans, Sections, and
Elevations. A purely practical work, intended for Architects, Joiners, Cabinet
Makers, Marble Workers, Decorators; as well as for the owners of houses who
wish to have them ornamented by artisans of their own choice. Half-imperial,
cloth, £2 12s. 6d.

DAVIDSON (ELLIS A.)—

PRETTY ARTS FOR THE EMPLOYMENT OF
LEISURE HOURS. A Book for Ladies. With Illustrations. Demy 8vo, 6s.

THE AMATEUR HOUSE CARPENTER: a Guide in
Building, Making, and Repairing. With numerous Illustrations, drawn on Wood
by the Author. Royal 8vo, 10s. 6d.

DAVISON (THE MISSES)—

TRIQUETI MARBLES IN THE ALBERT MEMORIAL
CHAPEL, WINDSOR. A Series of Photographs. Dedicated by express permission to Her Majesty the Queen. The Work consists of 117 Photographs, with
descriptive Letterpress, mounted on 49 sheets of cardboard, half-imperial. Price
£10 10s.

DE COIN (COLONEL ROBERT L.)—

HISTORY AND CULTIVATION OF COTTON AND
TOBACCO. Post 8vo, cloth, 9s.

DE KONINCK (L. L.) and DIETZ (E.)—

PRACTICAL MANUAL OF CHEMICAL ASSAYING,
as applied to the Manufacture of Iron from its Ores, and to Cast Iron, Wrought
Iron, and Steel, as found in Commerce. Edited, with notes, by ROBERT MALLET.
Post 8vo, cloth, 6s.

DE POMAR (THE DUKE)—

FASHION AND PASSION; or, Life in Mayfair. New
Edition. Crown 8vo, 6s.

THE HEIR TO THE CROWN. Crown 8vo, 7s. 6d.

DE WORMS (BARON HENRY)—

ENGLAND'S POLICY IN THE EAST. An Account of
the Policy and Interest of England in the Eastern Question, as compared with
those of the other European Powers. Sixth Edition. To this Edition has been
added the Tripartite Treaty of 1856, and the Black Sea Treaty of 1871.
Sixth Edition. Demy 8vo, 5s.

DE WORMS (BARON HENRY) Continued—

THE AUSTRO-HUNGARIAN EMPIRE: A Poli-
tical Sketch of Men and Events since 1868. Revised and Corrected, with an
Additional Chapter on the Present Crisis in the East. With Maps. Second
Edition. Demy 8vo, cloth, 9s.

DICKENS (CHARLES)—See pages 19—22.

DYCE'S COLLECTION. A Catalogue of Printed Books and
Manuscripts bequeathed by the REV. ALEXANDER DYCE to the South Kensington
Museum. 2 vols. Royal 8vo, half-morocco, 14s.

A Collection of Paintings, Miniatures, Drawings, Engravings,
Rings, and Miscellaneous Objects, bequeathed by the REV. ALEXANDER DYCE
to the South Kensington Museum. Royal 8vo, half-morocco, 7s.

DICKENS (CHARLES)—Conducted by—

ALL THE YEAR ROUND. First Series. 20 vols.
Royal 8vo, cloth, 5s. 6d. each.

New Series. Vols. 1 to 22. Royal 8vo, cloth, 5s. 6d. each.

DIXON (W. HEPWORTH)—

BRITISH CYPRUS. Demy 8vo, with Frontispiece, 15s.

THE HOLY LAND. Fourth Edition. With 2 Steel and
12 Wood Engravings. Post 8vo, 10s. 6d.

DRAYSON (LIEUT.-COL. A. W.)—

THE CAUSE OF THE SUPPOSED PROPER MOTION
OF THE FIXED STARS, with other Geometrical Problems in Astronomy hitherto
unsolved. Demy 8vo, cloth, 10s.

THE CAUSE, DATE, AND DURATION OF THE
LAST GLACIAL EPOCH OF GEOLOGY, with an Investigation of a New
Movement of the Earth. Demy 8vo, cloth, 10s.

PRACTICAL MILITARY SURVEYING AND
SKETCHING. Fifth Edition. Post 8vo, cloth, 4s. 6d.

DYCE (WILLIAM), R.A.—

DRAWING-BOOK OF THE GOVERNMENT SCHOOL
OF DESIGN ; OR, ELEMENTARY OUTLINES OF ORNAMENT. Fifty
selected Plates. Folio, sewed, 5s. ; mounted, 18s.
Text to Ditto. Sewed, 6d.

ELLIOT (FRANCES)—

OLD COURT LIFE IN FRANCE. Third Edition.
Demy 8vo, cloth, 10s. 6d.

THE DIARY OF AN IDLE WOMAN IN ITALY.
Second Edition. Post 8vo, cloth, 6s.

PICTURES OF OLD ROME. New Edition. Post 8vo,
cloth, 6s.

ENGEL (CARL)—

A DESCRIPTIVE AND ILLUSTRATED CATALOGUE
OF THE MUSICAL INSTRUMENTS in the SOUTH KENSINGTON
MUSEUM, preceded by an Essay on the History of Musical Instruments. Second
Edition. Royal 8vo, half-morocco, 12s.

ESCOTT (T. H. S.)—

PILLARS OF THE EMPIRE : Short Biographical
Sketches. Demy 8vo, 10s. 6d.

EWALD (ALEXANDER CHARLES), F.S.A.—

THE LIFE AND TIMES OF PRINCE CHARLES
STUART, COUNT OF ALBANY, commonly called The Young Pretender.
From the State Papers and other Sources. Author of "The Life and Times of
Algernon Sydney," "The Crown and its Advisers," &c. 2 vols. Demy 8vo, £1 8s.

SIR ROBERT WALPOLE. A Political Biography,
1676–1745. Demy 8vo, 18s.

FALLOUX (COUNT DE), of the French Academy—

AUGUSTIN COCHIN. Translated from the French by
AUGUSTUS CRAVEN. Large crown 8vo, 9s.

FANE (VIOLET)—

DENZIL PLACE : a Story in Verse. Crown 8vo, cloth, 8s.

QUEEN OF THE FAIRIES (A Village Story), and other
Poems. By the Author of "Denzil Place." Crown 8vo, 6s.

ANTHONY BABINGTON : a Drama. By the Author of
"Denzil Place," "The Queen of the Fairies," &c. Crown 8vo, 6s.

FEARNLEY (W.), *late Principal of the Edinburgh Veterinary College; Author of " Lectures on the Examination of Horses as to Soundness"—*

LESSONS IN HORSE JUDGING, AND THE SUM-
MERING OF HUNTERS. With Illustrations. Crown 8vo, 4s.

FITZ-PATRICK (W. J.)—

LIFE OF CHARLES LEVER. 2 vols., demy 8vo. 30s.

FLEMING (GEORGE), F.R.C.S.—

ANIMAL PLAGUES : THEIR HISTORY, NATURE,
AND PREVENTION. 8vo, cloth, 15s.

HORSES AND HORSE-SHOEING : their Origin, History,
Uses, and Abuses. 210 Engravings. 8vo, cloth, £1 1s.

PRACTICAL HORSE-SHOEING : With 37 Illustrations.
Second Edition, enlarged. 8vo, sewed, 2s.

RABIES AND HYDROPHOBIA : THEIR HISTORY,
NATURE, CAUSES, SYMPTOMS, AND PREVENTION. With 8 Illustrations. 8vo, cloth, 15s.

A MANUAL OF VETERINARY SANITARY SCIENCE
AND POLICE. With 33 Illustrations. 2 vols. Demy 8vo, 36s.

FORSTER (JOHN)—

THE LIFE OF CHARLES DICKENS. Uniform with
the "C. D." Edition of his Works. With Numerous Illustrations. 2 vols. 7s.

THE LIFE OF CHARLES DICKENS. A New Edition,
uniform with the Library Edition. 1 vol. Post 8vo, 10s. 6d.

THE LIFE OF CHARLES DICKENS. With Portraits
and other Illustrations. 15th Thousand. 3 vols. 8vo, cloth, £2 2s.

A New Edition in 2 vols. Demy 8vo, uniform with the
Illustrated Edition of Dickens's Works. £1 8s.

SIR JOHN ELIOT : a Biography. With Portraits. New
and cheaper Edition. 2 vols. Post 8vo, cloth, 14s.

OLIVER GOLDSMITH : a Biography. Cheap Edition in
one volume. Small 8vo, cloth, 6s.

WALTER SAVAGE LANDOR : a Biography, 1775-1864.
With Portraits and Vignettes. A New and Revised Edition, in 1 vol. Demy 8vo, 12s.

FORTNUM (C. D. E.)—

A DESCRIPTIVE AND ILLUSTRATED CATALOGUE
OF THE BRONZES OF EUROPEAN ORIGIN in the SOUTH KEN-SINGTON MUSEUM, with an Introductory Notice. Royal 8vo, half-morocco, £1 10s.

A DESCRIPTIVE AND ILLUSTRATED CATALOGUE
OF MAIOLICA, HISPANO-MORESCO, PERSIAN, DAMASCUS,. AND RHODIAN WARES in. the SOUTH KENSINGTON MUSEUM. Royal 8vo, half-morocco, £2.

FRANCATELLI (C. E.)—

ROYAL CONFECTIONER : English and Foreign. A
Practical Treatise. With Coloured Illustrations. 3rd Edition. Post 8vo, cloth, 7s. 6d.

GILLMORE (PARKER)—

PRAIRIE AND FOREST : a Description of the Game of
North America, with personal Adventures in their pursuit. With numerous Illustrations. 8vo, cloth, 17s.

HALL (SIDNEY)—

A TRAVELLING ATLAS OF THE ENGLISH COUN-
TIES. Fifty Maps, coloured. New Edition, including the Railways, corrected up to the present date. Demy 8vo, in roan tuck, 10s. 6d.

HANCOCK (E. CAMPBELL)—

THE AMATEUR POTTERY AND GLASS PAINTER.
With Directions for Gilding, Chasing, Burnishing, Bronzing, and Ground Laying. Illustrated. Including Fac-similes from the Sketch-Book of N. H. J. WESTLAKE, F.S.A. With an Appendix. Demy 8vo, 5s.

HILL (MISS G.)—

THE PLEASURES AND PROFITS OF OUR LITTLE
POULTRY FARM. Small crown 8vo, 3s.

HITCHMAN (FRANCIS)—

THE PUBLIC LIFE OF THE EARL OF BEACONS-
FIELD. 2 vols. Demy 8vo, 32s.

HOLBEIN—

TWELVE HEADS AFTER HOLBEIN. Selected from
Drawings in Her Majesty's Collection at Windsor. Reproduced in Autotype, in portfolio. 36s.

HOVELACQUE (ABEL)—

THE SCIENCE OF LANGUAGE: LINGUISTICS,
PHILOLOGY, AND ETYMOLOGY. With Maps. Large crown 8vo, cloth, 5s. Being the first volume of "The Library of Contemporary Science."
(For list of other Works of the same Series, see page 24.)

HUMPHRIS (H. D.)—

PRINCIPLES OF PERSPECTIVE. Illustrated in a
Series of Examples. Oblong folio, half-bound, and Text 8vo, cloth, £1 1s.

JAGOR (F.)—

PHILIPPINE ISLANDS, THE. With numerous Illus-
trations and a Map. Demy 8vo, 16s.

JARRY (GENERAL)—

NAPIER (MAJ.-GEN. W. C. E.)—OUTPOST DUTY.
Translated, with TREATISES ON MILITARY RECONNAISSANCE AND ON ROAD-MAKING. Third Edition. Crown 8vo, 5s.

KELLEY, M.D. (E. G.)—

THE PHILOSOPHY OF EXISTENCE.—The Reality and
Romance of Histories. Demy 8vo, 16s.

KEMPIS (THOMAS Ã)—

OF THE IMITATION OF CHRIST. Four Books.
Beautifully Illustrated Edition. Demy 8vo, 16s.

KLACZKO (M. JULIAN)—

TWO CHANCELLORS: PRINCE GORTCHAKOF and
PRINCE BISMARCK. Translated by Mrs. Tait. New and cheaper edition, 6s.

LEFÈVRE (ANDRÉ)—

PHILOSOPHY, Historical and Critical. Translated, with
an Introduction, by A. W. KEANE, B.A. Large crown 8vo, 7s. 6d.

LEGGE (ALFRED OWEN)—

PIUS IX. The Story of his Life to the Restoration in
1850, with Glimpses of the National Movement in Italy. Author of "The Growth
of the Temporal Power in Italy." 2 vols. Demy 8vo, £1 12s.

LENNOX (LORD WILLIAM)—

FASHION THEN AND NOW. 2 vols. Demy 8vo, 28s.

LETOURNEAU (DR. CHARLES)—

BIOLOGY. Translated by William MacCall. With Illustrations. Large crown 8vo, 6s.

LUCAS (CAPTAIN)—

THE ZULUS AND THE BRITISH FRONTIER.
Demy 8vo, 16s.

CAMP LIFE AND SPORT IN SOUTH AFRICA.
With Episodes in Kaffir Warfare. With Illustrations. Demy 8vo, 12s.

LYTTON (ROBERT, LORD)—

POETICAL WORKS—COLLECTED EDITION. Complete in 5 vols.

FABLES IN SONG. 2 vols. Fcap. 8vo, 12s.
LUCILE. Fcap. 8vo, 6s.
THE WANDERER. Fcap. 8vo, 6s.
POEMS, HISTORICAL AND CHARACTERISTIC. Fcap. 6s.

MALLET (DR. J. W.)—

COTTON: THE CHEMICAL, &c., CONDITIONS OF
ITS SUCCESSFUL CULTIVATION. Post 8vo, cloth, 7s. 6d.

MALLET (ROBERT)—

GREAT NEAPOLITAN EARTHQUAKE OF 1857.
First Principles of Observational Seismology, as developed in the Report to the
Royal Society of London, of the Expedition made into the Interior of the Kingdom
of Naples, to investigate the circumstances of the great Earthquake of December,
1857. Maps and numerous Illustrations. 2 vols. Royal 8vo, cloth, £3 3s.

MASKELL (WILLIAM)—

A DESCRIPTION OF THE IVORIES, ANCIENT AND
MEDIÆVAL, in the SOUTH KENSINGTON MUSEUM, with a Preface.
With numerous Photographs and Woodcuts. Royal 8vo, half-morocco, £1 1s.

MAXSE (FITZH.)—

PRINCE BISMARCK'S LETTERS. Translated from.
the German. Second Edition. Small crown 8vo, cloth, 6s.

MAZADE (CHARLES DE)—

THE LIFE OF COUNT CAVOUR. Translated from
the French. Demy 8vo, 16s.

McCOAN (J. CARLILE)—

OUR NEW PROTECTORATE. TURKEY IN ASIA: ITS
GEOGRAPHY, RACES, RESOURCES, AND GOVERNMENT. With a Map showing
the Existing and Projected Public Works. 2 vols. large crown 8vo, 24s.

MELVILLE (G. J. WHYTE-)—

BLACK BUT COMELY; or, The Adventures of Jane Lee.
New and cheap Edition, in One Volume. Crown 8vo, 6s.

RIDING RECOLLECTIONS. With Illustrations by
EDGAR GIBERNE. Large crown 8vo. Sixth Edition. 12s.

MELVILLE (G. J. WHYTE-)—Continued.

ROSINE. With Illustrations. Demy 8vo. Uniform with
"Katerfelto," 16s.

ROY'S WIFE. New and Cheaper Edition. Crown 8vo, 6s.

SISTER LOUISE ; or, The Story of a Woman's Repentance.
With Illustrations by MIRIAM KERNS. Demy 8vo, 16s.

KATERFELTO : A Story of Exmoor. With 12 Illustrations
by COLONEL H. HOPE CREALOCKE. Fourth Edition. Large crown, 8s.

(For Cheap Editions of other Works, see page 25.)

MEREDITH (GEORGE)—

MODERN LOVE, AND POEMS OF THE ENGLISH
ROADSIDE, with Poems and Ballads. Fcap. 8vo, cloth, 6s.

MOLESWORTH (W. NASSAU)—

HISTORY OF ENGLAND FROM THE YEAR 1830
TO THE RESIGNATION OF THE GLADSTONE MINISTRY.
A Cheap Edition, carefully revised, and carried up to March, 1874. 3 vols.
crown 8vo, 18s.
A School Edition. Post 8vo, 7s. 6d.

MONTAGU (THE RIGHT HON. LORD ROBERT, M.P.)—

FOREIGN POLICY : ENGLAND AND THE EASTERN
QUESTION. Second Edition. Demy 8vo, 14s.

MORLEY (HENRY)—

ENGLISH WRITERS. Vol. I. Part I. THE CELTS
AND ANGLO-SAXONS. With an Introductory Sketch of the Four Periods of
English Literature. Part II. FROM THE CONQUEST TO CHAUCER.
(Making 2 vols.) 8vo, cloth, £1 2s.

** Each Part is indexed separately. The Two Parts complete the account of
English Literature during the Period of the Formation of the Language, or of
THE WRITERS BEFORE CHAUCER.

Vol. II. Part I. FROM CHAUCER TO DUNBAR.
8vo, cloth, 12s.

TABLES OF ENGLISH LITERATURE. Containing
20 Charts. Second Edition, with Index. Royal 4to, cloth, 12s.
In Three Parts. Parts I. and II., containing Three Charts, each 1s. 6d.
Part III., containing 14 Charts, 7s. Part III. also kept in Sections, 1, 2, and 5,
1s. 6d. each ; 3 and 4 together, 3s. **** The Charts sold separately.

MORLEY (JOHN)—

DIDEROT AND THE ENCYCLOPÆDISTS. 2 Vols.
demy 8vo, 26s.

CRITICAL MISCELLANIES. Second Series. France
in the Eighteenth Century—Robespierre—Turgot—Death of Mr. Mill—Mr. Mill
on Religion—On Popular Culture—Macaulay. Demy 8vo, cloth, 14s.

CRITICAL MISCELLANIES. First Series. Demy 8vo, 14s.

NEW UNIFORM EDITION.

VOLTAIRE. Large crown 8vo, 6s.

ROUSSEAU. Large crown 8vo, 9s.

CRITICAL MISCELLANIES. First Series. Large crown
8vo, 6s.

MORLEY (JOHN)—Continued.

CRITICAL MISCELLANIES. Second Series. [*In the Press.*

DIDEROT AND THE ENCYCLOPÆDISTS. Large crown 8vo, 12s.

ON COMPROMISE. New Edition. Crown 8vo, 3s. 6d.

STRUGGLE FOR NATIONAL EDUCATION. Third Edition. 8vo, cloth, 3s.

MORRIS (M. O'CONNOR)—

HIBERNICA VENATICA. With Portraits of the Marchioness of Waterford, the Marchioness of Ormonde, Lady Randolph Churchill, Hon. Mrs. Malone, Miss Persse (of Moyode Castle), Mrs. Stewart Duckett, and Miss Myra Watson. Large crown 8vo, 18s.

TRIVIATA ; or, Cross Road Chronicles of Passages in Irish Hunting History during the season of 1875-76. With Illustrations. Large crown 8vo, 16s.

MURPHY (J. M.)—

RAMBLES IN NORTH-WEST AMERICA. With Frontispiece and Map. 16s.

NEWTON (E. TULLEY, F.G.S.)—Assistant-Naturalist H.M. Geological Survey—

THE TYPICAL PARTS IN THE SKELETONS OF A CAT, DUCK, AND CODFISH, being a Catalogue with Comparative Descriptions arranged in a Tabular Form. Demy 8vo, cloth, 3s.

O'CONNELL (MRS. MORGAN JOHN)—

CHARLES BIANCONI. A Biography. 1786–1875. By his Daughter. With Illustrations. Demy 8vo, 10s. 6d..

OLIVER (PROFESSOR), F.R.S., &c.—

ILLUSTRATIONS OF THE PRINCIPAL NATURAL ORDERS OF THE VEGETABLE KINGDOM, PREPARED FOR THE SCIENCE AND ART DEPARTMENT, SOUTH KENSINGTON. Oblong 8vo, with 109 Plates. Price, plain, 16s. : coloured, £1 6s.

OZANNE (I. W.)—

THREE YEARS IN ROUMANIA. Large crown 8vo, 7s. 6d.

PIERCE (GILBERT A.)—

THE DICKENS DICTIONARY : a Key to the Characters and Principal Incidents in the Tales of Charles Dickens. With Additions by WILLIAM A. WHEELER. Large crown 8vo, 10s.6d.

PIM (B.) and SEEMAN (B.)—

DOTTINGS ON THE ROADSIDE IN PANAMA, NICARAGUA, AND MOSQUITO. With Plates and Maps. 8vo, cloth, 18s.

POLLEN (J. H.)—

ANCIENT AND MODERN FURNITURE AND WOODWORK IN THE SOUTH KENSINGTON MUSEUM. With an Introduction, and Illustrated with numerous Coloured Photographs and Woodcuts. Royal 8vo, half-morocco, £1 1s

POLLOK (LIEUT.-COLONEL)—

SPORT IN BRITISH BURMAH, ASSAM, AND THE
CASSYAH AND JYNTIAH HILLS. With Notes of Sport in the Hilly Districts of the Northern Division, Madras Presidency. 2 vols. Demy 8vo, with Illustrations and 2 Maps. 24s.

POYNTER (E. J.), R.A.—

TEN LECTURES ON ART. Large crown 8vo. 9s.

PRINSEP (VAL), A.R.A.—

IMPERIAL INDIA. Containing numerous Illustrations
and Maps made during a Tour to the Courts of the Principal Rajahs and Princes of India. Second Edition. Demy 8vo, 21s.

PUCKETT (R. CAMPBELL)—Head-Master of the Bath School of Art—

SCIOGRAPHY; or, Radial Projection of Shadows. New
Edition. Crown 8vo, cloth, 6s.

RANKEN (W. H. L.)—

THE DOMINION OF AUSTRALIA. An Account of
its Foundations. Post 8vo, cloth, 12s.

REDGRAVE (RICHARD)—

MANUAL AND CATECHISM ON COLOUR. 24mo,
cloth, 9d.

REDGRAVE (SAMUEL)—

A DESCRIPTIVE CATALOGUE OF THE HIS-
TORICAL COLLECTION OF WATER-COLOUR PAINTINGS IN THE SOUTH KENSINGTON MUSEUM. With an Introductory Notice by SAMUEL REDGRAVE. With numerous Chromo-lithographs and other Illustrations. Published for the Science and Art Department of the Committee of Council on Education. Royal 8vo, £1 1s.

RIDGE (DR. BENJAMIN)—

OURSELVES, OUR FOOD, AND OUR PHYSIC.
Twelfth Edition. Fcap. 8vo, cloth, 1s. 6d.

ROBINSON (C. E.)—

THE CRUISE OF THE *WIDGEON*: 700 Miles in
a Ten-Ton Yawl, from Swanage to Hamburg, through the Dutch Canals and the Zuyder Zee, German Ocean, and the River Elbe. With 4 Illustrations, drawn on Wood, by the Author. Second Edition. Large crown 8vo, 9s.

ROBINSON (J. C.)—

ITALIAN SCULPTURE OF THE MIDDLE AGES
AND PERIOD OF THE REVIVAL OF ART. A descriptive Catalogue of that Section of the South Kensington Museum comprising an Account of the Acquisitions from the Gigli and Campana Collections. With 20 Engravings. Royal 8vo, cloth, 7s. 6d.

ROBSON (GEORGE)—

ELEMENTARY BUILDING CONSTRUCTION. Illus-
trated by a Design for an Entrance, Lodge, and Gate. 15 Plates. Oblong folio, sewed, 8s.

ROBSON (REV. J. H., M.A., LL.M.)—late Foundation Scholar of Downing. College, Cambridge—

AN ELEMENTARY TREATISE ON ALGEBRA.
Post 8vo, 6s.

ROCK (THE VERY REV. CANON, D.D.)—

ON TEXTILE FABRICS. A Descriptive and Illustrated
Catalogue of the Collection of Church Vestments, Dresses, Silk Stuffs, Needlework,
and Tapestries in the South Kensington Museum. Royal 8vo, half-morocco,
£1 11s. 6d.

ROWLAND (ARTHUR)—

FARMING FOR PLEASURE AND PROFIT. Edited
by WILLIAM ABLETT.
Vol. I.—DAIRY-FARMING, MANAGEMENT OF COWS, &c. Large
crown 8vo, 5s.
Vol. II.—POULTRY-KEEPING. Large crown 8vo, 5s.
Vol. III.—TREE-PLANTING, for Ornamentation or Profit. Suitable to every
soil and situation. Large crown 8vo, 5s.

SALUSBURY (PHILIP H. B.)—Lieut. 1st Royal Cheshire Light Infantry—

TWO MONTHS WITH TCHERNAIEFF IN SERVIA.
Large crown 8vo, 9s.

SCHMID (HERMAN) and STIELER (KARL)—

BAVARIAN HIGHLANDS (THE) AND THE SALZ-
KAMMERGUT. Profusely illustrated by G. CLOSS, W. DIEZ, A. VON RAMBERG,
K. RAUP, J. G. STEFFAN, F. VOLTY, J. WATTER, and others. With an Account
of the Habits and Manners of the Hunters, Poachers, and Peasantry of these
Districts. Super-royal 4to, cloth, £1 5s.

SHIRREFF (EMILY)—

A SKETCH OF THE LIFE OF FRIEDRICH
FRÖBEL, together with a Notice of MADAME VON MARENHOLTZ BULOW's
Personal Recollections of F. FRÖBEL. Crown 8vo, sewn, 1s.

SHUTE (ANNA CLARA)—

POSTHUMOUS POEMS. Crown 8vo, cloth, 8s.

SKERTCHLY (J. A.)—

DAHOMEY AS IT IS: being a Narrative of Eight
Months' Residence in that Country, with a Full Account of the Notorious Annual
Customs, and the Social and Religious Institutions of the Ffons. With Illustra-
tions. 8vo, cloth, £1 1s.

SMITH (GOLDWIN)—

THE POLITICAL DESTINY OF CANADA. Crown
8vo, 5s.

*SMITHARD (MARIAN)—First-Class Diplomée from National Training
School, South Kensington—*

COOKERY FOR THE ARTIZAN AND OTHERS:
being a Selection of over Two Hundred Useful Receipts. Sewed, 1s.

SPALDING (CAPTAIN)—

KHIVA AND TURKESTAN, translated from the Russian,
with Map. Large crown 8vo, 9s.

ST. CLAIR (S. G. B., Captain late 21st Fusiliers) and CHARLES A. BROPHY—

TWELVE YEARS' RESIDENCE IN BULGARIA.
Revised Edition. Demy 8vo, 9s.

STORY (W. W.)—

ROBA DI ROMA. Seventh Edition, with Additions and
Portrait. Post 8vo, cloth, 10s. 6d.

THE PROPORTIONS OF THE HUMAN FRAME,
ACCORDING TO A NEW CANON. With Plates. Royal 8vo, cloth, 10s.

CASTLE ST. ANGELO. Uniform with "Roba di Roma."
With Illustrations. Large crown 8vo, 10s. 6d.

STREETER (E. W.)—

PRECIOUS STONES AND GEMS. Second Edition.
Demy 8vo, cloth 18s.; calf, 27s.

GOLD; OR, LEGAL REGULATIONS FOR THIS
METAL IN DIFFERENT COUNTRIES OF THE WORLD. Crown 8vo, cloth, 3s. 6d.

STUART-GLENNIE (JOHN STUART) M.A., Barrister-at-Law—

EUROPE AND ASIA : DISCUSSIONS OF THE
EASTERN QUESTION. In Travels through Independent, Turkish, and Austrian Illyria. With a Politico-Ethnographical Map. Demy 8vo, 14s.

TOPINARD (DR. PAUL)—

ANTHROPOLOGY. With a Preface by Professor PAUL
BROCA, Secretary of the Société d'Anthropologie, and Translated by ROBERT J. H. BARTLETT, M.D. With numerous Illustrations. Large crown 8vo, 7s. 6d.

TROLLOPE (ANTHONY)—

THE CHRONICLES OF BARSETSHIRE. A Uniform
Edition, consisting of 8 vols., large crown 8vo, handsomely printed, each vol. containing Frontispiece.

THE WARDEN.	THE SMALL HOUSE AT
BARCHESTER TOWERS.	ALLINGTON. 2 vols.
DR. THORNE.	LAST CHRONICLE OF
FRAMLEY PARSONAGE.	BARSET. 2 vols.

AUSTRALIA AND NEW ZEALAND. A Cheap Edition
with Maps. 2 vols. Small 8vo, cloth, 7s. 6d.

HUNTING SKETCHES. Cloth, 3s. 6d.

TRAVELLING SKETCHES. Cloth, 3s. 6d.

CLERGYMEN OF THE CHURCH OF ENGLAND.
3s. 6d.

SOUTH AFRICA. 2 vols. Large crown 8vo, with Maps.
Fourth Edition. £1 10s.

SOUTH AFRICA. 1 vol. Crown 8vo, 6s.
(For Cheap Editions of other Works, see page 25.)

VERON (EUGENE)—

ÆSTHETICS. Translated by W. H. ARMSTRONG. Large
crown 8vo, 7s. 6d.

WALMSLEY (HUGH MULLENEUX)—

THE LIFE OF SIR JOSHUA WALMSLEY. With
Portrait, demy 8vo, 14s.

WESTWOOD (J. O.), M.A., F.L.S., &c. &c.—

A DESCRIPTIVE AND ILLUSTRATED CATALOGUE
OF THE FICTILE IVORIES IN THE SOUTH KENSINGTON MUSEUM. With an Account of the Continental Collections of Classical and Mediæval Ivories. Royal 8vo, half-morocco, £1 4s.

WHEELER (G. P.)—

VISIT OF THE PRINCE OF WALES. A Chronicle of
H.R.H.'s Journeyings in India, Ceylon Spain, and Portugal. Large crown 8vo, 12s

WHITE (WALTER)—

HOLIDAYS IN TYROL : Kufstein, Klobenstein, and
Paneveggio. Large crown 8vo, 14s.

MONTH IN YORKSHIRE. Post 8vo. With a Map.
Fifth edition. 4s.

LONDONER'S WALK TO THE LAND'S END, AND
A TRIP TO THE SCILLY ISLES. Post 8vo. With 4 Maps. Third Edition. 4s.

WORNUM (R. N.)—

HOLBEIN (HANS)—LIFE. With Portrait and Illustrations. Imperial 8vo, cloth, £1 11s. 6d.

THE EPOCHS OF PAINTING. A Biographical and
Critical Essay on Painting and Painters of all Times and many Places. With
numerous Illustrations. Demy 8vo, cloth, £1.

ANALYSIS OF ORNAMENT : THE CHARACTER-
ISTICS OF STYLES. An Introduction to the Study of the History of Ornamental
Art. With many Illustrations. Sixth Edition. Royal 8vo, cloth, 8s.

WYON (F. W.)—

HISTORY OF GREAT BRITAIN DURING THE
REIGN OF QUEEN ANNE. 2 vols. Demy 8vo, £1 12s.

YOUNGE (C. D.)—

PARALLEL LIVES OF ANCIENT AND MODERN
HEROES. New Edition. 12mo, cloth, 4s. 6d.

AUSTRALIAN MEAT : RECIPES FOR COOKING AUS-
TRALIAN MEAT, with Directions for Preparing Sauces suitable for the same.
By a Cook. 12mo, sewed, 9d.

OFFICIAL HANDBOOK FOR THE NATIONAL TRAIN-
ING SCHOOL FOR COOKERY. Containing Lessons on Cookery ; forming
the Course of Instruction in the School. With List of Utensils Necessary, and
Lessons on Cleaning Utensils. Compiled by "R. O. C." Large crown 8vo.
Fourth Edition, 8s.

CEYLON : being a General Description of the Island, Historical,
Physical, Statistical. Containing the most Recent Information. With Map. By
an Officer, late of the Ceylon Rifles. 2 vols. Demy 8vo, £1 8s.

COLONIAL EXPERIENCES ; or, Incidents and Reminiscences
of Thirty-four Years in New Zealand. By an Old Colonist. With a Map.
Crown 8vo, 8s.

ELEMENTARY DRAWING-BOOK. Directions for Intro-
ducing the First Steps of Elementary Drawing in Schools and among Workmen.
Small 4to, cloth, 4s. 6d.

FORTNIGHTLY REVIEW.—First Series, May, 1865, to Dec.
1866. 6 vols. Cloth, 13s. each.

New Series, 1867 to 1872. In Half-yearly Volumes. Cloth,
13s. each.

From January, 1873, to June 30, 1879, in Half-yearly
Volumes. Cloth, 16s. each.

HOME LIFE. A Handbook and Elementary Instruction, containing Practical Suggestions addressed to Managers and Teachers of Schools, intended to show how the underlying principles of Home Duties or Domestic Economy may be the basis of National Primary Instruction. Crown 8vo, 3s.

PAST DAYS IN INDIA; or, Sporting Reminiscences of the Valley of the Saone and the Basin of Singrowlee. By a late CUSTOMS OFFICER, N.W. Provinces, India. Post 8vo, 10s. 6d.

SHOOTING ADVENTURES, CANINE LORE, AND SEA-FISHING TRIPS. By "WILDFOWLER," "SNAPSHOT." 2 vols. Large crown 8vo, 21s.

SHOOTING, YACHTING, AND SEA-FISHING TRIPS, at Home and on the Continent. Second Series. By "WILDFOWLER," "SNAPSHOT." 2 vols., crown 8vo, £1 1s.

SHOOTING AND FISHING TRIPS IN ENGLAND, FRANCE, ALSACE, BELGIUM, HOLLAND, AND BAVARIA. By "WILDFOWLER," "SNAPSHOT." New Edition, with Illustrations. Large crown 8vo, 8s.

UNIVERSAL CATALOGUE OF BOOKS ON ART. Compiled for the use of the National Art Library, and the Schools of Art in the United Kingdom. In 2 vols. Crown 4to, half-morocco, £2 2s.

SOUTH KENSINGTON MUSEUM SCIENCE AND ART HANDBOOKS.

Published for the Committee of Council on Education.

THE INDUSTRIAL ARTS IN SPAIN. By JUAN F. RIANO. Illustrated. Large crown 8vo, 4s.

GLASS. By ALEXANDER NESBITT. Illustrated. Large crown 8vo, 2s. 6d.

GOLD AND SILVER SMITHS' WORK. By JOHN HUNGERFORD POLLEN. With numerous Woodcuts. Large crown 8vo, 2s. 6d.

TAPESTRY. By ALFRED CHAMPEAUX. With Woodcuts. 2s. 6d.

BRONZES. By C. DRURY E. FORTNUM, F.S.A. With numerous Woodcuts. Large crown 8vo, 2s. 6d.

PLAIN WORDS ABOUT WATER. By A. H. CHURCH, M.A., Oxon. Large crown 8vo, sewed, 6d.

ANIMAL PRODUCTS: their Preparation, Commercial Uses and Value. By T. L. SIMMONDS. Large crown 8vo, 7s. 6d.

FOOD: A Short Account of the Sources, Constituents, and Uses of Food; intended chiefly as a Guide to the Food Collection in the Bethnal Green Museum. By A. H. CHURCH, M.A., Oxon. Large crown 8vo, 3s.

SCIENCE CONFERENCES. Delivered at the South Kensington Museum. Crown 8vo, 2 vols., 6s. each.
VOL. I.—Physics and Mechanics.
VOL. II.—Chemistry, Biology, Physical Geography, Geology, Mineralogy, and Meteorology.

ECONOMIC ENTOMOLOGY. By ANDREW MURRAY, F.L.S., APTERA. With numerous Illustrations. Large crown 8vo, 7s. 6d.

SOUTH KENSINGTON MUSEUM SCIENCE & ART HANDBOOKS—*Continued.*

HANDBOOK TO THE SPECIAL LOAN COLLECTION
of Scientific Apparatus. Large crown 8vo, 3s.

THE INDUSTRIAL ARTS : Historical Sketches. With 242
Illustrations. Demy 8vo, 7s. 6d.

TEXTILE FABRICS. By the Very Rev. DANIEL ROCK, D.D.
With numerous Woodcuts. Large crown 8vo, 2s. 6d.

IVORIES : ANCIENT AND MEDIÆVAL. By WILLIAM
MASKELL. With numerous Woodcuts. Large crown 8vo, 2s. 6d.

ANCIENT & MODERN FURNITURE & WOODWORK.
By JOHN HUNGERFORD POLLEN. With numerous Woodcuts. Large crown 8vo,
2s. 6d.

MAIOLICA. By C. DRURY E. FORTNUM, F.S.A. With
numerous Woodcuts. Large crown 8vo, 2s. 6d.

MUSICAL INSTRUMENTS. By CARL ENGEL. With numerous
Woodcuts. Large crown 8vo, 2s. 6d.

MANUAL OF DESIGN, compiled from the Writings and
Addresses of RICHARD REDGRAVE, R.A. By GILBERT R. REDGRAVE. With
Woodcuts. Large crown 8vo, 2s. 6d.

PERSIAN ART. By MAJOR R. MURDOCK SMITH, R.E. With
Additional Illustrations.   [*In the Press.*

FREE EVENING LECTURES. Delivered in connection with
the Special Loan Collection of Scientific Apparatus, 1876. Large crown 8vo, 8s.

CARLYLE'S (THOMAS) WORKS.
LIBRARY EDITION COMPLETE.
Handsomely printed in 34 vols. Demy 8vo, cloth, £15.

SARTOR RESARTUS. The Life and Opinions of Herr
Teufelsdrockh. With a Portrait, 7s. 6d.

THE FRENCH REVOLUTION. A History. 3 vols., each 9s.

LIFE OF FREDERICK SCHILLER AND EXAMINATION
OF HIS WORKS. With Supplement of 1872. Portrait and Plates, 9s. The Supplement *separately*, 2s.

CRITICAL AND MISCELLANEOUS ESSAYS. With Portrait.
6 vols., each 9s.

ON HEROES, HERO WORSHIP, AND THE HEROIC
IN HISTORY. 7s. 6d.

PAST AND PRESENT. 9s.

OLIVER CROMWELL'S LETTERS AND SPEECHES. With
Portraits. 5 vols., each 9s.

B

CARLYLE'S (THOMAS) WORKS—*Continued.*

LATTER-DAY PAMPHLETS. 9s.

LIFE OF JOHN STERLING. With Portrait, 9s.

HISTORY OF FREDERICK THE SECOND. 10 vols., each 9s.

TRANSLATIONS FROM THE GERMAN. 3 vols., each 9s.

GENERAL INDEX TO THE LIBRARY EDITION. 8vo, cloth, 6s.

EARLY KINGS OF NORWAY: also AN ESSAY ON THE PORTRAITS OF JOHN KNOX. Crown 8vo, with Portrait Illustrations, 7s. 6d.

CHEAP AND UNIFORM EDITION.

In 23 vols., Crown 8vo, cloth, £7 5s.

THE FRENCH REVOLUTION: A History. 2 vols., 12s.

OLIVER CROMWELL'S LET-TERS AND SPEECHES, with Eluci-dations, &c. 3 vols., 18s.

LIVES OF SCHILLER AND JOHN STERLING. 1 vol., 6s.

CRITICAL AND MISCELLA-NEOUS ESSAYS. 4 vols., £1 4s.

SARTOR RESARTUS AND LECTURES ON HEROES. 1 vol., 6s.

LATTER-DAY PAMPHLETS. 1 vol., 6s.

CHARTISM AND PAST AND PRESENT. 1 vol., 6s.

TRANSLATIONS FROM THE GERMAN OF MUSÆUS, TIECK, AND RICHTER. 1 vol., 6s.

WILHELM MEISTER, by Göthe. A Translation. 2 vols., 12s.

HISTORY OF FRIEDRICH THE SECOND, called Frederick the Great. Vols. I. and II., containing Part I.— "Friedrich till his Accession." 14s. Vols. III. and IV., containing Part II.— "The First Two Silesian Wars." 14s. Vols. V., VI., VII., completing the Work, £1 1s.

PEOPLE'S EDITION.

In 37 vols., small Crown 8vo. Price 2s. each vol., bound in cloth; or in sets of 37 vols. in 18, cloth gilt, for £3 14s.

SARTOR RESARTUS.

FRENCH REVOLUTION. 3 vols.

LIFE OF JOHN STERLING.

OLIVER CROMWELL'S LET-TERS AND SPEECHES. 5 vols.

ON HEROES AND HERO WORSHIP.

PAST AND PRESENT.

CRITICAL AND MISCELLA-NEOUS ESSAYS. 7 vols.

LATTER-DAY PAMPHLETS.

LIFE OF SCHILLER.

FREDERICK THE GREAT. 10 vols.

WILHELM MEISTER. 3 vols.

TRANSLATIONS FROM MU-SÆUS, TIECK, AND RICHTER. 2 vols.

THE EARLY KINGS OF NOR-WAY; also an Essay on the Portraits of John Knox, with Illustrations. Small crown 8vo. Bound up with the Index and uniform with the "People's Edition."

DICKENS'S (CHARLES) WORKS.

ORIGINAL EDITIONS.

In Demy 8vo.

THE MYSTERY OF EDWIN DROOD. With Illustrations
by S. L. Fildes, and a Portrait engraved by Baker. Cloth, 7s. 6d.

OUR MUTUAL FRIEND. With Forty Illustrations by Marcus
Stone. Cloth, £1 1s.

THE PICKWICK PAPERS. With Forty-three Illustrations
by Seymour and Phiz. Cloth, £1 1s.

NICHOLAS NICKLEBY. With Forty Illustrations by Phiz.
Cloth, £1 1s.

SKETCHES BY "BOZ." With Forty Illustrations by George
Cruikshank. Cloth, £1 1s.

MARTIN CHUZZLEWIT. With Forty Illustrations by Phiz.
Cloth, £1 1s.

DOMBEY AND SON. With Forty Illustrations by Phiz.
Cloth, £1 1s.

DAVID COPPERFIELD. With Forty Illustrations by Phiz.
Cloth, £1 1s.

BLEAK HOUSE. With Forty Illustrations by Phiz. Cloth,
£1 1s.

LITTLE DORRIT. With Forty Illustrations by Phiz. Cloth,
£1 1s.

THE OLD CURIOSITY SHOP. With Seventy-five Illus-
trations by George Cattermole and H. K. Browne. A New Edition. Uniform with
the other volumes, £1 1s.

BARNABY RUDGE: a Tale of the Riots of 'Eighty. With
Seventy-eight Illustrations by G. Cattermole and H. K. Browne. Uniform with the
other volumes, £1 1s.

CHRISTMAS BOOKS: Containing—The Christmas Carol;
The Cricket on the Hearth; The Chimes; The Battle of Life; The Haunted House.
With all the original Illustrations. Cloth, 12s.

OLIVER TWIST and TALE OF TWO CITIES. In one
volume. Cloth, £1 1s.

OLIVER TWIST. Separately. With Twenty-four Illustrations
by George Cruikshank.

A TALE OF TWO CITIES. Separately. With Sixteen Illustrations by Phiz. Cloth, 9s.

⁎⁎ The remainder of Dickens's Works were not originally printed in Demy 8vo.

DICKENS'S (CHARLES) WORKS—*Continued.*

LIBRARY EDITION.

In Post 8vo.   With the Original Illustrations, 30 vols., cloth, £12.

			s.	d.
PICKWICK PAPERS	43 Illustrns.,	2 vols. ..	16	o
NICHOLAS NICKLEBY	39	„ 2 vols. ..	16	o
MARTIN CHUZZLEWIT	40	„ 2 vols. ..	16	o
OLD CURIOSITY SHOP and REPRINTED PIECES	36	„ 2 vols. ..	16	o
BARNABY RUDGE and HARD TIMES..	36	„ 2 vols. ..	16	o
BLEAK HOUSE	40	„ 2 vols. ..	16	o
LITTLE DORRIT	40	„ 2 vols. ..	16	o
DOMBEY AND SON	38	„ 2 vols. ..	16	o
DAVID COPPERFIELD	38	„ 2 vols. ..	16	o
OUR MUTUAL FRIEND	40	„ 2 vols. ..	16	o
SKETCHES BY "BOZ"	39	„ 1 vol. ..	8	o
OLIVER TWIST	24	„ 1 vol. ..	8	o
CHRISTMAS BOOKS	17	„ 1 vol. ..	8	o
A TALE OF TWO CITIES	16	„ 1 vol. ..	8	o
GREAT EXPECTATIONS	8	„ 1 vol. ..	8	o
PICTURES FROM ITALY and AMERICAN NOTES	8	„ 1 vol. ..	8	o
UNCOMMERCIAL TRAVELLER	8	„ 1 vol. ..	8	o
CHILD'S HISTORY OF ENGLAND	8	„ 1 vol. ..	8	o
EDWIN DROOD and MISCELLANIES	12	„ 1 vol. ..	8	o
CHRISTMAS STORIES from "Household Words," &c..	14	„ 1 vol. ..	8	o

THE LIFE OF CHARLES DICKENS. By JOHN FORSTER. A New Edition. With Illustrations. Uniform with the Library Edition, post 8vo, of his Works. In one vol. 10s. 6d.

THE "CHARLES DICKENS" EDITION.

In Crown 8vo.   In 21 vols., cloth, with Illustrations, £3 9s. 6d.

			s.	d.
PICKWICK PAPERS	8 Illustrations		3	6
MARTIN CHUZZLEWIT	8	„	3	6
DOMBEY AND SON	8	„	3	6
NICHOLAS NICKLEBY	8	„	3	6
DAVID COPPERFIELD	8	„	3	6
BLEAK HOUSE	8	„	3	6
LITTLE DORRIT	8	„	3	6
OUR MUTUAL FRIEND	8	„	3	6
BARNABY RUDGE	8	„	3	6
OLD CURIOSITY SHOP	8	„	3	6
A CHILD'S HISTORY OF ENGLAND	4	„	3	6
EDWIN DROOD and OTHER STORIES	8	„	3	6
CHRISTMAS STORIES, from "Household Words" ..	8	„	3	6
TALE OF TWO CITIES	8	„	3	o
SKETCHES BY "BOZ"	8	„	3	o
AMERICAN NOTES and REPRINTED PIECES ..	8	„	3	o
CHRISTMAS BOOKS	8	„	3	o
OLIVER TWIST	8	„	3	o
GREAT EXPECTATIONS	8	„	3	o
HARD TIMES and PICTURES FROM ITALY ..	8	„	3	o
UNCOMMERCIAL TRAVELLER	4	„	3	o

THE LIFE OF CHARLES DICKENS. Uniform with this Edition, with Numerous Illustrations. 2 vols. 3s. 6d. each.

DICKENS'S (CHARLES) WORKS—*Continued.*

THE ILLUSTRATED LIBRARY EDITION.

Complete in 30 Volumes. Demy 8vo, 10s. each; or set, £15.

This Edition is printed on a finer paper and in a larger type than has been employed in any previous edition. The type has been cast especially for it, and the page is of a size to admit of the introduction of all the original illustrations.

No such attractive issue has been made of the writings of Mr. Dickens, which, various as have been the forms of publication adapted to the demands of an ever widely-increasing popularity, have never yet been worthily presented in a really handsome library form.

The collection comprises all the minor writings it was Mr. Dickens's wish to preserve.

SKETCHES BY "BOZ." With 40 Illustrations by George Cruikshank.

PICKWICK PAPERS. 2 vols. With 42 Illustrations by Phiz.

OLIVER TWIST. With 24 Illustrations by Cruikshank.

NICHOLAS NICKLEBY. 2 vols. With 40 Illustrations by Phiz.

OLD CURIOSITY SHOP and REPRINTED PIECES. 2 vols. With Illustrations by Cattermole, &c.

BARNABY RUDGE and HARD TIMES. 2 vols. With Illustrations by Cattermole, &c.

MARTIN CHUZZLEWIT. 2 vols. With 40 Illustrations by Phiz.

AMERICAN NOTES and PICTURES FROM ITALY. 1 vol. With 8 Illustrations.

DOMBEY AND SON. 2 vols. With 40 Illustrations by Phiz.

DAVID COPPERFIELD. 2 vols. With 40 Illustrations by Phiz.

BLEAK HOUSE. 2 vols. With 40 Illustrations by Phiz.

LITTLE DORRIT. 2 vols. With 40 Illustrations by Phiz.

A TALE OF TWO CITIES. With 16 Illustrations by Phiz.

THE UNCOMMERCIAL TRAVELLER. With 8 Illustrations by Marcus Stone.

GREAT EXPECTATIONS. With 8 Illustrations by Marcus Stone.

OUR MUTUAL FRIEND. 2 vols. With 40 Illustrations by Marcus Stone.

CHRISTMAS BOOKS. With 17 Illustrations by Sir Edwin Landseer, R.A., Maclise, R.A., &c. &c.

HISTORY OF ENGLAND. With 8 Illustrations by Marcus Stone.

CHRISTMAS STORIES. (From "Household Words" and "All the Year Round.") With 14 Illustrations.

EDWIN DROOD AND OTHER STORIES. With 12 Illustrations by S. L. Fildes.

DICKENS'S (CHARLES) WORKS—*Continued*—

HOUSEHOLD EDITION.

In Crown 4to vols.

21 Volumes completed.

OLIVER TWIST, with 28 Illustrations, cloth, 2s. 6d. ; paper, 1s. 9d.

MARTIN CHUZZLEWIT, with 59 Illustrations, cloth, 4s. ; paper, 3s.

DAVID COPPERFIELD, with 60 Illustrations and a Portrait, cloth, 4s. ; paper, 3s.

BLEAK HOUSE, with 61 Illustrations, cloth, 4s. ; paper, 3s.

LITTLE DORRIT, with 58 Illustrations, cloth, 4s. ; paper, 3s.

PICKWICK PAPERS, with 56 Illustrations, cloth, 4s. ; paper, 3s.

BARNABY RUDGE, with 46 Illustrations, cloth, 4s. ; paper, 3s.

A TALE OF TWO CITIES, with 25 Illustrations, cloth, 2s. 6d. ; paper, 1s. 9d.

OUR MUTUAL FRIEND, with 58 Illustrations, cloth, 4s. ; paper, 3s.

NICHOLAS NICKLEBY, with 59 Illustrations, cloth, 4s. ; paper, 3s.

GREAT EXPECTATIONS, with 26 Illustrations, cloth, 2s. 6d. ; paper, 1s. 9d.

OLD CURIOSITY SHOP, with 39 Illustrations, cloth, 4s. ; paper, 3s.

SKETCHES BY " BOZ," with 36 Illustrations, cloth, 2s. 6d. ; paper, 1s. 9d.

HARD TIMES, with 20 Illustrations, cloth, 2s. ; paper, 1s. 6d.

DOMBEY AND SON, with 61 Illustrations, cloth, 4s. ; paper, 3s.

UNCOMMERCIAL TRAVELLER, with 26 Illustrations, cloth, 2s. 6d.; paper, 1s. 9d.

CHRISTMAS BOOKS, with 28 Illustrations, cloth, 2s. 6d.; sewed, 1s. 9d.

THE HISTORY OF ENGLAND, with 15 Illustrations, cloth, 2s. 6d. ; paper, 1s. 9d.

AMERICAN NOTES and PICTURES FROM ITALY, with 18 New Illustrations, cloth, 2s. 6d. ; paper, 1s. 9d.

EDWIN DROOD; REPRINTED PIECES; and other STORIES, with 30 Illustrations, cloth, 4s. ; paper, 3s.

CHRISTMAS STORIES, with 23 Illustrations, cloth, 4s. ; paper 3s.

THE LIFE OF DICKENS. By John Forster. *In November.*

Messrs. CHAPMAN & HALL trust that by this Edition they will be enabled to place the works of the most popular British Author of the present day in the hands of all English readers.

PEOPLE'S EDITION.

PICKWICK PAPERS. In Boards. Illustrated. 2s.

SKETCHES BY BOZ. In Boards. Illustrated. 2s.

OLIVER TWIST. In Boards. Illustrated. 2s.

NICHOLAS NICKLEBY. In Boards. Illustrated. 2s.

MARTIN CHUZZLEWIT. In Boards. Illustrated. 2s.

DOMBEY AND SON. In Boards. Illustrated. 2s.

MR. DICKENS'S READINGS.

Fcap. 8vo, sewed.

CHRISTMAS CAROL IN PROSE. 1s. | STORY OF LITTLE DOMBEY. 1s.

CRICKET ON THE HEARTH. 1s. | POOR TRAVELLER, BOOTS AT THE HOLLY-TREE INN, and MRS.

CHIMES : A GOBLIN STORY. 1s. | GAMP. 1s.

A CHRISTMAS CAROL, with the Original Coloured Plates ;

being a reprint of the Original Edition. Small 8vo, red cloth, gilt edges, 5s.

THE LIBRARY

OF

CONTEMPORARY SCIENCE.

Some degree of truth has been admitted in the charge not unfrequently brought against the English, that they are assiduous rather than solid readers. They give themselves too much to the lighter forms of literature. Technical Science is almost exclusively restricted to its professed votaries, and, but for some of the Quarterlies and Monthlies, very little solid matter would come within the reach of the general public.

But the circulation enjoyed by many of these very periodicals, and the increase of the scientific journals, may be taken for sufficient proof that a taste for more serious subjects of study is now growing. Indeed there is good reason to believe that if strictly scientific subjects are not more universally cultivated, it is mainly because they are not rendered more accessible to the people. Such themes are treated either too elaborately, or in too forbidding a style, or else brought out in too costly a form to be easily available to all classes.

With the view of remedying this manifold and increasing inconvenience, we are glad to be able to take advantage of a comprehensive project recently set on foot in France, emphatically the land of Popular Science. The well-known publishers MM. Reinwald and Co., have made satisfactory arrangements with some of the leading *savants* of that country to supply an exhaustive series of works on each and all of the sciences of the day, treated in a style at once lucid, popular, and strictly methodic.

The names of MM. P. Broca, Secretary of the Société d'Anthropologie; Ch. Martins, Montpellier University; C. Vogt, University of Geneva; G. de Mortillet, Museum of Saint Germain; A. Guillemin, author of "Ciel" and "Phénomènes de la Physique;" A. Hovelacque, editor of the "Revue de Linguistique;" Dr. Dally, Dr. Letourneau, and many others, whose co-operation has already been secured, are a guarantee that their respective subjects will receive thorough treatment, and will in all cases be written up to the very latest discoveries, and kept in every respect fully abreast of the times.

We have, on our part, been fortunate in making such further arrangements with some of the best writers and recognised authorities here, as will enable us to present the series in a thoroughly English dress to the reading public of this country. In so doing we feel convinced that we are taking the best means of supplying a want that has long been deeply felt.

[OVER.

LIBRARY OF CONTEMPORARY SCIENCE—*Continued*—

The volumes in actual course of execution, or contemplated, will embrace such subjects as :

SCIENCE OF LANGUAGE. [*Published.*	PHYSICAL AND COMMERCIAL
BIOLOGY. ,,	GEOGRAPHY.
ANTHROPOLOGY. ,,	ARCHITECTURE.
ÆSTHETICS. ,,	CHEMISTRY.
PHILOSOPHY. ,,	EDUCATION.
COMPARATIVE MYTHOLOGY.	GENERAL ANATOMY.
ASTRONOMY.	ZOOLOGY.
PREHISTORIC ARCHÆOLOGY.	BOTANY.
ETHNOGRAPHY.	METEOROLOGY.
GEOLOGY.	HISTORY.
HYGIENE.	FINANCE.
POLITICAL ECONOMY.	MECHANICS.
	STATISTICS, &c. &c.

All the volumes, while complete and so far independent in themselves, will be of uniform appearance, slightly varying, according to the nature of the subject, in bulk and in price.

When finished they will form a Complete Collection of Standard Works of Reference on all the physical and mental sciences, thus fully justifying the general title chosen for the series—"LIBRARY OF CONTEMPORARY SCIENCE."

LEVER'S (CHARLES) WORKS.

THE ORIGINAL EDITION with THE ILLUSTRATIONS.

In 17 vols.   Demy 8vo.   Cloth, 6s. each.

CHEAP EDITION.

Fancy boards, 2s. 6d.

CHARLES O'MALLEY.	THE DALTONS.
TOM BURKE.	ROLAND CASHEL.
THE KNIGHT OF GWYNNE.	DAVENPORT DUNN.
MARTINS OF CROMARTIN.	DODD FAMILY.

Fancy boards, 2s.

THE O'DONOGHUE.	LORD KILGOBBIN.
FORTUNES OF GLENCORE.	LUTTRELL OF ARRAN.
HARRY LORREQUER.	RENT IN THE CLOUD and ST.
ONE OF THEM.	PATRICK'S EVE.
A DAY'S RIDE.	CON CREGAN.
JACK HINTON.	ARTHUR O'LEARY.
BARRINGTON.	THAT BOY OF NORCOTT'S.
TONY BUTLER.	CORNELIUS O'DOWD.
MAURICE TIERNAY.	SIR JASPER CAREW.
SIR BROOKE FOSBROOKE.	NUTS AND NUT-CRACKERS.
BRAMLEIGHS OF BISHOP'S	
FOLLY.	

Also in sets, 27 vols., cloth, for £4 4s.

TROLLOPE'S (ANTHONY) WORKS.

CHEAP EDITION.

Boards, 2s. 6d. ; *cloth,* 3s. 6d.

THE PRIME MINISTER.	PHINEAS REDUX.
PHINEAS FINN.	HE KNEW HE WAS RIGHT.
ORLEY FARM.	EUSTACE DIAMONDS.
CAN YOU FORGIVE HER!	

Boards, 2s. ; *cloth,* 3s.

VICAR OF BULLHAMPTON.	HARRY HOTSPUR.
RALPH THE HEIR.	RACHEL RAY.
THE BERTRAMS.	TALES OF ALL COUNTRIES
KELLYS AND O'KELLYS.	MARY GRESLEY.
McDERMOT OF BALLYCLORAN.	LOTTA SCHMIDT.
CASTLE RICHMOND.	LA VENDÉE.
BELTON ESTATE.	DOCTOR THORNE
MISS MACKENSIE.	IS HE POPENJOY!
LADY ANNA.	

WHYTE-MELVILLE'S WORKS.

CHEAP EDITION.

Crown 8vo, fancy boards, 2s. *each, or* 2s. 6d. *in cloth.*

UNCLE JOHN.

THE WHITE ROSE.

CERISE. A Tale of the Last Century.

BROOKES OF BRIDLEMERE.

"BONES AND I;" or, The Skeleton at Home.

"M., OR N." Similia Similibus Curantur.

CONTRABAND; or, A Losing Hazard.

MARKET HARBOROUGH; or, How Mr. Sawyer went to the Shires.

SARCHEDON. A Legend of the Great Queen.

SONGS AND VERSES.

SATANELLA. A Story of Punchestown.

THE TRUE CROSS. A Legend of the Church.

KATERFELTO. A Story of Exmoor.

SISTER LOUISE ; or, A Story of a Woman's Repentance.

ROSINE.

CHAPMAN & HALL'S

List of Books, Drawing Examples, Diagrams, Models, Instruments, &c.

INCLUDING

THOSE ISSUED UNDER THE AUTHORITY OF THE SCIENCE AND ART DEPARTMENT, SOUTH KENSINGTON, FOR THE USE OF SCHOOLS AND ART AND SCIENCE CLASSES.

BARTLEY (G. C. T.)—

CATALOGUE OF MODERN WORKS ON SCIENCE AND TECHNOLOGY. Post 8vo, sewed, 1s.

BENSON (W.)—

PRINCIPLES OF THE SCIENCE OF COLOUR. Small 4to, cloth, 15s.

MANUAL OF THE SCIENCE OF COLOUR. Coloured Frontispiece and Illustrations. 12mo, cloth, 2s. 6d.

BRADLEY (THOMAS)—of the Royal Military Academy, Woolwich—

ELEMENTS OF GEOMETRICAL DRAWING. In Two Parts, with 60 Plates. Oblong folio, half-bound, each part 16s.

Selections (from the above) of 20 Plates, for the use of the Royal Military Academy, Woolwich. Oblong folio, half-bound, 16s.

BURCHETT—

LINEAR PERSPECTIVE. With Illustrations. Post 8vo, cloth, 7s.

PRACTICAL GEOMETRY. Post 8vo, cloth, 5s.

DEFINITIONS OF GEOMETRY. Third Edition. 24mo, sewed, 5d.

CARROLL (JOHN)—

FREEHAND DRAWING LESSONS FOR THE BLACK BOARD. 6s.

CUBLEY (W. H.)—

A SYSTEM OF ELEMENTARY DRAWING. With Illustrations and Examples. Imperial 4to, sewed, 8s.

DAVISON (ELLIS A.)—

DRAWING FOR ELEMENTARY SCHOOLS. Post 8vo, cloth, 3s.

MODEL DRAWING. 12mo, cloth, 3s.

THE AMATEUR HOUSE CARPENTER: A Guide in Building, Making, and Repairing. With numerous Illustrations, drawn on Wood by the Author. Demy 8vo, 10s. 6d.

DELAMOTTE (P. H.)—

PROGRESSIVE DRAWING-BOOK FOR BEGINNERS. 12mo, 3s. 6d.

DICKSEE (J. R.)—

SCHOOL PERSPECTIVE. 8vo, cloth, 5s.

DYCE—
DRAWING-BOOK OF THE GOVERNMENT SCHOOL
OF DESIGN: ELEMENTARY OUTLINES OF ORNAMENT. 50 Plates.
Small folio, sewed, 5s.; mounted, 18s.

INTRODUCTION TO DITTO. Fcap. 8vo, 6d.

FOSTER (VERE)—
DRAWING-BOOKS :
(*a*) Forty-two Numbers, at 1d. each.
(*b*) Forty-six Numbers, at 3d. each. The set *b* includes the subjects in *a*.

DRAWING-CARDS :
Freehand Drawing : First Grade, Sets I., II., III., price 1s. each ; in cloth cases,
1s. 6d. each.
Second Grade, Set I., price 2s. ; in cloth case, 3s.

HENSLOW (PROFESSOR)—
ILLUSTRATIONS TO BE EMPLOYED IN THE
PRACTICAL LESSONS ON BOTANY. Prepared for South Kensington
Museum. Post 8vo, sewed, 6d.

JACOBSTHAL (E.)—
GRAMMATIK DER ORNAMENTE, in 7 Parts of 20
Plates each. Price, unmounted, £3 13s. 6d.; mounted on cardboard, £11 4s.
The Parts can be had separately.

JEWITT—
HANDBOOK OF PRACTICAL PERSPECTIVE. 18mo,
cloth, 1s. 6d.

KENNEDY (JOHN)—
FIRST GRADE PRACTICAL GEOMETRY. 12mo, 6d.

FREEHAND DRAWING-BOOK. 16mo, cloth, 1s. 6d.

LINDLEY (JOHN)—
SYMMETRY OF VEGETATION : Principles to be
observed in the delineation of Plants. 12mo, sewed, 1s.

MARSHALL—
HUMAN BODY. Text and Plates reduced from the large
Diagrams. 2 vols., cloth, £1 1s.

NEWTON (E. TULLEY, F.G.S.)—
THE TYPICAL PARTS IN THE SKELETONS OF A
CAT, DUCK, AND CODFISH, being a Catalogue with Comparative Descriptions arranged in a Tabular Form. Demy 8vo, 3s.

OLIVER (PROFESSOR)—
ILLUSTRATIONS OF THE VEGETABLE KINGDOM.
109 Plates. Oblong 8vo, cloth. Plain, 16s.; coloured, £1 6s.

PUCKETT (R. CAMPBELL)—
SCIOGRAPHY, OR RADIAL PROJECTION OF
SHADOWS. Crown 8vo, cloth, 6s.

REDGRAVE—
MANUAL AND CATECHISM ON COLOUR. Fifth
Edition. 24mo, sewed, 9d.

ROBSON (GEORGE)—
ELEMENTARY BUILDING CONSTRUCTION. Oblong
folio, sewed, 8s.

WALLIS (GEORGE)—
DRAWING-BOOK. Oblong, sewed, 3s. 6d.; mounted, 8s.

WORNUM (R. N.)—

THE CHARACTERISTICS OF STYLES: An Introduction to the Study of the History of Ornamental Art. Royal 8vo, cloth, 8s.

DIRECTIONS FOR INTRODUCING ELEMENTARY DRAWING IN SCHOOLS AND AMONG WORKMEN. Published at the Request of the Society of Arts. Small 4to, cloth, 4s. 6d.

DRAWING FOR YOUNG CHILDREN. Containing 150 Copies. 16mo, cloth, 3s. 6d.

EDUCATIONAL DIVISION OF SOUTH KENSINGTON MUSEUM: CLASSIFIED CATALOGUE OF. Ninth Edition. 8vo, 7s.

ELEMENTARY DRAWING COPY-BOOKS, for the use of Children from four years old and upwards, in Schools and Families. Compiled by a Student certificated by the Science and Art Department as an Art Teacher. Seven Books in 4to, sewed :

Book I. Letters, 8d.	Book IV. Objects, 8d.
,, II. Ditto, 8d.	,, V. Leaves, 8d.
,, III. Geometrical and Ornamental	,, VI. Birds, Animals, &c., 8d.
Forms, 8d.	,, VII. Leaves, Flowers, and Sprays, 8d.

** Or in Sets of Seven Books, 4s. 6d.

ENGINEER AND MACHINIST DRAWING-BOOK, 16 Parts, 71 Plates. Folio, £1 12s. ; mounted, £3 4s.

PRINCIPLES OF DECORATIVE ART. Folio, sewed, 1s.

DIAGRAM OF THE COLOURS OF THE SPECTRUM, with Explanatory Letterpress, on roller, 10s. 6d.

COPIES FOR OUTLINE DRAWING :

DYCE'S ELEMENTARY OUTLINES OF ORNAMENT, 50 Selected Plates, mounted back and front, 18s.; unmounted, sewed, 5s.

WEITBRICHT'S OUTLINES OF ORNAMENT, reproduced by Herman, 12 Plates, mounted back and front, 8s. 6d.; unmounted, 2s.

MORGHEN'S OUTLINES OF THE HUMAN FIGURE reproduced by Herman, 20 Plates, mounted back and front, 15s.; unmounted, 3s. 4d.

ONE SET OF FOUR PLATES, Outlines of Tarsia, from Gruner, mounted, 3s. 6d.; unmounted, 7d.

ALBERTOLLI'S FOLIAGE, one set of Four Plates, mounted, 3s. 6d.; unmounted, 5d.

OUTLINE OF TRAJAN FRIEZE, mounted, 1s.

WALLIS'S DRAWING-BOOK, mounted, 8s.; unmounted, 3s. 6d.

OUTLINE DRAWINGS OF FLOWERS, Eight Sheets, mounted, 3s. 6d.; unmounted, 8d.

COPIES FOR SHADED DRAWING :

COURSE OF DESIGN. By CH. BARGUE (French), 20 Selected Sheets, 11 at 2s., and 9 at 3s. each. £2 9s.

RENAISSANCE ROSETTE, mounted, 9d.

SHADED ORNAMENT, mounted, 1s. 2d.

PART OF A PILASTER FROM THE ALTAR OF ST. BIAGIO AT PISA, mounted, 2s.

GOTHIC PATERA, mounted, 1s.

RENAISSANCE SCROLL, Tomb in S. M. Dei Frari, Venice, mounted, 1s. 4d.

MOULDING OF SCULPTURED FOLIAGE, decorated, mounted, 1s. 4d.

ARCHITECTURAL STUDIES. By J. B. TRIPON. 10 Plates, £1.

COPIES FOR SHADED DRAWING—*Continued*—

> MECHANICAL STUDIES. By J. B. TRIPON. 15s. per dozen.
> FOLIATED SCROLL FROM THE VATICAN, unmounted, 5d.; mounted, 1s. 3d.
> TWELVE HEADS after Holbein, selected from his drawings in Her Majesty's Collection at Windsor. Reproduced in Autotype. Half-imperial, 36s.
> LESSONS IN SEPIA, 9s. per dozen, or 1s. each.
> SMALL SEPIA DRAWING COPIES, 9s. per dozen, or 1s. each.

COLOURED EXAMPLES :

> A SMALL DIAGRAM OF COLOUR, mounted, 1s. 6d.; unmounted, 9d.
> TWO PLATES OF ELEMENTARY DESIGN, unmounted, 1s.; mounted, 3s. 9d.
> PETUNIA, mounted, 3s. 9d.; unmounted, 2s. 9d.
> PELARGONIUM, mounted, 3s. 9d.; unmounted, 2s. 9d.
> CAMELLIA, mounted, 3s. 9d.; unmounted, 2s. 9d.
> NASTURTIUM, mounted, 3s. 9d.; unmounted, 2s. 9d.
> OLEANDER, mounted, 3s. 9d.; unmounted, 2s. 9d.
> TORRENIA ASIATICA. Mounted, 3s. 9d.; unmounted, 2s. 9d.
> PYNE'S LANDSCAPES IN CHROMO-LITHOGRAPHY (6), each, mounted, 7s. 6d.; or the set, £2 5s.
> COTMAN'S PENCIL LANDSCAPES (set of 9), mounted, 15s.
>   „   SEPIA DRAWINGS (set of 5), mounted, £1.
> ALLONGE'S LANDSCAPES IN CHARCOAL (6), at 4s. each, or the set, £1 4s.
> 4017. BOUQUET OF FLOWERS, LARGE ROSES, &c., 4s. 6d.

4018.	„	„	ROSES AND HEARTSEASE, 3s. 6d.
4020.	„	„	POPPIES, &c., 3s. 6d.
4039.	„	„	CHRYSANTHEMUMS, 4s. 6d.
4040.	„	„	LARGE CAMELLIAS, 4s. 6d.
4077.	„	„	LILAC AND GERANIUM, 3s. 6d.
4080.	„	„	CAMELLIA AND ROSE, 3s. 6d.
4082.	„	„	LARGE DAHLIAS, 4s. 6d.
4083.	„	„	ROSES AND LILIES, 4s. 6d.
4090.	„	„	ROSES AND SWEET PEAS, 3s. 6d.
4094.	„	„	LARGE ROSES AND HEARTSEASE, 4s.
4180.	„	„	LARGE BOUQUET OF LILAC, 6s. 6d.
4190.	„	„	DAHLIAS AND FUCHSIAS, 6s. 6d.

SOLID MODELS, &c. :

*Box of Models, £1 4s.
A Stand with a universal joint, to show the solid models, &c., £1 18s.
*One wire quadrangle, with a circle and cross within it, and one straight wire. One solid cube. One skeleton wire cube. One sphere. One cone. One cylinder. One hexagonal prism. £2 2s.
Skeleton cube in wood, 3s. 6d.
18-inch skeleton cube in wood, 12s
*Three objects of *form* in Pottery :

Indian Jar, }
Celadon Jar, } 18s. 6d.
Bottle, }

*Five selected Vases in Majolica Ware, £2 11s.
*Three selected Vases in Earthenware, 18s.
Imperial Deal Frames, glazed, without sunk rings, 10s. each.
*Davidson's Smaller Solid Models, in Box, £2, containing—

2 Square Slabs.	Octagon Prism.	Triangular Prism.
9 Oblong Blocks (steps).	Cylinder.	Pyramid, Equilateral.
2 Cubes.	Cone.	Pyramid, Isosceles.
4 Square Blocks.	Jointed Cross.	Square Block.

* Davidson's Advanced Drawing Models, £9.—The following is a brief description of the models :—An Obelisk—composed of 2 Octagonal Slabs, 26 and 20 inches across, and each 3 inches high ; 1 Cube, 12 inches edge ; 1 Monolith (forming

    * Models, &c., entered as sets, cannot be supplied singly.

SOLID MODELS, &c.—*Continued*—

the body of the obelisk), 3 feet high; 1 Pyramid, 6 inches base; the complete object is thus nearly 5 feet high. A Market Cross—composed of 3 Slabs, 24, 18, and 12 inches across, and each 3 inches high; 1 Upright, 3 feet high; 2 Cross Arms, united by mortise and tenon joints; complete height, 3 feet 9 inches. A Step-Ladder, 23 inches high. A Kitchen Table, 14½ inches high. A Chair to correspond. A Four-legged Stool, with projecting top and cross rails, height 14 inches. A Tub, with handles and projecting hoops, and the divisions between the staves plainly marked. A strong Trestle, 18 inches high. A Hollow Cylinder, 9 inches in diameter, and 12 inches long, divided lengthwise. A Hollow Sphere, 9 inches in diameter, divided into semi-spheres, one of which is again divided into quarters; the semi-sphere, when placed on the cylinder, gives the form and principles of shading a Dome, whilst one of the quarters placed on half the cylinder forms a Niche.

*Davidson's Apparatus for Teaching Practical Geometry (22 models), £5.

*Binn's Models for illustrating the elementary principles of orthographic projection as applied to mechanical drawing, in box, £1 10s.

Miller's Class Drawing Models.—These Models are particularly adapted for teaching large classes; the stand is very strong, and the universal joint will hold the Models in any position. *Wood Models*: Square Prism, 12 inches side, 18 inches high; Hexagonal Prism, 14 inches side, 18 inches high; Cube, 14 inches side; Cylinder, 13 inches diameter, 16 inches high; Hexagon Pyramid, 14 inches diameter, 22½ inches side: Square Pyramid, 14 inches side, 22½ inches side; Cone, 13 inches diameter, 22½ inches side; Skeleton Cube, 19 inches solid wood 1¾ inch square: Intersecting Circles, 19 inches solid wood 2¼ by 1½ inches. *Wire Models*: Triangular Prism, 17 inches side, 22 inches high; Square Prism, 14 inches side, 20 inches high; Hexagonal Prism, 16 inches diameter, 21 inches high; Cylinder, 14 inches diameter, 21 inches high; Hexagon Pyramid, 18 inches diameter, 24 inches high; Square Pyramid, 17 inches side, 24 inches high; Cone, 17 inches side, 24 inches high; Skeleton Cube, 19 inches side; Intersecting Circles, 19 inches side; Plain Circle, 19 inches side; Plain Square, 19 inches side. Table 27 inches by 21½ inches. Stand. The Set complete, £14 13s.

Vulcanite set square, 5s.

Large compasses with chalk-holder, 5s.

*Slip, two set squares and **T** square, 5s.

*Parkes's case of instruments, containing 6-inch compasses with pen and pencil leg, 5s.

*Prize instrument case, with 6-inch compasses, pen and pencil leg, 2 small compasses pen and scale, 18s.

6-inch compasses with shifting pen and point, 4s. 6d.

Small compass in case, 1s.

LARGE DIAGRAMS.

ASTRONOMICAL :

TWELVE SHEETS. By JOHN DREW, Ph. Dr., F.R.S.A. Prepared for the Committee of Council on Education. Sheets, £2 8s.; on rollers and varnished, £4 4s.

BOTANICAL :

NINE SHEETS. Illustrating a Practical Method of Teaching Botany. By Professor HENSLOW, F.L.S. £2; on rollers, and varnished, £3 3s.

CLASS.	DIVISION.	SECTION.	DIAGRAM.
Dicotyledon	Angiospermous ..	Thalamifloral	1
		Calycifloral	2 & 3
		Corollifloral	4
		Incomplete	5
	Gymnospermous ..	.. .. ..	6
Monocotyledons	Petaloid	Superior	7
		Inferior..	8
	Glumaceous.. ..	.. .. ..	9

ILLUSTRATIONS OF THE PRINCIPAL NATURAL ORDERS OF THE VEGETABLE KINGDOM. By Professor OLIVER, F.R.S., F.L.S. 70 Imperial sheets, containing examples of dried Plants, representing the different Orders. £5 5s. the set.

Catalogue and Index, 1s.

---

* Models, &c., entered as sets, cannot be supplied singly.

BUILDING CONSTRUCTION:

TEN SHEETS. By WILLIAM J. GLENNY, Professor of Drawing, King's College. In sets, £1 1s.

LAXTON'S EXAMPLES OF BUILDING CONSTRUCTION IN TWO DIVISIONS, containing 32 Imperial Plates, 20s.

BUSBRIDGE'S DRAWINGS OF BUILDING CONSTRUCTION. 11 Sheets. 2s. 9d. Mounted, 5s. 6d.

GEOLOGICAL:

DIAGRAM OF BRITISH STRATA. By H. W. BRISTOW, F.R.S., F.G.S. A Sheet, 4s.; on roller and varnished, 7s. 6d.

MECHANICAL:

DIAGRAMS OF THE MECHANICAL POWERS, AND THEIR APPLICATIONS IN MACHINERY AND THE ARTS GENERALLY. By DR. JOHN ANDERSON.
8 Diagrams, highly coloured on stout paper, 3 feet 6 inches by 2 feet 6 inches. Sheets £1 per set; mounted on rollers, £2.

DIAGRAMS OF THE STEAM-ENGINE. By Professor GOODEVE and Professor SHELLEY. Stout paper, 40 inches by 27 inches, highly coloured.
Sets of 41 Diagrams (52½ Sheets), £6 6s.; varnished and mounted on rollers, £11 11s.

MACHINE DETAILS. By Professor UNWIN. 16 Coloured Diagrams. Sheets, £2 2s.; mounted on rollers and varnished, £3 14s.

SELECTED EXAMPLES OF MACHINES, OF IRON AND WOOD (French). By STANISLAS PETTIT. 60 Sheets, £3 5s.; 13s. per dozen.

BUSBRIDGE'S DRAWINGS OF MACHINE CONSTRUCTION. 50 Sheets, 11s. Mounted, 25s.

LESSONS IN MECHANICAL DRAWING. By STANISLAS PETTIT. 1s. per dozen; also larger Sheets, more advanced copies, 2s. per dozen.

LESSONS IN ARCHITECTURAL DRAWING. By STANISLAS PETTIT. 1s. per dozen; also larger Sheets, more advanced copies, 2s. per dozen.

PHYSIOLOGICAL:

ELEVEN SHEETS. Illustrating Human Physiology, Life size and Coloured from Nature. Prepared under the direction of JOHN MARSHALL, F.R.S., F.R.C.S., &c. Each Sheet, 12s. 6d. On canvas and rollers, varnished, £1 1s.

1. THE SKELETON AND LIGAMENTS.
2. THE MUSCLES, JOINTS, AND ANIMAL MECHANICS.
3. THE VISCERA IN POSITION.—THE STRUCTURE OF THE LUNGS.
4. THE ORGANS OF CIRCULATION.
5. THE LYMPHATICS OR ABSORBENTS.
6. THE ORGANS OF DIGESTION.
7. THE BRAIN AND NERVES.—THE ORGANS OF THE VOICE.
8. THE ORGANS OF THE SENSES.
9. THE ORGANS OF THE SENSES.
10. THE MICROSCOPIC STRUCTURE OF THE TEXTURES AND ORGANS.
11. THE MICROSCOPIC STRUCTURE OF THE TEXTURES AND ORGANS.

HUMAN BODY, LIFE SIZE. By JOHN MARSHALL, F.R.S., F.R.C.S. Each Sheet, 12s. 6d.; on canvas and rollers, varnished, £1 1s. Explanatory Key, 1s.

1. THE SKELETON, Front View.
2. THE MUSCLES, Front View.
3. THE SKELETON, Back View.
4. THE MUSCLES, Back View.
5. THE SKELETON, Side View.
6. THE MUSCLES, Side View.
7. THE FEMALE SKELETON, Front View.

ZOOLOGICAL:

TEN SHEETS. Illustrating the Classification of Animals. By ROBERT PATTERSON. £2; on canvas and rollers, varnished, £3 10s.

The same, reduced in size on Royal paper, in 9 Sheets, uncoloured, 12s.

THE FORTNIGHTLY REVIEW.

Edited by JOHN MORLEY.

THE FORTNIGHTLY REVIEW is published on the 1st of every month (the issue on the 15th being suspended), and a Volume is completed every Six Months.

The following are among the Contributors:—

SIR RUTHERFORD ALCOCK.
PROFESSOR BAIN.
PROFESSOR BEESLY.
DR. BRIDGES.
HON. GEORGE C. BRODRICK.
SIR GEORGE CAMPBELL, M.P.
J. CHAMBERLAIN, M.P.
PROFESSOR SIDNEY COLVIN.
MONTAGUE COOKSON, Q.C.
L. H. COURTNEY, M.P.
G. H. DARWIN.
F. W. FARRAR.
PROFESSOR FAWCETT, M.P.
EDWARD A. FREEMAN.
MRS. GARRET-ANDERSON.
M. E. GRANT DUFF, M.P.
THOMAS HARE.
F. HARRISON.
LORD HOUGHTON.
PROFESSOR HUXLEY.
PROFESSOR JEVONS.
ÉMILE DE LAVELEYE.
T. E. CLIFFE LESLIE.
RIGHT HON. R. LOWE, M.P.
SIR JOHN LUBBOCK, M.P.

LORD LYTTON.
SIR H. S. MAINE.
DR. MAUDSLEY.
PROFESSOR MAX MÜLLER.
PROFESSOR HENRY MORLEY.
G. OSBORNE MORGAN, Q.C., M.P.
WILLIAM MORRIS.
F. W. NEWMAN.
W. G. PALGRAVE.
WALTER H. PATER.
RT. HON. LYON PLAYFAIR, M.P.
DANTE GABRIEL ROSSETTI.
HERBERT SPENCER.
HON. E. L. STANLEY.
SIR J. FITZJAMES STEPHEN, Q.C.
LESLIE STEPHEN.
J. HUTCHISON STIRLING
A. C. SWINBURNE.
DR. VON SYBEL.
J. A. SYMONDS.
W. T. THORNTON.
HON. LIONEL A. TOLLEMACHE.
ANTHONY TROLLOPE.
PROFESSOR TYNDALL.
THE EDITOR.

&c. &c. &c.

THE FORTNIGHTLY REVIEW *is published at 2s. 6d.*

CHAPMAN & HALL, 193, PICCADILLY.

CHARLES DICKENS AND EVANS,]   [CRYSTAL PALACE PRESS.